DEADLY
PLEASURE

BRENDA
JOYCE

St. Martin's Paperbacks

DEADLY PLEASURE

Copyright © 2002 by Brenda Joyce Dreams Unlimited, Inc.
Excerpts from *Deadly Affairs* and *Deadly Desire* copyright © 2002 by Brenda Joyce Dreams Unlimited, Inc.

ISBN: 0-312-97768-9

Printed in the United States of America

St. Martin's Paperbacks edition / March 2002

St. Martin's Paperbacks are published by St. Martin's Press, 175 Fifth Avenue, New York, NY 10010.

10 9 8 7 6 5 4 3 2 1

This one's for my mother,
not for the first time and not for the last.
For always being there, no matter what.
Thanks, Mom!

ONE

Stanford White was having a party, and for the first time in her life, Francesca had practically begged her mother to be allowed to attend, in an abrupt reversal of character and inclination. Indeed, ever since turning sixteen four years ago and being informally introduced to society, Francesca had determinedly avoided all such events.

Now, she paused with her mother, Julia Van Wyck Cahill, and her brother, Evan, inside the doorway of Madison Square's Rooftop Garden, which White had not only designed, as he was one of the city's most brilliant architects, but which he had also taken over for the evening's soiree. Guests in tuxedos and evening gowns continued to move past the Cahills as they arrived, filing around numerous gold-swagged tables, all with exotic floral arrangements and set about a large dance floor. Francesca was oddly breathless, but she told herself it was due to the rush, and she had to try hard indeed not to keep glancing repeatedly over her shoulder.

Still, the doorway remained just within the line of her vision.

"You are behaving most oddly, Francesca," Julia murmured, elegantly clad in a pale green evening gown and more diamond jewelry than most women would ever set their eyes upon, much less wear. "First, you insist upon attending the White fête, and now, you cannot keep your eyes in your head. And you are fidgeting. What is this about?"

Francesca managed to smile at her mother, the arriving guests a blur in the corner of her vision. "Mama, perhaps I am finally maturing? After all, I am twenty now. I have finally seen the error of my ways. It is really quite simple. You have been right and I have been wrong; a young lady should be social and charming, and neither a recluse nor a bluestocking."

Her brother, who knew she secretly attended Barnard College and often stayed up most of the night to study, began to choke.

Julia, who had been gazing at the crowd, remarking all those whom she knew—and she did know everybody—whipped her regard back to her daughter, her eyes wide with suspicion. Evan, tall, dark, and handsome, especially in his tuxedo, finally gave in to his laughter. Francesca gave him a very cross and dangerous look. It said, *Keep quiet or you shall suffer the consequences.*

"You are up to something," Julia stated firmly. "Of that I have no doubt. I am only hoping it is as simple as wanting to gawk at White. We have had enough drama and mystery these past few weeks to last a lifetime, I daresay."

Francesca smiled angelically at her mother, and as she was blond and blue-eyed, the effect was one of utter innocence. Her mother, she knew, referred to the terrible crime that had happened right under their very noses two weeks ago—their neighbor's child had been abducted out of his bed by a madman. Julia was also referring to the fact that Francesca had been up to her own nose in the criminal affair—but on the side of law and order and justice.

"I am not up to anything, Mama," she murmured now, a tiny white lie. It was no easy task keeping her mother ignorant of all that she did these days. "But of course, as White is quite notorious for his personal affairs and his rather lavish, if not self-indulgent, behavior, it will be most interesting to meet him." The truth was, Francesca could not care less about greeting their infamous host. Perhaps, before the events of the past few weeks, she might have sought such an opportunity. But White was *not* the reason she had come to the overly ostentatious party.

"And you will be polite but discreet when you do meet him," Julia advised. "I will not have him, in his unorthodox views, encouraging you in yours."

Evan chuckled again. "I fear you have made a vast mistake, Mama, and this is one event Fran should not be attending. I fear she and White just might get along—too well. What if he should decide to become her mentor?"

Francesca scowled at him. "Isn't Sarah Channing somewhere about, Evan?" she asked sweetly. "Shouldn't you attend your fiancée?" Evan had recently become engaged.

But Evan was not to be dissuaded. "Perhaps I will chaperon you, Fran. God forbid White should affect and even increase your independent thinking and ways. Then what would the world do!"

Had he been closer, she would have stepped upon his foot with her pointy heel. Just then, she felt sorry that he knew the first but not the last of her secrets, even though she did adore him. "Thank you, Evan, for your loyalty." Then she realized another guest was arriving, and she whirled to stare— only to be disappointed, as it was a gentleman she did not know.

Evan leaned close as Julia stepped away to speak with a couple who lived just down the avenue from the Cahill mansion. "Careful, Fran. You will give yourself away."

"I do not know what you mean." She batted her eyes at him.

"I think you do." He grinned and winked. "Mother will discern whom you are waiting for in all of two seconds if you continue to carry on so. And I do believe she has forbidden any interest on your part in our new police commissioner."

Rick Bragg had recently been appointed commissioner of police. The appointment was a controversial one, as their new mayor was a man of principle, having been elected on the platform of reform, determined to right the ills inflicted upon the city by Tammany Hall. As Seth Lowe's appointee, Bragg was expected to reform the notoriously corrupt police department, no easy task indeed. He hailed from the Texas Braggs, a fine and wealthy family, although he had been born in New York City in rather unfortunate and improper circumstances—that is, on the wrong side of the blanket. The tall, tawny-haired, darkly handsome, and very determined police commissioner had been educated at Columbia University and Harvard Law School, and he had, until recently, resided in Washington, D.C., where he had been in private practice. Francesca had met Bragg exactly two weeks ago when she had discovered the first of a series of extremely bizarre "ransom" notes left by the madman who had abducted Jonny Burton.

"I am hardly carrying on," she said, low, vastly irritated now. Evan knew her too well, but then, she was not adept at hiding her feelings—she had never had to do so before.

For she had never had feelings like this before.

"You are acting like all of the marriage-mad, love-struck females you so disdain," he said, giving her a direct glance, one filled with more mirth. "You are a woman after all, Fran."

She stared, wanting to protest that it was not true. But she could not deny being a woman, of course. Still, she had so prided herself on being different from the marriage-mad females her own age. Now, she remained mute. Because in the matter of a few days, in the course of one fantastic criminal investigation, her entire life had been turned upside down.

Evan patted her shoulder, which was bare, as she wore a peach chiffon gown with tiny cap sleeves that fell upon her upper arms. "You are cute, this way," he said, his tone rather patronizing. "It's nice, for a change, not to listen to you sermonizing about sweatshops and temperance, about the poor and the indigent, about Tammany Hall and everything else you can think of! Perhaps you are normal after all, Fran," he said, laughter in his dark blue eyes.

"I am not cute and I am not 'normal' and I am not being any *way*," Francesca huffed. "And nothing has changed," she declared, wishing that she meant it.

He grinned and walked away.

Francesca took a deep breath and glanced around, somewhat shaken—because Evan was right, no matter how she might pretend that he was not. And it was almost inexplicable. How *had* this happened? Francesca had spent most of her life avoiding the hobbies and pastimes enjoyed by other young women her age. She had discovered books at a very tender age—she was six when she began to read, and her love affair with the written word and all that it entailed had never ended. For Francesca Cahill was a bluestocking through and through—enrolling at Barnard College had hardly been a whim. In fact, knowing how her mother would react should she ever learn of Francesca's pursuit of a higher education made it a very serious act indeed. Fortunately her parents were very generous in regard to Francesca's spending; nor did they question her sudden inclination to purchase a new wardrobe. Francesca had also borrowed money from her sister.

But attaining her degree was only the beginning. Francesca was a reformer with a capital *R*. It ran in the family; her father, Andrew Cahill, a self-made millionaire, also championed dozens of charities and supported political candidates like Lowe, not just in New York City but all over the state and the country. She was proud of her intellect and her passion for reform. She had no time for or interest in parties, shopping, or marriage; she could barely understand why every other young woman she knew did. She actively belonged to five societies, all dedicated to fighting injustice and easing the poverty rampant in the city, and she had founded one society herself—the Ladies Society for the Eradication of Tenements. She had intended to write articles and books about the city's worst side of life in order to enlighten the ladies and gentlemen living so blithely and elegantly uptown. But her ambitions had, suddenly and drastically, changed. Two weeks ago. For Francesca had discovered her true calling in life.

Crime-solving.

It had been a most unfortunate yet fortuitous accident, stumbling upon that first "ransom" note. From that moment on, she had taken it upon herself to help the city's new police commissioner solve the ghastly crime of the small boy's abduction. Together, she and Rick Bragg had faced the gravest dangers, uncovering clue after clue, each one pointing to the likelihood that the boy was dead, but in the end, against all odds, little Jonny Burton had been found alive and safely returned home, to his waiting mother's arms.

Bragg could not have done it without Francesca. He had even said so.

Francesca smiled at the thought and found herself openly regarding the doorway, through which more guests continued to arrive. Her father had said Bragg would be at the White party tonight.

Of course, they were only friends. They had only just met. But soon there would be another crime for them to solve—together. How could there not be, in this city of hooks and crooks? In fact, yesterday Francesca had picked up the new calling cards she had ordered at Tiffany's, and she had already begun handing them out. They read:

> *Francesca Cahill*
> *Crime-Solver Extraordinaire*
> *No. 810 Fifth Avenue, New York City.*
> *All Cases Accepted, No Crime Too Small.*

"Where is your father? He promised me that he would stop at his club only briefly. He is late," Julia said, frowning, having returned to Francesca's side.

Francesca had to tear her gaze away from the doorway now, as she did not want her mother to become more suspicious of her than she already was. Stealing about the city—and into some of the worst wards—was no easy task in itself, but eluding Julia made it even more difficult. And Francesca had learned that in order to be an effective sleuth, one must travel quite freely about town, dealing with every possible kind of person. But more important, Julia had noticed Francesca's interest in Bragg and had told her daughter in no uncertain terms that a bastard was not acceptable as a suitor, never mind that he was educated, a gentleman, the police commissioner, and a Bragg.

Still, she was as anxious as a schoolgirl on her first date. And it was absurd. She was no marriage-mad ninny—she was a college student and a crime-solver. She must get a grip—and fast. By tomorrow at noon, in fact, when he came calling for her.

Yesterday, he had invited her for a drive in the country. Francesca smiled to herself. Clearly, he wished to now court her.

"Francesca, do look. There's White. I think I will wait for your father to greet him." Julian Van Wyck Cahill gripped Francesca's arm, not even looking at her, moving away from the doorway.

They paused behind several ladies and gentlemen, all surrounding Stanford White. He was a tall, heavyset man with a booming voice, somewhere in his middle years. Julia studied the group surrounding White. Two of the women were clearly not from their social circle. "Oh, dear," Julia said. "Are those women what I think they are?"

Francesca wanted to say yes. The two gorgeous women were probably very well-kept mistresses. "I wonder if they are White's?" she murmured. "I have heard he keeps an apartment not far from here for his dalliances."

"Chase all such thoughts from your mind!" Julia cried. Then, "And just where did you hear such a thing?"

"Evan," Francesca said sweetly. Her brother deserved a little nick.

"I shall certainly have a word with him. And what else did he say?" Julia demanded.

"Oh, here is Papa!" Francesca cried, turning away from her mother's speculative regard.

But Julia said, softly now, "I know you are up to something, dear, and we both know that sooner or later the truth will out."

Francesca's cheeks warmed. She waved gaily at her portly father. She was always pleased to see him.

Andrew Cahill had been raised on a farm in Illinois; he had made his fortune in meatpacking in Chicago. He had moved his family to New York when Francesca was eight. Now, he beamed at his youngest child and kissed her cheek. "In the nick of time, eh, Fran?"

"Your timing is impeccable, as always, Papa," she returned. Then, in a whisper, "I cannot believe Mama wished to come to a party given by White."

Andrew Cahill had plump cheeks and heavy gray-white sideburns. "Curiosity kills most cats, but it won't kill Mother." He turned to Julia. "Dear." He kissed her warmly. "That is quite the dress. I don't believe I've seen it before."

"If you think I shall forgive you for being late, you are wrong," Julia said, as warmly. "And yes, Andrew, the dress is brand-new."

"I like it."

Julia smiled. "I'm glad."

Francesca saw the look they exchanged and she turned away. Andrew spoke. "Ran into the commissioner on the way out of the club and had to speak with him."

Francesca stiffened instantly. She was all ears.

"No politics, tonight," Julia warned.

"What news, Papa?" It was hard not to speak Bragg's name.

"The rumor is true. Unbelievable!" Andrew exclaimed.

Her heart raced. "What rumor?" What could she have missed? She had seen Bragg yesterday, having decided to call on him at police headquarters—where she was now somewhat known—after picking up her new calling cards at Tiffany's.

"Rumor has it that he demoted all three hundred of the department's wardsmen. It's true!" Andrew exclaimed. His eyes were bright with excitement and he faced only his daughter. "Can you believe the nerve of that man?"

Francesca stared, feeling faint and giddy at the same time. Police reform was one of the burning issues facing the city. It had been for years, ever since Theodore Roosevelt had held the post of commissioner and had begun to make a few inroads on the existing system of graft and corruption. The entire city—well, all reformers like herself, as well as liberals, clerics, and journalists—was waiting with bated breath to see if Bragg would bring to heel the notorious institution. Francesca thought he might succeed. If anyone could reform the city police department, she thought it was Bragg, a man of true moral fiber and character, a man capable of swift, unremitting action. "How could he demote three hundred wardsmen?" she asked.

"We really did not speak. He said it would be in the papers on the morrow. He is here, by the way. We came up together," Andrew said.

Her heart stopped. Then she saw her father studying her, and she ducked her head. As much as she adored Papa—and he was always on her side—he and Mama talked. And too frequently, the subject they discussed was their children. Connie, Francesca's sister, had married Lord Neil Montrose four years ago, and recently Evan's engagement had been announced. So that now left Francesca. She had little doubt that she would be the featured topic of most of their remaining conversations, and it would only get worse once Evan was married.

"Do we have to discuss the police department tonight?" Julia said firmly. "Andrew, I must meet White. Francesca, on second thought, you stay here."

Francesca stiffened. "Mama, that is not fair."

Julia ignored her. "I am afraid she might get even more unusual ideas from White, Andrew. In fact, having seen some of the crowd present, I am not sure allowing her to come has been a good idea."

"Papa?" Francesca protested.

"For once I am in agreement with your mother," Andrew said, taking Julia's arm. "I did not like the idea of bringing you here tonight to begin with. We will be back shortly."

Francesca stared after them as they moved toward the distinguished but flamboyantly clad gentleman with the head of white hair who was holding court on the center of the dance floor. The two women who were not quite genteel remained in the crowd, and now Francesca saw a very severely dressed woman with hair cropped short also in the crowd—the woman looked rather mannish and very intelligent, too. Francesca wondered who she was.

Francesca suddenly squinted. A dark-haired gentleman clad in a black tuxedo stood beside White, speaking to a lady, his very white teeth flashing. The tall, swarthy gentleman was more than familiar, she realized with a start, staring openly. Wasn't that Bragg's half brother, Calder Hart?

"You took that extremely well," a voice said behind her.

Francesca no longer saw Calder Hart. Bragg's breath feathered her bare nape, sending chills up and down her spine. She turned and looked into a pair of darkly golden eyes.

He bowed, hiding a smile. "Good evening, Miss Cahill."

"Bragg." She tried to sound casual and she also tried to hide her own answering smile.

"Cahill." Rick Bragg nodded at Evan, who had suddenly materialized beside Francesca. She felt like kicking him—his timing was impeccably rotten. She gave him an annoyed look, but Evan ignored it.

"So what brings you here, Bragg?" Evan asked, somewhat coolly.

Bragg smiled. "The usual—an invitation." His gaze turned to Francesca. And it slid warmly over her face.

She knew she flushed as she smiled at him. Bragg wore a white dinner jacket and black evening trousers. His tawny hair, a blend of copper, gold, and blond, glinted from the light cast by the huge overhead chandeliers. All last week he had seemed exhausted during the investigation into the Burton Abduction. Tonight he radiated masculinity, virility, and good health.

He also seemed pleased to see her. Amusement flickered briefly in his eyes. "So what is the plan?"

"The plan?" she managed.

"Surely you have a plan. With which to thwart your mother and go and meet White?" More amusement made him smile slightly, briefly.

"There is no plan." She took a breath, amazed with herself for being so easily flustered. "I shall meekly accept my fate this night."

He laughed. "Meekly? I doubt that."

"You shall see a new side of me, I fear."

He chuckled again. "But perhaps I like the old side?"

She stopped smiling. Their gazes held. His smile faded.

Evan coughed. "No police business tonight?"

"Unfortunately, there is always police business to attend to," Bragg said, not even glancing at Evan.

Francesca wet her lips. "I was surprised to hear that you would be here tonight. This is the last place I would expect you to be."

"It is one of the very last places I wish to be." His gaze was direct. He spoke now as if her brother were not present.

"Then why?" Francesca asked with real curiosity. She knew how hard—and how late—Bragg worked. "I am surprised you are not at police headquarters."

He shrugged slightly. "Public relations."

"Public relations?" she murmured while her mind sped.

"I must hobnob with the city's finest," he said with a self-deprecating shrug.

And she understood. He had so much to do—and so little time in which to do it, for there was rarely longevity in a controversial appointment like his. Already the press had dragged him through hell and back. Just a week ago, he had been accused of incompetence for failing to find Jonny Burton's abductor. Yesterday he had been hailed a hero. She wondered how the press would treat his first real attempt to fight corruption within the police by demoting 300 detectives. "Did you really demote three hundred of your men?"

His mouth quirked. "No comment."

"Bragg!" She was smiling. "I am not employed by the *Tribune*."

So was he. "Thank God, and yes, I did."

She realized he had been teasing her, and it felt glorious. "And what do you think to accomplish? Oh ho, they must fear their leader now!"

He chuckled at her exuberance. "They have been reassigned—to foot patrol—in different precincts. It is a long story, Francesca. Hopefully a few good men will emerge from the current circumstance."

Suddenly Francesca realized most of the police department must hate him now as well as fear him. She shivered. "Be careful, Bragg." And suddenly she did not like this newest development at all.

His eyes widened fractionally with surprise when Evan

stepped somewhat between them. "Shall we get something to drink, Fran?"

She felt like kicking his shin or pinching his hand. "Why don't you get me a glass of champagne?" She smiled sweetly but gave him a dark look of annoyance.

"Why don't you come with me?" Evan returned, not budging, but staring at her.

Why did he think to protect her from Bragg? "Perhaps I am enjoying a conversation with the police commissioner," she returned.

"I must move on, in any case," Bragg said. He hesitated. "Francesca? May I have a private word with you?"

She was surprised, and any elation quickly vanished as she realized that his expression was grim. "Of course." She ignored her disapproving brother now and stepped aside with Bragg.

He sighed. "I was going to send a note."

Dread overcame her. "A . . . note?"

"I am afraid police affairs dictate my life these days. I must cancel our outing tomorrow."

She looked at him and felt as if someone had just ripped the rug out from under her feet. *"What?"*

"I am sorry. Perhaps another time." He smiled at her, but his gaze was searching and very somber.

Francesca pasted what felt like a stupendous and stupid grin upon her face—as she mustn't let him see her real feelings. "Of course. Of course affairs of the city would keep you preoccupied. Think nothing of it, Bragg."

"I thought you would understand," he said, his gaze holding onto hers.

"I am your biggest supporter," Francesca said firmly, "as you must know."

"And I appreciate it." He nodded at her and Evan both before turning to go.

Feeling as if a mule had just kicked her in the chest, Francesca watched Bragg being greeted heartily by other guests.

"So that is the lay of the land," Evan said accusingly. "I thought it was a silly flirtation, but it is not!"

Francesca hardly heard him. Bragg had canceled their outing. How could he? What did this mean?

It meant that he had police affairs to attend to.

No. Clearly, clearly, it meant that their kiss had meant
nothing to him at all.

Francesca closed her eyes tightly. She had been trying to
forget their one single devastating kiss. They had both thought
Jonny Burton to be dead at the time; they had both been grief-
stricken, frightened, and exhausted. Bragg also had been
drinking.

Still, he had kissed her in a way that no gentleman would
ever kiss a respectable lady, he had kissed her and touched
her and held her, and she had done all of those things to him
as well. Had he forgotten?

Had the kiss meant anything at all?

"You are in love with Bragg!" Evan cried.

Francesca was saved from answering him by the lions.

Ladies screamed. A few gentlemen cried out. White laughed
and with a megaphone began to greet his guests as men in
tights and gypsy shirts entered the dance floor using whips to
urge four lions on ahead of them. A woman in garters, black
hose, a few inches of skirt, and a corset appeared, holding a
large hoop. As she was mostly naked, a few gasps sounded.
A lion jumped through her hoop.

"I have promised you all an evening of entertainment,"
White was saying. "And by God, you shall have it!"

The lions were circling the perimeter of the stage at a faster
pace, urged on by the four men; one by one, taking turns,
each lion jumped through the woman's hoop. The guests began to applaud. Francesca hugged herself.

She was crushed. This would not do. They were only
friends, after all.

God damn it.

"You are upset. Has he led you on?" Evan demanded.
"That is who you were with the other night!"

Only a few days ago, when she had been out extremely
late, Evan had found her out. He had not been certain whether

to believe her or not when she had told him the truth—that she was working on the Burton Abduction. Francesca faced him angrily. "I am not upset. And no one has led me on. And don't you dare breathe a word of this to anyone!"

"Breathe a word of what?" Connie, her sister, appeared at their side, absolutely breathtaking in a pale orange gown and a choker of citrines. It was widely held that the Cahill sisters were as identical as twins, but that was not true. Francesca had always felt that her sister was by far the more beautiful of the pair. She was also stunningly elegant, no matter the time of day. "Now what are you up to, Fran?" Connie asked, but teasingly.

"She is carrying on with Bragg!" Evan said grimly. He turned his back on them and pushed into the crowd.

Connie's elegant brows lifted briefly, and then she turned to Francesca. "That is good news as far as I am concerned. You know I like the commissioner."

Francesca did not speak. Fortunately, Julia and Andrew were a short distance away and out of earshot. They were speaking with two other couples, their eyes, however, on the show. Connie did like Bragg. She had been delighted that, finally, at the ripe old age of twenty, Francesca was somewhat romantically inclined toward a gentleman.

Francesca gazed at her sister and was painfully reminded of the secret she kept from her. Last week, she had discovered Connie's husband in the throes of passion with another woman. But she had not said a word to her sister of Neil's affair and treachery.

It was still unbelievable. Francesca had adored her handsome, aristocratic brother-in-law from the moment she had laid eyes upon him, five years ago. And until last week, she had thought that he adored his wife. Clearly, she had been wrong.

"Oh, dear," Connie said, her eyes wide.

Francesca turned to look at the spectacle and saw the woman riding on the back of one of the lions in her scanty attire. "That looks dangerous," Francesca remarked tersely.

"It looks more than dangerous," Connie said. "So what is wrong, Fran?"

A few men whistled; the woman waved.

Francesca shoved her unhappy thoughts of Neil Montrose aside. "Bragg has canceled," Francesca said. Connie was the only one to know about their date.

"What?" Connie glanced at her quickly.

"I am a fool," Francesca said heavily. "And I am very disappointed." There, she had dared to admit it.

Suddenly the crowd was hushed. Francesca glanced at the stage. The woman was now hanging upside down on a trapeze, her knees locked over the bar. Her short skirts revealed most of her backside. Her breasts seemed about to be falling out of her very small boned top. The lions were seated now placidly in a row, and three of the four men had formed a human pyramid behind them, the fourth man maintaining the lions. Clearly the uppermost man was going to be plucked up by the woman acrobat.

"Oh, Fran, I am sure he had a valid reason. These things happen," Connie began, not taking her eyes off of the show.

"You are prejudiced," Francesca grumbled.

"But so are you!" Connie exclaimed. The crowd cried out.

Francesca's eyes widened. The uppermost man of the human pyramid had caught not the woman's hands but the bar she hung from, and he threw his own legs over it, so he also hung down as they swung wildly over the crowd. But the man and woman had their legs locked together, and they were back to back and head to head.

"Oh, my," Connie managed, her cheeks as pink as her dress.

Francesca stared, stunned. And suddenly the trapeze artists both reversed positions, and they were sitting on top of the trapeze—on top of each other's laps.

Someone whistled. A man shouted. Others applauded.

They pumped the swing—and their bodies—harder.

It was almost as if they were lovers on top of that trapeze. Francesca managed, "You don't think . . . They wouldn't dare . . . White wouldn't let them!"

"I think this is not decent," Connie breathed, yet she did not look away. In fact, she seemed mesmerized.

"Very indecent," someone drawled behind them.

Francesca stiffened in surprise and she and her sister turned almost as one. Calder Hart smiled at Francesca, and then he looked at Connie, his regard becoming speculative.

"You're Bragg's brother. We met the other day," Francesca managed, wanting to see what the trapeze artists were doing but almost afraid to peek. Connie had turned her wide-eyed attention back to the performers.

"Half brother," he said, with a nod. "Miss Cahill, I presume?"

Francesca nodded, extending her hand, when the crowd shouted. As he took it, she jerked around to see the two trapeze artists standing on the trapeze, facing each other now, swinging energetically back and forth.

Hart released her hand.

Francesca turned to face him, but he was staring at Connie, who still could not take her eyes away from the show.

Calder Hart laughed and shook his head, returning his gaze to Francesca. "You should be home, Miss Cahill. Home and in bed, where proper young ladies like you belong. And maybe you should take your sister—I presume she is your sister—with you."

"I am in shock," Francesca admitted.

"In shock—or titillated?" he asked, glancing sidelong at Connie again.

"I beg your pardon." Francesca finally stiffened. But she *was* titillated. How could she not be? She was thinking about Bragg. Was he as mesmerized as everyone else by the spectacle on the trapeze? Or was he annoyed or angry or even bored?

"*Is* this your sister?"

Francesca nodded. "I am sorry. Connie, Mr. Hart. My sister, Lady Montrose." Francesca pinched her arm.

Connie gasped and faced Calder Hart abruptly, clearly breathless and quite distracted. She gave him her hand while he looked her up and down, slowly and frankly. Francesca was simply stunned, but Connie didn't even notice. "I beg your pardon. I have never seen such a thing. I am speechless," Connie confessed rapidly.

He was wry. "That is obvious." He bowed over her hand. "Might I assume that any efforts on my part to extol your beauty would now be a sheer waste of my breath and time?"

Connie glanced briefly at him. "I beg your pardon?" She hadn't heard a word he'd said.

"I thought so," he said with some mockery. He touched his chest as if he had been wounded.

"He is Bragg's half brother," Francesca offered.

"And a good friend of White's," Calder Hart added, staring at Connie as if awaiting her reaction to this bit of news. When she said nothing, he shrugged and grinned.

Francesca stared at him thoughtfully. If he was White's friend, clearly he was used to this kind of exhibition. "Why does White wish to shock society?"

He grinned at her. "You shall have to ask him that. It has been a pleasure, ladies. I do hope to have the pleasure again— soon."

Francesca found herself rather speechless, but it did not matter, as he bowed his head and disappeared into the crowd too quickly for her to have a chance to respond. Connie didn't even notice. The man on the trapeze had slipped beneath and through the woman's legs and now he stood *behind* her, pumping the trapeze. The crowd roared, while the woman on the bar seemed to be in the throes of ecstasy.

Francesca poked Connie with her elbow—a quite unlady-like gesture. "You were rude!" she exclaimed.

"Was I?" Connie managed. She did not even look at Francesca.

"There you are!" It was Julia, and Andrew was on her heels. "We are leaving! I have seen quite enough. We are leaving this instant. White should be arrested for this!"

Francesca had had enough as it was. "That's fine." She glanced at Connie.

"I had better go find Neil," Connie whispered unsteadily, referring to her husband.

Before she could leave, Francesca gripped her hand. "Con?" She was thinking about the way Calder Hart had kept staring at her sister. It was making her uneasy now—in retrospect.

Connie's breathing was shallow. "I'm fine. I'll see if Neil wants to stay or leave."

Francesca nodded. "All right."

Suddenly Connie squeezed her hand and leaned close. "And don't worry. The fat lady hasn't sung yet." She smiled. "Bragg will be back."

Francesca thought about Bragg and her heart sank. "Thank you," she said. But Francesca knew Connie was wrong.

Half the crowd had decided to leave, and from the murmurs and whispers around her it was clear that White's departing guests were shocked and scandalized. Some, like Julia, were very angry at being duped into attending such an immoral and lax display.

The elevators were full. Francesca found herself in one corner, her parents in another. Evan had decided to stay. Julia was very angry with him.

Francesca wondered if Connie and Neil would remain for the rest of the evening. As angry as she was with Neil for having taken Eliza Burton as his lover, she doubted he would be so disrespectful of Connie now as to spend the rest of the evening with her in the throes of such immoral entertainment. Francesca felt certain Neil would take his wife home.

As the elevator cage was opened, the crowd surged out. "Francesca?" her father called.

"I'm fine, Papa," Francesca said, following the crowd through the exit doors. She couldn't see her parents but knew they were somewhere on her left.

Outside, a blast of cold air enveloped her in spite of the fur-lined cape she wore. It hadn't snowed in days; it was too cold. The city was breaking its own record low temperatures.

Horses and carriages lined Madison Avenue between 26th and 27th Streets. The broughams and coaches were double-parked, along with a few motorcars. Hansoms cruised the av-

enue, looking for or carrying fares. Pedestrians swarmed the
sidewalk in front of the Garden, but the surrounding blocks
were rather deserted, due to the cold. Francesca slipped on a
patch of treacherous ice as people pushed past her, looking
for either a cab or their coach; she did not see her parents in
the crush. "Papa?" She righted herself carefully and gingerly
made her way to the curb. The Cahill brougham was just
ahead.

Someone grabbed her arm, hard.

Francesca whirled, knowing it wasn't either of her parents.
A pair of black eyes met hers from beneath a huge fur-
trimmed hood.

For one instant Francesca stood there, shocked that someone would grab her and unable to determine whether the person was a man or a woman. She was about to demand that
she be released when the person said, "Miss Cahill?"

It was a woman. Francesca relaxed slightly. "Yes?"

"*Please.*" The woman's single word was an emotionally
distressed plea. "Please. *Please help me,*" she said.

TWO

Astonished, Francesca could only stare. As she did so, the woman pressed something into her hand and begged again, "Please." She turned, slipping and sliding away as she fled into the crowd.

"Wait," Francesca began, coming to her senses.

"Francesca?" her father called from the street behind her.

Her heart was racing and she was breathless. Francesca opened her palm, keeping her back to Andrew as he called for her again. The woman had crushed a card into her palm, and even with all of the street lamps, it was too hard to read in the dark. Francesca quickly slid the card into her beaded purse.

She inhaled with excitement and turned, moving toward the waiting brougham. Her father regarded her closely as she approached. "Did that woman accost you? Are you all right?"

Francesca smiled at him, and it was genuine. "No, no, it was a case of mistaken identity," she said.

A woman was in trouble. Desperately so, if her tone was any indication of her straits. And she wanted Francesca's help.

It was not until she had reached the sanctuary of her bedroom that Francesca could dig into her purse and produce the calling card. On the front was the woman's name, Miss Georgette de Labouche, and her address, which was 28 West 24th Street. She lived only a few blocks from Madison Square.

Francesca turned the card over, and the laboriously printed words, all in block letters, leaped out at her. There were four.

HELP.
COME IMMEDIATELY.
TONIGHT.

Francesca exhaled harshly, amazed. What was this?

She finally removed her elbow-length white evening gloves, kicking off her delicate high-heeled green satin slippers. Was this a trick?

She knew no one except, perhaps, Evan, who might play such a prank on her, and he would not do so at such an hour. For clearly this note was urging her to return to Madison Square then and there. Francesca glanced over at the large bronze clock set on an ebonized maple bureau. It was ten past ten.

For a single gentlewoman, it was late. Single gentlewomen did not rush about the city alone and unescorted at such an hour. If they were out, they were at a dinner party or a ball, or perhaps the opera or ballet.

Of course, she was not like the other young single women in this city.

Why had Miss Georgette de Labouche singled her out for her pleas? God, even her name, which meant "Georgette of the mouth," was a joke.

Was she an actress? Francesca began to pace, her mint green evening gown, a combination of silk and chiffon, rustling about her legs. Then she halted. Dear God, that woman had been frightened and terribly distraught. Francesca would bet her life on it.

Which meant she must respond to the woman's plea for help.

Francesca hurried to her closet, throwing it open. Their home, built only a few years ago, had all of the most modern conveniences, including electricity, closets, indoor plumbing, and one telephone—which was in her father's study downstairs. Set back behind a large circular drive and huge lawns on Fifth Avenue, facing Central Park, it had been dubbed the Marble Palace by someone in the press, for the vast use of that particular stone. There was no marble, though, in Francesca's large and beautifully appointed bedroom, except for the mantel over the fireplace and one marble-topped table in front of the beige damask sofa and blue-upon-blue sitting chairs.

She pulled a dove gray suit from her closet and fumbled with the buttons on the back of her dress, not wanting to call for a maid. The house's single telephone was downstairs. Was her father in the library even now? It was his favorite room, his sanctuary, and he might be reading a journal there before bed. Francesca was thinking about calling Bragg.

Of course, he was not at home. He was at the Rooftop Garden—wasn't he?

Somehow, Francesca just knew he would not have remained for very long at Stanford White's shocking fête. Perhaps he had gone to his office at 300 Mulberry Street, to work well into the night, as she knew he so often did.

Still, if she called Bragg, she might be relinquishing her very first case, giving it into his control. Trembling with worry and excitement she struggled out of her evening gown. She had to do this, and she must not tell Bragg—who had rebuffed her anyway. Still, she could not help recalling what had happened last week when she had gone out late like this, alone.

Evan had discovered her delinquency and to this day remained skeptical of her, thinking her to have a *tendre* for someone she had dared to go out to meet. Bragg had actually caught her in the act of returning home well past midnight, and he, too, had assumed the worst. And to make matters even worse, earlier in the week Neil had caught her coming in on Sunday dressed in the disguise of one of the maids' clothing. He, too, assumed her to have taken a lover.

Francesca had to smile a little, because her reputation was rapidly turning into shambles, yet that was the furthest thing from the truth. Except, of course, for the kiss she and Bragg had shared.

Francesca forced it from her mind. Going out alone at this late hour was not a good idea for far more basic reasons than the damage it would do to her reputation.

The city was crawling with the worst, most offensive, and most dangerous elements at night. It was no place for any lady, no matter her new line of work.

It crossed Francesca's mind that, given her new although

somewhat secret profession, she must immediately purchase
a gun.

Francesca finished dressing. Georgette de Labouche's plea
could be a trick or a trap. And while Francesca didn't really
think it was a trap, she had to consider the possibility.
Therefore, it would be so much better to wait until the morning to venture back to Madison Square. Yet Francesca knew
she would not wait, because she believed Georgette de Labouche to be truly in trouble.

Therefore, she needed help. She just could not go out and
about alone in the late-night hour. Joel Kennedy would be
perfect for the night's work. Even though he was only ten
years old, he knew the city intimately and was brilliant at
getting out of jams.

She would fetch Joel on her way downtown.

Relieved, Francesca smiled to herself.

Joel lived with his mother, a seamstress who worked for the
clothing manufacturer Moe Levy, and his two younger brothers and his younger sister on 10th Street and Avenue A. He
was a little hoodlum, adept at picking pockets and cutting
purses. He was even in Bragg's Rogues' Gallery, an album
of photographs of the city's most wanted criminals, male and
female, begun by one of Bragg's notorious predecessors, Tom
Byrnes.

Francesca and Joel had met purely by chance when she
was investigating Jonny Burton's abduction, and when Joel
had saved her from a thug, exposing his true nature, an odd
bond had been formed between them. In fact, as he knew the
ins and outs of the city so well, especially the slums of downtown, Francesca had turned to him repeatedly for guidance
and help. Francesca wasn't sure she would have ferreted out
the madman who had abducted Jonny without Joel at her side.
And she had grown fond of the little boy in the past two
weeks. He was hardly all bad. If he ever gave up his life of
crime, he would be a wonderful child. Of that she had no
doubt.

However, Francesca had seen the poverty in which he and

his family lived. She had seen how hard his young mother, Maggie, worked to support her four children. She had seen how much Joel cared for his two brothers and sister, although he would never admit it. Francesca knew he would not give up a lucrative, if risky, way of life anytime soon.

The cab, which she had flagged down on Fifth Avenue after sneaking out of the house through the kitchens, paused in front of No. 201, the building where Joel and his family lived. Francesca hesitated. Was she to go up and knock on the Kennedys' door? Maggie would be angry. What mother would let her son out and about at this hour?

Francesca realized she had no choice but to try to explain. In any case, a woman in trouble was waiting desperately for her, and that spurred her on as little else could.

She gave the driver a dollar. "Please wait," she said firmly, "as I will be but a few minutes." She had run this game before, with no success. After she had paid her last driver to wait for her, and handsomely, he had taken off anyway, stranding her in the worst section of bordellos and gambling halls. She smiled. "If you are here when I return, I shall pay you a double fare at my destination."

His eyes widened. "I'll be here, ma'am," he said.

Francesca knew he would. She was proud of herself—she was not the kind of woman to make the same mistake twice. She slipped from the hansom, sliding on the ice beneath her feet, and somehow made it to the front door of No. 201. Once inside the tiny cramped entryway, which could not allow more than three bodies at once, if crammed together like sardines, she was faced with severe blackness and many foul and obnoxious odors.

Francesca climbed the stairs, wishing she had a candle or even a match, it crossing her mind now that she needed to travel about the city with a small cache of useful items in a larger purse. Mentally, she added matches to her list of one small gun. And she resolved to find a way to help the Kennedys.

She found their apartment and knocked.

The door was opened almost instantly, and to Francesca's

surprise, she realized that Maggie hadn't been sleeping, in spite of the long hours she kept at the factory. One light was on in the single room that was a living room and a kitchen. A tub in the corner told Francesca it was also where everyone bathed; a mat on the floor told her Maggie also slept there. A single open door was to the rear of the room, where the three children must be sleeping.

Francesca saw a pile of beautiful fabric on the kitchen table, along with a sewing machine, a pincushion, and several spools of thread. A paper pattern was on the second of two chairs, folded in half.

Maggie Kennedy's tired blue eyes registered surprise as their gazes met through the cracked but still-chained door. "Miss Cahill?"

Francesca smiled. "I am so sorry to call at such an hour," she said, stunned to realize that Maggie was working and clearly not for Moe Levy at this hour.

"Is something wrong? Are you . . . alone?" Maggie was glancing behind her into the dark hall. She did not remove the chain or open the door and invite Francesca in.

"Yes, someone is in trouble. Dire trouble, I fear." Francesca hesitated. "I am afraid to run about at this hour alone, and my parents would murder me directly if they ever knew I was not safely at home. Is there any chance I might employ Joel as a guide?" That last request was a sudden inspiration. She would pay Joel handsomely for his efforts, she decided, pleased. It would, to use a common saying, kill two birds with one throw.

"He isn't here," Maggie said, anguish briefly flitting across her face. "He keeps his own hours. Paddy says he left just before I got home, which was an hour ago. I'm afraid I can't help you." She hesitated, as if uncertain what to do or say next.

Francesca's heart lurched and she realized how dearly she had been counting on having Joel at her side while she investigated Georgette de Labouche's plea for help. She would have to go on alone. There was no other choice.

"Then thank you very much," Francesca said on a deep

breath. Her gaze slipped past the red-haired woman with the pretty but tired face to the beautiful sky blue satin on the table. "That will be a lovely dress."

"Yes, it will." Maggie did not smile. "If you ever need a gown custom-made, please call. My work is superior and my prices are cheaper than anyone else's in this city, I assure you of that."

Francesca started, realizing that Maggie worked for herself with serious resolve when she was not at the factory. In that moment, she decided to have several gowns made. "I do need some new gowns for the spring, and I will call, immediately."

Maggie's eyes brightened. "You will not be sorry," she said. Then, "Let me get you a candle so you can make your way downstairs. You may return it another time." She closed the door abruptly.

Francesca was cloaked in darkness. This woman was so destitute that she would only loan her a penny candle. It broke Francesca's heart.

The door opened, this time without the chain, and Maggie handed her a small lit candle, and perhaps the barest smile passed over her face. "Good night, Miss Cahill," she said, and the door closed abruptly again.

Francesca murmured to the sheet of scarred and ill-painted wood, "Good night." She turned and hurried downstairs, the candle, no thicker than her pinkie, shedding only the tiniest pool of light on the narrow and uneven stairway. But it was enough for Francesca to avoid someone's rotten and half-eaten potato.

Her cabbie was waiting. Francesca was briefly exultant—her play had worked! She climbed into the hansom and gave the driver Georgette de Labouche's address. The cab moved forward, the horse's harness jingling, his hooves clopping on the cobblestones. In the distance, somewhere, Francesca heard the horns of a fire wagon. The plea *was* odd. She prayed she was not walking into some kind of trap. Her intuition told her that all was not as it should be.

Suddenly something banged hard on the side of the hansom. Francesca flinched, as did the driver, glancing over his shoulder. The black mare in the traces paid no heed. "Hey! Bugger off!" he shouted to someone or something on the running boards.

An opulent carriage drawn by four matching bays passed them on their left.

Francesca was amazed as the door beside her opened and a small bundled-up figure she recognized catapulted himself onto the seat beside her. "Ow, it's cold!" Joel cried.

Francesca reached across him to close the door firmly. "Driver, it is a friend; we are fine."

The driver said something incoherent and unpleasant beneath his breath. The horse's hooves clattered on the cobblestones as they turned onto 14th Street, heading west. The traffic was light now, consisting of a trolley and a few other cabs, moving in both directions.

Francesca faced the dark-haired boy with the strikingly white skin. "Joel?"

He was rubbing his hands, wrapped in rags, together. He grinned. "Who else, lady, would be driving around my ward in a fancy rig like this?"

She beamed. "I have been looking for you."

"Of course you have," he said, a proud boast. He grinned at her.

"No, really. I need to hire you, Joel. I need your services," she said, and even as she spoke it hit her then that she did need him, and badly, but as far more than a guide. She needed him to help her as a guide but also in so many other ways! Francesca didn't want to call upon his unique talents in her new avocation, absolutely not, but he was shrewd and street-smart, and in just two weeks she had already learned so much from him.

"Joel, I am offering you employment," she said. This was not the time to think about her mother's silver, she reminded herself. A week ago Joel had briefly worked in the Cahill stables and her mother's finest silver had disappeared. Both Julia and Mrs. Ryan were furious and certain Joel was to blame. He denied it.

"I hate horses," he said.

"No, you are scared of them," Francesca corrected gently.
He sighed. "Don't like working in no stable, lady."

"Did I say anything about working in a stable? I wish to
hire you as my assistant," she said.

A salary was quickly negotiated. "I will pay you two dollars
a week. Plus meals." Francesca smiled, knowing she was offering him a quarter more than the job of stable boy paid.

"Three, plus meals, an' a bed, too, when I need it."

She blinked. "Three dollars a week? You are only ten years
old!"

"Three dollars, an' meals, an' a bed, an' you got yourself
a handshake, lady," he said.

"Very well," Francesca sighed. Then, eagerly, "We are on
our first case." She quickly told him what had happened, pro-
ducing Georgette's card as she did so. "What do you think?"

His face screwed up as he reached for the woman's calling
card. "Something stinks. Something ain't right." He squinted
at the calling card.

Francesca hadn't truly wanted to have her suspicions confirmed. "Joel, you can't read."

He smiled at her. "Actually, me ma's been teachin' me for
a few years now an' I can read a little."

Francesca was aghast. "You told me you could not read!"

"Well, I didn't know you an' there were foxes everywhere
an' I was mindin' my own business!" he cried.

Francesca took back Georgette de Labouche's card rather
grimly. "You know, Joel, I am a very honest woman. And if
you are working for me, you will have to get over this propensity of yours to . . . to . . . alter the truth." He had lied to
her—blatantly—and not for the first time.

He gave her a gap-toothed smile. "Wut's propenty?"

"Propensity. It means inclination." The hansom was halting. "Uh-oh." Her heart lurched with undue and unnerving
force. "We are here, Joel."

He patted her hand. "Don't worry, lady. If you want, I will
go in first, make sure it's all on the up-'n'-up."

Francesca paid the driver. "No. This is my very first case.

We will go in together." She smiled, hoping it looked brave. But her courage seemed to be failing her now.

The moment she used the knocker, footsteps could be heard at a rapid pace in the hall beyond the door, hurrying to them. The door was thrust open immediately.

Francesca was greeted with the sight of a buxom woman in her early thirties, her dyed and curled red hair pinned up, clad in a well-made suit, although the jacket had been designed to show off an undue amount of cleavage. The woman was wearing large aquamarine drop earrings, a huge aquamarine-and-diamond pin in the shape of a butterfly, and three rings, all gems. Her face was pretty and quite made up. Instantly, Francesca knew she was not greeting a gentlewoman.

Francesca peered past the woman almost immediately and saw a wood-floored hall beyond the small entry, stairs that led upstairs just behind the woman. The door directly at the end of the hall was closed, but light spilled out beneath it. The hall itself was dimly lit.

"You came! Thank God, Miss Cahill—who's that?" Her tone changed, becoming one of abject suspicion as she stared down at Joel.

"I'm her assistant," Joel announced, slipping beneath the woman's arm as she held open the door and ducking into the entry.

Francesca made another mental note—Joel should know to let her do all the speaking. "Miss de Labouche?"

"Yes, yes, do come in!" the woman cried, indicating that she had indeed been the one to hand Francesca the note, but she faced Joel. "Stop right there, young man," she said sternly.

Joel slid his rag-clad hands into the pockets of his big wool coat and he shrugged. Georgette de Labouche shut the door behind Francesca. "Thank God you have come, but you should have come alone!"

The woman was in a panic. There was no mistaking the

signs—panic was in her eyes and in her tone and written all over her face as well.

"Perhaps we should start from the beginning," Francesca said kindly.

"There is no time!"

Francesca began unbuttoning her fur-lined cloak. "Very well. Shall we sit down somewhere and begin?"

Georgette hesitated, glancing at Joel. Then, "We can go in there." She pointed at the closed door at the end of the hall, where light glared out from beneath it. Clearly the room beyond was brilliantly lit. "But the boy stays right here." She glared at Joel. "You don't move, buster. You got that?"

Joel made a funny face. "I got one boss and that's Miss Cahill."

"Don't talk back to me!" Georgette cried.

Francesca put a hand on her arm and smiled reassuringly. "I can see you are upset. We shall speak privately, have no fear." She looked at Joel. "Joel, your job is to assist me— when I need assistance. Right now, please stay here in the entry and wait for me until I ask you to do otherwise."

His gaze was searching. Francesca realized he was trying to decide what her words really meant—as if she were speaking in code.

"Stay right here," Francesca reiterated. She smiled at Georgette, who was wringing her bejeweled hands. The redhead looked close to tears. "He'll be fine," Francesca said, hoping she spoke the truth. While originally the idea of Joel as an assistant had seemed wonderful, Francesca wasn't quite sure she could trust him to do as she asked. Which made him a loose cannon indeed. She did not want to mismanage her first case because of the little boy.

Georgette led the way briskly down the hall.

Francesca asked, speaking to her rigid but small shoulders, "How did you know to contact me, Miss de Labouche?"

She glanced over her shoulder, her hand on the knob of the closed door. "You gave me one of your cards outside of Tiffany's yesterday. It was an unusual card. I tucked it away.

But I never thought I'd have need of it, and certainly not a day later!"

Francesca met her dark brown eyes. The woman was crying. "It will be all right," she said softly.

Georgette turned and thrust the door somewhat open, stepping inside. Instinct caused unease to assail Francesca, and she hesitated for a moment before slipping past Georgette, who instantly slammed the door closed behind her—locking it.

But Francesca only flinched at the sound of the lock clicking, because directly in the middle of the room was a man. A gentleman, by the looks of him. He was lying on his abdomen, on the highly polished wood floor, his face turned to one side, in a pool of dark red blood.

Francesca muffled her very own gasp. "Is he . . . ?"

"He's dead," Georgette said flatly. "And I need you to help me get rid of the body."

THREE

Francesca gasped. Surely she had misheard Georgette de Labouche. "What?"

"We must get rid of the body. You have to help me! And
the first thing we must do is send the boy away!" Georgette
cried, as if Francesca were a dolt.

Francesca could hardly believe her ears. This was her very
first official case. And it was not just any case; it was a homicide, the gravest of crimes. A murder had been committed,
and Francesca intended to get to the bottom of it. But this
woman was asking her not to solve the crime, but help hide
it. The situation might have been comical had a man not been
murdered and lying there dead at their feet.

"Didn't you hear a word I said? If the police find him,
they will throw me in the cooler for sure!" Georgette stabbed
at the air, near hysteria.

Francesca took a deep, calming breath. She glanced once
more at the dead man at their feet. Her stomach heaved. She
had seen corpses before, of course, but they had been in their
Sunday best and carefully arranged on the satin bed of a beautiful coffin. "Miss de Labouche? Who is this man? And . . .
did you kill him?"

"See! Even you think I did it!" Georgette whirled, pacing,
her bosom heaving.

Francesca tried to peer more closely at the dead man. "Is
that a hole I see in the back of his head?" She wondered if
she might retch. She must control the urge. "Was he shot? Or
beaten with a stick?"

Georgette whirled. "I would never hurt Paul. He was a
dear, dear friend."

Francesca was relieved as she faced Georgette, no longer
studying the man. But she had seen right away that he was

well dressed, right down to the tips of his shiny new Oxford shoes. She had noticed a gold watch fob in a gray vest where his dark wool jacket was open. The suit, the watch, and the shoes were all of a very fine quality indeed. "A dear, dear friend," Francesca repeated. "You are his mistress?"

Georgette did not flush. "Obviously," she snapped. "Will you or will you not help me dispose of the body?"

"So now you wish to *dispose* of the body?" Francesca gaped. "Miss de Labouche, this man is not a mouse in a trap. He is a human being and the victim of a terrible crime. We must inform the police. A man has been murdered. In cold blood, I might add—from the look of things."

"Of course it was in cold blood!" Georgette cried, and she sank down on a red velvet chair, moaning and holding her face with her hands.

Francesca took another glance at the body. He had removed his overcoat and top hat; both items lay on another chair with a silver-tipped cane. She estimated his age as early fifties. Then she walked over to Georgette and laid her palm reassuringly on her plump but narrow shoulder. "I am sorry for your loss," she said softly.

Georgette did not speak. She moaned again and said, "I am going straight to the Tombs; I can see it now!"

"No one has accused you of any crime, Miss de Labouche. What happened?" Francesca knew she did not have a lot of time in which to ask questions. In fact, if she was a truly honorable citizen, she would rush off to call the police in that instant. But she preferred to ask some questions first—before the police began their investigation.

An image of Bragg flashed through her mind. They had worked quite closely together to solve the abduction of Jonny Burton. Something stirred in her heart. He had even admitted, once, reluctantly, how helpful she had been. She wondered if they would work together again, to solve this newer and even more dastardly crime.

Georgette looked up. "I was in my bath," she finally said. "Paul comes every Tuesday and Friday evening. His full name is Paul Randall," she added. "I heard him come in, or

I thought I did. I expected him to come upstairs. I had a surprise waiting for him." Tears filled her eyes.

"A surprise?" Francesca asked, wishing she had a notepad. First thing tomorrow she would begin acquiring the tools of her new trade.

"I was in the bath, Miss Cahill. With champagne and other . . . things."

Francesca stiffened. "Oh." Things? Did she dare ask what those things were? She was dying of curiosity, and then she reminded herself that as a now-professional sleuth, of course she must ask. "What kind of things?"

Georgette blinked. "Toys. Devices. You know."

Francesca thought her heart had slowed. "Toys? You mean like rubber ducks?"

Georgette sighed in exasperation and shook her head, standing. "You gentlewomen are all the same! No wonder men like Paul come to women like me! Not rubber ducks, my dear. Toys. *Sex* toys. You know. Objects that bring extra pleasure. If you'd like, I can show them to you?" She stared rather coyly.

Francesca tried not to gasp as her cheeks flamed. She was stunned. She hadn't known that such objects existed, and in any case, what could they be and how were they used? She fought to get a grip. "I see." Her cheeks remained hot. Would Connie know anything about sex toys? Francesca doubted it, but she was the only person Francesca dared to ask. "So you were in the bath and then what happened?" She tried to sound brisk, professional.

"Many minutes passed as I lingered there, with the toys." She briefly smiled at Francesca, some kind of insinuation hanging there. Francesca did not quite know what she meant. "Of course he would come to find me; I know him so well. But he did not, and suddenly, I was concerned. And it was just at that point when I heard a sharp, loud crack. One sound. A crack. And I knew it was a gunshot."

Francesca had had an image of Georgette alone in the bath together with different-sized rubber ducks, the best her sud-

denly infertile imagination could do. She shoved that rather
unwelcome image aside. "And?"

"And? I leaped up, put on a robe, and ran downstairs,
calling for Paul. I was praying that the sound I had heard
meant something else. When I reached the entry, the door
was wide open, so I closed it."

Francesca had a thought. "What about the staff?"

"I have no staff on Tuesday and Friday evenings, for obvious reasons, reasons of privacy."

"Of course," Francesca said.

"After I closed the door I turned, and the parlor door was
wide open and I saw him. Oh, God! It was so horrid; you
just cannot imagine how horrid it was!" She cried out, a sob-
like sound, and covered her face with her hands once again.

Francesca patted the woman's shoulder again. "I am so
sorry."

Georgette looked up at her tearfully. "Are you?"

"Yes," Francesca said quietly, earnestly. "An innocent man
is dead. This is a ghastly crime. I am terribly sorry, and I
promise you, Miss de Labouche, that I will find out who
perpetrated this deadly and foul deed."

Georgette said, "I only want to hide the body. Paul is dead.
Finding whoever did this will not bring him back." Her mouth
trembled again.

"We *must* tell the police," Francesca reiterated firmly. "So
you ran to him? Was he still alive? Did he say anything?"

Georgette shook her head and briefly closed her eyes. "He
was dead. His eyes were wide open, sightless, and there was
so much blood!" She moaned and sank down again, but this
time on the red brocade sofa.

Francesca looked at the dead man. His eyes were closed.
"Did you touch him?"

Georgette nodded and whispered, "I closed his eyes, I just
had to, but that is all."

Francesca nodded, folding her arms. She studied the dead
man, Paul, for another moment, then glanced at Georgette,
who remained motionless on the sofa, hunched over in apparent misery. Francesca glanced around. "The only way to

enter this room is via that single door from the hall?"

Georgette nodded.

"And you are certain you did not see anyone?"

She nodded again.

Francesca glanced at the clock on the mantel. It was a quarter to midnight. Georgette had accosted her on the street outside of Madison Square Garden at half past nine, approximately. Perhaps it had even been fifteen or twenty minutes past the hour. "At what time did the murder occur? At what time did you enter your bath? How long were you in it before you heard the shot?"

"It was six-thirty when I began to prepare to bathe. I was expecting Paul at seven. He is usually prompt. He was probably murdered a few moments past seven."

"Miss Labouche. This is very important. Did Mr. Randall have any enemies? Can you think of anyone who might want him dead?"

"Only his wife," the redhead said, her regard sullen.

"I am in earnest," Francesca returned. "Are you?"

Georgette de Labouche grimaced. "He had no real enemies. He was not the type of man to provoke anyone, Miss Cahill. He had retired from his position as manager of a textile company five years ago. We met shortly afterward. He was a simple man. His life revolved around his children and his wife, his golf, his club—and me."

Francesca was the one to nod, thoughtfully. Then she sighed. "Well, I may have more questions for you, Miss de Labouche, but for the moment, that is enough. I must call the police. Do you have a telephone?"

Georgette looked at her. "They will think I am the one. A murder like this is always blamed on the mistress."

"I do not think they will think you are the one," Francesca said, meaning it. "We must inform the police. We *must*."

"Fine," Georgette said, appearing very unhappy. "I do not have a telephone. While you go, I shall go upstairs and try to compose myself. Perhaps I shall lie down."

"I think that is a good idea," Francesca said. She hesitated. Bragg's house was only a few blocks away. Should she go

out on the street and wave down a roundsman or go over to
Bragg's? Eventually he would be informed of the murder anyway.

Of course she must go directly to Bragg. Otherwise there
would be pointless questions and delay as she dealt with the
patrolmen who would answer her call.

Of course, he had rebuffed her earlier, and she should not
be pleased about their sharing another case. And she was not
pleased—this was *her* case. She had found it first.

"I will see you to the door," Georgette said abruptly, standing.

There was something in the woman's tone that made Francesca start, and suspicion filled her. Georgette had said at least
three times that she wanted to hide the body. Francesca realized she should stay and *guard* the body while sending Joel
for help. Even though it was unlikely that the woman could
remove and hide the body in the half hour or so that it would
take the police commissioner to arrive.

"I am sending Joel round the block to the police commissioner's house," Francesca announced, watching her closely.
"He is a personal friend of mine," she added.

Georgette blanched, and without a word—but looking
even unhappier than before—she ran from the room.

As she did so, Joel fell into the room, clearly having had
his ear pressed to the closed parlor door the entire time.
"Hell!" he cried, eyes wide. "Look it that! Cold as a wagon
tire, Miss Cahill, a real stiff for your first crime." He grinned
at her. "An' a real to-do gent by the look of him."

"Yes, he appears to be a gentleman." Francesca was stern.
"Joel, if you are to be my assistant, eavesdropping is not
allowed."

"Eavesdroppin'? Wut the hell is that?"

"It is spying," she said, coming forward. "You spied on a
private conversation between myself and Miss de Labouche."

"I was lookin' out for you, lady," he said fiercely. "That's
me job."

She looked into his almost-black eyes and melted. "You
were?"

He nodded. Then, "Did you peek in his purse?"

She stiffened. "We are not stealing a dead man's purse!"

"Why not? He's dead. He can't use the spondulicks!"

"Spondulicks?" Sometimes conversing with Joel was like trying to comprehend a foreign language.

"He's dead. He can't spend a dime."

"We are not stealing from the corpse!" Francesca cried, meaning it. "Now listen carefully. Tomorrow we will sit down and go over some rules. Rules of your employment. But right now, I need you to go over to the police commissioner's house and tell him what has happened. If he is not there, tell Peter, his man." She hesitated, glancing behind her at the dead man. God, she would be alone with the corpse while Joel was gone. It was not a comforting thought.

Of course, Georgette was upstairs, so she would not really be alone.

"And you should hurry," Francesca added.

"Right," Joel said, turning to go.

"Wait!" She caught the shoulder of his jacket. "Do you know where you're going?"

Joel grinned at her. "Sure do. Madison and Twenty-fourth Street."

She stared. "How would you know where Bragg lives?"

He shrugged. "Whole world knows. Ain't no secret. Back in a flash." He hurried away.

Francesca stood very still, watching him leave the house. And then she felt truly alone.

She shivered.

The house was so quiet that she could hear the clock ticking on the mantel. It almost felt as if there were eyes trained on her back—the dead man's eyes. But of course, they were closed—and he was dead.

Fortunately, she did not believe in ghosts. Still, Francesca hurried down the dimly lit hall, wishing it were more brightly lit, relieved to leave the room with the corpse. She checked the front door. It was locked. That made her feel a bit better.

She cracked open the only other door on the hall, other than the parlor door, and glanced into a small dining room.

It was cast in shadow. She vaguely made out an oak table and four chairs, a floral arrangement, and a sideboard with knickknacks. A kitchen had to be on the other side of the alcove. Francesca hesitated.

If there was a kitchen door that led to a garden out back or the street out front, she wanted to make sure it was locked. She was very nervous now. And why not? She was guarding the corpse of a man who had been murdered less than five hours ago.

Francesca looked up at the dark stairs. "Miss de Labouche?" she called.

There was no answer.

"Georgette?" she tried again, with the same lack of success.

Francesca glanced behind her. The parlor remained so brilliantly lit, and the dead body in the pool of blood remained a grotesquely eye-catching spectacle. Francesca realized just how nervous she was.

That was it. She dashed through the small dining alcove, trying not to consider that the murderer might still be in the house—of course that made no sense—and she found herself in the kitchen. This house did not have electricity, and it was a moment before Francesca turned on one gaslight. There was a back door. It was locked.

She sighed in abject relief.

When she heard something.

Instinct caused Francesca to turn off the light and crouch down beside the doorway to the dining alcove. She had not closed the dining room door, and she could just glimpse the hall beyond.

She heard something again. God damn it, but it was the front door, she was certain of it, being carefully closed.

Francesca ducked completely behind the kitchen doorway, now perspiring madly. Joel had left about five minutes ago. Maybe, maybe, he could run from here to Bragg's in five minutes. But there was just no way that he was already returning, alone or with Bragg, and anyway, they would have to knock.

She trembled and heard a floorboard creak.

Someone had entered the house. Someone was in the hall. Someone who was not announcing himself—someone who had a key.

She heard more soft footsteps.

Francesca went blank. But she had to know who the intruder was. She thought he had walked past the dining room doorway, but she wasn't sure. Keeping on all fours now, she peered around the kitchen doorway and into the dining room.

Just in time to glimpse a man's silhouette as he walked past while in the hall.

Francesca ducked back. She heard the man halt. And there was a very soft, barely audible expletive, followed by absolute silence.

She imagined he had seen the body and that was what had stopped him in his tracks and caused him to curse. Was he staring at it now?

Suddenly she heard brisk footsteps returning. Francesca did not dare peer around the corner again, as much as she wanted to. She held her breath, afraid he might feel her presence, afraid he might change course and discover her hiding in the other room.

The front door opened and closed.

Francesca jumped up and ran into the dining room and shoved aside the draperies to peer onto the street, her pulse racing wildly. A very nice gig was pulling away from the curb, a single man its occupant—the driver. He was too far away for her to make out any features.

Francesca stared. Who in blazes had just walked into Georgette de Labouche's house in order to stare at her dead lover? Who would do such a thing, then turn around without a word and leave?

What in tarnation was going on?

Francesca quickly returned to the scene, less shaken now and very perplexed. Why hadn't the intruder cried out for help? Why hadn't he called for Georgette? Had he expected to see

Paul dead upon the floor? Or was he just very good at hiding his surprise?

She glanced first at the dead man, then at the clock on the mantel. It was fifteen minutes past the hour; if Bragg had been at home, he should arrive here at any moment. Francesca inhaled hard.

She stared at the corpse. Of course, she should not touch anything, but now that the moment of danger had passed, her senses were returning to her. She hadn't asked Georgette where he lived. Had his whole life really been his wife, his children, his game of golf, and his club, and his mistress? Clearly he had had enemies. These were all very important, if not crucial, questions.

Francesca knew she should leave the body undisturbed. She slowly approached it.

Well, what the hell. This was her first case and she was determined to solve it—alone. She gingerly reached out and flipped the man's jacket farther open. There was a bulge in his trouser pocket. A billfold. That would tell her something.

She reached for it, but unless she stepped into the drying blood on the floor, she could not quite reach. Bragg was very sharp, and he did not miss a thing—she did not want him to remark blood on her patent boots. She strained to reach the man's pocket. It was no easy task to maintain her balance and keep the toes of her ankle boots out of the blood. Francesca tugged on the material of the trousers and finally slipped two fingers inside them. She was sweating, and her body felt as stiff as a board. She felt the hard leather edge of his billfold beneath two of her fingertips.

She felt triumphant, and she strained to get a better grip, tugging the billfold out of the trousers. The moment it slid free, she smiled, only to watch it fall from her two fingers into the blood.

"Damn it."

Francesca stiffened, surprised at how loud her own words sounded in the presence of the dead man. She swallowed hard and took the wallet, stood, looked around, saw nothing with which to wipe off the blood, and sighed. She opened it.

He was carrying quite a bit of cash, which she ignored. There were several calling cards in the wallet. The first one read:

MR. PAUL RANDALL
89 EAST 57th STREET
NEW YORK CITY

Francesca wanted to take the card, but she filed the information away instead. And then she looked past all of his personal cards and she gasped. The last card read:

CALDER HART, PRESIDENT
HART INDUSTRIES & SHIPPING CO.
NO. 1 BRIDGE STREET
NEW YORK CITY

And scrawled in pen on the card was another address, which Francesca could not quite make out. It was either 973 or 978 Fifth Avenue.

Francesca stared at Calder Hart's card, as if that might bring meaning to the fact that she had found it in the dead man's wallet. Of course, this meant nothing, other than that Paul Randall had met Calder Hart at least once.

Did they have business dealings? Were they friends?

Francesca heard the front door open and slam and she heard multiple pairs of footsteps coming down the hall.

Without debate, she tucked Calder Hart's card into her bodice beneath her suit jacket and then she quickly redeposited Paul Randall's wallet in the pocket of his trousers where she had found it, all the while praying that she was not obstructing a criminal investigation. Bragg had once threatened her with such charges. Then she stepped away from the body, breathlessly, and when she faced the door Bragg was barreling through it.

He saw her, he saw the body, and he stopped in his tracks. His face was a comical arrangement of anger and resignation.

Actually, it wasn't comical at all, Francesca decided nervously.

"There's the bloke," Joel said cheerfully, ducking past Bragg and coming to stand between Francesca and the dead man. He pointed at the corpse. "Colder than friggin' ice." He grinned.

Peter, Bragg's huge, towering personal servant, stood behind him, looking more like a bodyguard than a valet. He was six-foot-six and had to be 240 pounds, all of it muscle. But then, Francesca had come to the conclusion that he was quite the jack-of-all-trades.

Their gazes locked.

"I can explain," Francesca said quickly.

Bragg's jaw tightened. His face was hard now, dangerously so. "This shall be good," he finally said. "Of that I have no doubt."

FOUR

She could not seem to tear her gaze away from his.

"I am waiting, Francesca," he said softly, and somehow his tone with its bare drawl was dangerous. "I am waiting for a plausible explanation. How did you happen to be here, in this house, with this corpse?" His brilliant gaze finally left her and moved over Paul Randall. "A newly murdered corpse, from the look of it."

"It is all rather simple, and very plausible, too!" she cried, aware of the parlor being impossibly warm. She wished to fan herself. His calm demeanor felt threatening.

As if he had not heard her, he turned. "Find me a roundsman, call headquarters, and I would like at least one detective on the scene—now. And Kennedy can wait in the hall," he spoke to Peter in a slightly sharper tone, and the big man nodded and left, with a reluctant Joel in tow.

Francesca backed up discreetly as Bragg spoke. He was angry, quite obviously, and she was no fool—she knew his anger had less to do with being roused out of bed to solve a murder than with finding her there with the victim. It was like waiting for a tornado to strike and all the while watching it coming.

Was he concerned for her—or merely irritated?

He gave her a very dark look and approached the victim, squatting down beside him and clearly looking at the head wound. "I am waiting, Francesca," he said, not looking up.

"Very well!" Somehow she threw her hands up in the air. "As I was leaving the Garden a woman pressed a card with a note into my hand, quite desperately, begging me for help. I was with my parents and I could not read the note until I returned home. Her name is Georgette de Labouche, and she lives here. She did not say what she wanted, but the note was quite clear—she begged me to come here immediately, to-night."

Bragg had easily retrieved Randall's wallet from his trousers and now stood, glancing through it. "So you stole out of your parents' house at the midnight hour to meet a stranger, merely because she gave you a note asking you to do so?" He stared at the white calling cards in his hand. His expression briefly changed, but Francesca could not fathom the light that flitted through his topaz eyes.

"She sounded desperate, Bragg," Francesca said nervously. "How could I deny her?"

He faced her. "Very easily, actually. Did it not occur to you that this could be a trick of some sort, or a trap? And where is Miss de Labouche?"

"She is upstairs, and yes, of course I considered the unsavory possibility—as remote as it seemed—that this might be a trap."

"Did you touch *anything,* Francesca?" Bragg asked, turning over the wallet.

She prayed he would not notice the bloodstains. "No." And she felt her cheeks heating.

"There is blood on your shoes. There is blood on the wallet," he said, remaining calm. But his gaze was piercing.

She grimaced, uncertain of what to say, what to do. She did not like lying, but she did not like being put on the carpet this way, either.

He waited, his patience vast.

"Yes!" she cried. "Of course I peeked into his wallet!" Should she tell him she had taken Calder Hart's card from it? But it was her very best lead!

"It is a crime to interfere with a criminal investigation," he said less softly.

"I know, and I am so sorry, but after the intruder I could not seem to help myself!"

"The intruder?" Bragg asked sharply.

Francesca nodded eagerly. "Bragg, shortly after Joel left, someone entered the house. A man. I did not get a good look at him, as I was hiding in the kitchen after going there to make sure any back doors were locked. But he clearly went up the hall, saw the body, said not a word, except for a single curse, and he left. Just like that." She was breathless, having spoken far too rapidly.

"Christ," Bragg said. He slapped the wallet down onto the low table before the couch and paced to her, confronting her. "What if that was the killer? Jesus, Francesca, why do you have to put yourself directly in the face of danger, time after time? Will you ever learn?"

She knew she was wide-eyed. His proximity was doing two things to her: it was increasing her anxiety and increasing her tension. "But you do not care," she heard herself say, and then she wished, fervently, that she could take the words back.

"What?" He stared. "Of course I care. You are my friend and the last thing I wish to do is attend your funeral!" His last sentence ratcheted up in volume until the final words were almost shouted. "I leave you at an orgiastic spectacle—which is bad enough. And then what do you do? You wind up in a stranger's home with a fresh corpse! One day, you will drive some poor man insane with his fear for you!"

Francesca kept recalling now how he had broken their engagement for the morrow. She lifted both brows. "Well, at least you can be assured that that poor man will not be yourself."

He blinked. "I beg your pardon?"

"Nothing," she mumbled, turning away.

But he gripped her arm. "No, I want to know what that comment meant. And I want to know this instant."

She faced him. "Commissioner, you are manhandling me."

He dropped his hand. "I am sorry. But I had assumed you would return to a normal life, now that the Burton abduction has been solved." He shook his head. "I can see that I have assumed wrongly."

She said softly, "You should know me better than that, Bragg."

He stared.

Then she said, "You can be irksome, too."

His eyes widened. "I can be irksome?"

"Yes."

"And how is that?" He folded his arms across his broad chest.

"Well, when one plans one's entire day over an event and then, quite summarily, that event is canceled, why, that is rather irksome, wouldn't you agree?" Her tone was sugary, her smile sweet.

His hands found his hips. "I see. I see now what your temper is about. You are upset because I cannot take you driving tomorrow. It is a matter of your female disposition." He started to smile.

"I have made other plans. And there is no such thing as a female disposition."

"The library?" he suggested. "To study? For your self-exams?"

He was wisely ignoring the subject of female dispositions. Now she flushed. Only Connie and Evan knew that she secretly attended college, and once, when Bragg had almost caught her, she had told him she liked to test herself on the subjects she studied by herself. "I have other callers," she said, a lie.

"Francesca, enough. I am sorry you do not understand the pressure I am under in my position as commissioner of police. I promise that one day we will have our outing." He glanced at her a final time and turned back to the corpse. His shoulders seemed rigid now.

One day they would have their outing? Francesca was disbelieving. Had she so misunderstood his intentions? It did not sound as if he had any interest in her at all; it did not sound as if he intended to court her, not now, not tomorrow, not *ever.*

I must not be disappointed, she managed, turning away. *I have a case to solve, an important case, my first, and it is* murder.

"What did you take from the wallet, Francesca?" Bragg asked, somewhat wearily, now moving about the room, his gaze going everywhere.

"Nothing," she lied. She shoved her disappointment aside. Of course, she would have to tell him about Calder Hart's card, but maybe Hart would provide a clue and she would solve the case—first, without Bragg's help. And never mind that she had somewhat fancifully imagined the two of them solving this case together.

"What happened when you arrived at the house?" Bragg asked, looking underneath seat cushions and pillows now.

Francesca walked away from him and the corpse and sat down in a far chair. "What are you looking for?" She could not help being curious.

"Often the killer leaves evidence behind, and often in a homicide that evidence is the weapon that was used to murder the victim." He walked over to a table filled with photographs and bric-a-brac. "I shall not be surprised if we recover the murder weapon within half a city block of this house."

Francesca filed away that interesting piece of information.

"Please tell me what happened when you arrived?" Bragg said, now looking in corners of the room and behind the single window's draperies, which pooled on the floor.

"Miss de Labouche was quite distraught when I arrived," Francesca said, wishing she could help him look for the gun. "She was unhappy that I had brought Joel," she added.

He faced her, hands on his hips. "And how did our little 'kid' appear on the scene?"

"I do think he has mended his ways, Bragg," Francesca said, in reference to Bragg labeling Joel a "kid," which meant a child cutpurse.

He snorted. "So he just showed up here?"

"I sought him out. I was afraid to wander about the city alone."

He smiled at her. It was an "I told you so" smile.

"The moment I arrived she showed me the body—then asked me to help her hide it," Francesca said with wide and innocent-looking eyes, well aware of the reaction her dramatic statement would cause.

"What?" he exclaimed. "Jesus! And she is upstairs?" He started for the door.

"She did not do it, Bragg." Francesca stood up. "She is—was—Randall's mistress and she is afraid you will think she did it, which is why she was desperate to hide the body."

"And you believe her? Francesca, you are too naive."

"She was in the bath when she heard a shot ring out! With sex toys, I might add."

That stopped him in his tracks. He looked at her and she looked back.

Francesca said, breathlessly, "I am merely repeating exactly what she told me."

"I see." He seemed somewhat flushed. Then, "Do you have any idea what you are talking about?"

She shook her head. "No. But she assured me the toys were not rubber ducks."

He stared. And his stare was direct.

Francesca thought about the bathtub upstairs and the toys that might still be in it, devices that would give extra pleasure to their owner. She swallowed hard. "Do you know what she is talking about?" she heard herself ask.

"Yes. It is time to talk to Miss de Labouche." He stalked out of the parlor.

She ran after him. "The murder occurred around seven o'clock this evening," Francesca added to his broad shoulders.

He regarded her at the bottom of the stairwell. "So you have already interviewed the suspect?"

"I consider her a witness," Francesca retorted.

"You are not a policeman," Bragg said firmly. "And what you consider is neither here nor there. I mean it, Francesca," he warned. "This case is *not* your affair."

How many times would he hurt her feelings in one evening? she wondered. "I helped you solve the Burton Abduction," she said, not as firmly. "You admitted so yourself."

"Yes, you did. And for that I am forever grateful. But, and I do mean *but,* Francesca, you will *not* help me solve the Randall Killing; you will *not.*" His eyes blazed. "Not even if I have to keep you under lock and key in your home."

She folded her arms across her breasts and did not rebut him.

"But what?" he demanded.

She couldn't quite smile. "Miss de Labouche is my client," Francesca said. Which wasn't quite true, as their arrangement wasn't quite official. But Francesca felt certain that they had an understanding; besides, Miss de Labouche would undoubtedly agree to retain her as a crime-solver if Francesca offered her services for free.

And she watched as the blood pressure Bragg had spoken of soared.

He bounded up the stairs ahead of her, without a word.

Francesca followed. On the second floor's landing he whirled and they collided. "Go downstairs," he said tightly.

She did not really want to fight. "Very well. But you do not have to be so mean-spirited, Bragg."

His response was, "My hair has turned gray in the two weeks since we have met."

Francesca smiled as he turned away; absurdly, she was somewhat pleased.

She heard him calling for Miss de Labouche. There was only one bedroom on top of the stairs, which was not unusual, as clearly this was a large townhouse that had been subdivided into several apartments. The lady of the house did not answer.

As Bragg finally pushed open the door to the bedroom, Francesca glanced into the separate bathing room. Signs of a hastily disrupted bath were everywhere: a small stool contained an open bottle of champagne and two glasses, one half-full, a towel lay in a heap upon the floor, and candles had been burned down to their wicks. The bathroom, while small, had been painted a dusky shade of pink, and it was quite pretty. A colorful painted screen was in one corner, and wall pegs contained several lacy peignoirs. There was no toilet, which was in an adjacent and separate chamber.

Francesca stared down. In the porcelain tub, a tub that stood on gilt claw feet, floating in the two inches of leftover water, was a large plastic object in a nondescript color. But there was absolutely nothing nondescript about its shape and there was no mistaking what it was meant to represent. As Francesca stared, she felt herself warm.

Good God. Now she understood.

"She isn't here and there is a back stairs which leads to the kitchen—she is gone," Bragg said darkly, pausing on the threshold of the bathroom.

"Oh," Francesca said, backing out and brushing past him in her haste.

So that was what a sex toy was. She simply could not get over it. Her mind spun.

"Oh, Christ," Bragg said, stepping out of the bathroom.

She could not look him in the eye. "Well, she was most definitely in the bath."

"That does not mean she did not kill her lover," Bragg returned, far too evenly.

Still not looking at him, Francesca poked her head inside the bedroom, which was a red room with many Chinese paintings on the walls, gold velvet draperies, and an Oriental screen. The bed was large, also done up in red, and it dominated the room. It was perfectly made up.

Francesca left the bedroom, glancing briefly down the back stairs. In the dark, and in her fear, she had never noticed stairs that led to and from the kitchen. "She was in the bath, Bragg, *exactly* as she said she was," Francesca said.

He sighed, placing his hand on her shoulder and guiding her downstairs, the back way. Voices could now be heard in the foyer in the front of the apartment. "Francesca, you are young. And genteel. Perhaps she bathed *after* killing her lover."

Bragg was one of the smartest men she knew; he was also very perceptive. Surely he had seen that plastic object floating in the bath? She said, harshly, "She bathed with her toy, Bragg."

They had reached the kitchen. Francesca turned on the light as Bragg repeated, "As I said, perhaps she bathed after killing Randall."

Francesca finally understood his meaning and she stared. "But that is sickly!"

"Yes, it is." He left her standing in the kitchen as he went through the dining alcove and into the front hall.

Francesca forced herself to recover from her shock. She ran after him and found him telling two patrolmen to cordon off the area immediately, with another two officers awaiting their instructions. "I believe the murder was committed with a small weapon, a lady's pistol, perhaps, or a gentleman's derringer. I want a search conducted now. The house, the grounds, the entire city block if need be, but I expect that weapon to be found tonight." The first two roundsmen quickly left, the expressions on their faces severe and determined.

Francesca grimaced. She had forgotten, but if Bragg had demoted 300 officers, the entire department was in chaos, and undoubtedly in abject fear of Bragg as well. She glanced at the other two men standing stiffly before Bragg, waiting for their orders. They did not seem happy. But clearly they would jump through a hoop if he so commanded it.

Two plainclothes detectives came through the front door, one of whom Francesca recognized as Inspector Murphy, a man with a big belly and thick sideburns. "The corpse is in the parlor," Bragg said. "But first, we also must locate Georgette de Labouche, the mistress of the house. You may not arrest her, but she is to be brought downtown for questioning by myself, personally. Francesca, please describe Miss de Labouche."

"Bragg," she began, in protest.

Murphy had just recognized Francesca and the portly man's eyes widened briefly. Bragg said, "Describe Miss de Labouche, please. Time is of the utmost importance now."

Francesca was almost certain that Georgette had not killed Paul Randall. She said, "She is about thirty, plump and pleasing, with curly red hair and brown eyes. She was wearing a blue suit, the jacket of which was rather daring. Also, large aquamarine drop earrings and a big aquamarine butterfly pin. She had several large rings on both hands, one of which might have been a garnet set in silver, not gold."

"Thank you," Bragg said. To Murphy, "She can't have

gone far. Put the word out. I want her in my office before the sun comes up. Begin by speaking with the neighbors. Someone may have seen her leaving, and we must learn when Randall arrived."

"Yes, sir," he said, exiting the house. From his tone, Francesca was surprised that he did not salute.

"I should like to see the victim," the other detective said.

"Please," Bragg returned with a gesture.

The detective left them to go into the parlor. Horses' hooves sounded on the cobblestones of the street outside. Francesca also heard wagon tires. She moved and glanced out the window beside the front door. A police wagon had arrived, and wardsmen were jumping out. Someone had already placed a sawhorse on one end of the block, and she saw another patrolman dragging a second barricade to the front of the house. Lights had appeared in the windows of the houses just across the street. Francesca saw several neighboring tenants in those windows, and one was shoved open. A man shouted, "What the hell is going on?"

"Peter?" Bragg intoned.

Francesca turned, startled, and she saw the big man step out of the shadows by the stairs. She had not even realized he was present. He had one hand on Joel Kennedy's small shoulder. Joel gave her an annoyed look, which turned to a pleading one. The silent language he spoke was unmistakable—he wanted to get away from the police as soon as possible, if not sooner. She smiled at him reassuringly.

He scowled and said, low, "Bugger all coppers."

"Please take Miss Cahill home and see to it that she does go home," Bragg said, ignoring Joel's comment. "The boy may go as well." Bragg glanced at her and briefly their gazes held.

Francesca was dismayed. She did not want to go. Not when Georgette had run away, not when the murder weapon had yet to be found, not when Bragg would soon huddle with Murphy and that other detective to discuss the case. And what about the neighbors? She wanted to hear what they might say!

This was *her* case. Yet she was being excluded.

"Good night, Francesca," Bragg said firmly.

She stared mutely at him for a moment. Then she nodded, realizing she had no choice but to leave—as he was not giving her one. But tomorrow, why, that was a brand-new day—one filled with exciting possibilities. "Good night, Bragg." She was sweet.

As she followed Peter to the door, Bragg said, "And, Francesca?"

She paused, regarding him innocently.

"If your *client* contacts you, I am certain you will inform me immediately," he said.

She mustered up another too-nice smile. "Of course," she replied.

"I mean it," he said, a warning.

"As do I."

FIVE

The moment she awoke she recalled that she had her very first case and so much to do that she doubted it could all be done in a day. Too many questions to count flooded her instantly racing mind: Had Georgette de Labouche been found? What was Calder Hart's relationship with the deceased? Had a neighbor seen or heard anything?

And who hated Paul Randall enough to want him dead?

Francesca was determined to solve the murder, thus proving to Bragg once and for all how invaluable she was, and she blinked her eyes open, imagining how, in a week or so, he would once again thank her for her indispensable help— and perhaps even confess that he could not have managed the investigation without her.

She smiled.

But it was not Bragg standing at the foot of her bed, smiling back at her. Her sister, Connie, clad in a beautiful rose-and-cream-striped ensemble, stood at the foot of her bed, as radiant as ever, smiling with bemusement. "Good morning, sleepyhead. That must be some dream, Francesca, to put such a smile on your face!"

Francesca sat up with a wide and inelegant yawn. "It was."

"Let me guess. Our dashing new police commissioner?" Connie teased.

Francesca sobered. There was one problem—she was not a police officer, and Rick Bragg was determined to keep her out of the investigation. It was as if their teamwork during the Burton Affair had never occurred. Somehow, she would have to sleuth very discreetly indeed. Until he realized how invaluable she was. "What are you doing here and what time is it?" Francesca flung the heavy quilts and blankets aside, glancing at her partially drawn draperies as she did so. Outside, the sun was up and high. She had overslept.

"It is past ten, and I admit to being simply shocked that I have found you loitering abed like any other of your unwed peers." Connie smiled again, arms folded.

"It was a late night," Francesca admitted. She and her sister were as close as could be, and Francesca was pleased to find her sister waiting for her to wake up. Perhaps their closeness could be explained by the fact that there was so little or no sibling rivalry between them because they were so different, in spite of their nearly identical looks. While Francesca was the bluestocking and reformer in the family, Connie was an indisputably perfect hostess, an elegant wife, and the doting mother of two darling little girls. As young girls, Francesca had studied and Connie had gone to tea parties with Julia. As much as Francesca had sought to avoid suitors, Connie had encouraged them even before her informal debut. Francesca had always, secretly, known she would postpone marriage for as long as possible; Connie had always, openly, dreamed of whom she might wed and prayed it would be as soon as she was old enough. She had been seventeen when she had met Neil Montrose, and they had been married a year later. She was only twenty-two now.

"I see that it must have been a very late night," Connie was saying. "Have you been up until dawn studying?"

Francesca grinned as she stood, shivering a bit in her pale blue silk nightgown. "No. I have my first case, Con!" she exclaimed, keeping her voice down but unable to contain or even hide her excitement.

"Your first what?" Connie asked with a furrowed brow.

"My first case." When Connie failed to understand, Francesca said, perplexed, "Con, as a crime-solver. Remember?"

Connie blinked. "What?"

Francesca could not believe Connie did not understand. She was already reaching for the purse she had used last night. She handed Connie one of her calling cards. "Didn't I show these to you? I picked them up at Tiffany's on Thursday." Connie would be the first person she would show her new cards to—after Bragg.

The card read:

FRANCESCA CAHILL
CRIME-SOLVER EXTRAORDINAIRE
NO. 810 FIFTH AVENUE, NEW YORK CITY
ALL CASES ACCEPTED, NO CRIME TOO SMALL

Connie gasped. "Oh, dear. When I said you should become a crime-solver, I was in jest, Francesca. What about your studies?" Clearly she was alarmed. Her sky-blue eyes were hugely wide.

Francesca blinked and retrieved her card, tucking it safely away. "My studies shall not suffer, I may assure you of that."

"What do you mean, you have your first case? And what is it?" Connie demanded nervously. Then, "Mama will kill us both when she learns of this!"

"Mama is not going to learn of this," Francesca said, her tone becoming even lower. It also contained a warning.

Connie gave her a disbelieving look. "No one can keep a secret from Mama for very long. She knows everything of import that pertains to anybody she deems a significant part of her life."

That was more than true. Julia was, beyond a doubt, one of the shrewdest and most powerful women in the city. She knew all of the city's leaders, both gentlemen and ladies. She more than knew the city's elite; she was an active force behind almost any important social, political, or charitable scene or encounter. When she wished to, she could move mountains. Better yet, when she wished it, the mountain *always* came to her.

"I do not like this," Connie said.

"I am sorry. But don't worry. Perhaps I shouldn't have told you. So. What are you doing here—and on a Saturday morning?" Francesca suddenly realized just how odd this visit was. "Isn't Neil at home?" Her heart lurched as she spoke. It was far too early for Neil to be out philandering, wasn't it?

Francesca remained in disbelief every time she thought about her brother-in-law and his affair. God, he had been, up until her awful discovery, the noblest gentleman she had ever met. In fact, Francesca had thought him to be perfect in every way, including as a husband.

Connie had looked away. "Yes. Neil is at home." Her voice was so soft it was almost inaudible.

Francesca saw the troubled look upon her sister's face and hated herself for not blurting out what she knew. And there was no possibility of Francesca having made a mistake; she had actually caught Neil in the act. Of course, Francesca was aware that his lover was about to depart for Europe for the rest of the year. And that would be the end of the affair, Francesca thought. So perhaps this would all simply disappear.

But she did not think so. A few days ago Connie had quite bitten her head off for prying into her personal life. She had been so explicit, demanding that Francesca mind her own affairs. Never had Connie been so angry.

Connie had never before spoken to Fran in such a way.

Francesca was not certain whether Connie knew, but clearly she sensed that something was amiss. Francesca smiled a little now. "So, you have come to share a late breakfast with me?" Connie was a dedicated wife and mother, and her not being at home on a Saturday morning with her infant daughter, three-year-old Charlotte, and Neil was a sure sign of the distress brewing in her life.

Connie returned her smile. "I thought it would be fun to go shopping. Besides, Neil is going out to lunch and Charlotte has a birthday party to attend."

Francesca merely stared. The sister she knew would take both of her daughters to the party and hobnob with the other mothers there—all of whom were young, newly married high-society wives.

"I have come to fetch you so we can spend all of our money, have lunch at Sherry's or the Plaza Hotel, and have the most wonderful time!" Connie cried, but the smile on her face did not reach her eyes.

Francesca looked at her. Connie knew she hated shopping, but her face was so earnest now, and her eyes were so clearly unhappy, filled with dismay, and perhaps also with fear. Francesca took her hand. "Oh, Con. I can't. I'm so sorry."

"Whyever not?" Connie cried.

She hesitated. "My case. I must interview several people." Paul Randall's widow was first on her list; second was Calder Hart. She would also enlist Joel to go down to Mulberry Street and try to ferret out information regarding any progress Bragg had made thus far in his investigation.

"You are going to spend the day sleuthing?" Connie asked with a bit of surprise.

Francesca nodded brightly. "But please, do not use that word in this house!"

"Mama is in her apartments. She will not come down for another two hours and you know it."

"There is always a first time."

"I doubt it. Very well. I shall accompany you," Connie said flatly.

"What?" Francesca was sure she had misheard.

"I will accompany you," Connie smiled. "This shall be fun, actually." Her smile faded. "And it will keep my mind off of . . . things."

Francesca stared. "You mean Neil." The words just popped out, of their own accord.

Connie's face stiffened. "I did not say that." She turned away, then back. "Please, Fran. I promise not to interfere, I will act as your steadfast companion, if that is what you want."

Francesca wanted to say no. She did not want to drag Connie along, especially because, if something dangerous did arise, she would be responsible for her sister's welfare—and removing herself from danger had proved to be enough of a task in itself in the recent past. Also, she could not reveal to Connie that she was investigating a murder. Francesca had no doubt that Connie would have a conniption fit at the mere usage of a word like *murder*. She would also run straight to Neil with the information, no matter the state of their marriage. She might even tell on her to Bragg.

But then it crossed her racing mind that Calder Hart had taken something of an interest in her sister—she had seen it in his eyes. And it might not be so easy gaining an audience with him—if she were alone.

She hated using Connie. But how could it hurt—this one single time?

Besides, a killer was out there, a killer who had to be brought to justice.

"Very well," Francesca said, realizing she would have to put off her visit to Randall's widow, for if Connie came along, the cat would be out of the bag. "But on one condition. You must swear that whatever transpires this day, you shall tell no one, Con, no one, and that includes both Neil and Bragg."

Connie raised her right hand, as if her left were on the Bible while she was being sworn in to a public office. "I swear," she said.

Somehow, Francesca was not relieved.

Connie's four-in-hand, a very elegant black coach, paused before the entrance to No. 973 Fifth Avenue, about ten blocks uptown from the Cahill residence. "This cannot be it," Francesca announced.

"That scribble is a three and not an eight; this must be it," Connie returned, her hands inside of a rose-colored mink muff that matched both her ensemble and her coat.

Francesca stared at the huge mansion they faced. It was at least five stories high, and it was the only house on the block, the property taking up at least half of it. The rest of the lots were vacant, although one showed some signs of imminent construction. Sweeping lawns, now covered with snow, surrounded the house; a frozen pond and a guest cottage were in the back, as were tennis courts and a large stable. "This house is larger than our own. Could Calder Hart be that well off?"

"Perhaps he has ten children," Connie said. She rapped on the window of the coachman's cab. "Clark, please pull up in front of the house."

"He did not act like a married man the other night," Francesca said, and the moment she spoke she regretted her words, as she was thinking about Neil's behavior.

Connie glanced at her. "He spoke with us for a minute or two. How could you tell anything in that period of time— during such a circus?" She blushed at the memory.

Francesca wondered what Connie would say if she told her about her client's interest in sex toys and baths. "Unlike yourself, I was paying attention to Mr. Hart. I found him more interesting than that spectacle arranged for us by the very dissolute Mr. White."

Connie flushed deeply. "I paid attention to Mr. Hart as well."

"Balderdash. You could not take your eyes off of the performers."

"Francesca, that is rude," Connie said primly.

"I'm sorry. It was . . . titillating, to use Calder Hart's word." She patted her sister's arm.

"It was hardly titillating. It was shocking and scandalous," Connie said firmly.

"So you and Neil left?" Francesca had to ask, trying not to sound sly. Their brougham paused in front of the entrance to Hart's stone mansion. Not surprisingly, a life-size statue of a stag graced the roof of the house just above the temple front that was the entrance.

"Actually, we stayed a bit longer." Connie's jaw tightened. "I had some trouble finding Neil in the crush."

Francesca did not like the sound of that. Had his lover been present? Or had Neil been merely conversing with other guests? Francesca prayed that was the case.

Connie gave her a bright smile as Clark opened their door. "Shall we? Onward and upward to whatever it is that you are seeking?"

Francesca smiled and she stepped out of the carriage behind her sister, the coachman steadying her so she would not slip. She shivered in spite of her fur-lined coat. "This weather is enough to make one fantasize about Newport in the summer," Francesca said. She had nothing against the beach, but she did not like Newport when it was a retreat for the city's most artificial and most wealthy citizens. The most enchanting time of year was now, in the midst of a snowy winter, when

one could take long solitary walks upon the beach, and the
city itself was like a ghost town.

Connie was already knocking on the door. It was opened
promptly by a manservant. "Shall I give him my card or shall
you give him yours?" Connie asked.

Francesca was already handing her brand-new card to the
butler, answer enough. "Please tell Mr. Hart that the Cahill
sisters have come calling."

When the butler left, they both glanced around. The foyer,
which boasted a black-and-white grid pattern of marble floors,
was large enough to host a small ball. Francesca had never
seen such an oversized entry. The domed ceiling above them
had been painted in a fresco, and clearly the subject was re-
ligious—people and angels and perhaps even devils were being swept up into heaven, or was it hell? As the sky was
painted blue, Francesca hoped, fervently, that it was heaven,
but the men, women and children seemed to be screaming,
indicating that the experience was not a pleasant one—and
perhaps the subject matter was the end of the world, the effect
was so macabre.

She shivered.

Black marble columns were at both ends of the huge room,
and at the far end, in between them, were two life-size statues
of nude women. Francesca simply stared.

While the statues were beautiful, neither hands nor leaves
covered anyone's private parts. And both women were fleshy
and voluptuous. One woman seemed to be running, as if pursued. Her long tresses were flowing about her ample hips and
full breasts, and she seemed to be afraid, gazing over her
shoulder, her eyes wide. Francesca tore her gaze away and
met Connie's wide eyes. They looked at each other and said
not a word.

A long moment passed. Connie said, low, "Look at the
paintings."

Francesca hadn't even noticed the two huge paintings on
the two facing walls. She stared at an extremely graphic and
realistic painting of a man in armor upon his back, perhaps
dying, clearly wounded—a horse walking by him or even

trotting upon him. She gave her sister a glance and walked over to the art.

"*The Conversion of Saint Paul*," she whispered, reading the name of the painting aloud. It was powerful and disturbing and she shivered again.

Connie joined her and said, low, "Is he an atheist, do you think? I doubt the Church would approve of such a painting."

"I hardly know the man," Francesca said.

Footsteps sounded. They were brisk, assured. "What a pleasant surprise."

They both turned quickly, in unison, as if two small girls with their hands in someone's cookie jar.

Calder Hart was grinning. "And you are both admiring my Caravaggio?"

Francesca managed to hold out her hand. "Mr. Hart. Hello. Thank you for seeing us. And yes, we were admiring your art."

"Really?" He bowed over her hand and looked at Connie, rather frankly. "Most of my guests find this painting, among others, to be rather irreligious, if not scandalous and shocking." He smiled as if that amused him.

"It is somewhat irreverent," Connie murmured. "Good day, Mr. Hart."

"Please, you must call me Calder." He bowed over her hand, and there was a gleam in his eyes. "Does it shock *you*?" he asked.

Connie tugged her hand from his as if he had held it for too long, which he had not. "It does not shock me, but I would never hang it in my own home," she said, surprising Francesca with her uncustomary bluntness.

"So you do not care for it?" Hart asked.

"No, I do not."

"And if your husband wished to own it?"

She stared at Hart. "Why, he should then own it. But I would never allow him to hang it in a public room, much less the entrance of our house."

"Oh ho. You disapprove of me. Perhaps I need some guidance then, by a woman like yourself."

Connie said, "You are unattached, Mr. Hart? There is no good woman who currently offers you the guidance you have spoken of?"

"I am a bachelor, if that is what you are asking. Confirmed, I might add." He grinned.

"What a shame," Connie said, as if she meant it. Francesca knew she did.

"Really? Most women seem pleased when they learn I am unequivocally available." His grin widened. It was so devilish.

"Most single women," Connie corrected.

His grin widened and he laughed. "Even the proper married ones," he corrected.

Connie's body stiffened. "I beg your pardon. A proper married woman would only care that you are a catch if she had a friend or a sister to match you to."

He looked at her. "In your circle, perhaps." Clearly, he did not believe her.

Francesca looked from one to the other as their rapid exchange occurred and did not like what was happening. The painting no longer disturbed Connie; clearly, she was disturbed by their host, who was flirting with her and not even hiding it. In fact, Hart was acting as if flirtation were hardly on his mind, for he looked at her sister as if she were his next prey. And *that* was simply unacceptable.

"Mr. Hart? Might we have a word with you?" Francesca interrupted them.

"Of course, Miss Cahill." He faced Francesca, then said, "And do you also find the conversion of one of the Catholic Church's most popular and sacred saints irreverent and shocking?"

She wet her lips. "I find it disturbing, but I have yet to think about why. Still, the artist is clearly a master, and the work is riveting."

He nodded with approval. "I agree." He glanced at Connie. "I am an avid collector. I should love to give you a tour of the house and the many masterpieces I have spent years acquiring. Perhaps I might change your opinion of art that does not neatly fit into the lives of most denizens of this city, like yourself." He smiled at her.

"I doubt we have time for such a tour, Mr. Hart," Connie said, and there was no mistaking that her *we* was a rebuttal to his *you*, which Francesca felt certain had not been intended as a plural pronoun.

He covered his heart with one hand and he was laughing. "Perhaps, in time, you will have a change of heart." He then smiled at Francesca. "No pun intended, ladies. Do come with me." He turned.

Francesca's gaze met Connie's. She gave her a look, one that she meant to be reassuring. Connie's answering regard was both grim and annoyed, and maybe also angry. Her eyes seemed to say, *This is just not right!*

Francesca smiled a little and took her sister's hand and they followed Calder Hart across the huge entry and into another vast room, this one a salon.

At first, Francesca saw only a dozen or more seating arrangements, the furnishings exotic. There were brocades, damask, and silks everywhere, striped patterns competing with paisleys, with few, if any, solid-colored fabrics anywhere. Two huge throne-like chairs seemed to be covered in real zebra skins. The salon was a kaleidoscope of warmth— of shades of red, gold, and amber, except, of course, for the two astonishing zebra chairs. The walls were painted a burnt orange; huge crystal chandeliers were overhead, and two of the room's many rugs were leopard skins. Standing there in the midst of the eclectic room, Francesca felt as if she had entered another world, perhaps in the Middle East, or maybe even another time, centuries ago in Byzantium.

Connie poked her, her cheeks aflame.

Francesca followed her gaze and gasped.

The room was so busy that she hadn't even noticed the paintings on the wall. The one Connie pointed at caused Francesca to stare, gaping. A curly-haired brunette lounged sensually amid rumpled white silk sheets. She was nude, flushed, even satisfied, and the way she was sprawling left very little to the imagination. The artist had rendered every inch of her with precision and the utmost care, although fortunately, her loins were covered. Still, the oil painting was excessive, graphic, and shocking.

Francesca had never seen anything like it.

Connie turned away, sitting down abruptly on a gold-print damask chair. She clasped her hands in her lap.

Francesca tore her gaze from the woman and looked at Calder Hart. His gaze was on Connie, and it was speculative now, while Connie stared at her hands. Francesca stared at their host. Did he like to shock his guests and the world in general? Or did he so love his art that he just did not care what anyone thought of him? And why would a bachelor build a home like this? How lonely it must be to float around in this vast, exotic palace with only servants for company.

He realized she was staring and he gestured. "Shall we sit?"

Francesca nodded and sat down beside her sister on a red love seat with burgundy cording. Hart took an armchair that was facing them both. Francesca tried to organize her thoughts. She had been so distracted since entering the house that she had almost forgotten why she was there in the first place. She had come to solve a murder, and the first order of business was to learn of his relationship with the recently deceased Paul Randall.

"So, Miss Cahill, how may I help you . . . and your sister?" Hart asked. "I assume this is not a social call, as you presented me with the most unique calling card."

Francesca and Connie exchanged glances. "No, I am sorry to say this is not a social call."

He smiled and said, "I am dismayed."

"Perhaps another time," Francesca said.

"Yes, perhaps I will have the honor of taking you and your sister to lunch sometime. Say, this week?" He did not glance at Connie.

But Connie spoke before Francesca could respond. "That is extremely kind of you, Mr. Hart, but my calendar is full, this coming week."

"Then in the week afterward?" He smiled at her, and it

was a smile that was very potent indeed. Francesca wondered if she had ever met any man with more charisma. At the least, she had never met anyone so ruthless in his use of it before.

"I shall have to check my book," Connie said ruefully. Francesca knew she was only being polite and had no intention of having lunch with their host.

"Please do," Hart said, apparently not dissuaded. He turned to Francesca. "How may I help you?"

Francesca straightened. "I have recently acquired a client, Mr. Hart. Miss Georgette de Labouche. I wondered if you were acquainted with her?"

If he knew Miss de Labouche, if her name was at all familiar, he gave no sign. Nor did he smile at its comical interpretation. "No. And what is this about?"

Francesca hesitated. How best to proceed? "Miss de Labouche is a dear *friend* of Paul Randall. I believe you are an acquaintance of his?" Francesca smiled.

He did not return her smile. His tone changed, becoming cool. "I know Randall," he said.

"How?" Francesca asked eagerly. "Do you have business dealings? Are you friends?"

Hart stood. "I hardly see how this is any business of yours, Miss Cahill."

Francesca was stunned by his change in personality. "Am I somehow intruding?"

"Yes, you are," he said bluntly.

Connie stood. "Francesca, perhaps we should leave. I fear we have overstayed our welcome."

Francesca ignored her, her eyes glued to Hart's. Hart also ignored her sister now. "Mr. Hart, I apologize if I am intruding, but your relationship to Paul Randall might very well be crucial to my investigation."

"And just what the hell are you investigating. Miss Cahill?" he demanded.

She wet her lips. "Paul Randall is dead, Mr. Hart," she finally said. "And I am investigating his murder."

Connie gasped. Francesca only vaguely heard her, because she was watching Hart so closely. Of course, she did not

suspect him of anything, except perhaps of being a friend or
associate of Randall. But his expression changed. Something
passed through his eyes, so quickly she could not tell what
the emotion was. Had it been surprise? Or something else,
something she was not astute enough to recognize?

Calder Hart stared grimly at her.

"He was murdered last night, Mr. Hart," Francesca said.
"I am sorry to be the one to tell you, but now you can see
why I must know the nature of your relationship."

Hart turned away. He crossed the room. Not far from
where they sat was a silver liquor cart. Francesca's eyes widened as she watched him pour a drink, then slam down half
of it. "Mr. Hart?"

He remained with his back to her, and he finished the
whiskey. Then he refilled the glass.

Connie plucked her sister's sleeve. She was standing, and
her eyes were wide with disapproval. "I think it is time for
us to go," she said low.

Francesca shook her head.

Hart turned. He held up his glass as if in a toast. "You
have made my day, Miss Cahill," he said then, and his smile
was more than mocking. It was a sneer. "Randall is dead.
Hurrah." He drank.

Connie surprised everyone then, perhaps even herself. She
moved swiftly forward, to Hart's side, and she took the glass
from his hand. "You are upset. I apologize for my sister, who
means no harm—but sometimes suffers from terrible lapses
in grace and common sense. Please. Sit down. Let me call
your man, Mr. Hart."

"How kind you are," he mocked. He tilted up her chin. "I
wonder how far your kindness would go—given the right
circumstances?"

Francesca understood his meaning and she gasped. Connie
did not pull away for a moment, and she stared as if hyp-
notized at their host.

Hart released her. He smiled and looked at Francesca. "The
answer to your question is a simple one. And now that Randall is dead, I have no problem answering it."

Connie backed away from Hart. She was white. Francesca took her hand tightly. This man was frightening.

"I am his son," Calder Hart said. *"His bastard son."* He smiled at them both, and it was chilling.

SIX

Francesca stared at Hart, horrified.

He was Randall's son?

"Dear God," Connie whispered, white with the very same shock.

"Mr. Hart! I am so sorry; I had no idea," Francesca began, wringing her hands. Her mind was racing, and it was filled with accusations, mostly directed at herself. She had just told a man that his father was dead, and she would regret her lapse forever. But how could she have known? And why hadn't Bragg been round to inform Hart of the murder? Surely Bragg knew that Randall was his half brother's father!

"You are sorry that Randall is dead, or for having been the bearer of such *ill* tidings?" Hart asked coolly.

"Both," Francesca whispered, mortified.

Connie stepped between them. "We have bungled terribly!" she cried. "I can only beg your forgiveness, and if I had known what Francesca was up to, I would have never allowed it!" She shot Francesca a furious glare. It said, *How could you?*

"I had no idea," Francesca repeated. "Mr. Hart, do sit down. Let us bring you some tea."

He laughed at her. The sound wasn't pleasant, not at all.

"We are leaving," Connie said firmly, glaring again at Francesca. She faced Calder Hart. "Is there anything we can do to help you through this terrible time?"

His gaze moved over her. Before, when he had looked at Connie, no matter how reprehensible his intentions—if indeed he did have intentions—somehow, his interest and virility had combined to make him more fascinating. Now, his look was ice-cold. It was the look of a man who, perhaps, had no conscience. It was almost reptilian.

He said, "I can think of numerous ways in which you might comfort me, my dear Lady Montrose."

Connie flushed.

The comment was so rude that even Francesca was silent.

Connie grimaced, and without a word, she turned and marched away, crossing the salon and heading for the door.

Francesca stared at Hart.

"Good day," he said to her abruptly—as rudely.

A sharp rebuke for his terrible behavior was on the tip of her tongue. She wondered if he had enjoyed so discomfiting her sister. But then she thought of how he had just learned that his father was dead, and she held her tongue.

"Mr. Hart, sir."

Francesca turned and saw the butler at the door of the salon where Connie was about to exit. He said, "The commissioner of police is here to see you, sir."

Francesca's heart seemed to go right through Hart's roof.

"My day just gets better and better," Hart said caustically. "Show the dear police commissioner in."

Francesca knew she had to leave and debated the slim possibility that she might do so without encountering Bragg. Was there another exit to the room? She saw a series of huge doors ahead, clearly leading to another room. How she yearned to beeline for them.

Bragg strode into the salon.

Francesca arranged her expression into one that she fervently hoped resembled passive innocence. She tried to come up with a credible excuse for calling on Hart, and failed. Bragg faltered with surprise the moment he saw her.

Hart was pouring another drink. "Your paramour beat you to it, Rick," he said. "The news is out; the king is dead. Long live the king."

Bragg looked from his half brother to Francesca and back. Then his gaze slammed onto Francesca. "No," he said, shaking his head as if he just could not believe it—as if he were seeing things.

"It was an innocent mistake," Francesca cried. "Please, Bragg, do not leap to the wrong conclusions!"

"I am trying very hard not to do just that," he said. Francesca winced.

Hart chuckled. "The taming of the shrew. This should be an enjoyable little family drama, one I shall cherish from the sidelines."

Bragg looked at him. "Shut up, Hart. As you are in dire straits."

"What? Will you arrest your own brother? And for what? A few timely barbs?" Hart drank, but leisurely now. His eyes appeared black as he watched his brother coolly.

Bragg approached Francesca. Their gazes locked. "I am debating, Francesca, very seriously, taking you downtown. Perhaps then you will understand the gravity of the situation."

"Connie and I are going shopping," she began.

"That is not true!" Connie cried from the doorway. She was still angry with Francesca.

Francesca sent her a baleful look. Then, "I am so sorry!"

"Go outside. Wait for me in the foyer. I will discuss this with you privately, after I have spoken with Calder."

"Yes," Francesca said meekly, debating running for Connie's carriage and home. Of course, defying him right now might not be the best of ideas. She flew across the room. As she left, she felt as if she had just escaped the executioner.

In the entry, Connie stared accusingly at her. "You are investigating a *murder*, Fran?"

She wanted to be defensive, but she was too shaken. "I will never forgive myself," she whispered, "for telling Hart about his father that way."

"You should not forgive yourself," Connie snapped. "Even if he is a most reprehensible man."

Francesca looked at her and then heard raised voices coming from the salon. She became still. They were arguing.

Yes, she was terribly sorry for telling Hart about his father, but the mistake had been an innocent one. However, she would die to know what they were speaking about. And there was no mistaking that the conversation coming from the other room was an argument, one that was escalating even as she thought about it.

"I would give anything to be a fly on the wall in that room right now," Francesca whispered, looking at her sister.

"No," Connie said, shaking her head. "We are waiting for the police commissioner *right here.*"

Francesca ignored her. It was as if her feet had wings—and a mind of their own. She ran into an adjacent room, which turned out to be a smaller but equally opulent salon. The huge double doors she had seen from the other salon faced her, and she ran to them, ignoring Connie's cry of protest. Francesca pinned her ear to the wood and strained to hear. Connie approached.

"You should be throttled! Have you no decency? Their conversation is a private one!" Connie cried.

"Ssh," Francesca hissed, trying to hear the two men.

Connie hesitated, then said, softly, "What is going on?"

Francesca wet her lips. "Hart denies killing Randall."

Connie gasped, and then she laid her ear against the door as well.

"I did not kill him, if that is why you are here," Hart said indifferently. He turned to the bar cart. "Drink?"

"Have I suggested that you killed Randall?" Bragg asked coolly.

Hart took his time, pouring Bragg the drink he had not asked for and stepping over to him in order to hand it to him. His smile was feral. "I know you well, or do you forget? After all, we are *brothers.*"

Bragg smiled, but it was solely a baring of his teeth. He put the drink down, untouched. "You do not know me at all, Calder, and do not fool yourself, in spite of the fact that we are *half* brothers."

Hart laughed at that. "I know you. My brother the crusader, ever on the wings of Lady Justice, her sister Liberty, and the pursuit of happiness as a God-given right for all."

"The right is a constitutional one."

"Not according to Rick Bragg."

"Do you not even have one whit of remorse for your selfishness?"

"Have you not ever regretted being the slave of moral rectitude?"

Bragg said, "Of course I have."

"And honest, disgustingly honest. How can I compete?" Hart mocked.

"Only *you* have made this a competition," Bragg returned evenly.

"As always, the fault is mine." Hart sighed with immense melodrama. "Wouldn't you say it is odd that this is the very first time you have set foot in my home? Would you care for a tour?"

"It is hardly odd, as I only just returned to New York City to accept my appointment as police commissioner. It is hardly odd, as you damn well know that we do not frequent the same circles. And as far as a tour goes, when I have a need to see your house, it will be for official reasons, not social ones, and you shall be the very first to know."

"Oh, dear, I had forgotten; my world is too debauched for you."

"It is," Bragg agreed. "But only because you strive so hard to be so shameless."

"I think you are jealous," Hart taunted.

"Of what? Of what would I be jealous? Surely not your debauchery."

There was silence. Hart was smiling. He made an expansive gesture, indicating his home and its expensive furnishings and objets d'art.

Bragg laughed, the sound as cold and unpleasant as Hart's previous laughter. "Why would I be jealous of a man who has no heart and no moral fiber? I do admire your intelligence, Calder, and I always have. But I cannot admire anyone who has stolen and cheated and slept his way to wealth and position."

"And how else would you have a poor bastard like myself achieve anything?" Hart asked with a shrug.

"Rathe offered to bankroll you in a start when you dropped out of Princeton. I know it for a fact," Bragg said, referring to his own father, Rathe Bragg. Then, "And we are off the topic. Way off. I am here on official police business, Calder."

"No, for this is so much better, I think. Have they told you?"

Bragg stiffened. "Has who told me what?"

"Has your father told you the news?"

Bragg became wary. "What news?"

"Apparently they have decided that life in Texas no longer suits them now that Lucy and Shoz are married and have settled down." Lucy was Rathe and Grace's eldest child and Bragg's half sister. They had five other children, all boys. "Apparently young Nicholas is thinking of following in your footsteps at Columbia next year. He has made an early application. Rathe and Grace are returning to New York with Nicholas, Hugh, and Colin, and they intend to stay with me while they reopen their home." Hart smiled and it was wide. "I believe Grace wishes for Rathe to sell the house and build a new one, smaller but uptown here on Fifth."

There was a short, surprised, and tamped-down silence. "I have heard nothing," Bragg said quietly, at last.

"I just cannot believe that beloved Rathe failed to tell his own *real* son of his plans! Of course, we both knew that their decision to stay in Texas after Lucy's wedding would not last for long."

"Yes," Bragg said, his jaw flexed.

Hart laughed. "I am sure you will hear from him soon. They plan on coming up to town in another month or so."

Bragg smiled then. It did not reach his eyes. "How many points does this little coup of yours score—in your mind?"

"I don't know. I had forgotten what score we were left at."

"You have never forgotten the score," Bragg said brusquely, "and we both know it."

Hart smirked and lifted his glass in a salute. "Bragg five hundred, Hart ten. I am catching up. Hurrah, hurrah."

Bragg ignored that. "Let's get back to the business at hand so I can leave. I would not mind ending my day today at a reasonable hour—in spite of Randall's death."

"And to think I thought you could not wait to leave me,

as your little crime solver awaits you in the next room." Hart
laughed.

"I suggest you cease with your innuendos about Francesca," Bragg said harshly.

"What? Will you lock me up or punch me?"

"The latter is becoming a difficult notion to resist, Calder.
Francesca Cahill means well. She is also a young lady—
meaning she is naïve in a way you cannot even imagine.
Leave her be, and do not shatter her illusions."

"So now you are her champion," Hart chuckled. "This is
rich indeed!"

"I am no one's champion; I merely do what must be
done—what is right." His eyes were almost black now.
"Where were you, Calder, last night, between five and nine
P.M.?" Bragg snapped, clearly in a foul temper now.

Hart laughed. "So I was right after all, knowing you as
well as I do. Hart eleven, Bragg five hundred. You have come
to see if your monstrously immoral brother has an alibi."

"Do you?" He smiled too nicely and waited.

"I fear that I do. Thus I now ruin your day. Tsk-tsk."

Anger flashed in Bragg's eyes. "Let's get this over with,
why don't we? As I have more to do than to stand here and
spar with you. Just tell me where you were during those hours
and whom you were with."

"Very well." He drank. "I was at my office until six-ten.
My secretary can attest to that. His name is Brad Lewis."

"And after that?"

"I was in my carriage, with my driver, Raoul. He left me
around seven P.M."

His eyes narrowed. "Where?"

"At apartments on Third Avenue and Forty-eighth Street."
Hart grinned at him.

"Let me guess. Your mistress?"

"Hell, no. I keep *her* uptown, on Fourth Avenue, in a very
fine manner. These ladies have an arrangement with their
landlord, I believe. Their names are Rose and Daisy. Jones,
I think, is their last name. They are sisters." He laughed at
that. "Or so they say."

"You mean they are whores."

He shrugged. "They are adept, and that is what counts."

"At what time did you leave the . . . sisters?"

"A few minutes before nine. I was at White's little fête, remember? That started at nine; I was actually rather prompt. I stayed until midnight, then went home."

"When was the last time that you saw Randall?" Bragg asked.

"Tuesday night." Hart shrugged.

"Really? I didn't know the two of you had formed a friendship."

"We hadn't." Hart looked at his watch. "I have appointments downtown, Bragg."

"How timely. I will be but a moment more. Why did you see him, and where did this meeting take place?"

"As I am sure you will learn of it eventually, I will save you the time and the trouble of sleuthing. We met for dinner at the Republican Club, of which he is a member. As to why I saw him, it is none of your business. The meeting was extremely brief, actually." Hart smiled, as if that memory was amusing.

"Actually, your relationship with him *is* my business, because he has been murdered, and you are at the top of my suspect list." Bragg smiled—with pleasure.

"How loyal you are."

"We both know how much you hated him. And I suppose the question is, did you hate him enough to murder him?"

"I have never kept my feelings a secret. I rarely do." Hart finished his second drink of the morning. "And now I must go. Oh—and the answer is no."

"Do not even think of leaving town, Hart. You are both an important link in my investigation as well as a suspect, and if you leave the city, I will have to call in the U.S. Marshal. I would also have to place you in custody."

Hart pretended to shudder. "Oh, dear, and what would I do then?"

"I want your word," Bragg said, ignoring his remark, "that

you will not leave the city until I have given you permission to do so."

Hart stared. "You have it, then. But I find it hard to believe that you would accept my word on anything."

"Normally, I would not. But your father has been murdered, Hart, in cold blood. And as much as you claim to despise him, I believe that, if you did not kill him yourself, you do have some small conscience somewhere in that black heart of yours, and you will want to see this matter resolved more than anyone, even the widow." Bragg nodded and walked out.

Hart stared after him. "You are wrong," he said. But he spoke only to himself.

Francesca straightened breathlessly and faced her sister, who was wide-eyed. Did Bragg really suspect Hart of murdering his own father? And why did they seem to so dislike each other?

Connie whispered, "I feel sorry for Mr. Hart."

Francesca stiffened. She did not like her sister having sympathetic feelings toward Hart.

And Bragg had seemed to defend her. While Hart kept making odd little remarks about her relationship with Bragg. Did he see or sense something that Francesca had also thought to be happening between them? She smiled a little then, to herself.

Then she realized that Bragg would be looking for her. Her eyes widened. "Come, Con," she said, grabbing her hand and half-dragging her across the salon as quickly as she could.

But she was a bit late. Bragg stood in the entry, arms folded across his chest, his expression dark. But he wasn't staring at the doorway they had just run through; he seemed to be staring at the floor. Francesca halted, trying not to sound out of breath.

Bragg was grim as he looked up at her. Francesca flinched but did not look away. Instantly she knew he was preoccupied, the unpleasant exchange with Hart firmly on his mind.

She decided to take advantage of his preoccupation. She

touched his sleeve. "I apologize. I had no idea that Hart was Randall's son."

He met her gaze. "I know you didn't, Francesca. You would not hurt a fly, if it could be avoided."

She smiled a little at him. "Are . . . are you all right?"

His gaze was direct. "I am fine."

She knew it was a lie. Briefly, she touched his sleeve.

He seemed surprised. Stirring, he said, "How much did you overhear?"

"Just . . . a little." Was he so disturbed now that he did not realize she had been snooping in the other room? Francesca was ashamed of her behavior, but on the other hand, her heart melted for Bragg now. She did not think he hated Hart, but Hart clearly hated—or wanted to hate—him. "Hart is jealous of you, Bragg," she said softly. "It is obvious."

His brows lifted. "I doubt it. He has become one of the city's millionaires. Prior to my appointment here, I worked as a lawyer in D.C., and half of my cases were criminal ones—defending those I believed to be innocent of the charges leveled against them. It was not a lucrative practice, Francesca. Hart has more now, in this brief moment, than I will ever have."

"I admire you, Bragg," she said, and then she flushed, as the words had just popped out, but they were so very true. His nobility moved her in so many ways, and perhaps it was one of the reasons she found him so attractive. Of course, he was a strikingly handsome man.

He started and their gazes locked.

Francesca did not move. She forgot that they were not alone. He said, softly, "Do not put me on a pedestal."

"I won't," she returned as softly.

He smiled then; so did she.

Connie coughed, behind them, but Francesca remained motionless. She didn't really hear Connie. Her heart was racing now. She had the oddest feeling that Bragg was going to reach out for her, perhaps to touch her.

But he did not. Instead, his hands found the pockets of his dark trousers. "The admiration is mutual," he said finally, as if he had not heard Connie, either. And then it was as if he came to his senses. He frowned. "You have interfered with my investigation, Francesca. I simply cannot allow it."

She swallowed. "I know. And I am sorry."

"Really? I do not think you have one sorry bone in your body," he said, but he was not angry.

She inhaled hard, debating reminding him that she did have a client, and then she decided against it. "Do you really think Calder Hart murdered his own father?"

His expression closed. "It is my moral duty to keep an open mind and consider all the possibilities."

He was not going to confide his true feelings to her. "Did you find Georgette de Labouche?"

"No."

"The gun?" She was hopeful now.

He eyed her. "Francesca, what do I have to do to get you to return to your studies at Barnard College and to your life as a reforming woman?"

She froze. "What?"

"I do believe you heard me."

"How . . . how did you find out . . . about my studies?" she gasped.

He smiled and it was affectionate. "Francesca, I am a policeman. Do you really think we would investigate the Burton Abduction together as we did and I would not learn all that is significant about you?"

She could only stare.

Bragg turned to Connie in the interim. "Surely you do not approve of your sister's new avocation?"

Connie was grim—and vocal. "I most certainly do not."

"Good. Then I have an ally." He faced Francesca. "Stay away from Hart. Trust me. He is a dangerous man." He glanced at Connie. "You should stay away from him as well, Lady Montrose. I highly recommend it."

Connie flushed. "Why would I do otherwise? I do not know the man. He is hardly a friend of mine or Neil's."

"Good." Bragg looked at Francesca. "I take it you have not heard from Miss de Labouche?"

Francesca shook her head. "No, I have not."

He studied her, saw the truth, and smiled at her.

It so warmed Francesca, inside and out.

"Well, I must be going," Bragg said. "Francesca, enjoy your day of *shopping*." He gave her a stern look as they all started for the door, where a servant waited for them.

"I despise shopping," Francesca said, her mind racing. She must get rid of Connie if she wished to do any more sleuthing that day.

"Take her shopping," Bragg said firmly to Connie as the doorman opened the front door for them all. Bragg's motor-car, a handsome cream-colored Daimler, was parked behind Connie's coach.

"I will," Connie promised him. "Good day, Commissioner, and again, I am so sorry for all that we have done."

Bragg nodded to them both, and it seemed to Francesca that his gaze lingered a bit longer upon her than was necessary. She followed her sister into their coach but craned her neck in order to watch Bragg as he cranked the roadster to a start, climbed in, and shifted into gear. Their coachman let him pull out first.

Francesca sighed. The moment she did so she blushed and glanced quickly at her sister. Connie was smiling. "You are so obvious, Fran."

"He is merely a friend. Do not think anything else," Francesca warned.

"Very well," Connie returned. She leaned forward to give their driver instructions.

"And I refuse to go shopping. Let's go home," Francesca said, with ulterior motives. "As I have been pinched this day, so to speak, I may as well use my time to good advantage and get some studying done."

Connie told their coachman to take them home and she glanced curiously at Francesca. "Pinched?"

Francesca grinned. "That means bagged. You know— caught by the police."

Connie rolled her eyes. Then, as their carriage moved onto Fifth Avenue, going uptown, as Fifth headed north, she stared pensively out the window, her expression changing. She seemed sad.

Francesca briefly closed her eyes, wishing she could help her sister. But the only person who could help Connie was Neil. "Perhaps Mama can be enticed into going shopping with you," she suggested.

Connie did not turn from the frozen landscape that was Central Park. Even in the inclement weather, several horseback riders and carriages were enjoying the day on the track. "I do not wish to spend the day with Mama."

"Well, what time will Neil be home? And Charlotte?"

Connie hesitated.

"Con?"

Now it was her sister's turn to sigh, but the sound was very different from Francesca's, belabored, if you will. "I don't know. He wasn't certain. He has been so . . . distracted of late."

Francesca nodded. "Yes, I think so."

Finally Connie looked at her. "So you have noticed."

Francesca felt some small nagging guilt. "I have."

"I have noticed that the two of you seem to be at odds," Connie remarked tersely.

Francesca blinked. "What?"

"What are you two fighting about? You have always adored Neil." Connie's voice quavered. "The other night at Evan's engagement party, it was as if the two of you could not stand each other."

Francesca was rigid with tension. "Well, Neil thinks I am having an affair."

"What?" Connie gasped.

Francesca nodded seriously. "So does Evan, and Bragg did, too, for a time."

"What?" Connie said again.

"My sleuthing had me out and about at some very unusual hours during the Burton Affair," Francesca said, her heart pounding. "I could not tell Neil what I was doing, and he leaped to the wrong conclusion. Thus we fought."

Connie regarded her with amazement. "Neil never said a word."

"He promised me he would not." Just as she, Francesca, had failed to promise him that she would keep her own silence as to what he knew—which was the real reason they were at odds now.

"Well . . . ," Connie trailed off, clearly relieved. "Oddly, I thought there might be another reason for your dissension."

Francesca stared, realizing now that Connie suspected everything and that she had somehow surmised the real reason for Francesca's quarrel with Neil. *I should tell her,* Francesca thought in a panic. If ever there was a moment, it was then. *Perhaps she would be better off having her suspicions confirmed. Perhaps knowing the truth, instead of worrying about it, would be a relief, of sorts. For then she could repair her marriage, not just for her own sake, but for that of her two daughters.*

But Bragg had once told her that words spoken too lightly could never be taken back. His wisdom held her back now. What should she do?

It would be a relief for everyone to have Neil's sordid past put behind them, Francesca thought glumly. But Francesca had already had a great internal debate, and she had decided not to say anything to Connie, no matter how she might ache to do so. For Francesca would want to be told the truth if she were in her sister's shoes, but Connie was not Francesca—they were as different as night and day.

Francesca felt certain that even as worried as she now was, Connie would not want to know the truth.

"Why are you staring at me like that?" Connie asked, cutting into Francesca's thoughts.

Francesca swallowed hard. "I am sorry. I did not mean to stare." Quickly Francesca looked away.

But Connie gripped her knee. "Fran? What is it?"

Startled, Francesca gasped. "What?"

Connie was starkly pale. Briefly, she closed her eyes. "There is something else, isn't there? There is another reason for the dissension between you and Neil." She opened her eyes. "There is something you are not telling me. Isn't there?"

Francesca was in shock. Was Connie asking her for the truth? Did Connie want to know? What should she do? Her panic increased. "Con . . . ," she began, a protest.

"Isn't there?" And it was a harsh demand.

Francesca stared. She had to wet her lips in order to speak. What she would not do was lie. "Yes," she said.

SEVEN

Connie's eyes widened, and Francesca saw fear there. Then Connie glanced away. Their brougham was approaching the block where the Cahill mansion was. "What is it?" Connie asked tersely. "What is it that you're not telling me?"

Francesca reached out and took her hand, forcing her sister to meet her eyes again. Her own pulse was racing wildly—she so feared doing the wrong thing now. "Connie, if there was something amiss, something I know about that you, perhaps, should also know about, would you want me to tell you what I know?"

Connie was rigid and breathless. She stared, and the moment became an endless one. "Is this about Neil?"

Francesca hesitated.

"It is, isn't it?" Connie pulled her hands free of Francesca's and stared out her window. Another endless moment passed. Francesca did not speak. She could not blurt out the fact of Neil's adultery, not unless she was certain her sister was ready to face the truth. "You know, I have changed my mind. I will go shopping with you!" she exclaimed. "And I have a wonderful idea! Let's call on Sarah Channing and ask her to join us." Sarah was Evan's fiancée. The engagement was a recent one and quite against Evan's will. "Sarah is the most amazing artist. We will undoubtedly find her feverishly at work in her studio. I doubt she is inclined toward shopping, but she will surely want to get to know her future sisters-in-law better."

The coach had halted in front of the huge limestone house that was the Cahill home. Connie turned to Francesca. "There is another woman," she said.

Francesca, in the act of rising, sank back down on the leather squab. She wet her lips. "You . . . know."

Connie stared, her expression one of dread and anguish. "No. I don't know. But somehow you do."

Her heart hurt her now, because her words would hurt her sister unbearably, even if she were only the messenger. "Yes. I know. I saw him . . . with someone . . . another woman."

Connie did not speak. She seemed carved out of stone. In a few small moments, she had become an unbearably lovely and frozen ivory statue.

"I am so sorry," Francesca whispered. And the statement seemed to hang there, tautly, between them.

How small the carriage had become.

How silent the day.

And Connie made a harsh sound. "How long have you known?" Her eyes glazed over. "He adores the girls. He adores me. I do not understand!"

Francesca took her hand. "I don't understand, either. I haven't known for very long. Perhaps a week or so. I didn't think you would want to know; I didn't think I should say anything."

"Are you certain?" Connie asked with desperation. "Are you certain? Perhaps you misconstrued the situation."

Francesca was silent, feeling for her sister—having already wept copiously herself. "I am certain. I was snooping," she said, trembling. "I saw him clearly."

Connie hugged herself. "I think I shall die," she said.

"No, Con, you will not die! Neil does love you, I am certain of it, and you will fix this madness; I am certain of that, too!" Francesca cried.

Connie stared. Tears began to fill her sky blue eyes. A tear slid down her face.

"Neil does love you," Francesca insisted, wishing she could somehow spare her sister the brutal pain she must just now be experiencing and praying her own words were true.

Connie said, "I have to know. I have to know who he was with."

Francesca hesitated. "Eliza Burton."

*   *   *

Francesca slipped somberly into the house, a large marble-floored hall with Corinthian pillars set at intervals about the room. Marble panels divided the walls, and a high ceiling depicted a fresco of a pastoral scene. Francesca felt shaken and depressed. Connie had asked her if anyone else knew, and Francesca had said she thought not. Bragg knew. But she had not seen the point in making her sister more anxious by telling her of that. She had promised not to breathe a word of Neil's affair to anyone, not even Evan, and especially not their mother.

Francesca somehow smiled at the doorman and handed off her muff, her hat, which she unpinned, and her fur-lined coat to a manservant. The house was very quiet. But Mama was undoubtedly on her way to a ladies' luncheon, Evan would be long since gone by now, and perhaps, just perhaps, she had the house to herself. Francesca started toward the library.

It was early. As soon as she looked at the morning's news-paper—which she had forgotten to do when she had awoken, due to Connie's unexpected visit—she would hail a cab and go find Joel. They had all afternoon to continue their inves-tigation into Randall's murder. Francesca thought a safe place to start might be with Georgette de Labouche's neighbors, if she managed to be very discreet. She did not dare visit the widow now. She was afraid to run into Bragg and the police there.

She stepped into her father's study, which also happened to be her favorite room in the entire house. With its gold-cloth-covered walls and stained-glass windows, with its dark wood accents and warm, comfortable furnishings, it was a most inviting sanctuary. Now she blinked in surprise. Andrew Cahill sat at his desk, engrossed in writing a letter. He did not look up, not even hearing her.

She left the door ajar and smiled fondly at him. "Papa, I did not see the second carriage, and I did not realize you were home."

Cahill started and looked up. His smile answered that of his daughter. "Good day, Francesca. I noticed you slept quite late this morning."

In a way, it was a question, one asked very mildly. Francesca was not alarmed—had Julia asked the very same question, she would be anxious and afraid of being found out.
"Yes, I did. It was delicious, too, I might add. Perhaps I will
acquire a new and lazy habit."

Cahill laughed. "That would astonish me to no end."

Francesca smiled back at him and walked over to the
couch, which faced the fireplace. On the cushions she saw
the *Tribune* and the *Times.* She sat down, reaching for the
former, and quickly scanned the headlines. Randall's murder
had not made the news, apparently—she was certain it would
be on the front page of the *Tribune,* although perhaps not the
Times—but Bragg had made the news. She stiffened. "Bragg
Wreaks Havoc on Police Affairs," the headline screamed. The
subtitle read: "Hundreds of Officers Demoted in Attempt to
Halt Corruption."

She glanced quickly at the *Times.* "Three Hundred Detectives Demoted and Demoralized," she read. And then, "Reas-
signment will break graft in wards or destroy crime-fighting
ability."

"Bragg has certainly taken the tiger by the tail," Andrew
commented, standing and coming over to her. "He is a cou-
rageous man."

Francesca was thrilled, although she did not like the *Times'*
suggestion that Bragg might be hurting the capabilities of the
city's police. "Will he survive this brave act of his, Papa?"

"We shall see. But by transferring these officers to different precincts he has dealt a severe blow to the system of graft
and corruption that is synonymous with police protection."

Francesca understood. "The detectives from a single ward
take payoffs and bribes from the saloons, brothel keepers, and
gambling halls in their ward, By demoting them and reas-
signing them to an unfamiliar ward, it will be difficult for
them to immediately devise a new system of graft and corruption. How clever. How bold."

"Bragg is not very popular in his own department right
now," Cahill commented. "And if you read the *Times,* one
journalist suggests he has gone too far too quickly and that

crime will actually blossom in this new environment."

"I am sure Bragg does not care about his popularity—or lack thereof," Francesca said fiercely. "But should his own men come to despise him, well, that does worry me a bit."

"He needs to appoint his new chief of police, and soon."

"Yes, he does. But how to find an ally among the existing ranks? Everyone is so corrupt!" Francesca exclaimed. "Unless he promotes a man who is weak and incompetent."

"Well, he cannot bring in someone new. As it is, Bragg was performing two jobs during the Burton Affair. He has enough on his plate fighting the corruption within the department; he really cannot fight crime on the streets, too."

Francesca agreed with that; on the other hand, she knew Bragg now, and she did not think he would stop fighting those most dastardly crimes executed on the street. She wished she could tell her father about the Randall murder, but she could not. Not if it was not in the morning's papers. "Well, I believe Bragg has done the right thing. He has shaken up the police department, and it is a beginning. I do not think he would ever do such a thing if it would jeopardize the police's abilities to fight crime in any way."

Cahill took a seat on the plush moss-colored sofa with its many patterned pillows. "You are so loyal and supportive of Rick Bragg," he remarked.

Francesca kept her face straight and was resolved not to blush. "We are friends now, Papa. We did solve the Burton Affair together."

He patted her knee. "I know. And I am proud of you, although I hope you never so endanger yourself again. Of course, after being held a prisoner all day by that madman, I know you will never attempt to solve any crime again." He looked her right in the eye.

She glanced away, unable to hold the eye contact. "Well . . ." She could not—would not—lie to her father. He was her favorite person in the entire world.

"Francesca!" he exclaimed. "Surely you have learned your lesson?"

She was imploring. "Papa, if I saw a crime committed, and

no one was about except for myself and the criminal, you know I would do what I felt was right."

He sighed. "Yes, I do, but you must restrain yourself when the choice involves placing yourself in harm's way!"

"I realize that. Still, if I saw a big man beating a small child, I would attempt to stop him, even if he might beat me." She meant it.

"How did I ever come by such a bold, brave, and determined daughter? Francesca, you know I am in complete agreement with you on most subjects, but do promise me you will stay out of Bragg's way from now on." His eyes narrowed a bit at the mention of Bragg's name now.

She stood up, twisting her hands. "Please don't make me promise that, Papa."

He leaped to his feet. "But you must!"

"I cannot. I simply cannot."

He was incredulous. "I do not know if I should ask this or not, but I shall. Is your refusal to make such a promise about justice, Francesca, or does it have something to do with Bragg as a man?"

She flushed, and opened her mouth to say that it was about justice, but no words came out.

"I see." Andrew was grim.

"We are just friends, Papa," she tried. "Truly."

He nodded, for a moment silent. "I am a good friend of Rick's. I truly admire him. I respect him. But he is not for you, Francesca."

She stared, dismayed. Julia had declared the exact same thing. "Why? Because he is illegitimate?"

Andrew was surprised. "Your mother told you that?"

She nodded.

"Actually, that is a bit of a cloud, but no, that is not why. You will have to trust me on this. He is not for you, Francesca, so do not go losing your heart to a man who can never return it."

His words were the most severe blow. "Why are you saying this to me?"

"Because I sense that I must." He patted her shoulder. "I am sorry to upset you, dear."

"Did Bragg say something about me? Has he indicated that he could never . . . become fond of me? Is there someone else?"

"Francesca, I know that you are not for him—and that he is not for you—and let us leave it at that."

She wanted to cry but couldn't. She didn't. She was too stunned—and too upset.

"Now. I have a favor to ask of you," Andrew said, changing the subject.

Francesca hardly heard him. She wished she knew why her father was being so adamant. But he was wrong—wasn't he?

Still, as fond of her as Bragg sometimes seemed, he had canceled their outing for that day, in no uncertain terms. Taking her out at another time had not even seemed to be remotely on his mind.

Her spirits, already low due to her blunder with Calder Hart and having to tell Connie about Neil, sank even lower. "What is it, Papa?"

"It is about Evan," Andrew said, now grim.

Francesca sat down on the edge of the sofa. "And?"

"He has not spoken to me since his engagement party. It has been a week now. He avoids me, and will do no more than nod in greeting or mutter a curt word. I know he is angry about the engagement and my refusal to pay his debts, but Francesca, he is my son. This cannot go on. You must speak with him. If anyone can make him see how he needs to change and mend his ways—and how Sarah Channing will help him to do so—it is you." Andrew halted, his speech having been an impassioned one.

Evan was furious at being forced to marry Sarah Channing, a woman he did not love. Their father had told him that he would not pay the vast sum of Evan's gambling debts if he did not marry Sarah. Francesca had been dismayed, of course; she wanted Evan to marry for love. She had even tried to champion his cause, but her father was adamant and he had refused to even consider changing his mind about the engagement. Now Evan was not speaking with Andrew. "Of course I will speak with him, Papa," Francesca said.

Andrew brightened. "I knew that you would."

"I will speak with him, but this once, I disagree with you completely. Sarah and Evan do not suit, and their engagement—and forthcoming marriage—is an utterly terrible mistake," Francesca said.

Her father told her he would not need the second coach as he would spend the afternoon going over paperwork that he had not had a chance to do during the week at his downtown office.

What luck, Francesca thought as the coach fought the Saturday afternoon traffic on the Upper East Side. Electric trolleys, hansoms, and other elegant broughams fought for the right-of-way at every intersection. On 57th Street a police officer in his blue serge uniform was directing the traffic, but no one seemed to pay him any mind, with various gentlemen dashing about on foot through the coaches and the occasional motorcar. Bells sounded and a horn blared. Frankly, Francesca did not like using cabs and trolleys to get around the city when she was in the more unsavory and crime-ridden neighborhoods. On the Lower East Side, even when in disguise, somehow she stood out like a sore thumb. One terrible and frightening encounter during the Burton Affair had taught her that.

Georgette de Labouche's neighborhood, however, did not distress her. Should she not find Joel, she would venture on by herself.

The traffic changed in the lower thirties, the fine coaches and carriages with their wealthy occupants disappearing, and by the time her driver was approaching 10th Street and Avenue A, most of the traffic belonged to carters, consisting of wagons filled with merchandise and wares. Vendors were hawking odd items like mittens and earmuffs, as well as toasted pretzels and spicy pigs' ears, to the pedestrians swarming the streets, in spite of the cold. Those passing by were so bundled up it was hard to make out anyone's gender, but Francesca knew that at this hour it was mostly poor immigrant women with too many children to look after to be able to go off to work in a factory or sweatshop.

There were one, two, or three saloons on every block now. All of the establishments were doing a brisk business indeed. Inebriated patrons, both male and female, lurched about the streets. Francesca couldn't help recalling Bragg's quandary. The high-minded citizens of the city, including the clergy, were adamantly opposed to the saloons operating in defiance of the Blue Laws on Sundays. Yet the police had a long history of looking the other way. Bragg was under some pressure to force closings on the Sabbath and uphold the city's law against drinking on that day.

He had so much on his plate, but her anxiety now had little to do with his job. If only her father had explained why he insisted she stay away from Bragg romantically. Clearly Andrew knew something that she did not.

"Miss Cahill? We are here, Number Two-oh-one Avenue A," her driver said, having opened the partition between them so he could speak to her.

"Oh! Thank you," Francesca said, starting. She turned to get out of the carriage only to see Joel there, grinning at her.

"Where you been all day, lady?" he asked, shivering, his hands in the pockets of his baggy, ragged coat. "I been waitin' an' waitin'."

Francesca beamed. "I should have known! Climb in. We are going to snoop around Miss de Labouche's apartment and see if we can learn anything."

Joel climbed into the carriage beside her while Francesca gave their driver the new address. "It's two o'clock," the boy complained.

"I know. I stopped at Calder Hart's at noon." Francesca told him a bit of what had happened.

Joel listened intently. "Miz Cahill, you got to avoid the commissioner. I seen how pissed he was last night. He don't want you involved in this one."

"I am aware of that, but it is too late, because I am already involved," Francesca said firmly. "Have you heard anything, Joel? Is there any 'word' on the 'street'?"

"Not down here, there wouldn't be," Joel said. "But I'll sniff it out for you when we get to what's-her-name's house."

"That would be wonderful," Francesca said with a smile, and she patted his hand.

But Joel stiffened, his gaze directed out the window. "Hell," he said. "Ain't that your brother?"

"What?" Francesca peered past him.

They had turned onto Broadway and were traveling briskly uptown, following closely behind an omnibus. Francesca looked into a nearby carriage and she froze.

Evan was in the passenger seat, and so was a woman she recognized.

It was not his fiancée, Sarah Channing. It was his mistress, the gorgeous and renowned stage actress Grace Conway, and from the look of things, the affair was not over, oh no.

Francesca stared in absolute disbelief.

Georgette de Labouche's house had become the scene of a criminal investigation, and a uniformed policeman guarded the house to prevent intruders from entering and disturbing any evidence. There was no sign of any further activity at the house, which relieved Francesca.

Still, as they knocked upon the first of the neighbors' doors, Francesca kept thinking about her brother. She adored him. He was one of her best friends. She respected him; she admired him—she did, in spite of the confession he had made to her so recently that he was astonishingly in debt, due to his penchant for gambling. Many men gambled, and Francesca knew that once this huge debt was paid off, Evan would mend his ways. Their father had promised to pay off the sum now that Evan was engaged.

How could he be out and about with his mistress? If he was now engaged, he owed Sarah Channing his loyalty as well as his heart. Francesca remained shocked at what she had seen.

And there had been no mistaking the fact that it was Evan

and the stage actress, whom Francesca had glimpsed upon one other occasion, several months ago.

Suddenly, as she banged the door knocker again, a thought struck her. What if Evan was with Grace Conway simply to break things off?

Relief flooded Francesca. Her brother was a man of fine character indeed. Of course that was why he was with the gorgeous actress!

A tired-looking housemaid in an ill-fitting black dress opened the door.

Francesca smiled, handing her a calling card. "Is the master or mistress of the house in?"

The maid nodded and closed the door, not saying a word. Francesca fidgeted, glancing at Joel. He sighed. "Ain't no real fun in bein' off the crook," he commented. "Sort of dull, ain't it?"

Francesca did not know precisely what he meant by "off the crook." "We have only just begun our investigation. Joel, have you ever heard of two sisters, Daisy and Rose Jones? They are women of ill repute."

"Nope, but shady ladies are everywhere. Want me to make 'em fer you?"

"Find out what you can today. I believe they reside somewhere on Forty-eighth Street and Third. If we have time, we shall pay the Randalls a visit after this, as long as no police are in sight, and tomorrow we can call on the two sisters."

"Why?"

She grimaced a little. "Well, Bragg seems to think a certain gentleman is a possible suspect for his murder. His alibi consists of his having been with the two women I have just mentioned." She did not want to tell Joel that Hart was a suspect.

Joel grinned. "Two, eh?"

Francesca did flush. That was a thought she had been trying to ignore. "I'm sure he was only visiting one of the sisters," she said firmly.

Joel laughed and shook his head.

The front door of the house suddenly opened and her card was pressed into her gloved palm. "They be out," the maid said, and she shut the door in Francesca's face.

Francesca blinked. "How rude!" she exclaimed.

"Now what?"

Francesca didn't even hear him. Using her fist, she banged sharply on the door again. This time, her several knocks were not answered.

Clearly the maid had no intention of answering, as clearly her employers had instructed her that they would not receive Francesca.

"Leatherhead is sure interested in us, or you," Joel remarked.

"Bragg is here?" Francesca gasped, whirling.

"No, lady, I mean the copper on the stoop of the Labouche flat."

Francesca realized that the police officer guarding Georgette's house was studying them openly. She gave him what she hoped was an imperious glance, and she left Georgette's closest neighbor. Unfortunately, the next two nearest neighbors also refused to speak with Francesca. Their servants returned her calling card, with murmurs of indisposition and regret.

Francesca was at a loss. "Surely someone has seen something!" she cried in exasperation.

"Plenty a' folks saw plenty," Joel said knowingly. "You wait here. I'll be back in a spot."

"Joel," she began, about to ask him what he intended. But he flew around the corner of the house where they were standing, into the narrow foot of space between two brick buildings. Francesca knew tiny yards were out back, undoubtedly hung with clotheslines that were empty now, on such a cold winter day.

She shivered. Maybe she should give up for the rest of the day. Not only did she want to speak with Evan, but she knew she must go to Connie's to see how her sister was faring. Francesca prayed she was somehow managing, and knew she could not be. Her own reaction to the knowledge of Montrose's affair had been anguish and heartbreak. For her sister, it could only be much, much worse.

"Can I help you?"

Francesca started and turned. Her eyes widened—the obnoxious reporter from the *Sun* faced her, grinning. His name was Arthur Kurland, and he was a balding man in his thirties who had the best timing for appearing where he was not wanted.

"Miss Cahill, isn't it?"

She had stiffened. "Hello, Mr. Kurland, and unless you have any new information on Randall's murder, no, you cannot help me."

He grinned at her. "Have I offended you in any way? By your tone, I take it that I have."

She lifted her chin even higher. "I do not like being followed—or spied upon."

"I only do my job." He was sly. "Commissioner's not far from here."

She could not respond. She knew very well that Bragg lived only a few blocks away, and Kurland knew she knew, as well. After all, he had seen her entering Bragg's residence—alone—at a rather unusual hour just a week or so ago. He had also seen her leaving it—in a very disheveled state. "I am sure Bragg is in his office at police headquarters," she said coldly.

"His mistress is still missing," Arthur Kurland commented. "But they found the gun. A small, pearl-handled derringer. The kind ladies use."

"Or fancy gentlemen," Francesca said.

He nodded. "Yeah, them, too."

Francesca had to ask. "Are there any other developments?"

"I'll trade," he said. "There is, but you have to give me something, too."

Francesca was aghast. "Why, that is blackmail!"

He chuckled. "You are so young, Miss Cahill, too young to be a sleuth."

She blinked. "How—how did you know?"

"It's my job to know what happens on the street, as far as crime goes. And what I have suggested is not blackmail. It's called trading information and it's done all the time in my profession."

Francesca considered that—but what could she tell him, and did he really have information to share with her? "Who goes first?"

"You do."

"But what if this is a trick?"

"Then you shall learn a relatively painless lesson—but you will never trust me again, and that might not be in my better interest."

She absorbed that. "Miss de Labouche is my client."

He chuckled again. "Not good enough, Miss Cahill."

"Miss de Labouche wanted to hide the body," she said.

His expression did not change. "Not much better, Miss Cahill. Or may I call you Francesca?"

"You may not," she said sharply. "I think it is your turn," she said.

"Not until you give me something I do not know."

Francesca was riddled with tension. She dared not say more. And Calder Hart was on her mind now.

"Why did Bragg—and you and your sister—call on Calder Hart this morning? The Calder Hart of Hart Industries? One of the city's wealthiest—and most infamous—citizens?"

Francesca gasped. "You are spying upon me!"

"Why? How is he involved in this?"

Francesca turned away. "Good day, Mr. Kurland."

He gripped her arm and she cried out. "One of the neighbors here saw a dark, quite dangerous-looking man leaving this apartment before eight o'clock on the evening of the murder."

Francesca stared. Dark and dangerous in appearance—the description fit Calder Hart perfectly.

"It's your turn," Kurland said harshly.

"I . . ." she began, and stopped.

"How is Hart involved? What is his connection to Randall? I will find out, Miss Cahill, you do know that, but you owe me now."

Her cheeks burned. Was it public information? Surely it had to be a matter of public record. She hesitated.

"Well?" the reporter demanded.

She sighed. "He is Randall's son."

EIGHT

Somehow, Francesca had to be wrong.

But she had seen them together. She had caught them in the act.

Or so she claimed.

Connie loved her husband's study. Even when he was not in it, every inch of the masculine room, with its dark woods and green and gold appointments, reminded her of him. The books he loved to read—many of which he had brought with him from England—filled the floor-to-ceiling bookcase on one wall. Shakespeare and Chaucer vied with Tolstoy and Dostoyevsky. The two landscape paintings hanging over the mantel above the fireplace came from Neil's ancestral home in Devon, and they were masterpieces. The large studded leather armchair behind the massive desk where he worked had been his father's, and it hailed from sixteenth-century Spain. Recently Connie had taken to sitting there when Neil was not at home. There, in that huge throne-like chair, she could smell his cigars, his horses, his cologne, and she could even feel his presence.

She did not sit there now.

She had known something was very wrong. She had known it for some time now. But Francesca had to be wrong.

Her sister often was.

No one meant better, but no one, more often than not, leaped to the wrong conclusions or blundered into the wrong situation.

Connie turned away from Neil's desk. She was trembling like a leaf. She was breathless, her lungs constricted, making the usual intake of air impossible. *Francesca had to be wrong.* She could not have actually seen what she had thought she had.

But who could make such a mistake?

Neil's study was on the second floor of their large house, which took up a corner of the block overlooking both Madison Avenue and 62d Street. The lot had been vacant when they had become engaged, and both the vacant lot and the house, which they had built subsequently, had been a wedding gift from her father. Neil's office had catty-corner windows, overlooking both the large busy avenue with its nearly incessant traffic and the shady, tree-lined side street, as quiet as the avenue was not. Connie heard a familiar sound from outside and she flinched.

For she recognized, as she always did, the crunch of his coach's tires on the cobblestones of the short drive belonging to their house. She recognized the tinkling of the bells on the matching grays. She recognized Joseph's cry of, "Whoa there, now!"

Her body tightened up impossibly. *I must not cry,* she thought.

She moved from Neil's desk, where she had been standing like a statue, her mind going round and round in circles, for hours and hours—or so it seemed. She paused and glanced down at 62d Street, where their driveway curved into the house, past a small front garden. She could see Neil from behind as he walked away from the carriage, disappearing from her view before entering the house.

Her heart seemed to be choking her now. She reminded herself that this was a terrible mistake. For surely her husband loved her the way that she loved him.

She had loved him from the moment she had first laid her eyes upon him, five long years ago. Or was it five lifetimes ago?

Of course, he had terrified her, too. Because he was so perfect, and never in her wildest dreams had she imagined that she would land a husband so noble, so handsome, so intelligent, and so worldly. In the first year of their marriage, he had made her feel all of fourteen again. In that year, she had felt clumsy and gauche.

Of course, she was no longer that naïve child-bride. She

was an adult woman, the mother of two, adept at running their home, caring for their daughters, and attending whatever functions Neil chose. She also supported the requisite charities, holding her own charitable functions twice a year. Universally she was considered to be an ideal wife and mother. Her friends frequently asked how she managed to do it all, and so well.

Her answer had always been that it was easy, when one had the kind of marriage that she had.

Now, Connie inhaled. But just what kind of marriage did she actually have? The answer was terrifying; she dismissed the question.

Somehow, she put one foot after the other, and she made it to the door. She opened it.

A housemaid was passing by. "Dottie? Please ask Lord Montrose to come to his study."

"Yes, ma'am," the maid said, and then she stopped and glanced wide-eyed at Connie a second time. "Lady Montrose? Are you ill?"

Connie realized she was clinging to the door, as if afraid she might fall down. And perhaps she would, if she did let go. Somehow she detached herself from the door and stood upright. "I am fine, Dottie. Thank you." She walked back into the study. She felt odd, as if she were floating.

In fact, her life felt odd now, odd and unreal. *How many times had she thought to herself that Neil was the perfect husband?*

Abruptly tears filled her eyes and she imagined Neil with another woman, in an act that should never be performed outside of the bonds of love and marriage. How could Francesca have made such a terrible mistake? Francesca had stated that she had seen them together on the sofa, in the dark, in a state of dishabille. She had implied that they had been making love. Did that necessarily mean that they had? And it had been dark. Perhaps it had not even been Neil.

Connie felt her stomach turn over, hard. No, it had not been a mistake. Neil had been aloof lately. And they had not made love in months. She was ill.

"Connie?"

She flinched at the sound of his voice. And slowly she turned to face him, the man she loved with all of her heart and then some.

Neil Montrose was a big man and he filled up the doorway. He was impeccably clad, yet somehow the effort seemed careless. His suit jacket was open, his tie just slightly askew. When one added to his dark but blue-eyed good looks, his tall, muscular build, the effect was rakish and disarming. He was smiling, and he had a cleft chin.

And his smile disappeared. "What is it? Are you ill? Connie, do sit down." He rushed to her.

She said, "Don't touch me." And she was aghast, appalled—it was as if another woman had spoken in that harsh, uncharacteristic tone.

He halted in his tracks, dropping his hands. Hands that had covered almost every inch of her body; hands that knew her intimately, hands that had, ultimately, brought her so much pleasure—once she had realized that there was so much pleasure to be had and so little shame within the bonds of marriage.

His jaw flexed. "What is it?" he asked again, but this time more coolly.

"Do you love her?" she heard herself ask—very coldly.

He straightened. He was so much taller than she was—Connie was not even five-foot-three, and Montrose was six-foot-four. "I beg your pardon?"

"I do think you heard me. Do you love her?" She felt her mouth stretch into a mirthless smile. "Or did you merely think to amuse yourself—and destroy me?"

"I see," he said. "You have had a conversation with your sister." His eyes were hooded now. They no longer seemed to be Neil's eyes.

Inside, her heart began to break. Connie thought she could feel each shard as it peeled off. It hurt so. It was so hard to breathe. "Yes. Francesca told me."

"How meddlesome she has become."

"So you do not deny it?"

He stared at her.

Connie waited.

"And if I did?" he asked slowly.

She could not breathe now. Connie said, "I would not believe you." And once more, she had astonished—and terrified—herself.

"I see." He turned away.

This was her chance. She opened her mouth and sucked down oxygen, dizzy and faint, clutching his desk—no, it was a chair in front of the desk—determined to compose herself before he turned back again. She thought she must resemble a fish out of water, dying pitifully, pathetically. How pitiful he would think her if he saw her now, like this.

He turned. "Are you not going to scream and shout? Weep, cry, and carry on?" His words were cautious.

"No. Just tell me how long it has been. For how long has Eliza Burton—whom I have entertained in this house—been your mistress?" Her exterior calm amazed her.

"Not long." He did flush. "When the Burtons were over, she was not my . . . mistress. She has never been . . . my mistress."

"I see. There is a difference between a lover and a mistress." She turned her back on him. He did not speak. Did he see how badly she was shaking? Could he know that inside of her brain she was screaming—the worst, most reprehensible and unladylike profanities? At him? Surely he knew. *"Do you love her?"* She had to know.

"No."

Connie nodded, not facing him. "Do you love me?" The moment she spoke, she knew how foolish her words were. Of course he did not love her. If he did, he would not have committed adultery.

"Yes."

She slowly turned. His gaze was on her, watchful, unblinking. He reminded her now of a hawk, no, an owl. And she was the mouse he wished to devour.

But she was already devoured. She was dead, inside, and

she would never be alive again. For he did not love her, and the proof was his treachery. "Why?"

It was such a simple question. It was the most profound question in the world.

"You would not understand."

She finally let her gaze slide over him, as the pressure to cry built up inside of her, in her chest and in her heart, behind her eyes. She would not cry, though, not in front of him. Not now, not tomorrow, not ever. "Maybe you might try to explain." But she already knew the answer. *She wasn't perfect enough.*

"I don't think so," he said, and his tone took her by surprise, because it was harsh. "I am sorry," he said, his jaw flexing. "It will not happen again. Will you forgive me?" he asked.

Of course she would. He was her husband, until death did they part. "No," Connie said. "I will not forgive you, Neil."

His eyes widened.

She walked out.

Her mind raced. Had Calder Hart been at Georgette de Labouche's on the evening of the murder? Not for one instant did Francesca believe him to be the murderer. She refused to believe it. He was rather immoral and perhaps something of a blackguard, but he was Bragg's brother and he simply could not be a killer.

But a neighbor had seen someone who resembled Hart leaving the apartment—before eight o'clock. And that did not bode well for Hart.

But he had an alibi. Which was why she and Joel were now on their way to find and interview the Jones sisters, whom Hart claimed to have been with until nine that evening, instead of calling upon Randall's widow to pay their regrets. That condolence call would have to wait until the morrow.

"Hey, lady," Joel said loudly.

Francesca realized he had been trying to get her attention ever since they had left that horrid reporter standing in the street by Georgette de Labouche's house. He was tugging on her sleeve. "I'm sorry, Joel. I was thinking."

"Stone-cold deaf," he grumbled. "Don't you want to know what I copped from the neighbors?" he asked.

Francesca started. "I do hope you don't mean you have stolen something," she said cautiously.

"Hell, no! You asked me to find out who seen wut." He grinned.

She leaned forward eagerly as they approached 48th Street. "Someone saw something?"

"Nope. But the tart's got family."

"What?" Francesca breathed.

"She's got a brother. Mark Anthony. An' he's here in the city; he's downtown somewhere."

Disappointment seared her. "This is a joke," she said flatly.

His whole face furrowed with puzzlement. "Ain't no joke. She got a brother. Mark Anthony. Big gambler type."

"Mark Anthony was one of Caesar's generals, Joel," Francesca said. "Someone was jesting with you."

He scowled. "Caesar? Never heard of him. This Anthony fellow has a flat somewhere down Broadway, and now and then he visits Labouche. She's his sister," he insisted. "He even brings her gifts from time to time. They be real close. Sunday dinners usually. He's the only family she seems to have."

Maybe it wasn't a joke, Francesca thought. Maybe adopting ridiculous names ran in the family, or some such thing. "Do we know where to find Mr. Anthony?" she asked.

"I'll find him," Joel said confidently.

Francesca smiled and patted his head of thick black curls. "That was a job well done," she said fondly. "You shall make a fine assistant indeed."

"You think so?" he said, beaming and unable to contain it.

"Yes, I do."

He began to whistle. Francesca gazed out the window, considering another question. She herself had seen an intruder in Miss de Labouche's apartment, but that had been around midnight. Could it have been Hart?

It was truly hard to say. Her glimpse had been so brief—not even a full second—and in the dark. Francesca felt certain she could not identify the intruder.

If it had been Hart, then he was not the murderer—because he would not have gone back to simply stare at the man he had just killed and then walked away. Francesca was certain that whoever had entered the apartment while she was hiding in the kitchen was innocent of Randall's murder—but somehow involved in Randall's life. The killer would not return to the scene of the crime.

Francesca realized her spirits were even lower now than they had been upon leaving her house an hour or so ago. It had been one blow, it seemed, after another. First her father's insistence that Bragg was not for her, which continued to dismay her to no end. Francesca felt certain that her father knew something that he was refusing to share with her. And whatever that something was, she would have to ferret it out. Unfortunately, her feelings for Bragg remained, leaving her no other choice.

Having had to tell Connie about Neil also continued to haunt her. Francesca could only imagine the extent of her sister's heartbreak. And now she had just seen Evan with the actress who was his mistress. If only Evan could leave well enough alone! Kurland remained a mere annoyance—she thought she could manage him—but Hart had suddenly become even more of a suspect in the Randall murder than he already was.

Of course, she did not know Hart, not at all, so she should not care—but she did. He was Bragg's brother, and because she cared about Bragg, that made her, in a way, Hart's friend and ally—never mind the hostility between the two brothers. Whatever their mutual animosity was about, it was juvenile, and Francesca realized she intended to see them mend both their rift and their ways.

She smiled then at the idea, her mood lifting. It was a wonderful ambition, to see Hart and Bragg patch things up—

why, perhaps she might even help them to become friends!

The coach was halting. "We're here," Francesca said to Joel, glancing down the block. A line of shops seemed to be on the street and basement level of the avenue. A cobbler's was directly before them, a small grocery on one side, a lock-smith on the other. A busy saloon was on the street corner. Laughter and shouts came from it. Five thugs were swilling beer, standing by the lamppost, just outside of the saloon's open doors. A policeman also stood there, swilling beer with the five rowdies. It was a shameful sight with the copper in his uniform.

"Let's see if we can find out where the Jones sisters live." Francesca felt uneasy at the scene facing them now. "Is that copper drunk?" she managed, gawking. "It isn't even five o'clock in the afternoon!"

"Drunk as a skunk, an' that will be easy, if you got an eagle on you." Joel jumped down to the frozen street, nar-rowly avoiding a pile of manure and other garbage.

"I do," Francesca said, dismounting carefully from the coach. The conversation on the corner, which had been drunken and animated, abruptly ceased. Francesca knew her coach—and her person—had been seen. She tensed, prepar-ing for lewd remarks, and when one of the men whistled—the sound insulting—she fled down the steps and into the safety of the cobbler's shop.

A small man with a beard was pounding on a pair of leather soles on the rough wood counter where he was work-ing. It faced the street. Behind him, a rack was filled with shoes, some mended, some needing repair. A small room was behind that, and Francesca glimpsed a woman at a stove and a baby in a bassinet.

Francesca knew that the cobbler lived behind his storefront shop with his family, and perhaps several other families as well, in terrible tenement conditions—the kind of conditions that she and others in the city wished to improve. But now was not the time to think of reform, and Francesca managed a firm smile as the cobbler set aside his leather soles, watch-ing her rather curiously.

"Hello. I am looking for two women, Daisy and Rose Jones? I wonder if you could help me?" Francesca asked, opening her purse.

"English no good. Shoes fix?" he said with a heavy Slavic accent.

"No, no, I do not need any shoes fixed. I am looking for two women, Daisy and Rose Jones?"

"Shoes fix," he said, smiling at her. He pointed at her feet.

Francesca realized he did not understand a word that she was saying.

"He's a Jew an' he don't speak English," Joel said, making a face.

She blinked at Joel, realizing he was bigoted—like so many in the city. She was about to reprimand him—and give him a lecture on equal rights, using the Declaration of Independence as an example of what God intended—when the baby in the back began crying. Francesca smiled at the cobbler and handed him five dollars. "I do not need my shoes fixed," she said. "But buy your family something healthy to eat."

"Shoes fix," he said, smiling.

A thin woman with plump cheeks came out from the room behind the store, holding her baby, who was nursing now. "Two doors down," she said, her English that of a native New Yorker.

"You know the sisters?" Francesca asked.

The woman—who was probably Francesca's age but looked twenty years older—nodded. "But you don't want to go up there, ma'am."

"Why not?"

"It's a bordello," she said, weariness in her eyes.

"Oh," Francesca said, flushing. She should not be surprised. It had been clear why Hart had been with whichever sister he had been calling on. Still, having a mistress and visiting a bordello seemed vastly different to Francesca, the latter somehow depraved. Was she going to step inside a house of ill repute?

Of course she was! She was dying to know what it was like.

Francesca thanked her and left, going two doors down as she had been instructed to do. She knocked on the door. A big black man opened it, saw her, and shut it, and for the second time that day Francesca had a door slammed in her face.

"They'll never let you in," Joel said. "Not unless you pay 'em big, lady. An' I mean *big*."

"Why not?" She knocked again.

" 'Cause I know this house. They're busy and lots of gents come here. Gents from your side o' town." He was sly.

She felt herself flush. "Then I'll pay."

This time a woman cracked the door, leaving several chains on. Their eyes met.

"What do you want?" the woman said. She was older, in her forties, her hair dyed almost black. Francesca saw that she had blue eyes and nice skin, in spite of the heavy makeup she wore.

"I need to speak with Daisy and Rose Jones," Francesca said, smiling in a friendly manner.

"I've never heard of them." The door slammed closed.

But Francesca had heard girlish laughter, the tinkling of crystal glasses, and lower, deeper masculine voices. She knocked again.

The door was opened so quickly that it was clear to Francesca that the woman had been waiting for her to knock. Quickly Francesca said, "I will pay to speak with them." She strained to see beyond the woman but could not make out anything other than the soft peach glow of the lighting inside.

"Then that will be fifty dollars for the two girls."

"What?" Francesca gasped, shocked.

"They're my best." The woman's blue eyes were sharp and hard. "Twenty each apiece, but fifty for the two at once. That's the price. It's printed right on the menu, but first-time customers do not get to see the menu unless I have decided they are on the up-and-up." She stared at Francesca.

Francesca stared back. There was a menu? The door was slammed in her face, again.

She knocked, growing angry. The door was immediately opened.

"I don't understand," she said. "This is not a restaurant."

"Some think it is," the woman said, and she suddenly smiled. "We're not much different from an eatery. We've got prices. You want to talk, that's your affair, and that's not on the menu. You have to buy what's on the menu. Daisy's twenty, straight missionary-style sex. So is Rose. Together, they're fifty, with the extra ten being for Gentleman's Delight. The prices don't change, sorry. You want to talk to them both you have to pay what the menu says. Of course, if you want something special, the price is even higher and it has to be arranged first with me."

Francesca gasped. And what was a Gentleman's Delight? She should not wonder, of course, she should not even think about it, but how could she not?

The door began to close.

Francesca shoved her hand between it and the jamb. "I'll give you fifty dollars, even though I simply wish to speak with the girls."

The woman smiled. "Come in." She opened the door, glancing at Joel. "He can come in, too, but if he steals anything, you'll have to pay."

"Joel won't take a thing," Francesca promised breathlessly, and the next thing she knew, she was standing in a hall with salmon-colored walls, and the door closed behind her.

"They happen to be free," the madam said, leading her and Joel to a stairway. The woman's name was Mrs. Pinke. "Rose just finished a customer, and Daisy is waiting for a regular at six."

Francesca didn't speak. She was straining to see down the hall and into a parlor with a decor that was mostly red. She glimpsed a very beautiful and fully dressed young woman reading on a sofa, although her dress was daring and bare.

The male voices Francesca had heard earlier were silenced now. "Where is everyone?"

"Upstairs." The woman smiled over her shoulder at Francesca. "Discretion is widely requested in this house."

"Is that why you have not asked my name?" Francesca asked.

"If you wished for me to know your name, you would have told me what it is," Mrs. Pinke said firmly.

Francesca absorbed that. "Am I the first to request an audience with Daisy and Rose?" she asked as they reached the landing. She heard a woman giggling from behind closed doors.

"An audience. Yes, you are the first," Mrs. Pinke said with a shake of her head and an amused smile.

So the police had yet to question the sisters. Francesca was thrilled at the thought.

But she also remained disappointed. Where were the half-clad girls? And she had been hoping to see some gentlemen lounging about as they waited for their paramours. Then she realized that perhaps this was for the best. For what if she ran into someone she knew—or someone who knew her? "Did you whisk away the gentlemen calling today on my account?" Francesca suddenly asked.

"They whisked themselves away," Mrs. Pinke said, knocking upon a door. She gave Francesca a glance. "You are a clever young lady. You will have thirty minutes. I must request that you pay in advance."

Francesca dug into her purse as the door was opened, and then she forgot what she was about. One of the most beautiful women she had ever seen stood there, and she was, for all intents and purposes, naked. Her peignoir was sheer and she wore nothing beneath it but hose and black garters.

"Daisy, the young lady wishes to *speak* with you and Rose." Mrs. Pinke nodded at Francesca and turned away, clutching the money she had taken from Francesca's hand.

Francesca suddenly realized that Joel was standing there gaping. She covered his eyes with her hands. "You wait for me downstairs," she cried.

"Hey, let me go," Joel protested. "I got rights!"

"Go downstairs right this minute, or you shall cease being my assistant," Francesca said. And over her shoulder, "Miss . . . er . . . Jones. Please put on some clothing."

Daisy seemed perplexed and she yawned, turning and sauntering away, but not before Francesca had glanced into a pair of bright blue eyes—which had not the flat light of boredom or even stupidity, but the sharp bright light of curiosity and intelligence. As Joel grudgingly departed, Francesca thought, *This woman plays dumb, but she is not dumb at all.*

Francesca stepped into the room and closed the door.

Daisy had slipped on a silk robe. It was a soft ivory, which matched both her naturally platinum hair and the pallor of her skin. On other women, the effect might be draining. Upon her, it was luminous. Her pale coloring somehow accentuated her high cheekbones, her exquisite features, her brilliantly blue eyes, and the pink lushness of her full mouth.

Instantly Francesca understood Calder Hart's reason for coming to this woman. She was simply breathtaking, and he would be powerless in the face of her beauty.

"I've never had a woman customer before," Daisy said softly. She did not speak like a woman from the streets. Her voice was cultivated. "Tell me what you want me to do." She smiled.

Francesca stiffened. "I am not a customer. I am paying you—and Rose—to answer a few questions."

Daisy nodded and shrugged then, as if indifferent. But her eyes remained bright, even though she glanced down so Francesca could not look into them.

"Where is Rose?" Francesca asked.

"She's coming—finishing with a customer, I suppose." Daisy sat down in a big green chair, crossing her long legs. The bedroom was quite nice, actually, boasting a four-poster bed and a fireplace. "What kind of questions?'

Francesca looked around briefly, having expected sex toys perhaps, but she saw nothing out of the ordinary. She took the room's only other chair. "You are a friend of Calder Hart's?"

"I have never heard of him," Daisy said in her soft voice.

Francesca realized instantly that she had been conned. Discretion was the name of this game, and even though she had paid fifty dollars to speak with the two girls, they would never admit to knowing Calder Hart—or, worse, to his being a customer.

Suddenly the door behind Francesca opened and another woman stepped inside. Francesca turned and blinked at another breathtaking girl, this one sultry, with waist-length black hair, the palest skin, and big green eyes. Daisy was small and petite. Rose was tall and voluptuous. Fortunately, she was already clad in a silk wrapper, although it hardly reached her thighs.

"Perhaps you can tell me about your relationship with Calder Hart," Francesca said.

Rose blinked. Like Daisy, her eyes were bright and inquisitive. She said, "Who?"

"This will not do. Hart may be in trouble. He mentioned both your names, and I need to know if he was telling the truth or not."

"Are you his wife?" Daisy asked, her gaze direct.

"No." Francesca felt herself blush at the notion. "He is not married." She watched Rose stand behind Daisy's chair, and there was something protective about the motion.

Daisy shrugged. "What do you mean by 'friend,'?"

"Is he a customer?" Francesca asked bluntly. "When did you last see him?"

"We don't know him," Rose said firmly.

Francesca stared, noticing that Rose had slipped her palm onto Daisy's shoulder. The gesture was intimate, and Francesca felt herself flushing. She knew these women were not sisters, and she was beginning to think that they were more than friends.

"And what if I tell you that Hart may wind up charged with murder? Will that change your minds?" Francesca asked.

Daisy's face tightened and she glanced up at Rose. Rose looked down at her. They held hands.

"Maybe we do know Hart," Rose said slowly. "Why would

our knowing him or not change his being charged with murder or not?"

"I promise you that if he is your customer, he will not mind you corroborating the fact. He has already confessed to seeing the both of you recently, and that is all I can really say. I must know when you last saw him, exactly," Francesca said.

"Confessed?" Daisy asked. Her tone was mild; the question was not.

"He has told the police," Francesca said softly.

They did not look at each other now, but Francesca saw Rose's grip on Daisy's hand tighten.

"I have no reason to lie," Francesca cried.

"We do." It was Rose who spoke, but only after Daisy had squeezed her hand. "Is that all?"

"When did you last see him?" Francesca asked again, firmly. Then, "Please."

They stared at her mutely.

"You must tell me the truth," Francesca tried. "I am his friend."

Daisy looked up at Rose. "I think she is telling the truth. Her eyes are honest."

Rose nodded. "He is our *friend*," she said. "He's here on a regular basis."

This wasn't quite Francesca's business, but she said, "Whom does he visit?"

Daisy smiled a little, and it was a fond smile. "Both of us."

Francesca stared, her cheeks heating. "Not at the same time, surely."

"At the same time," Daisy said, still smiling. "But surely that has little to do with the murder you referred to."

Francesca swallowed. "I suppose it doesn't. . . . Excuse me. *How* is it possible?"

Rose suddenly smiled. "It's very possible. Especially for a man like Calder. He is tireless."

"And kind," Daisy added softly.

Francesca started. She would have never dreamed in a

thousand years that anyone would call Hart kind. "Are we speaking about the same man?"

Rose nodded. "There are men who come here who think they are gentlemen, but they are not. A girl died last month—she was beaten so badly by her *friend*. And it wasn't the first time."

Francesca stood, shaken by what Rose had just revealed. "Why do you do what you do? Clearly you are both genteel and educated. I can see it in your eyes and hear it in your voices."

Daisy glanced up at Rose. Rose said, "You would not understand. But not every woman wishes to marry a man and become a slave to his wishes and those of his household and his children."

Francesca stared. In that single moment, she felt as if she had more in common with Daisy and Rose than she did with most of her peers. "I do understand," she said slowly. "But . . . how can you be . . . intimate . . . with strangers?"

Daisy smiled. "It's only hard the first few times. And when we have someone like Calder, it's quite lovely."

Her intimate use of his first name spoke volumes. "Please. When was he last here?"

They looked at each other. Daisy slipped to her feet and Rose put her arm around her. "Last night."

Relief flooded Francesca. This was the answer she had been praying for. "What time did he arrive? What time did he leave?"

They shared another glance. "He arrived around seven, I think." Daisy spoke again. "He left just before nine." She smiled then, as if at a memory she liked. "He said he had a party to attend."

Francesca blushed, for she imagined what the memory was about, but she was exultant. Hart had an alibi and it was the truth. "Would you tell this to the police?" she had asked, when a sudden commotion downstairs made her pause while both girls paled and turned to each other.

The front door sounded as if it had slammed open, and the cry went up, "Police!"

Doors were banging. Women were crying out; men were cursing. Footsteps sounded, and it was as if an army were rushing up the stairs. And Francesca heard several men shouting, "Police! Open up! Police! This is a raid! Open up!"

Daisy and Rose fled through a window, onto a fire escape, not grabbing a thing.

Francesca was about to follow when she saw three policemen appear at the bottom of the outdoors ladder on the street below, grinning at the two women, waiting to arrest them. She turned, hesitating, as a banging began on the bedroom door. How could this be happening now? Francesca only knew that she must not be found in the bordello, oh no. She could imagine Bragg's wrath.

Having no choice, she leaped underneath the four-poster bed and crouched there, trembling and breathless. She heard the front door open and saw three pairs of black shoes entering the room, almost at once.

"Where are they?" Bragg said.

She cringed. *This could not be happening. Bragg could not be there.*

"Room's empty, sir. Maybe this isn't the right room."

"Search it," Bragg snapped, and he turned and strode out.

Francesca did not breathe. There was no relief. Sweat poured down her body now, in pools and rivulets.

Objects were tossed around. A closet door was opened. Francesca closed her eyes and prayed.

And then she knew that she had been discovered.

Slowly she opened her eyes, only to find a policeman on all fours, staring at her with a grin. "I found me something, Harry," he said.

Francesca moaned.

He pulled her out from under the bed.

NINE

"You are hurting me!" Francesca cried as the policeman hustled her downstairs. His grip on her elbow was ruthless and uncompromising.

"Shut up," the policeman said. His breath was sour. "Before I give you one good." He winked lewdly at her.

Francesca realized what he was mistakenly thinking. "You think I am a . . . ," she gasped, unable to finish her sentence. "I am a lady!"

He laughed. "And I'm Santa Claus."

Mortified, Francesca stumbled down the last two steps.

"Release Miss Cahill immediately."

The policeman detaining Francesca dropped his hand so quickly it was as if he had been shot.

At the sound of Bragg's sharp voice, Francesca's gaze flew to the hall by the front door. It was wide open, and Bragg stood on the threshold, in his dark suit and overcoat, backlit by the winter sun. It did riotous things to his tawny hair. Beyond him, Francesca saw numerous ill-clad women being loaded into a police wagon, most of them shouting and protesting. Mrs. Pinke stood on the street, her arms folded across her bosom, furiously arguing with a detective in a worsted suit and a badge. Two officers stood on either side of her, looking bored.

Francesca glared at the police officer as she reached the landing, rubbing her elbow. "You have bruised me," she said. "And I will not tolerate such brutality from our city's finest."

"Francesca," Bragg warned.

She cringed a little and faced him. That was when she saw Joel standing behind him, in the grasp of a detective in a shabby suit. He looked miserable. And his expression seemed to blame her for his being once again in the hands of the police.

But he could not be as miserable as she was, just then. "Hello, Bragg," she managed, newly breathless.

"Are you all right?" His gaze scanned her from head to toe.

She nodded, surprised, having expected more in the way of anger from him. "I suppose I deserved being mistaken for a trollop." Was he concerned that she had been hurt?

"Yes, you do." Bragg turned as another uniformed officer led Daisy and Rose up to him from the street. Both women were shivering violently in their thin silk robes and high-heeled slippers. "Are these the two women?"

"Suppose so. Caught 'em coming down the fire escape from the bedroom you said they was in," the policeman said. "But they won't say their names."

"Find them two blankets," Bragg ordered. Francesca watched him carefully. If Daisy's ethereal beauty or the bare length of Rose's shapely legs overcame him, he gave no sign. He said, "Are you Daisy and Rose?"

Daisy's mouth was firmly pressed together. Rose said, "No. An' who the fuck are you?"

Francesca flinched. Rose had changed her enunciation, and it was as if she had been born and raised in the trash-filled gutter just outside of where they all stood.

"I am the highest authority in this city, after the mayor," Bragg said coldly. "I am the police commissioner."

Rose shook off the officer and stepped forward, and as she did so, her short robe fell open, revealing not a stitch of any clothing beneath. She pressed against Bragg. "Well, why didn't you say so? For the police commissioner, it's free. Anything you want," she purred.

Bragg's expression did not change; Francesca wanted to slap the other woman silly. Instead, she felt her cheeks go on fire—and then she noticed Rose's hand, sliding over Bragg's thigh. It was perilously close to his groin.

Francesca was stunned. And an instant later she was furious.

Bragg stepped away from the brunette. "Take her and her

friend to the Tombs. If they behave, my office, eight A.M."
He turned his back on Rose.

Francesca took a deep breath. She had been about to
pounce on the other woman for touching Bragg in such a
manner!

Rose spat.

Bragg said, not turning, "Separate them. Separate cells—
and no communication."

Rose said to his back, "Fuck you. But only in your dreams,
copper!"

"Please, stop it, Rose," Daisy whispered, tugging on her
hand.

"Get them out of here," Bragg said to another policeman.
Then to a third, "Make sure the establishment is empty; then
lock it up. Board up all of the windows and the front door.
There will be no more business in this whorehouse."

Francesca looked from his set face to Daisy and Rose, who
were being walked across the street to the police wagon. The
girls were arm-in-arm, but now it was more of an effort to
shield each other from the cold than it was about intimacy or
love. As if feeling eyes upon her, Daisy flung a glance over
her shoulder. Her gaze locked with Francesca's. And in her
gaze there was a plea.

Francesca hesitated, then nodded at her. What she hoped
to communicate was that she would try to help them if she
could.

Daisy smiled in relief.

Francesca realized that Bragg had noticed the exchange.
He said, "You may give me a ride to police headquarters.
Dickens, escort Miss Cahill and the kid to their brougham,
and have them wait for me there."

Francesca realized she was wide-eyed. She tried to remain
composed. Why did he wish to ride with her? Unfortunately,
she knew his motives were not social ones. "Do you not have
a vehicle, Bragg?"

He ignored her and walked out of the bordello and over
to Mrs. Pinke, the only woman now left standing on the street.
She had a fur-lined cloak draped over her shoulders. As Fran-

cesca was led toward her coach, she strained to hear their exchange.

"Have you had a change of heart?" Bragg asked the madam.

"If you mean will I reveal the names of any of my customers, the answer is no."

He smiled at her and it was dangerous enough to make Francesca shiver. "But protecting your customers no longer matters, as you shall never be open for business again."

Mrs. Pinke stuttered and then said, "You will never survive in this city, Commissioner. I beg you, give me a private audience."

"Why? To offer me several thousand dollars? I cannot be bought, Mrs. Pinke, unlike my predecessors. You have a choice. It is a simple one. You may rot in the Tombs and face charges for pimping, prostitution, fraud, blackmail, bribing a police officer, and anything else I can think of successfully prosecuting you for, or you may tell me everything I wish to know, and you will get off with a warning."

She stared. "And my establishment?"

He smiled. "You are out of business, Mrs. Pinke, and from my point of view, it is one less nest of corruption that this city and its inhabitants have to suffer with."

Mrs. Pinke trembled. "I have a lawyer, Bragg. A damned good one!"

Bragg turned his back on her. "Throw her in the wagon." Then his gaze settled on Francesca, who was poised to climb up into her own coach, and narrowed with speculation and intent.

Her heart turned over hard.

And she thought, *He is all business; he is about to lay into me now. I am such a fool, because seeing him makes me happy.*

Bragg strode over to her coach. He held open the door. Francesca smiled at him. He did not smile back.

Her own smile faded. She tried to think of a truly good reason for her to have beaten him at his own game, and she failed.

He followed her inside.

*   *   *

They traveled a few blocks in silence. Joel sat on the seat facing them, and occasionally, as the coach bounced over a rut, Bragg's knee touched Francesca's. She stole several sideways peeks at his profile. He seemed very preoccupied.

"Bragg? I do have good news," she finally said, nervously.

He turned so he was partially facing her. "How did you know about Daisy and Rose? Did you speak with Calder since I last left you?"

Francesca bit her lip. Even though Joel was in the coach with them, she was acutely aware of Bragg's proximity. He was such a masculine and powerful man that he somehow dominated the space inside of the brougham, making it seem very small indeed. "No."

"I see. You were eavesdropping on Calder and myself."

She hesitated. "It is because I care."

He shook his head. "Do the ends always justify the means?" he asked.

She paled. "Of course not."

"Then why? Of course, this is a huge part of your charm. This is what makes you unique and unlike any other woman I have ever known. But it is also frustrating. I never know when I shall open a door and Francesca Cahill will pop up— like a jack-in-the-box." He did not smile.

But he didn't seem terribly angry. He wasn't shouting. In fact, his tone was fairly mild. She smiled a little. "So, I am unique?" She did like the sound of that.

"Terribly, tirelessly so." He finally smiled.

And Francesca was elated. He was the only man, other than her father, who understood her and appreciated her for being a different kind of woman. "Thank you, Bragg," she said.

He sighed. "I have come here to chastise you, and somehow I have wound up flattering you. Only you, Francesca."

"I don't mind." She grinned and almost took his hand. Wisely, she restrained herself. Then, "Why aren't you angrier with me?"

He seemed slightly amused. "Do you wish me to be angry?"

"You were angry last night," she pointed out.

"I found you with a corpse!" he exclaimed. "It was the last thing I expected."

"And you were angry this morning."

"Yes, I was. As my preference is not to have you involved in my work. However, I have had some time to think about it. You were extremely helpful in the Burton investigation, Francesca." His eyes narrowed.

She flushed with pleasure and reached out to touch his hand. The moment she did so, she shivered and dropped her palm. "You know I only have the best of intentions. You know that, like yourself, I am appalled by injustice."

He smiled a little and shook his head. "Yes. I know. Which is why I have done some thinking and have decided that perhaps you might have a role in this case after all." His gaze slowly lifted to hers.

His look was odd, but it was only later that Francesca recalled it. She was elated, ecstatic even. "You do? You wish my help? Shall we be a team, then?" she cried.

"Do you truly believe Miss de Labouche to be your client?"

Francesca hesitated. Now was not the time to dissemble. "I am certain she will agree if I offer my services for free."

He smiled. Then, somberly, "She approached you in the first place. And she is still missing, Francesca. She is a prime suspect in this case even if you believe her to be innocent. I must question her."

Francesca understood. She almost clapped her hands together in her excitement. "You want me to find her."

"Immediately," he said. "I have put a detective on it, but he already has a huge case on his hands. You have heard about the theft of Mrs. Graff's jewels?"

"I think so," Francesca said.

"Then I realized that this is so unorthodox, perhaps you should work on your own—reporting directly to me and me alone."

She was so thrilled she was reeling.

"Peter is a jack-of-all-trades. If you have need of an assistant, he could help you, Francesca."

She blinked at him. "I have an assistant. Joel." She glanced at him, but he was staring out the window at the passing street, appearing bored by their conversation—when Francesca knew he was listening intently to their every word.

Bragg's eyes widened. "Joel—the kid—is now your assistant?"

She nodded proudly. "I have hired him. And do not worry, Bragg; he has given up his criminal ways and he can be trusted completely."

Bragg groaned.

But her mind was racing. With Peter at her side, she could face down the worst thugs—perhaps even a half a dozen of them at one time. "Perhaps, just perhaps, I might use Peter, from time to time." She narrowed her eyes. "Is he to spy on me?"

"No." Bragg smiled. "He is to protect you, Francesca, and keep you out of harm's way."

She smiled back at him, sweetly. "I did manage to fend for myself during the Burton Affair."

"You managed to escape several extreme situations by a hair's breadth," he returned evenly.

That was true. "I will find Georgette de Labouche for you, Bragg," she decided. As quickly, she decided not to tell him about her best lead, Georgette's brother, Marcus Anthony. "But she might refuse to speak with you."

"Then she will speak with you, and you shall be my eyes and ears."

Francesca smiled happily. "This is my dream come true," she blurted; then she wished she had not been so open.

"Perhaps you will decide sleuthing does not suit you after all," he said.

"I doubt it." Sleuthing would always suit her, especially with Bragg at her side. "Don't you want to know what Daisy and Rose told me?" She was somewhat coy now.

"Please," he said, lifting a hand.

"First of all, they are nice women and not at all what you think them to be." She truly intended to impress this fact upon him before their ride was through. "They should not be incarcerated, Bragg."

He faced her fully. "Francesca, they are not *nice* women, they are *prostitutes*, and solicitation for the purposes they solicit for is against the law."

"No." She touched his hand reflexively. This time, she took a moment to feel the texture of his skin. "Rose changed when she was with you. Before, when we were alone, she spoke as if she came from a fine family and had attended fine schools. I swear those two women were gentlewomen before they chose this life. I am certain of it."

"And what difference does it make? They are prostitutes now. They offer their bodies for a price." He stared. "They make their livelihood by breaking the law, Francesca."

She stared back. He was right—but so was she. "You are the one who told me, not very long ago, that nothing is black or white—that there is always some shade of gray to be found in every situation."

He sighed. "Touché. I concede."

"You do?" She was pleased and smiling openly.

Briefly he smiled back. "In fact, I did notice instantly, in spite of Rose's vulgarities, that they were not the harlots one encounters in a bordello. I suspect they had an unusual arrangement with Mrs. Pinke. Knowing my brother, I can say I truly expected no less."

Francesca couldn't help seeing Calder Hart in a very compromising position with both women. She said brightly, "In any case, I do have wonderful news. Hart was there last night." She paused and flushed. "He was with both Daisy and Rose, as he said, until almost nine. He even told the women he had a party to attend."

Bragg eyed her.

She stared back, blushing hotly.

"Are you warm, Francesca?" Bragg asked softly.

She tensed. His tone had changed, becoming soft and sensual. It caused an immediate reaction within her, making her breathless, as if afflicted with anticipation. "I am . . . somewhat surprised . . . that is all. Your brother is . . ." She stopped.

"Immoral, depraved, cunning, and very selfish," Bragg finished for her.

"Daisy said he is kind."

Bragg laughed. "Only to get what he wants. If he wanted Daisy in a certain manner, then trust me, he would be kind."

"Perhaps you do not know your brother as well as you think," Francesca suggested, rubbing her arms.

He stiffened at once. "Do you now *defend* my reprehensible *half* brother? Are you now his *champion*?"

She flinched. "Of course not! I mean, I do not think he is quite so bad!"

"All women fall in love with Calder. I see that you are no exception," he said rigidly.

She inhaled, stunned. His reaction to her simple and innocent suggestion was so swift, so intense. "I am not in love with Calder Hart!" she exclaimed. And she felt like hitting him over the head with a plywood board. She almost exclaimed, "I am in love with you, you foolish man!"

"For your sake, I hope that is the truth," Bragg said. "As he is incapable of loving *anyone* but himself."

Francesca was unmoving. Had she just admitted to herself that she was in love with Bragg? She began to tremble; she did not know whether to be aghast or elated.

"What is it?" Bragg asked.

She recovered, swallowing with difficulty. "It is the truth. He is your brother, and that is why I am fond of him, if I am fond of him at all," she managed.

Bragg stared out of the window. They were approaching 23rd Street. He seemed sullen now.

Francesca folded her arms across her breasts. "I do not wish to argue, Bragg. Why, we are a team now!"

"We are not arguing. Just stay away from Hart."

"I promise," she said. Was she really, truly, in love?

Her heart was telling her now, in no uncertain terms, that there was only one possible answer.

He turned to study her. "I mean it."

She swallowed. "So do I." Did she? If she had to choose between Bragg's friendship and an association with Hart, there was no question of what her choice would be. However, right now, there was no choice to make—there was merely a case to solve and an astounding revelation to ponder. She was in love. *She was in love with Rick Bragg.*

But was it truly so surprising? He was a devastating man, handsome in a very unique way, with his dark complexion and tawny hair and his high, high cheekbones. He was also extremely powerful, and not simply because he was currently New York City's police commissioner. His power came from within, and it had everything to do with his intelligence, his ethics, and his ambition. She was already so proud of him— and they had only just met. In short, given all that they had in common, he was so perfect for her.

Bragg was regarding her quite closely. Francesca started as she realized it, hoping that he could not be guessing her thoughts.

She straightened, smiled, and said, "Well, Hart does have an alibi." Her voice came out high in pitch with nervous tension.

Bragg looked at her. "Are you all right?"

"Truly, I am fine!" But she wasn't fine; she was in love with the most amazing man.

"Those two women are bought and paid for by Calder, Francesca. They would never say anything he did not wish for them to say."

She gaped, successfully diverted from her stunning thoughts. "You—you do not believe them? You think he has . . . he has . . . *bribed* them to claim that he was with them last night?" She was shocked.

"Do you not understand life at all, Francesca?" Bragg asked angrily. "I fear that one day your trust and naïveté will truly hurt you. Calder has millions. He is a powerful man. If two prostitutes, whom he frequents, claim he was with them last night, it is a meaningless claim. Of course they will say whatever Hart wishes them to say. They will not go against him, and neither will Madam Pinke, and I doubt Calder even had to bribe them—as that is a crime and he is hardly so stupid."

Francesca stared. His features were hard now, his eyes flashing. "But it might be true—and I think it is," she finally said, but now she wasn't so certain.

"It might be true," Bragg agreed. "And for Calder's sake, I hope it is true, but I doubt we will ever know for certain whether or not he was with the girls last night."

"Then why have you sent them to the Tombs?"

"Because I am an officer of the law, they have broken the law—and it is my duty to try to get to the truth. Perhaps Daisy will break. She strikes me as softer than Rose. Clearly, in this case, as they are so attached to one another, divide and conquer is the best course of action. If they are lying, perhaps a night that is cold and foodless and unpleasant—and spent separately—will make one of them speak out."

"But it is cruel."

"Perhaps. But what is worse is allowing Randall's killer to get off scot-free," Bragg said.

Francesca did not agree. "I have decided that I like Daisy and Rose. I detest seeing them sent to the Tombs."

His brows arched. "Really?"

"Yes, really." She met his golden stare. "Unlike other people in this city, I keep an open mind. Sometimes rules are made to be broken."

"And when should the law be ignored, or even flouted?"

"That is an ancient question, one of philosophy, and we could sit here all day and all night debating it," Francesca pointed out.

"Yes, we could." Bragg shook his head, but he smiled. "I do not think this is about likes or dislikes. You are interested in Daisy and Rose because they are so different from anyone you have ever known, because they are so different from yourself. And until you understand what they are about, you will grapple with the subject of how two women from genteel backgrounds could become what they have become. Am I right?"

She blinked at him. "Perhaps. Perhaps you know me very well, Bragg, considering our acquaintance is so short." Her heart began to beat hard.

"I have already told you, I am an extremely astute judge of character." He was smiling.

So was she. And somehow, their gazes locked. Francesca felt herself becoming breathless, all over again, her smile fading. There was no one she wished to be with more. Even arguing about the two prostitutes was somehow exciting with Bragg. Surely there was no mistaking the tension between them now, and she felt certain it was not one-sided. She hesitated, but only for a fraction of a moment, then blurted, "Was police business the real reason you canceled our drive in the country?"

"No," he said.

She inhaled. She had wanted an answer—but not that one. "Why?" she whispered.

His jaw flexed; his entire face tightened. He leaned forward and slid open the window partition between their cab and the coachman. "Driver, turn right on Houston," he said.

She wondered if he intended to answer her.

He finally looked at her. Something flickered in his eyes, but she could not define what it was or what it signified. He said, "I realized after impulsively suggesting a drive in the country that my behavior was entirely inappropriate—and misleading. I apologize, Francesca."

She was trying, desperately, to keep her head above water, but she was sinking fast. "Inappropriate? But how?"

He glanced away. "My only intention has been to offer you friendship, Francesca, from the moment we met. Again, if I have misled you, I apologize."

Francesca was speechless.

After dropping Bragg at police headquarters, she had assured Joel that their day was done, taking him not home, but several blocks from his flat. "Let's plan to continue our work tomorrow," Francesca told him with a smile.

"What time?" Joel asked eagerly.

"How about ten? Could you come uptown and meet me at my house?" Joel already knew where she lived, as she had briefly found him employment in the stables there. However, he did not like horses, and it had not worked out.

"You bet." He grinned. Then his expression changed and he hesitated instead of leaping out of the coach.

Francesca looked into his dark eyes with their long, sooty lashes. "Is there something you want to say?" she asked.

He hesitated, then blurted, "Lady, I got to tell you, it's a trick!"

She blinked. "Whatever are you talking about?"

He sighed. "The copper. The copper you are all cow-eyes for."

Francesca digested his words and felt her cheeks warm. "Joel, first of all, I am not 'cow-eyes' for Rick Bragg." What a lie! "And secondly, I have not a clue as to what you mean."

"He couldn't look straight at you when he said it. He don't mean it at all!"

Instantly she became apprehensive. "He didn't mean what?"

"That you be his partner and all. That he wants you an' him to be a team an' you need to report to him like you was a leatherhead yerself."

She stared.

"It's a trick," Joel said fiercely. "He's got somethin' up his sleeve, an ace in the hole, an' you should know it."

"But why would he suggest we work together at all? Why would he ask me to locate an important part of this case— Miss de Labouche? How could that be a trick? We need to speak with her, Joel. Surely you know that."

"It's a trick, and I don't get it, meself." He nodded at her; then his expression changed. "Sorry, lady." He leaped from the coach.

Francesca stared after him for a moment, her mind spinning. And suddenly she sat up straight, simply breathless. *Did Bragg want her off the case?*

Did he think to ask her to chase Miss de Labouche so she

would stay out of his way? So she would stay out of the principal part of his investigation?

Her heart was drumming now. *My God,* Francesca saw the light! He thought to send her on a mostly wild-goose chase, so he could solve the murder by himself!

Well, it would not do! Oh, no!

"Joel!" She opened her door and poked her head out; he stopped in his tracks. "You are a very clever boy indeed!" she called.

He beamed at her.

Less than half an hour later, Francesca stared up at the Montrose residence. She remained anxious and worried about her sister, and she simply had to speak with her. Calling on Connie now would help her rein in her very wayward thoughts as well. For the more she thought about it, the more she thought that Joel was right and Bragg was trying to divert her from the real investigation. Worse, beneath her anger there was real dread and fear—she could not forget Bragg's firm avowal of his platonic intentions toward her.

Why?

Did he not find her attractive?

Or did he think her far too eccentric, and even mannish, for his tastes?

She tried to compose herself. She did have a job to do. She was committed to solving this case, with or without Bragg as a partner.

"Miss Cahill?"

Francesca realized that one of the doormen had seen her carriage and had come out of the house to open the door for her. She tried to smile at Williams and thought she failed. She allowed him to help her down from the coach and to the cobblestones of the courtyard.

The Montrose home was a four-story stone building the color of sand. The short cobbled drive formed a small U around an island that, in the spring and summer, was abloom with flowering shrubs and two stately elm trees. The drive disappeared beneath an archway, ending in a small interior courtyard, which was framed by tall and bare maple trees. The house had been built around the courtyard, and its entrance was at the far side, which was where her carriage had now parked.

Both Connie and Neil were home, Francesca saw, for their two conveyances, a big brougham and a smaller gig, were standing in front of the house. The Montrose coat of arms was sculpted in stone and painted red, blue, and silver above the front door of the house. A lion with his paw upon a globe sat there atop a banner that read, "In honor all things."

Francesca was ushered inside. The foyer was bright and airy, with gleaming beige marble floors and shockingly white plastered walls. Several Montrose family portraits of centuries-old ancestors hung on the walls. She smiled at the doorman, this time firmly. "Will you tell my sister that I am here? I will wait in the salon," she said.

The doorman nodded and left.

Francesca wandered into a lush room just off of the foyer, the furnishings mostly yellows and gold. While Connie entered and moved about the Cahill home quite as she pleased, Francesca had decided long ago not to do so in her sister's home. Even as a naïve and young sister to the bride and in-law to the groom, she had sensed she might walk in on something she had no wish to interrupt.

Francesca did not sit. Shortly after their engagement, Neil had commissioned a portrait of her sister, and it was almost full-size. It hung on the far wall, dominating it. Connie was so lovely in her lavender ball gown, beaming at the artist. She radiated excitement and happiness; she radiated joy.

"How dare you set foot in this house?"

At the sound of Montrose's voice, Francesca whirled, her heart dropping precariously, as if to the floor.

He strode to her, absolutely livid. "Did you hear me, Francesca?"

She did cringe. "Neil."

"I asked you to mind your own affairs. I clearly stipulated that you not interfere in my marriage and my life!" he thundered.

Francesca felt tears well up in her eyes. Montrose was frightening. But what was so much worse was that, just a few weeks ago, she had adored him so—the result of an instant infatuation that had begun the moment she had laid her eyes upon him when she was but fifteen. In the past two weeks, her illusions had been severely shattered. Her heart had also been broken. But had they now come to this? To hostility and shouts, to accusations and strife?

"How dare you shout at me?" Francesca stammered. Being coherent in his presence had always been a problem for her. Even now, feeling about him as she did, he was the most attractive man she had ever seen. He had a huge and magnetic presence. Francesca knew most women found him devastating; it had always been obvious.

"How dare I shout at you? How dare you destroy my marriage—my life!" he roared.

She gasped, taking another step backward—but he only came forward, towering over her. "I have destroyed nothing, Neil! I did not coerce you into having an affair! If something has been tainted—or destroyed—you have only yourself to blame for it!"

"Do you think I do not know that!" he shouted furiously. "Do you think me a fool? I know I have made the worst mistake of my life! But did you have to intervene? I asked you not to say a word. And you promised me you would not. Are you satisfied now? Are you?" It was a demand. His turquoise eyes had become a fascinating shade of green. Somehow, his hands gripped her shoulders and it was not pleasant.

"Please release me," she managed, shaken and shaking. He did so instantly. She backed away, hugging herself. "How could I be satisfied? How?" she asked in a whisper. "I am not satisfied; I am horrified!" she cried.

"I think you are satisfied," he said darkly. "I think this is what you have *always* wanted."

"What?" she gasped. "I do not have a clue as to what you are speaking about!"

"No? I think you do." He stared. His face was ruddy. Montrose had nearly black hair and turquoise eyes; his skin was pale, even in the summer. But his light complexion was hardly effeminate, as he was such a big, virile man. Francesca had never seen him flushed like this before. "I think you know *exactly* what I am speaking about."

She shivered. "I don't. I have to go." She started past him.

He gripped her shoulder, whirling her about, and he did not unhand her this time. "You have always wanted to be in your sister's shoes, and do not think I have not always known it."

Francesca gasped. She could not speak—she could only stare.

Because he was right, in a way. She had always wondered what it would have been like if she had been the older sister—the one to wed Neil. Until the past two weeks, she had always thought, secretly, deep in her heart, that should she have been the older one, she would have been the happiest woman on earth.

"If you are asking me if I have always admired you, then the answer is yes," she said. "I was turning fifteen when we met, Neil. My admiration for you was quite natural."

"I would call it infatuation," he snapped.

Francesca felt herself turn red. "No." But it *had* been an infatuation, albeit a harmless and innocent one. "I have adored you and the girls, I love my sister, so do not ever again suggest I have told Connie about your affairs with some kind of horrid intent!"

Francesca tried to move past him, but he barred her way. "Let me go!" she cried, near tears.

"I wish to throttle you, Francesca," he stated coldly. "I do not know if I am more angry with you—or myself."

She blinked up at him through sudden tears.

Suddenly he released her with a harsh sound, one very much like a groan.

"I have always admired you, Neil," she cried softly, through tears. "But my admiration for you took a turn for the worse when I saw you with Eliza! It was truly like being woken up with ice-cold water on your face! How could you even suggest that I have been secretly in love with you—and that I would do anything, anything, to hurt your marriage, my sister, and my nieces? Dear God, that makes you a reprehensible man!"

"But I am already reprehensible, am I not?" he mocked, his hands at last curled up into fists on his narrow hips. "So what difference does it make what I now do? The saint has become a sinner, and that will never change."

She stared. "Balderdash. In time, this will pass. And you know it as well as I do. I can only pray that somehow you and my sister will find a way to truly forgive and forget, and forge an even greater bond." Neil made another harsh sound. "But I do wish you had never broken my sister's heart!"

Suddenly he demanded, "Has it ever occurred to you that my heart is the broken one?"

She had been frightened, but now she was stunned. "What?" she whispered. "No, it most certainly has not!"

"You are a busybody, but you hardly know everything." He turned away. "Enough, Francesca. I don't know why you are here—and I do not care."

His words somehow hurt her. "Neil—"

"Get out of this house," he said flatly, walking away now.

"Neil!" Francesca cried, stunned.

He did not turn as he paused on the threshold of the room. His broad back remained rigidly facing her. He ground out, "Get out of this house, Francesca, before I bodily remove you from it."

She backed away.

Not turning, he said, "You are not welcome here. *Not ever again.* Have I made myself clear?"

Francesca was disbelieving and speechless.

"Get out!" he roared, whirling.

Francesca ran.

TEN

The last place Francesca wished to be was at the opera house.

But Signora Valciaolo was renowned throughout Europe, and she was making her American debut at the Metropolitan Opera House that night. The Cahills kept a box at the Metropolitan, having given up their membership at the Academy of Music several years earlier, and plans for this particular evening had been made months ago. A grand—and late—supper would follow at Delmonico's.

Francesca sat beside her father, who was actually reading a newspaper, as the opera house filled up. Julia was in the huge lobby downstairs, circulating among the opera aficionados, most of whom were her friends. Francesca was seriously ill.

It was an illness of the heart, but it was making her physically sick as well. She hadn't been able to eat a thing before leaving the house, causing her mother to raise both brows at her, and she wondered if she would make it through the evening without disgracing herself.

Neil could not have meant it. He had spoken in anger. They had been friends for years. In fact, he had stated unequivocally that he considered her his little sister. And technically, she had become his sister, once he had wed Connie.

He appeared to detest her now. But surely, in time, he would forgive her for telling Connie what was only the truth.

Too late, she realized she could not manage such hostility rejection from her brother-in-law. Too late, she realized that five years of affection did not die in one fell swoop. She could not hate him, not even knowing what a cad he was, and his words had cut her heart in two.

She only wanted Neil and Connie to repair their marriage; she only wanted for their life to go back to where it had so recently been. And what had his comment about *his* having a broken heart meant?

Neil and Connie were supposed to join them at the opera. Francesca was terrified of facing him now; she could not imagine how she could act as if nothing were amiss between them. The only advantage to Neil and Connie's joining them was that Francesca would finally see her sister and, she hoped, find a private moment with her to discover how she was handling the burden of the truth.

Francesca had tried to call Connie on the telephone just before leaving for the opera, but a servant had said that Lady Montrose was not taking any calls.

That worried Francesca. Connie would always take a telephone call from her sister.

"Hello, Andrew. Hello, Francesca."

Francesca turned and saw Sarah Channing and her mother. It was the rather distracted but very amiable Mrs. Channing who had spoken.

Andrew got to his feet to kiss Mrs. Channing's hand and Sarah's cheek. "Hello, Lillibet. Sarah. My dear, you are lovely tonight," Andrew said with a fond smile at his future daughter-in-law.

Sarah smiled back but said nothing. She was a rather plain and nondescript young woman, petite, with dark hair and eyes. As usual, she wore her red evening gown carelessly— it was outdated, far too flamboyant for her nature, and the color overwhelmed her. Francesca knew Sarah enough to know that she was not even aware of what she wore or how it looked, and Francesca also guessed Sarah's mother was the one who had asked her to wear the ugly dress.

"Hello," Francesca managed to them both. She now had a splitting headache, as Sarah's presence was a potent reminder to her of the words she must have with Evan about his mistress.

"Francesca, how lovely you also look," Mrs. Channing said, allowing Sarah to slip into the seat beside Francesca. "Peach is such a perfect color for you. And where is Julia?" she asked Andrew.

Francesca glanced again at Sarah, trying to smile.

Sarah did not smile back. "Francesca?"

"I am fine," Francesca said quickly, realizing that Sarah had quickly ascertained that something was wrong without even speaking with her. Sarah was the classic case of appearances being absolutely deceiving. She appeared very meek and shy, and indeed, she was a very quiet young lady. But she was a passionate and brilliant artist, and her work expressed her feelings and views more than a million words ever could.

Evan had never even seen her art.

Sarah merely smiled, with encouragement, it seemed, and she patted Francesca's hand comfortingly.

Francesca shot to her feet, anxiety overcoming her. "I must take some air; I will be right back," she said as Julia entered their box.

"Do hurry, Francesca," Julia said, resplendent in a dark red chiffon gown and numerous rubies to match. "You know the curtain rises precisely at eight."

Francesca nodded and hurried through the heavy velvet draperies and into the hall behind the opera. Escaping the Cahill box was a vast relief. She paused and quite collapsed against the wall.

She could not bear it if Neil now despised her, but it was a little late to realize that. Had she done the wrong thing in telling Connie about his affair with Eliza? Connie had already suspected an affair, Francesca felt certain. That afternoon, Connie had *wanted* to hear the truth. Hadn't she? Should she have lied to her sister?

"Fran? Curtain's up in five minutes," Evan said, sauntering down the hall with two young ladies whom Francesca vaguely recognized. They were casting longing glances at her brother, who seemed oblivious to their adoration. He was grinning at Francesca.

"I'd like a word with you," she said tersely.

His eyes widened. "Whoa! Have I done something to upset you?"

Francesca swallowed hard. She must not take out her distress on her brother, as he was hardly to blame for Neil's wrath. She nodded to the two young ladies. "Privately."

Both women turned to Evan, who bowed slightly at them. Francesca watched them hurry away, the brunette casting a long and hopeful glance over her shoulder at Evan. He did not notice; he was studying Francesca. "What is it, Fran? Have you been crying?"

It was on the tip of her tongue to tell him about Neil's affair and Connie's dilemma; she did not. What if they wished for the entire incident to be kept private, even from the family? She stiffened. "No, I have not been crying, but I am quite distraught."

"Surely not because of me," he said. He was tall, dark-haired, and good-looking. He had the sunniest disposition of anyone Francesca knew; Evan rarely lost his temper, and he was usually smiling.

"I have a lot on my mind, so my dour mood has little to do with you," she said.

"Whew! That is a relief." He chucked her under the chin. "C'mon, Fran, it can't be that bad."

"I saw you with Grace Conway."

"What?" He stiffened instantly, his eyes widening.

"On Broadway, in a carriage, downtown," Francesca said. "Do not deny it."

He began to flush. "How do you even know Grace . . . er, Grace Conway?"

"Evan, I am not a fool. I know you have had a string of mistresses, and I saw you with her ages ago. An inquiry or two quickly revealed that she is a rather acclaimed stage actress. And a very beautiful one, too, I might add," Francesca said.

He was flushing darkly now. "Leave it to you, Fran. Is nothing sacred? Can I not have any secrets? Must you always snoop?"

She crossed her arms. "You are engaged now, Evan. You are engaged to a very fine woman. I only pray that you were with Miss Conway in order to tell her that your affair is over."

"What I do, and what I do not do, is none of your affair,

Fran—not when it comes to my private life," he said harshly, and he turned on his heel and began striding away from her.

Francesca was shocked. She ran after him, grabbing his arm. "You mean, you will not break it off now that you are about to be married?"

He whirled to face her, shrugging her off. "That is my personal affair, Fran. It is not yours!"

She stared at him, shocked.

"Besides," he said angrily, "you know I do not love Sarah. You know that Father is *blackmailing* me into this marriage, so how can you take *their* side?"

"I am not on their side," she managed. *And it was true. Andrew would only pay Evan's debts upon his marriage to Sarah Channing.* "No one is more against your marriage to Sarah Channing than I. I have never seen two people more mismatched! You know I begged Father to change his mind, and you know it is hopeless. I wish nothing more than for you to marry for love. But you are engaged now, Evan. And right is right and wrong is wrong. Cheating on your fiancée is wrong. You must give Sarah your heart as well as your loyalty."

He gave her a look of disgust and walked away, leaving her standing there in the now-empty hall.

She had never seen him send anyone such a look before, much less herself.

And from behind all the closed doors, Francesca heard Signora Valciaolo begin to sing.

Francesca slipped into her family's box as unobtrusively as possible. It was impossible not to notice that Evan's shoulders were stiffly and angrily set as he sat beside Sarah, between her and her mother. It was also impossible not to notice how empty their box was. Connie and Neil had not yet arrived.

As Francesca slipped into her seat between Sarah and her own mother, she knew in her heart that they would not be coming.

Everyone was raptly involved in the Italian soprano's per-

formance of a star-crossed lover, except for Francesca. Her
misery seemed to have escalated.

There was a stirring in the crowd surrounding her, like a
ripple in a heretofore-placid pond. Francesca followed the re-
directed attention of the opera attendees, and she saw a tall
man entering a box at the other end of the mezzanine. She
recognized him instantly.

Calder Hart was darkly devastating in his black tuxedo as
he bent to kiss the cheek of a woman Francesca recognized
but did not recall by name. She was a petite and beautiful
brunette, recently widowed, and the heiress to both her husband's and her deceased father's fortunes. Her box was full;
clearly Calder was but one of her dozen guests.

Francesca trained her opera glasses on the pair. Calder was
still standing, and he remained bent over the widow, who was
whispering into his ear. Francesca followed her gloved arm
to her hand and saw that she had it on his waist. She stiffened.
Was this another of his lovers, then? And just how many
women could one man dally with?

Calder Hart suddenly straightened and turned to stare in
her direction. Francesca quickly lowered her opera glasses—
which had been trained quite obviously on him—and she felt
herself flush. The distance between them consisted of five
boxes, and she could make out his features clearly enough.
Their gazes met.

He smiled, somewhat sardonically, and bowed.

She flushed again and trained her glasses quickly on the
virtuoso star of the evening's performance.

Julia turned to gaze at her.

Francesca ignored her mother now. What did that bow
signify?

Still holding her glasses, she peeked out of the corner of
her eye, first to the right and then to the left. Good God.
People were looking at her, and not just ladies but also gentlemen.

Francesca tried to focus on the drama unfolding on the
stage below. It was an impossible feat. She decided that Calder was as reprehensible as Bragg claimed. For some odd

reason, he was toying with her, for that was what his mild yet somehow sinister flirtation seemed to be.

Finally Francesca gave up. She tweaked the direction of her glasses and directed them upon the widow's box—upon him.

He was watching the performance intently, she saw, clearly rapt, but his widowed lady friend was sitting so close to him that their bodies had to be touching. If they were not already lovers, they would become so, soon.

Francesca jerked her glasses back to Signora Valciaolo. Several interminable minutes passed, during which she felt several stares, not the least of which was Julia's. And that was so odd. Francesca's mother truly adored the opera; in fact, she was a devout fan of all the arts. Never did her attention waver from an opera, a ballet, or a musical. At least, not until this night.

"Francesca?" Sarah whispered in her ear.

Francesca lowered her glasses and turned toward Sarah. "Yes?"

"Who is that man?"

Francesca hoped she did not blush. She followed Sarah's gaze. Hart remained as he had been before, thoroughly immersed in what was clearly a spectacular opera, although Francesca could not enjoy it. She turned back to Sarah. "His name is Calder Hart. Why?"

"I think he is taken with you. He keeps looking over here," Sarah said in a low tone that could not be overheard.

Francesca blinked at her. Then, "If he is taken with anyone, it is . . ." She stopped. She realized Julia was attempting to eavesdrop, and she had been about to insist that Hart's interest currently lay, inappropriately, with her sister. She leaned closer. "You are wrong. And in any case, Hart is the kind of cad who plays the field. He is never set upon one single woman."

Sarah's eyes widened and then she shook her head. "That is too bad. I felt certain he is rather preoccupied with you. Is he the same Calder Hart who is a renowned art collector? The one who spent a fortune last month in London on Ingres's *Grande Odalisque*?"

Francesca blinked at her. "He is an art collector. But I have no idea whether he purchased this painting you are speaking about."

Sarah was flushed with excitement. "If you know him, Francesca, perhaps, if it is no bother, at some time, in the future, you might persuade him to show us his collection? I have heard it is one of the finest in the world."

Francesca was about to agree when Julia took her hand, in warning. She nodded at Sarah, meaning that, in the future, she would try, and she gave her mother an apologetic glance for being so rude during the opera.

It was midnight when they entered the house, without Evan. After supper, he had dutifully escorted his fiancée and her mother across the park and home. Francesca did not think that he would be returning to the house; she suspected he would sojourn to one of his clubs, a cabaret, or a popular downtown restaurant, as he usually did. Perhaps he would even go to his mistress. That last thought remained dismaying.

"Good night, my dear," Andrew said, kissing her cheek. "I shall see you in the morning." He smiled and trudged up the wide white alabaster staircase, leaving Francesca standing in the foyer with her mother.

She was desperate. She wished to immediately learn if Connie had called or dropped off a note. She smiled at Julia. "Good night, Mama."

"Francesca, whatever is wrong with you, dear?"

She had been about to dash for the stairs and her room, where any notes or messages would have been left on her desk. "I am just a bit under the weather," she replied, trying to smile. "I suppose I have another touch of the flu."

"The last time you said that was only a few days ago," Julia remarked. "And you were up to your ears in that terrible Burton Affair." She was handing off her magnificent sable coat to a servant. Her long black gloves followed, but she did not take her eyes off of Francesca.

Francesca's coat was peach-colored silk brocade with a mink lining. It matched her evening gown precisely. She removed it, handing it to a waiting servant avoiding her mother's probing eyes. "Well," she said slowly, "a little boy's life was at stake, and I could not sit idly by and do nothing when I knew I could be of help."

Julia tilted up her chin. "What are you up to, Francesca? Tell me the truth. For I can see so much worry in your eyes, and it is quite unsettling."

Francesca stared at her, and as her mother was the exact same height as she was—which was five feet, five inches tall—they stood eye-to-eye. "Nothing," she finally whispered. Deception now felt impossible. Francesca detested having to lie to anyone, much less to a member of her own family.

Julia released her. "You would lie to my face, Francesca?" she asked quietly.

"Oh, Mama. No, I am sorry. I would not." Francesca wrung her hands. She was trapped. She was worried about her sister, but she dared not breathe a word of that to her mother—even though sooner, rather than later, Julia would find out everything; of that Francesca had no doubt. It was better to try to fob her off with half of the truth, as she seemed to already have surmised it, anyway. She sighed. "Perhaps I have been helping Bragg, just a bit, on another case."

Julia seemed genuinely stunned. "What?!"

Francesca looked at her. "But—you did not know?"

"I pride myself on knowing just about everything that happens under this roof, but no, Francesca, I did not know. It has only been a week since that Burton Abduction!" she cried, clearly surprised, and not pleasantly.

"I know we only closed the case a few days ago. I am sorry. But Mama, I know I can help—"

"I will not have it!" Julia cried firmly. "I will not. You placed your life in danger. Francesca, this will not do. You are a genteel young lady. Instead, you consort with the police and hoodlums and even that child pickpocket. Who absconded with my silver, I might add." Her hands found her hips.

The misunderstanding regarding Joel had to be cleared up right away, especially as he would be about the house now, in his new position as her assistant. "Mama, Joel Kennedy did not take your silver. I am certain of it."

"Mrs. Ryan feels differently, Francesca, and I do not wish to discuss the stolen silver now."

"But I do! He has become a friend, and his family is so poor. I hope to employ him as an errand boy," she said, a tiny white lie.

"What? You will do no such thing! I do not want to see hide nor hair of that little thief in this house. I mean it, Francesca."

"We have a crook in our midst, Mother, in our *employ*. But have no fear. I shall uncover the culprit and clear Joel's name." Francesca meant it, even though she did not have a clue as to how she would find the time to do so. Not when Connie needed her so, with her marriage in the dire straits it now was in, and not with the commitments she had made to find Georgette de Labouche and, more importantly, to find Paul Randall's killer and clear her name. Even the mere thought of all that filled her plate was enough to make her mind spin crazily. Francesca felt dizzy. Could she possibly be in over her head?

She had a bad feeling. Now, after the Burton Abduction, it was one she recognized, too well. She shook it off.

Julia was pacing across the spacious room with its inlaid plaster panels. Then, turning, she said, "I thought this was about your sister."

Francesca felt the blood draining from her face. "What?" She prayed she had misheard; she knew she had not.

"I thought this was about your sister," Julia repeated, staring.

Francesca wondered if her mother had gypsy blood, enabling her to read minds—yet Julia Van Wyck Cahill prided herself on her aristocratic background, as her ancestry could be traced back to her Dutch forefathers in New Amsterdam and her noble French forefathers in the years before the French Revolution. "Why would you think it is about Connie?" Francesca asked cautiously.

"Because I am her mother and it is obvious that she is distressed, and has been so for some time. I know how close you two are, and I know she confides in you—if she chooses to confide in anyone at all. Is something wrong, Francesca?" Julia approached. Her own blue eyes, so much like her daughter's, reflected genuine worry now. "Should I be concerned?" She stared.

Francesca inhaled, not looking away. "Mama, I cannot say. I wish I could, but I cannot."

Julia finally nodded. "If you tell me that there is no illness involved, that Connie, Montrose, and the girls are all in good health, then I shall wait until Connie chooses to tell me herself what the matter might be."

"There is no illness," Francesca whispered, thinking of how much like a sickness a broken heart was.

Julia seemed to accept that. "If one has one's health, Francesca, one can succeed, and thwart all obstacles, in the end."

Francesca nodded. "I suppose so."

Julia cupped her shoulder. "I do not like seeing you this distressed, either."

Francesca shrugged. "It will pass."

"Yes, it will." Julia studied her closely. "So Mr. Hart has remembered you from your previous meeting at the White party at the Rooftop Garden last night."

Francesca stiffened with surprise—and instantly she knew where this was leading. And she reprimanded herself for not having realized that Julia would have noticed their meeting the other night at Madison Square Garden. Julia never missed anything! It was as if she had eyes in the back of her head and ears in other people's purses. "Why do you say that, Mama?" she asked cautiously.

Julia smiled. "He quite singled you out tonight for his attentions. He turned to look at you several times. I did not mistake it, Francesca. In fact, quite a few of my friends have commented to me upon his interest."

Francesca could hardly believe their conversation. "Mama, you cannot possibly be thinking what I think you are thinking."

"I am." Julia smiled. "He is one of the city's wealthiest bachelors. Do you know that he trades with China? He also owns the city's largest insurance company. I realize he has a certain rather notorious reputation, but Francesca, he is young—only twenty-six. He is merely sowing his wild oats, and once he has been brought to the altar, I am certain he will settle down."

How could her mother be thinking, even for a moment, that Calder Hart was taken with her? And that he might marry her? Briefly Francesca recalled Sarah Channing's comments and wondered if she had somehow missed something. Then she thought about his flirtation with her sister and knew that Julia and Sarah were both wrong. Besides, she wasn't marrying him—he was Bragg's half brother. In fact, right now, she wasn't marrying anyone. "I do not think anyone will bring him to the altar, Mama," Francesca whispered, but something inside her had become nervous and jittery.

"Nonsense. All men must marry eventually, and he is hardly an exception to the rule. Why not you?" Julia smiled again. Clearly she was thrilled with this most recent development.

Francesca folded her arms tightly across her chest. Julia had to be stopped, immediately. A very vivid image of Bragg was flashing in her mind, and he was angry. Was it only a few hours ago that he had accused her, erroneously, of having fallen in love with Calder? Francesca had not had any time to dwell on that conversation, but now it seemed to her that he had been very unhappy and perhaps even jealous of the notion. Which made no sense, as he only wished to be her friend.

"I have decided to never wed," Francesca said firmly, thinking not about Calder Hart, but his half brother, Rick Bragg, who had stated that his only intentions toward her were platonic ones. "And you cannot dissuade me, Mama."

"Please, Francesca, stop it. That is absurd!" Julia exclaimed.

"It is hardly absurd. You cannot force me to wed. I prefer to remain a spinster. I shall live here, with you and Papa, participating in my clubs in the hopes of reforming this city." Francesca meant her every word. Indeed, the idea was quickly growing upon her. She elaborated, "One day, when you are both old, and I am here, taking care of you, you shall be very happy with my decision indeed."

"You will not remain a spinster," Julia said, horrified. "Only you, Francesca, would come up with such a ghastly notion. I simply will not have it."

"I am not joking, Mama."

"Neither am I."

"Besides, you will not succeed in marrying me off, not easily, anyway." She did not feel quite as triumphant as she had thought she might be as she played a trump card.

"Francesca, are you serious? Do you know how many inquiries I receive, on a daily basis, about you?"

"From your friends?" She shook her head. "Not from their sons." Francesca usually avoided all thoughts on the subject of socializing for the purpose of marriage. Thinking now about it caused the smallest incision to open up in the vicinity of her heart.

"What is this about?" Julia cried. She touched her cheek. "Dear, what is this about?"

Francesca grimaced. "I am not a fool. I am well aware that I am considered odd. I have been called eccentric, even mannish, not that I care." She shrugged.

And reminded herself that she did not care. And it was mostly true.

The problem was, inside of herself, there was a tiny part of her that did care and that yearned, quite desperately, to be as idolized and longed for as Connie.

Julia gaped.

"I know what they say about me behind my back." Francesca smiled bravely. "Connie and I may look like twins, but that does not fool anybody. So you see, you are wrong. Your friends might think me suitable for their sons, but those boys do not find me suitable as a bride. And as for Calder Hart?

Trust me, he is not interested in me, not that way."

"Francesca, darling, how could you be thinking such things?" Julia pulled her close. "No one is calling you such names behind your back."

Francesca only smiled. She wasn't about to argue this point, and she had heard, quite clearly, just a few weeks ago, two young ladies calling her both eccentric and mannish, not to mention snooty as well. Besides, she knew how different she was from other young ladies her age. Even as a child she had always known she was quite different from all the other little girls.

"Francesca, I must get these terrible concepts out of your head. You are a catch. You are beautiful, intelligent, from a fine family, and you have an inheritance. Trust me. There is no issue as far as finding you a husband."

Francesca pulled away. "Mama. I do not want to find a husband. And you cannot force me to the altar."

Julia smiled, and it was somewhat sly. "Not even if Calder Hart were the lucky groom?"

Francesca stiffened. "Not even Calder Hart would entice me into wedlock." She was grim. "Mama, I doubt you will think he is so eligible when I tell you that he is Bragg's half brother."

Julia's expression changed. "But . . . how could that be?" And then comprehension flooded her face.

"They have the same mother." Francesca could not feel triumphant, but the fact that Bragg's mother had been a woman of ill repute and that he was a bastard was the reason Julia had told Francesca in no uncertain terms that he was not for her. "He is illegitimate as well."

Julia had paled.

"So, you see, Calder Hart is not for me."

"Perhaps not, but perhaps you are wrong," Julia said.

"What? You have disqualified Bragg because of his lineage, so surely Hart must be disqualified, too!" Francesca exclaimed.

"I must discuss it with your father," Julia said thoughtfully.

"I don't understand!" Francesca cried.

"Bragg is penniless. He is a civil servant—"

"He was a lawyer before he accepted this appointment," Francesca shot, furious now.

"A lawyer defending hoodlums and crooks," Julia said. "A lawyer taking on the lowliest cases—and receiving little or no compensation for his work."

Francesca could not believe her mother had known about Bragg's past. "How, in God's name, did you learn about this?"

"When I saw the way you were looking at him, I made it my business to learn more about him." She shrugged. "And believe me, I know his defense of the poor, the needy, and the insane only makes him more attractive to you," she said with a sigh.

"He is a champion of the underdog. Of course I find that attractive—the world needs more selfless men like Bragg. But Hart would be acceptable, reputation and all, because he is *rich*?" Francesca was aghast.

"I said I would discuss it with your father," Julia returned. "But your husband must be able to provide for you in the manner you are accustomed to."

"Connie married Neil! Montrose was penniless—and Papa gave them a fortune!" Francesca nearly shouted.

"All British noblemen are impoverished. Montrose brought a noble lineage, not to mention his many titles, to the union. And he is a gentleman."

"So is Bragg. Oh, forgive me! He is penniless, he has no title, and he is a bastard! Shall we lynch him now, Mother? As clearly he is too awful to circulate among *our* kind." She glared.

"Do not speak to me in such a manner, Francesca," Julia warned. "I admire your idealism, but in time, you will come to understand the ways of the world. Bragg is not for you. And I am sorry you are still fervent about him."

"Fervent?" She was near tears. "No. You have no idea how I feel, not about him and not about anything. Never mind. Because this hypocrisy of yours is far too unsettling. I am going to bed!" Francesca turned.

And she heard her mother say, softly, behind her, "One day, you will thank me for all of my efforts, darling. They are all on your behalf."

Francesca ran up the stairs. She did not think so.

And once within her room, with the door securely locked behind her, she thought about her sister and ran to her desk. She tossed aside her notes and notebooks, but there was no note from Connie on her desk, nor any message lying there hidden among her papers; there was no word at all.

ELEVEN

Francesca found her father alone in the breakfast room, where cheerfully papered walls in a canary yellow print provided a sense of intimacy and warmth, and two large windows overlooked the lawns and gardens behind the house, now covered with ice-crusted snow. The sideboard was laden with covered dishes that Francesca knew contained eggs, sausages, waffles, and breakfast rolls. Coffee, milk, freshly squeezed juice, fruit, and jellies and jams also graced the sideboard. Andrew was immersed in the *Tribune*; clearly he was already finished with the *Times*. As Francesca poured herself a cup of coffee from a silver pitcher, he laid the paper briefly aside.

"Good morning, Papa." She smiled although she remained as worried as ever, wishing fervently for some word from Connie. The sound of silence had become ominous. Francesca did not think she had slept more than an hour or two all night, alternately replaying the conversation with Julia in her mind and worrying about her sister. She remained angry with her mother for her unfairness and hypocrisy regarding Calder Hart and Rick Bragg.

"Sleep well?" her father asked, with a warm smile.

"Yes." Francesca sat down. There was no point in telling him that she had tossed and turned all night, as she did not want to answer any pointed questions. She took a sip of her coffee and her glance slid to the front page of the *New York Times*. It read:

MURDER IN HOME OF MISTRESS
PAUL RANDALL DEAD

She set her cup down and scanned the subtitle, which offered little other than the fact that no suspects had yet been identified, although the mistress had disappeared. But then, the *Times* was the least sensational and the most objective of the city newspapers.

"Did you know Mr. Randall, Papa?" she asked.

"I met him some years ago, playing golf, I believe, in Sagaponack. A rather quiet fellow, if I recall correctly, a typical middle-class gentleman." He sipped his tea. "Apparently Paul Randall was killed Friday night. Shot in the back of the head while at the home of his mistress." Andrew shook his head. "It is hard to believe that he had a mistress, having met the fellow, although I did hear that he was quite a wild man when he was young."

Francesca assumed he had been sowing his wild oats, to use her mother's expression, when he had fathered Calder Hart, and she took another sip of her coffee. Her father thrust a different paper toward her. "Did you see this?" he asked. It was the *Sun*.

She saw the leading headline and choked.

POLICE COMMISSIONER INVOLVED IN RANDALL KILLING

"Oh my God!" Francesca cried, setting the cup down and reaching for the *Sun*. "What is this?" And her eyes widened as Arthur Kurland's name jumped out at her from the byline.

"This reporter certainly did his homework," Andrew said. "Apparently Randall is the father of Bragg's half brother, Calder Hart. You met him, I believe, at the Stanford White affair."

His tone was a bit odd and Francesca tore her gaze from the stunning headline as she was instantly pricked with guilt. She prayed that this terrible headline was not her fault. But how would she have known that Kurland would connect Hart and Bragg? She had only told him that Randall was Hart's father.

She was sick now, as well as miserable.

And she took one look at her father's calm expression and knew that he and Julia had had a talk last night before bed.

"Yes, I did," she managed. She scanned the subtitle and grew increasingly appalled:

BRAGG'S RECUSAL COULD BE IMMINENT

"That is quite the story," Andrew remarked as Francesca began to read. "The reporter is demanding Bragg recuse himself from the investigation, because of his relationship with Calder Hart."

"It's worse than that," Francesca whispered. "Kurland claims that Hart and Randall dined together on Tuesday night at Hart's club and that they had a huge argument. He claims there were witnesses, and that Hart was so angry he walked out on his own father." Francesca looked up. She could feel how wide her own eyes were. "He is suggesting, without saying it directly, that Hart might have murdered his own father!" she cried. "And he says directly that Bragg has yet to identify any suspects and Hart has yet to be brought to headquarters for questioning. It is an accusation—of negligence . . . and more!"

Andrew nodded grimly. "Hart's reputation won't help him much, if this begins to snowball. Perhaps Rick had better consider recusing himself from this one, before the gossip turns to recriminations."

Would Bragg once again be skewered by the press as he worked diligently on an investigation? For Francesca knew better than anyone else did how hard he worked and how determined he was—she knew how committed he was to the attainment of justice. She was frightened, and not for herself.

"I don't think Hart's a killer, Papa, and, in fact, I am not sure he even hated his father, as much as he would like the world to think otherwise."

Andrew regarded her. "And how would you know so much about Calder Hart—when you only met him Friday?" he asked.

She hesitated. Finally, at something of a loss, she said, "Bragg is my friend. Hart is his brother. Need I truly say more?"

"Undoubtedly you could," Andrew said calmly. "Francesca, please do not get yourself too involved in Bragg's life."

She laid the paper down. "Why?"

"I cannot tell you why. I'm sorry."

Francesca stared, trying to see into his eyes. His words were an echo of her own words to her mother last night. Was Andrew keeping a confidence of Bragg's, the way she was with Connie? It certainly seemed so. "And if I become 'too involved' in Hart's life?"

"I should not like that, either." Andrew slapped his napkin down. "Your mother finds him suitable for you; I do not. He is a notorious womanizer, and worse than that, he shows very little respect for anyone or anything. I find it hard to like a man who seems intent on shocking the world with his every utterance and action. I do not like him, I do not trust him, and I should not like for you to set your cap on him as your mother has for you."

"I am not setting my cap on anyone," Francesca said tersely, her heart sinking at her father's words. Clearly Julia had made up her mind, and the frightening part was, she usually got her way. "I tried to tell Julia that last night. Well, thank God you are not on her side."

"Not in this, at least. And I have put my foot down in no uncertain terms." He hesitated. "It is a shame, really, about Bragg."

She tensed. "Why?"

"Because he is such an honorable man and, if things were different, I am quite certain the two of you would suit one another very well indeed." He stood. "But things are not different." He held her gaze. "And they will never be different, Francesca."

It felt like a death knell. "I wish I knew why," she tried, knowing it would be futile.

He came around and kissed her forehead. "I am sure he will tell you himself, if the need arises—but hopefully, it will not."

Francesca could only watch him leave the breakfast room, and when he was gone, she cradled her forehead on her hands, briefly despairing. Bragg had a secret, clearly, and she was afraid of what it might be.

Before departing to call upon Mrs. Randall, Francesca tried telephoning Connie again. This time, there was no answer, and she was thoroughly alarmed. Why hadn't a servant picked up the telephone?

True, they only had one telephone, and like the Cahills', that telephone was in the study. It was possible no one had heard it ringing. Possible, but not likely. The Montrose household was a busy one, and they had a dozen in staff, at the least.

Francesca wrote Connie a note, sealed it in an envelope, and gave it to a stable boy to deliver, with precise instructions—it was to be handed directly to Lady Montrose and not her husband. If Lady Montrose was not available, it was to be handed to Mrs. Partridge, the girls' nanny, and she was to deliver it personally herself.

Francesca reminded herself that, even though it felt like an eternity had passed since she had last seen her sister, it had only been yesterday in the late afternoon. In all likelihood, all was well, and she was imagining all kinds of terrible scenarios.

And what could be happening? For all Francesca knew, Connie had taken to her rooms to nurse her broken heart. Still, she had confronted Montrose, and every instinct Francesca had told her that was only the tip of this particular iceberg.

Joel was waiting for her outside of the Cahill mansion's front gates. Briefly Francesca's spirits lifted; she was happy to see him. The Randall residence was on 57th Street, between Lexington and Fourth Avenues. Francesca hailed a hansom, not wanting to alert anyone in her family where she was off to. As she and Joel got out, she instantly saw Bragg's handsome motorcar double-parked alongside a waiting coach, and she hesitated.

"Now what do we do?" Joel asked by her side. "Copper won't like this." He shook his dark head.

Her heart seemed to do a series of somersaults. "Let me think," she said tersely. There was no denying that her first reaction to the sight of his roadster and the knowledge that he was at the Randalls' was a nervous excitement and a real elation—it seemed as if their paths were meant to coincide. But following her initial response was a different kind of anxiety. Francesca reminded herself that she had every right to pay Mrs. Randall her respects. And she was now a bona fide part of the police investigation, if she played along with Bragg and pretended that she believed he had enlisted her to find Miss de Labouche. Surely her clever mind could concoct a plausible and convincing explanation as to why the search for Georgette de Labouche had led her there.

She sucked up any dwindling courage and knocked on the door of the red brick Victorian townhouse. A maid answered it immediately.

Francesca gave her a calling card and waited in the small, shadowed foyer while Joel glanced curiously around and the maid presented it to the widow. She could see that her father was right—Paul Randall had led a very genteel but usual life, neither poor nor wealthy, but somewhere in between. His home was pleasant but small; it was one-half of the brick house she had entered. A narrow staircase led to the bedrooms upstairs—there were probably three. She could glance into the dining room, where a table and chairs seated six. He undoubtedly had two or three servants; the maid would also be a laundress and perhaps even a cook. His coachman would also serve as valet. The wood floors beneath her feet needed a new stain and a bit of repair, but they were acceptable. Francesca could smell a Sunday dinner cooking. Roasted guinea hens, unless she missed her guess.

At the end of the hall was the parlor, and the door was now closed. The maid reappeared from within it. "You may come with me, miss," she said, blinking at Joel.

Francesca moved down the hall, giving Joel a look, that meant children were to be seen and not heard—especially when on an investigation. She was ushered into an overdone parlor, crammed with too many chairs and tables but just one somewhat frayed red sofa. Popular art vied for one's attention with framed photographs and many collectibles. Mrs. Randall sat on the sofa, clutching a handkerchief, her eyes swollen and red. She was a plump woman who had probably been quite pretty in her youth. A rather plain blond girl, about Francesca's age, stood behind her mother, her thin hand on her shoulder. She, too, appeared heartbroken, and her nose was red and swollen, as were her eyes. Bragg had been sitting in an armchair, but he stood as Francesca was shown into the room. He wore his usual dark and finely cut suit, but his overcoat was draped upon the back of the chair.

She smiled tentatively at him.

He said, "Good morning, Miss Cahill. I was wondering how long it would take you to call upon Mrs. Randall." His amber eyes were filled with warmth and good humor. He was neither disturbed to see her present, nor angry about the day's newspapers. Francesca was pleased to see him well rested and in good spirits. Their gazes met.

"I am here on official business, Commissioner," she said, hiding a bigger smile and inclining her head. She did not want him to ascertain her true feelings for him now.

He glanced at Joel. "Joel," he said, in way of a reluctant greeting.

Joel gave him a dark and scowling look.

Francesca touched his shoulder in a quieting manner. He crossed his arms and moved farther away from Bragg. She sighed but could not blame Joel for his attitude toward the police. He was, after all, a pickpocket.

She approached the heavyset widow. "Mrs. Randall? I am here to pay my condolences. I am so very sorry for your loss."

Henrietta Randall nodded. "I do not understand, Miss Cahill," she said. "We have not met. You do not know Mary. Your card says you are a crime-solver? Did you somehow know my husband?"

Francesca did not glance at Bragg now. "Actually, I did not, but I have been retained to find his murderer."

Henrietta Randall blinked. "By whom?"

"I am afraid my client wishes to remain anonymous,"

Francesca said firmly. She glanced at Bragg. He was studying
her, and his expression, while rather impassive, contained another hint of his earlier good humor. Clearly he approved of
the tack she had chosen to take; she could not tell the widow
that she worked for the mistress. Francesca knew she should
be angry with him for his trying to divert her from the real
work at hand, but it was impossible; she had to smile at him.

Why did he have to look so good this early in the day?
Why did his mere presence have to dominate and warm the
room? Even when she was not looking at him, she was
acutely aware of him being there, his attention somehow
trained upon her.

"I do not wish to interrupt your interview with the commissioner," she began, looking far too directly into his eyes.

"You are not interrupting," Bragg said, with a wave of his
hand. He did not look away. "In fact, I am done here, and on
my way out."

Francesca started, dismayed.

He gave her an odd look, which she thought contained a
warning, just for her, and he handed Henrietta Randall his
business card. "Mrs. Randall. Rest assured I shall find your
husband's murderer. And in a timely manner. If you have any
further thoughts based on our conversation, please get in
touch with me immediately—at any time, either at my office
or at my home. I will come by instantly. No thought is too
small or too inane, Mrs. Randall. You might think something
is irrelevant when I shall think it a great clue." He smiled at
her, then glanced at Mary. "You, as well, Miss Randall."

Mary nodded, but said, "We have told you everything.
There is simply nothing more to tell."

Henrietta started to cry. Mary clasped her hand tightly. She
had a wide but narrow mouth, which was pursed very tightly.
Her hair was pulled back tightly in an unfashionable and unkempt chignon.

"Miss Cahill." Bragg smiled and inclined his head.

"Good day, then," Francesca managed, watching him walk
out. She knew he had tried to tell her something privately,
and the fact thrilled her. Unfortunately, she did not know what

he had intended to communicate. When he was gone, she gave herself a mental kick and smiled at her hostess and her daughter. "May I ask a few questions?"

"Please," Henrietta said.

"Do you know who wished to kill your husband?"

"No one wished to kill my husband," Henrietta said firmly. "He was well liked, a kind man."

"Mother!" Mary cried out in exasperation. "Why do you keep saying that?" She looked angrily at Francesca. "I told the police commissioner, and I will tell you, too. One person hated my father."

Francesca thought she knew who that one person was. "And that is?"

"His bastard, Calder Hart. My half brother," she practically spat.

So animosity was a family affair, Francesca thought. She glanced at Henrietta. "Do you feel the same way?"

Henrietta nodded, her gaze downcast, tears sliding down her face. "He has always hated us all."

"Why? Why did Hart hate his father so?" Francesca asked, although the answer seemed obvious. Still, she wished to hear it from either Henrietta or her daughter.

"Why?" Mary was incredulous. "Why? I'll tell you why! Because he was a mistake, because Father never wanted him, not then, and not now!"

"Did your father hate Hart, as well?" Francesca felt she had to ask. The family drama was terribly compelling.

"My father did not hate anyone!" Mary cried. "He was a good man, as good as gold! He only thought to please people, and help them. He was a saint!"

Francesca blinked. She supposed she would be speaking of her own father in the same way, she decided, if he had just died. "I am so sorry," she said again.

Mary sat down beside her mother, crying now into her hands. Her sobs were huge and torn from deep within her. The sobbing turned to terrible moans. Watching her, Francesca felt hugely sympathetic. She could only imagine her own grief when the day came that her father passed on. She knew it was time to leave.

"Perhaps we can finish this another time?" Henrietta asked. She stood. "As you can see, Mary is inconsolable. She was the apple of Paul's eye. His little girl. We all loved him so; but she, even more."

Francesca nodded. She whispered, "Mary? I so understand. I adore my own father, too."

Mary paused, looking up, her face covered with tears. "Then you know I shall never be the same," she whispered in real anguish.

"Yes, I know."

Mary covered her face, weeping again.

Henrietta walked out from behind the table in front of the sofa, clearly wishing Francesca to leave them to their mourning.

"Mrs. Randall? How old is Mary?"

"She is eighteen," Henrietta said, walking Francesca to the door.

And Hart was twenty-six—for Francesca knew he was two years younger than Bragg was. "You have a son, do you not?" Francesca asked.

"Yes, Bill arrived home yesterday afternoon. He attends university in Philadelphia," she said. Then, proudly, "He will graduate this summer."

Francesca smiled. So Bill Randall was older—and he was about twenty-one. Five years separated Randall's affair with Hart's mother and the birth of his first legitimate child. Francesca wondered when Henrietta had learned that Randall had had a mistress and an illegitimate child, but that did not quite pertain to this case. Had she known about Georgette de Labouche? As it was all over the morning's papers, Francesca suspected she knew now.

"I would like to speak with him, too, if I may," Francesca said.

"He's asleep. Why don't you come by later this afternoon? We will be through with our dinner by four," Henrietta said.

"Thank you." Francesca shook her hand and found herself

in the hall with Joel. Their gazes met. She shook her head, warning him not to speak yet, and they walked slowly to the foyer, Francesca thinking about the brief and unenlightening conversation she had just had.

"Miss Cahill?"

Francesca turned at the sound of Mary's shrill voice.

The very thin, rather gawky blonde hurried to her. "I didn't want to speak in front of my mother," she said fiercely. She glared at Joel. "Who is *that*?"

"He is my assistant. He runs errands for me." Francesca had become alert. "What is it? What is it that you wish to tell me?"

"I *know* Hart killed my father—and I know why!" she cried.

"You do?" Francesca asked, surprised.

"Yes, I do," Mary hissed, low and urgently. "Hart was blackmailing my father, Miss Cahill. I overheard them on the day of the murder, speaking on the street outside of this house. They were arguing about money, the money Hart was demanding my father pay him, the money my father was refusing to pay!"

Francesca stared, the wheels of her mind turning rapidly. "But what could Hart be blackmailing your father for?"

Mary made a disparaging sound. "Who knows? Does it even matter?" She stared. "He is evil, Miss Cahill, evil, just like the Devil. He doesn't need a reason to torment and torture anyone. He does it with pure joy."

Francesca looked into her eyes. They were burning with hatred. She drew back, a reaction she could not control. The depth of hostility had frightened her. Somehow, she patted the girl's bony shoulder. "Thank you, Mary. Thank you very much."

"Do not thank me." Mary started to cry again, the sobs frightening, as they so racked her thin body. "Just bring me justice, Miss Cahill. *Bring me justice,*" she said.

Francesca stepped outside with Joel and faltered. Bragg stood beside his Daimler automobile, speaking with a roundsman.

He saw her and waved at her, clearly indicating that she come over.

So this was what his silent communication had meant. He had been waiting for her, and Francesca hurried to him, smiling, Joel not following.

The roundsman nodded and with a stiff hand to his forehead said, "Yes, sir," and left them.

Bragg eyed her.

"Do you now have your troops saluting you, Bragg?" she teased.

He laughed. "That is hardly a regulation, Francesca. How are you?"

She thought about Connie—and her mother and the secret Bragg had to be keeping—and she felt her expression fall.

"Is something wrong?"

"Is anything right?" she returned, trying to be arch.

He studied her. Then, "Let me give you a lift. Any progress regarding Miss de Labouche?"

"No," Francesca said, following him to the passenger car door. What if Joel was wrong about Bragg's wild-goose chase? "I am debating the many possibilities that exist as to where she has gone, and Joel is also working on it."

He nodded at her, not looking at her, as he opened the door for her. "And I am sure you will succeed," he said.

Joel was right, she thought, staring at Bragg. He was trying to send her on a wild-goose chase! She glanced over her shoulder at Joel, who stood beside the townhouse's front steps, his hands in his pockets. He gave her a warning look, which was easy to read. It said, *Don't tell the copper a thing!*

Bragg had opened the door for her, but she did not get in. She fought her need to demand the truth from Bragg. She reminded herself that having a mission given by him, even a bogus one, helped her enormously in her investigation. "Have you spoken with Daisy and Rose this morning?" she managed.

His gaze whipped to hers as he heard how odd and tight her tone was. "Yes, I did. At eight o'clock. They hold to their story. I interviewed them separately, and if they are lying,

they are doing an excellent job of it." He regarded her quiz-
zically. "Is something wrong?"

"Whatever could be wrong?" She smiled far too archly.
"Come, Joel."

He slowly approached the car while Bragg stared at her,
clearly not believing her words. "I'll meet you, if you need
me later," he said.

"I am sure that I do need you. Bragg will be more than
happy to give you a ride, won't you, Bragg?" She smiled at
him.

"Please," Bragg said, clearly reluctant.

"I'll meet you uptown," Joel said with a scowl. He turned
and broke into a run.

"Joel!" Francesca cried.

"Later, lady," he said, disappearing around the block.

Francesca faced Bragg with her hands on her hips. "There.
Look at what you have done."

He seemed to be trying not to chuckle. "Just what have I
done? Kennedy did not want a ride—it had nothing to do
with me."

"You could have been more pleasant," she said hotly.

"Are you angry with me, Francesca?" he asked cautiously.
"And if so, why?"

Instead of answering, she slipped into the plush leather
seat, staring straight ahead. Should she be angry with him for
his pretending to want her help? Yes, she should. But she
must keep her anger to herself.

Besides, that was more annoying than anything else.
Knowing Bragg as she did, he probably thought to keep her
out of harm's way by sending her after Georgette. Her anger
ran deeper than that. Why had he told her yesterday that he
wished merely to be friends?

"No, I am not angry with you." Francesca sighed. "Perhaps
Hart was with them, as he claims he was."

"I still hope so." He smiled at her again and it reached his
golden eyes.

In that moment, she realized he was the most attractive
man she had ever met, and that included Hart and Montrose,

two other magnificent men. She had heard somewhere that the Braggs had Apache blood, and she could see it clearly in his extraordinarily high cheekbones. His golden coloring—the eyes, the sun-kissed skin, the hair—combined with his unusual features made him far more than good-looking; he was striking, in a most original manner. "You are quite chipper, today."

"It is Sunday. I enjoy Sundays—especially when I have a feisty crime-solver extraordinaire to investigate a murder with." He was teasing her now.

"Bragg! What is going on?"

He sighed. "Francesca, I am usually in a good frame of mind. It is only when I am extremely pressed and tired that I become somewhat grim." Then he added, "Besides, I have had some time to adjust to the fact that every time I turn around, I will find you in my shadow." His eyes twinkled now. He continued to lean over her door.

"You did ask for my help," she pointed out, then bit her lip.

"Yes, I did." He looked away. Joel was so very right.

"Bragg, have you seen the morning's papers?"

He slammed her door closed. "Yes, I have."

She was surprised.

"I learn quickly, Francesca. And I learned during the Burton Affair that I must have a thick skin—and do what I think is right—if I am to succeed in this appointment. If I let every headline-hungry reporter ruin my day, I may as well find a new means of employment now."

She felt grim—for him. His burdens were great—and unfair. But she supposed it came with such a public and controversial job. "Will you rescue yourself from the Randall investigation, Bragg?"

He smiled. "No."

She wondered what would happen if Hart became even more of a suspect than Kurland claimed he was. "Kurland wishes to hang Hart even as we speak."

"I don't think so. Kurland wants to sell newspapers." He

gave her another lingering glance and walked to the front of the roadster, pulling on his driving gloves.

Francesca felt a thrill, in spite of his words yesterday. That look had been impossibly warm. How could she be mistaken? Bragg was fond of her. She felt so certain. She so wanted to ask him just what was holding him back—but she was too afraid of the answer to dare to do so. She watched him cranking the car. The engine came to life.

He hurried around the nose and climbed in. He eased out into the heavy traffic passing by them. A huge lorry was causing quite a traffic jam.

"Why did you leave me alone with Mrs. Randall and her daughter?"

He looked over his shoulder and then passed a four-in-hand, zipping in front of an old-fashioned and shabby gig. "I think you know why."

She did, and it pleased her immensely. "You felt I would have more success with the two women than you would."

He grinned. "And what have you learned?"

"Hart was blackmailing Randall."

Bragg almost swerved into an electric trolley. "Francesca! Must you always be so dramatic?"

"Sorry." She grinned, even though she gripped the sides of her seat.

"Please elaborate." He slowed as they crept into the very busy Fourth Avenue intersection. A policeman saw the Daimler, obviously recognized it, and halted all other traffic. He waved Bragg through.

"Mary says she overheard Hart and her father arguing on the street on the day of the murder—in the morning. She says Hart was blackmailing Randall, and they were arguing over money." She looked at him.

He returned her look. "That is impossible."

"That Hart would blackmail his own father?"

"No. It is impossible that they argued Friday morning here in New York."

Francesca twisted in the seat. "Why?"

"Hart could not have been in the city before early Friday

afternoon. He had business in Baltimore, I know, because I saw him there Thursday night, as I had business there as well. Trains do not run north to New York after eleven P.M."

"Are you certain?" Francesca asked, the implication dawning upon her now.

"Yes."

She wondered what had taken him so briefly to Baltimore. "Bragg, you do realize this means Mary is lying?"

"I do. And interestingly, she chose to lie to you. She said not a word to me." He gave her another long look.

"Whatever that means," Francesca said, returning his gaze. It was impossible not to feel that they were partners now. Their discussion of the case was a frank one, and he was including her, not excluding her. It was amazing, but in spite of all of her worries, not the least of which involved Bragg's feelings for her, in that moment she felt so pleased to be with him, even thrilled.

She might almost expect birds to break into song around them, it felt like that kind of day. Except, of course, that they were in the dead of winter.

He turned onto Madison Avenue, where they were crushed between an omnibus, a coach, and a trolley. The traffic was very slow. "She was very shy in my presence," he mused. "She strikes me as quite a mouse. I am quite certain she is afraid of men, or even resentful of them, the exception being her dear and departed father."

Francesca blinked. "She adored Randall, that is clear. She was not shy with me, Bragg. In fact, she was very voluble— and very angry. She despises Hart."

"An apparent family condition." Then, "She might despise all men."

Francesca hesitated, then said, "I am not defending Calder. But . . . I do not quite believe that he hates his father, and I believe his callous reaction to the news of his murder was a cover for other, more complicated feelings."

Bragg stared. "So now it is 'Calder'?"

She flushed. "Please. You almost sound jealous, Bragg."

"Jealous? Francesca, have you lost your mind? I am not jealous of my brother. Not in the least."

She sincerely doubted that. In fact, whenever she mentioned Hart's name it seemed to set Bragg off. Even though it was misplaced, Francesca hoped that some of Bragg's jealousy involved her. It felt as if that was the case. "Well, that is good." She smiled but turned away so he would not see, looking out her window, and said, "As you have nothing to be jealous of."

He was silent.

She stole a glance at him.

He turned and caught her eye. Their gazes held, and it seemed potent.

Francesca turned away, breathless. Sharing a case was wonderful, but she wanted so much more. Perhaps she should take on another investigation—one of her own.

She tensed at the thought. She remained afraid now, afraid of what she would find if she dared to delve into Bragg's life. Besides, it felt wrong. If he wanted her to know something, he would tell her directly; she felt sure of it.

And they were friends now. That much was clear. Surely when the time was right, he would tell her whatever it was that was holding him back.

"So what is distracting you, Francesca?" he asked softly.

She jerked, startled.

"You have seemed very anxious today. What is it? Can I help?"

Francesca hesitated and then blurted, "Oh, Bragg! It is family matters."

"Oh." He hesitated. "I am happy to lend a shoulder," he said with a small smile. "Even though I know you despise weepy females."

They were on 61st Street. From where they idled in the creeping traffic Francesca could see the Montrose house. She imagined using his shoulder to cry upon. Perhaps she should engage in some theatrics. She sighed, knowing she could not be that coy. "Well, I do believe Evan is still carrying on with his mistress."

"He is not married," Bragg said.

"But he is engaged! His affair should end!" She stared at him.

Bragg said, with a smile, "From your point of view, perhaps. I doubt he feels compelled to be loyal to Miss Channing until after his vows are said."

"But . . . is that how you would think?" She was stunned by what he had said. It did not sound like the man she had come to know so well.

"No, that is not how I think, not at all. But it is how many men think."

Oddly, she felt relieved. She didn't need to know Bragg better to know that he would be the most loyal and faithful of men.

"Is that the extent of your worries?"

"Hardly." She looked away, afraid he might guess that he was at the top of her list. Then, abruptly, she half-turned and faced him. "Bragg? I had to tell Connie about Montrose."

He whirled his head. "What!"

"Bragg, the gig!" she shouted.

He turned his attention to the road, slamming on his brakes. The gig had eased out from behind another carriage, right in front of them. Bragg looked back at her. "You don't mean what I think you do, do you?"

"She has been suspicious, I am certain, and then she asked me directly what I knew. I could not lie."

"Oh, Francesca." He shook his head.

"You do not think I did the right thing?" She gripped his arm. Their gazes locked. "But how could I lie to Connie?"

"I do not know. Perhaps you might have been evasive. What I do know is that it is better to stay out of the private lives of other people, especially married ones." His gaze was somber. It washed over her now.

"I told her yesterday afternoon. Bragg, I have called the house repeatedly, and I cannot reach her! Yesterday she was not taking calls; this morning, no one answered. I am worried. I probably shouldn't be, but I am." She smiled grimly.

"I am worried, too," he said, not words she wanted to hear.

She glanced at him. "I had hoped you would say something encouraging."

"Your sister is not as strong as you are, Francesca, and she loves Montrose deeply."

"Connie is very strong," Francesca began, but even as she spoke, she wondered if she believed her own contention. "She has been determined to follow in Mama's footsteps ever since she was a child, and she is doing a wonderful job of it."

"Perhaps your mother has been the determined one," he said.

"What?"

"I suspect your mother has wished for her eldest daughter to be a perfect copy of herself."

Francesca stared. "Well, of course she has, but Connie has wanted Mama's way of life, too."

He said, "Life has a way of making those who least wish it face their worst fears."

She gazed at his strikingly chiseled profile. "Bragg, that is so dark."

"I have found it to be the truth," he returned, and there was something in his tone that made her stare.

She swallowed. "Have you been forced to face your worst fears?"

He did not look away from her eyes. "In part."

She inhaled; she did not like his answer, oh no. Worse, she saw something dark and sad, perhaps even tragic, there in his own gaze, and it frightened her. Her impulse was to reach for his hand.

Fortunately, he was driving, and his hands were occupied, so she did not.

He smiled a bit then. "Connie has you, and her family; she will be fine."

Francesca didn't know whether he really meant it or not. "Montrose threw me out of the house. He told me I am never welcome there again."

Bragg shifted and gazed unwaveringly at her. He did not speak.

She flushed. "It is very hurtful."

"I am sure that it is."

She became angry. "I had hoped for some sympathy from you."

"You will not find it where Montrose is concerned." He gazed rigidly at the road.

Francesca looked away. She was aware of an enmity between Montrose and Bragg. "Is this because you still have feelings for Eliza yourself?" She had to ask. Many years ago, when Bragg was in Columbia University, he had a torrid affair with Eliza, just before her marriage to Burton. And even after all of these years, they had remained friends.

Eliza Burton had a penchant for involving herself with spectacular men, Francesca thought sourly.

"I am fond of Eliza. But she is only a friend. We have been through this before," he said. He gripped the leather-bound steering wheel and stared straight ahead. "But I am also fond of you."

Francesca did not know what to say, and she wasn't given a chance to respond. He said, "I feel protective of you, Francesca. And Montrose is a cad. Has he not proven that? You should not admire him now."

"Yes, he has proven himself reprehensible, Bragg. But he has been hurt, too. I am sure of it." She would not mention that he had even said so.

"God! You defend everyone. Now, you defend Montrose!"

"No, I do not defend everyone, just those whom I care about. How could it be otherwise?"

He turned and leveled a stare at her. It seemed heated.

"And you know I care for him only as I do for Evan," she said hotly.

He looked back at the road. "You are a unique woman. With your studies and your liberalism, your passionate views about reform—yet for a bluestocking, somehow, you attract the most virile men. Oddly, you seem to surround yourself with them."

Francesca could only blink at him. What was he talking about! Montrose was her brother-in-law, and she had only just met Hart, who was an acquaintance, and it had only been two weeks since Bragg had walked right into the forefront of her life.

They were approaching the intersection at 62d Street. Francesca forgot all about his odd statement. She *had* to speak to Connie.

Bragg said, as if reading her mind, "Do you want me to stop?"

She hesitated. She desperately wanted to go up to that door—but what if Montrose was at home? She did not feel up to facing him yet again. She said, "He was so angry, Bragg."

"You are afraid of Montrose?" He was incredulous.

She nodded. "I know. It is silly. I know he would never hurt me, but his temper—it was stunning."

"Do you want me to go ask to see your sister?"

She faced him. "Yes. Please. I will wait in the car. Simply tell her she must see me!"

Bragg abruptly veered to the left. A coachman behind them shouted at him. He ignored it.

Francesca twisted her hands in her muff. She really hoped that she would not have to see Neil again; she hoped he was not at home.

Bragg turned into the short driveway that belonged to her sister and Neil. He drove through the arch and into the interior courtyard, where he stopped the car. One coach was parked in the drive. Francesca prayed that meant that Connie was home and Neil was not.

"Wait here," Brag said, jumping out.

"Bragg?"

He paused before striding up the three short front steps.

"Thank you."

He nodded and used the knocker.

Francesca hesitated, watching, and there was no answer. God, was she truly afraid of Montrose in a temper? Yes, she was, but such cowardice would not do. After all, he would never strike her—even though his words had hurt her more than any physical blow. She slowly got out of the car.

Bragg glanced at her. "Courage in company?" he asked. A smile registered in his eyes.

"Will you still respect me?" she countered.

He did smile then. "I shall always respect you, Francesca, and I do not blame you for being afraid of Montrose, given the situation. I would be furious with you if I were him. Actually, I am surprised he did not try to throttle you."

She could not help herself. "And if he had?"

He paused, his golden eyes intent. "Are you seeking a champion, Francesca?" he asked softly.

She felt herself warm inside. "And if I am?"

His answer was a smile. The moment of locked gazes became a long one. Francesca heard herself sigh.

He gave her a look, perhaps amused, and used the door knocker again. "Is no one home? What of the staff?"

Instantly Francesca became alarmed. "Try one more time. If there is no answer, then something is terribly wrong, and we shall have to try to find a way into the house!"

"Breaking and entering is a crime," he said mildly, banging now with his gloved fist. "But I doubt that would deter you."

"It would not. But why is there no answer?" Francesca asked, wringing her hands. "This is too strange, and I have a horrid feeling of dread."

"I am sure there is a reasonable explanation," Bragg began, squeezing her hand, when suddenly the door was thrust open—and they were faced not with a servant, but Montrose.

He towered over them, in his shirtsleeves, unshaven and unkempt. "You!" he said to Francesca. And he began to slam the door closed.

Bragg blocked it with his hip. "We wish a word with your wife, Montrose," he said coldly. "Do let us in."

"Get a warrant," Montrose said harshly.

"I shall," Bragg said calmly.

Montrose stared.

Bragg stared back.

Montrose turned his eyes on Francesca, and they were filled with rage, frustration, and despair. "I am afraid," he said, biting off each word in his anger, "that my *wife* is not receiving callers. Not here, not today."

"Why not?" Francesca gasped. "What have you done with her?"

"What have I done?" he roared. "You! You are the one, God damn it, Francesca! Your meddling is to blame!"

"Where is Lady Montrose?" Bragg cut in.

Montrose turned to stare at him. "I don't know," he said.

"What?" Francesca whispered, in growing horror. "What did you say?"

"I don't know!" he shouted. "Connie has taken the girls and they have simply disappeared!"

TWELVE

Francesca felt the ground tilt wildly beneath her feet. She felt Bragg grip her arm, but she only had eyes for Montrose. "No. Connie cannot have disappeared. That is impossible."

"And you are to blame," Neil ground out, jabbing his hand at her. He turned and stalked into the entrance hall, not bothering to close the front door.

Francesca finally looked at Bragg, still in shock. "She must have taken the girls out for the day. I am sure of it."

Bragg's gaze was soft with compassion. "Francesca," he began, as softly.

Montrose whirled. "An outing? She has left me, Francesca; she has stolen the girls and left me!"

Francesca did not dare approach him. He seemed unhinged in his rage. "Neil," she spoke very calmly, "I know my sister. She would never do such a thing. Connie is very proper."

He cried, "She took a trunk for herself and one each for the girls! She has left me, Francesca. And I do not know where she has gone." Suddenly he turned his back on her, his shoulders shaking.

Francesca's instinct was to rush to him and comfort him. Bragg detained her with his hand.

She glanced briefly at him. "She will be back, Neil. I am certain of it."

He made a harsh, disparaging sound.

Francesca finally shook Bragg off. She felt his displeasure but ignored it and slowly crossed the room. "Neil? Why don't you go to your rooms? I will send a servant up with a supper tray and a glass of brandy." She knew cognac was his favorite drink.

He glanced at her. "I am hardly hungry. And I have dismissed the servants for the day."

Their eyes held. She saw his panic now, so clearly, and

his desperation. "I will find her, Neil. She will be back."

And the anger in his eyes changed, turning into something softer. He shook his head. "I have treated you in the worst way, and you think to be kind? And to offer me hope?"

"Yes, I do," she said.

He stared. "Francesca, I so wish you had let my life alone."

"I wish you had not had an affair with another woman."

"You have no idea what my life is like, what I feel in my heart, not for anyone, including your sister."

"But how complicated can it possibly be?" she asked, meaning her every word.

"Very," he returned flatly.

She stared again. It was obvious that Neil did care deeply for, and perhaps even loved, her sister. It was as obvious that something was terribly wrong in their relationship and that it was hardly as simple as his having had a wandering eye.

Neil was the one to turn away, and his head was hanging. "I have a terrible feeling about this," he said.

"Don't." Francesca touched his arm. "Don't predict the future; don't predict the worst."

"I cannot help myself." He looked directly at her. "I fear that my marriage is over," he said.

Bragg's Daimler motorcar idled in the large circular driveway in front of the Cahill mansion. Francesca sat with her hands inside of her fox fur muff, this one matching the trim upon her tan coat. Her mind would not stop. Neil was wrong, Connie had not left him, and if she had, it was temporary. The sister Francesca knew would never do such a thing.

Bragg took her arm and pulled her hand from the muff and clasped it. "She will turn up, sooner rather than later," he said, his gaze searching.

Francesca turned to him gratefully. "Please don't hand me fodder. Tell me what you really think." She clung to his palm. It felt strong, amazingly so. This was a man, she thought, whom she could depend upon.

"I have already told you. I think Connie is fragile, more so than anyone suspects, and I am worried about her."

"Bragg!" she cried, her heart racing with alarm.

"But I am not worried about her welfare. She is in a hotel somewhere with the girls, a lavish suite, warm and comfortable and well fed."

Francesca prayed that he was right. "Well, I cannot imagine where else she would go. But why didn't she come home, here?" she asked as he released her hand.

"Pride. And the desire to put a distance between herself and her husband." His gaze slid over her features slowly.

Francesca became distracted. She felt flustered, and it seemed to reach right into her heart. "I am not going to say a word to Mama or Papa, for they will be far too worried. But I shall recruit Evan, and Joel, and we shall begin canvassing every single hotel in this city."

"You could do that," Bragg agreed. "But perhaps you might want to give Connie some privacy now."

She stared. "You are joking, right?"

"No, Francesca. Clearly she wishes to be alone. When she has a need to be with her family, I have little doubt that she will make her whereabouts known." He smiled. "It is only a suggestion."

He was right. Francesca sighed. Then she said, peevishly, "Why are you always so wise?"

He grinned. "I am a bit older than you."

"Only eight years."

He narrowed his gaze. "I do not recall telling you my age."

She did grin, too. "I am a sleuth, remember?"

"How could I forget?" He rolled his eyes theatrically and she laughed.

He sobered. "You become too serious and too intense when there is a crisis. I do not like seeing you so worried. You cannot carry the world upon your small shoulders, Francesca."

"I can try," she said, aiming for levity. But he did not smile at her remark. She hesitated, then said, "I feel the same way about you, Bragg." And her words were not a spontaneous utterance.

Their eyes held. He hesitated, then, as if he had not heard

her, "I am going to have another chat with my half brother.
If you have need of me, even tonight, Francesca, do not hesitate to call. I will be answering my telephone." He got out
of the roadster and went around the front in order to open
her door for her.

She smiled at him before getting out. "I appreciate that,
Bragg."

"Say hello to your parents for me," he said.

Francesca murmured an affirmative and walked to her
door. She felt him watching her as she did so. It was a good
feeling, having him watch her walk to her door to make sure
she got safely inside, and she thought about the extent of his
concern for her family and herself. Was it really due only to
their friendship? She refused to believe so.

But she could not handle another mystery now. Her feelings for Bragg and his avowal of his intentions of friendship
had to be put aside. No matter that Connie probably was in
some posh hotel with the girls, Francesca desperately wanted
to speak to her. And they had a killer to find.

Francesca saw no one as she crossed the entry hall. Her
parents were to be avoided at all costs—either one of them
would take one look at her face and know that something was
terribly wrong. Instead, Francesca hurried up the stairs.

Evan had an entire half of the house to himself. The house
had been built in such a way that it was two houses combined,
not one, so that Evan could live there with his family, once
he had one. It was not an unusual arrangement. Mrs. Astor
had done so for her son. Evan had his own separate entrance
on 62d Street, a beautiful curving drive surrounded by his
own lawns and gardens. One day, when he did have children,
they would be able to run from their father's property to their
grandfather's, for no fence separated them.

And one did not have to enter Evan's apartments from the
street. Stairs from his residence entered the Cahill mansion
on the second landing. Francesca now used those stairs to
descend into his entry hall, a spacious marble-floored room
that very much resembled the hall in her own home, except
it was about a third the size.

A servant smiled at her. "Miss Cahill?"

"Is my brother about?" Francesca asked, finally removing her coat.

"He is in the library."

Francesca nodded and hurried down the hall, past a large formal salon and a smaller music room. The door to the library was open. It was a bright airy room, the walls papered in a soft pastel green, the ceiling nearly white. The desk, the single bookcase, and several tables were all dark wood, and a dark green marble mantel was over the fireplace. Evan sat on the sofa in front of it, his head in his hands.

Francesca stopped abruptly. He had shrugged out of a black tuxedo jacket—the very one he had worn to the opera last night. His silver silk vest hung open, and his white shirt-sleeves were rolled up. He also wore his tuxedo trousers. A glass of scotch sat on the low table by his knees, as did a cummerbund and a pair of gold, onyx, and diamond cuff links.

"You are just getting in?" she gasped. It was two in the afternoon!

He did not look up. "Go away, Francesca," he said.

She stiffened. "And you are drunk?"

He finally sat up, only to slump against the back of the couch, his disinterested blue gaze on her. "I am three sheets to the wind, but is it your concern?"

She came forward. "Why? And of course it is my concern; you are my brother and I adore you!"

He waved at her. "You are such a good sister, Fran." He was not mocking, as Evan had nary a sardonic bone in his body.

She sat down beside him. "You seem so unhappy," she whispered.

"Do I?" His thick, slashing black brows lifted. "Good God, why would I be unhappy? Because I owe almost two hundred thousand dollars in gaming debts, which Father will not pay, or because, in less than six months, I shall stand at the altar and vow to love, honor, and cherish a woman I have not even the slightest affection for? God!" He groaned.

She was trembling now and she took his hand before it could claim the whiskey glass. "You might come to love Sarah in time," she whispered, but she knew he would not. Evan preferred vamps and coquettes. The women he turned his attentions on were all gorgeous, if not flamboyant—even the eligible young ladies. Sarah was a brilliant artist, but she was a mouse in comparison to the others. And they were opposites. They had nothing in common.

But had he said what she thought he had?

"Let us hope," he said with a despondent shrug.

"Perhaps you should try to get to know her, Evan. Perhaps you should visit her studio. If you saw her art, why, you might very well change your mind about her."

He gave her a dark look. "I am marrying a woman, not a masterpiece, my dear Fran. What difference could her talents make?"

Francesca sighed. "She is a woman of passion. Hidden passion, but passion nonetheless."

He laughed. "You really believe that?" He laughed again. "I am sorry, Fran. But you are so naïve. So terribly naïve." He patted her head.

"Oh, stop it," she snapped. "I am not as naïve as you think." She pushed his hand away.

"You think Bragg is a knight in shining armor," he replied evenly.

"Hardly."

"You are in love with him."

"Not true."

"You think to outfox Mama and have your way and become Mrs. Police Commissioner." He was triumphant. He lifted his glass in a toast and sipped. "Mama will never allow it."

"I have seen sex toys," she said flatly.

He choked. "What?" Scotch spilled all over his hand.

"You heard." She tried not to laugh at him.

"Bragg?" His eyes were popping from his head. "I shall kill him, Fran, if he has so much as touched you!"

"No, you will not, because my relationship with him is

none of your affair. Besides, the toys were not his. They belong to a possible murder suspect."

"What?" He was on his feet. To his credit, he held his liquor well and hardly staggered. "Do not even begin to tell me you are getting yourself in something untoward and dangerous again! Have you not learned your lesson?"

"Yes, I have." She also stood. "Evan, Connie has taken the girls and left Montrose."

He froze.

"And I do not know where she has gone. Montrose is furious—with me—and we must not tell Mama or Papa," Francesca said, rapidly but firmly. It crossed her mind that she had promised Papa that she would speak with Evan about his behavior toward their father, but now was clearly not the time.

He took her shoulders in his hands. "You had better explain yourself," he said. And he no longer appeared inebriated at all.

"I been wonderin' where you been," Joel said when she met him two hours later, again outside of the house. Francesca had just concluded Sunday dinner with her parents. Evan had refused to join them, preferring to sleep off his night of excess instead, after warning Francesca never to interfere in anyone's private lives again. And he did mean Connie's. Clearly, like Neil, he blamed Francesca for the entire disastrous separation. If that was what it was.

Francesca still believed Connie would change her mind, come to her senses, and return home, hopefully at any moment. Evan agreed with Bragg. She should be left alone, and they would hear from her when she wanted to see them.

Often Connie, Neil, and the girls joined them for Sunday dinner. Montrose had telephoned with their excuses. Mama had looked directly at Francesca while relating this, a question in her eyes. Francesca had smiled innocently back. Julia was clearly suspicious.

Francesca had asked her parents if she could use the smaller of their two carriages in order to make some social calls. Now she directed their driver back to the Randall residence. "I have been a busy bee. Joel, we must locate Miss de Labouche. Have you heard anything at all about the Randall murder? Have you discovered Mr. Anthony's whereabouts?"

"Nope," he said, rubbing his wool-clad arms. "Anthony must be a strange duck. No one seems to know where he lives. An' he ain't been around town these past few nights. His favorite saloon is Willard's, on West Broadway. They ain't seen him since Friday."

Francesca looked at him. Friday—the night of the murder. "Is that unusual?"

Joel nodded. "He's in just about every night, at least for a hand or two."

Francesca faced him squarely. "Does Mr. Anthony have an honest profession?"

Joel grinned. "Like I said, he gambles." He added, "An' I heard he runs a good con."

"He is a con man?" she gasped.

"Looks like it," Joel said with a shrug.

Francesca sighed. Anthony was hardly an honest man, apparently, and his sister did not have the purest of reputations. What if Bragg was right? What if Georgette was a possible suspect? For not only had she disappeared, but it seemed as if her brother had as well.

"But a friend o' mine got out of the Tombs this mornin'. She was hauled in for a reefing she didn't even do! Bess knows yer new friends." Joel was sly.

"Daisy and Rose?" Francesca guessed, with renewed excitement. She had no idea what *reefing* meant and right then did not care. "Do tell!"

"She heard 'em talkin' in the caboose. Guess what?" Joel leaned close and whispered, as if afraid their coachman would overhear, "Hart's lyin'. He ain't been with them two Friday night. They had other johns."

Francesca stared at Joel. "Oh, dear," she said, her heart sinking.

*   *   *

Henrietta Randall was indisposed when Francesca called, just
before five that afternoon. Apparently she had left word with
her maid and her son, for Francesca was promptly ushered
into the very same parlor where she had been a few hours
before, but this time Joel accompanied her. The maid informed her that Mr. Randall would be right down.

"Funny room," Joel said, wrinkling up his nose while
touching a porcelain dolphin with a gold braid around his
body. "What the heck is that?"

"Most people think it is a fish, but it is actually a mammal,
as it breathes air. It is called a porpoise, Joel." Francesca
paced, then stiffened as a man her own age appeared in the
door.

"Miss Cahill?" He smiled a little at her. He was of medium
height, with dark brown hair, and neither attractive nor
homely but somewhere in between.

"Hello. You must be Bill Randall." Francesca smiled
warmly. She handed him one of her cards, and as he read it,
she said, "I am so sorry about your father."

He tucked her card in the pocket of his leisure jacket and
walked into the room. His regard was distraught, even pained.
"And will you solve the crime?"

"I hope so," Francesca said evenly.

He smiled a bit. "You seem very young to be a sleuth."

"I think we are almost the same age."

"I am twenty-one."

"I am twenty," she said.

They smiled. He invited her to sit and asked if she wished
for some refreshments. Francesca declined. "We have just had
our Sunday dinner."

He nodded. "How can I help you? And who is the boy?"

"Joel is my assistant. He is very intimate with the city, and
he was instrumental in helping me in my last investigation."
Joel smiled at that.

Bill's eyes widened. "For some odd reason, I just assumed
this was your first case."

"No." She shook her head firmly. "I worked closely with
the police to solve the Burton Abduction." She let him absorb

that. It had been called the crime of the century at the time, and he seemed dutifully impressed. "Do you have any idea of who would want to kill your father?" Francesca asked.

He stood. "I believe Mary has already told you who hated our father enough to murder him—in cold blood." His eyes flashed.

"So you are in agreement with her?"

"Yes."

"Do you also think Calder Hart is evil?"

"Did Mary say that?" He shrugged. "He is a bastard, and by that, I do not refer to his birth. He enjoys hurting other people—he has enjoyed hurting this family immensely."

Francesca was uncomfortable now. She hoped that Bill Randall was exaggerating. Still, she imagined Hart might have a cruel side. "How has he hurt this family? Other than by murdering your father—if, indeed, he was the one to shoot him."

Bill stared, somewhat coldly. "He appeared here on our doorstep one day, introducing himself. My mother's world ended, then and there. Is that not enough?"

Francesca could imagine the shock of such an event—a man or boy appearing in a family's midst and announcing that he was a part of it. "When was this?"

"What does that have to do with my father's murder?"

"I am trying to comprehend Calder Hart," Francesca said. But she could not help wondering now if Bill had hated his own father for hurting his mother so.

"It was ten years ago. I will never forget the day, a very hot summer day, and we were packing in order to leave for our holiday in the Adirondacks. I was eleven years old. Needless to say, our vacation—our summer—was ruined."

"It must have been a shock."

Bill said nothing.

"Have you seen the day's papers?"

Bill eyed her and said abruptly, "Yes."

"Specifically, the *Times*?"

"What is it that you are trying to ask, Miss Cahill?" He was not friendly now.

Francesca hesitated. "I wish to know how much you know about your father's private life."

"I knew about his mistress. I've known for some time. Several years, I think."

Francesca got to her feet. She did not want to jump to conclusions, but perhaps Bill had a motive for murder, too. "Does your mother know? Does Mary know?"

His jaw tightened. "Why?"

"I am trying to solve a very complicated puzzle, Bill. Please bear with me."

He sighed. "Mother has known for years. It has been a huge cross to bear. But Mary, well, she so adores Father that she has been kept in the dark. I do not think she knew about that harlot until this morning."

Francesca was grim. Again, it was obvious that Bill had not been forgiving of his father's indiscretions. And what about the wounded and aggrieved wife? Francesca thought to dismiss Henrietta as a possible murderess. She had met the woman, and the widow had seemed stricken by her loss, in spite of all the pain Randall had caused her. And she had also known about Georgette for years, so what motive could there be? Still, Francesca knew she must not jump to any conclusions yet. "I am sorry. Mary must be devastated." This might explain her having called her father a saint earlier, Francesca thought.

"She *is* devastated. I do not think she truly comprehends that Father had a secret life."

"Mary claims Hart was blackmailing your father. Did you know about that?"

Bill laughed without mirth. "She is crazy. Hart, blackmailing Father? If that is the case, no one has told me."

Francesca was somewhat relieved.

"So, you are rooting for the prime suspect, Miss Cahill?"

"Am I so obvious?"

"Yes."

"I am a friend of his brother, and I also think he is not what he would like the world to think he is," she said.

"If you think that way, then I doubt you will solve this case," Bill said sharply, with some anger.

Francesca was taken aback, and she stared at him.

His expression changed. "I apologize; that was rude," he said contritely. "In spite of the fact that I did not approve of my father's secret life, I am as upset as anyone in this household." He was rueful.

Francesca smiled politely, but now, she wondered if it was true.

Suddenly Mary walked into the room. She was pale, her expression drawn. Her eyes glittered. "Bill, Hart was blackmailing Papa," she said, clearly having been outside the door, eavesdropping. "You have been away. You do not know what has been going on around here." She sent Francesca an angry glance.

Bill walked over to her. "Why don't you go to your room and lie down? I will handle Miss Cahill. Do you want some laudanum?" he asked, his tone somewhere between kind and firm.

Did he seek to soothe his sister—or send her away from the room? Francesca wondered.

Mary's face crumpled. "No. Maybe. I don't know. Please believe me. Hart told Papa he would tell the world that he is his bastard son and, worse, the extent of his debts. I heard them. Papa was crushed, frightened. Hart was amused." She turned to Francesca. "I hate him. He is the one. There is no doubt!"

"I can understand why you feel as you do," Francesca said quietly. This was not looking good, she decided. First Hart's alibi being disproved, if Joel's friend was right, and now this blackmail scenario. Unfortunately, Francesca could see Hart toying with Randall in just such a manner as Mary described.

Still, she had lied about having witnessed a conversation on the street the morning of the murder. But why?

"Can you?" Mary asked with belligerence. She shook her head, tears suddenly falling, and she wrenched free of her brother. She ran from the room.

Bill began to follow her, calling out. As he hurried past

Francesca, she blinked. There was something so familiar about the way he strode toward the door, from this particular angle.

It made her feel as if she were in a situation she had been in once before.

The slim shoulders, the dark hair, the narrow, swift stride. It was like déjà vu.

He cursed. Softly, and almost inaudibly, beneath his breath.

Francesca stiffened as comprehension struck with the force of a bolt of lightning.

Bill Randall turned. "I am sorry. I do apologize. Is there anything else I can do for you, Miss Cahill?"

She could hardly breathe. For she was staring at the man who had been the silent intruder in Georgette de Labouche's home just hours after the murder had taken place.

THIRTEEN

SUNDAY, FEBRUARY 2, 1902—6:00 P.M.

Francesca was in a state. Once out on the street, she paused beneath the glow of a street lamp, hardly able to think clearly. It had begun to snow, and big, fat flakes dusted her shoulders and danced in the light's halo.

"What is it? What's wrong?" Joel asked, tugging on the sleeve of her fur-lined coat.

She hardly heard him. Bill Randall had walked into Georgette de Labouche's house around midnight, looked at his father's body, cursed, and walked out. How incredible; how strange.

He could not be the killer.

But somehow, he had known that the body was there. He had not been surprised to find it, his behavior indicated that he had expected to find it, and the fact that he had not run directly to the police added to the mystery.

Was he protecting someone?

Was he an accomplice?

Instantly both Mary and Henrietta shot to the top of her list of suspects. Still, Mary had *adored* her father. And Henrietta had known about her husband's mistress for years.

Francesca felt Joel's hand on her arm. She looked down at him.

"What is it?" he repeated insistently. "If I'm to be your assistant, you have got to tell me."

She bent close to his ear. "Randall's the one who came into the house when I was hiding in the kitchen."

"Hell no!" Joel cried. Then, eyes narrowed, "Now ain't that odd."

"Very. Joel, he lied. If I am right, Bill Randall lied, and he was in the city on the night of the murder." She thought about that. Was there any way a murderer would return to the

scene like that? Francesca did not think so. How unusual this
case had become.

"Joel, I am sending you home. I shall hire a hansom while
my driver takes you back." Her first instinct was to run to
Bragg and tell him all that had transpired in the past few
hours. But she hesitated. She had a few questions to ask Hart.
It was just past six in the evening. She might be able to catch
Hart at home now, but later he would undoubtedly be out.
She also did not think she should call on him at a late and
unusual hour.

But she could call on Bragg at any time.

"I don't need to be home yet," Joel protested.

"It's Sunday. You should go home and help your mother."
She paused. "I have two classes tomorrow morning," she said
reflectively. "Can you meet me at my house around noon?
We shall spend the afternoon investigating. We must find a
way to speak with the Randalls again, and we must find
Georgette de Labouche," she added vehemently. "Even I wish
to speak with her again."

"I can spend the mornin' while you're in school askin'
around. She had to have friends. Someone has to know where
she is," Joel said.

Francesca beamed at him and patted his back. "That would
be wonderful," she said. "Or perhaps you can locate her
brother."

After he had climbed into the carriage, she closed the
coach door and told Jennings to meet her at Hart's after dropping Joel at his Avenue A flat. The coach rolled off; Francesca stepped into the street to look for a cab. And it was
just her luck, a hansom was approaching and it was empty.
Her hand shot up and she flagged it down.

Francesca was suddenly nervous as she was greeted at Hart's
front door by the white-haired butler whom she recognized
from the other day. She managed a tight smile. "Is Mr. Hart
at home?"

"Mr. Hart is not receiving callers."

She flushed but did not move. Perhaps he was entertaining

a lady "friend." She hesitated, then said quickly, "It is urgent. Terribly so. Are you certain that he will not see me?" She held her muff with one hand, and with her other one she opened her purse to retrieve a calling card.

"Miss Cahill," the Englishman said, clearly recognizing her as well, "Mr. Hart *is* indisposed."

She did not like the sound of that, and somehow her gaze met that of the butler. "I hope he is not unwell," she breathed.

The man hesitated, obviously conflicted about breaching his sense of professional propriety. "He is indisposed, madam," he repeated firmly, clearly wishing to close the door but not about to do so unless she had turned to leave first.

"He is ill?" Francesca boldly stepped past the butler, into the huge hall with its nude sculptures and its shockingly irreligious painting by the artist Caravaggio.

"Madam, he has been most precise; he will not receive anyone."

"Like hell I won't."

Francesca muffled a gasp and saw Hart at the far end of the hall, standing there in trousers and a loosely belted smoking jacket. His grin was lopsided and somehow dangerous; Francesca tensed instantly.

"Do come in, Miss Cahill. Oh, Alfred. Did I mention that the Cahill sisters are always an exception to my rules?"

Alfred bowed. "You did not, sir."

"Next time, then, you shall know to *always* admit either one of them." Hart grinned at her again.

Francesca stared. He was unshaven and holding a thick cigar. Beneath the velvet and paisley jacket, his shirt was badly rumpled. His thick, dark hair was waving over his forehead. Even his trousers were terribly wrinkled, yet he was disturbingly attractive. But that was not the problem; her every instinct told her that something was wrong.

Her instincts also told her to proceed with the utmost caution indeed.

"Do come in, Miss Cahill." He smiled and it was as if he had dishonorable intentions. He seemed to be laughing at her.

"Thank you," Francesca managed rigidly. She handed her

coat, muff, gloves, and hat to Alfred, then began crossing the large room. Hart didn't move. He leaned now against the brass railing of the wide, sweeping staircase at the hall's other end, watching her as she approached. She felt flustered and did not like it, not at all.

Why did she feel as if she were entering the wolf's den? And that he was regarding her as if she might become a tasty meal?

He grinned again. He had one dimple to Bragg's two, but it was identical. "What a pleasant surprise."

The moment she had reached his side she could smell the whiskey and she was dismayed. "Have you been drinking?"

"Of course." He looped her arm in his. "I am celebrating, or have you forgotten?"

Francesca was practically enfolded against his side. He was a muscular man, a bit larger of frame than Bragg was, although the brothers were nearly the same in size and height. She tried to put an inch between them, but he held her so tightly, walking her back into the house, that she gave up. "You are inebriated," she said unsteadily, and it flashed through her mind that the brothers had more in common than they would ever admit. The last time she had been around a foxed man, it had been Bragg—and look at what had happened. They had shared the most reckless and devastating kiss.

"I am drunk," he said cheerfully. "And feeling no pain." He smiled warmly at her.

Her heart fluttered in response. And in that moment as he smiled into her eyes, she understood. She understood why he could have any woman that he wished; his charm was magnetic, mesmerizing, and fatal to its recipient. She wondered if he even knew that he was turning the full force of his charisma upon her now. She did not think so. She had the feeling it was habit. "I do not think you should drink any more," she whispered. "And would you please release my arm?"

"Why?" he asked, leading her into a large and spectacular library. Most studies were sanctuaries for their owners, but not this one. Books and artwork, both canvases and sculptures, filled the room. But so did a half a dozen seating arrangements. One massive desk was at its farthest corner, clearly where Hart worked.

The art consisted of landscapes, portraits, nudes, and depictions from mythology and religion. No style dominated; one landscape was impressionistic, another realistic.

"Because you are embracing me," she said tartly.

He laughed and turned her so she was in his arms. "And that is a terrible crime?" he asked, gazing into her eyes.

She ducked free and was almost swamped by a tide of relief. "We are strangers!"

"Really? But you are in love with my brother. That hardly makes us strangers, my sweet Francesca." His eyes were laughing now.

She swallowed. "Think what you like. I—"

"I always do." He walked away from her, and there was more relief.

Francesca reached for the collar of her shirtwaist. She lifted it away from her throat, where her pulse hummed. She felt certain he enjoyed toying with her.

He turned from a beautiful bar, all marble and mirrors, now holding a glass. "Hot?" His eyes gleamed.

"Yes. No. Mr. Hart, I wish a word with you."

He laughed and drank.

"Is that funny?"

"Life is funny, is it not?" Briefly the smile disappeared and he stared at the glass he held. "Funny, unpredictable . . . insane."

She sensed his pain. She knew it ran deep. "You do not have to drink like a fish, Mr. Hart. Perhaps you should throw in the towel and weep?"

He stared at her. No charm emanated from him now. His gaze was frigidly cold. "Weep for what? Are you suggesting—dare you to suggest—I weep for Randall?"

She nodded, clasping her hands tightly.

"Like hell," he said. "Like goddamn hell." He lifted the glass and hurled it across the room with all of his might.

Francesca cried out as it exploded at the far end, against a stunning canvas, a floral arrangement done in oils.

"Shit. Get out of here," he said, not looking at her. "Run away; cower and tremble; hide!" He turned back to the bar. He was the one who was trembling now.

Francesca fought for courage and found it. "I don't think you should be alone right now, Mr. Hart."

He was pouring another drink. He turned, leaning one narrow hip on the marble countertop. He had not recovered all of his composure, she thought, for he seemed to be a bit breathless.

"Oh, so now you wish to comfort me?" He was mocking.

"Yes, but not in the way your tone suggests." Francesca remained unmoving. If she moved, she did fear she might flee.

"Why not? You are a rather unusual woman. Odd, eccentric even. I daresay you have no use for rules and social dictums." He stared, his gaze intent, brilliant.

She inhaled. "Yes, I am rather eccentric, I agree. And many rules are to be bent or broken—but not all."

He put the glass down and slowly moved toward her. Francesca became so stiff she could not move, even had she wanted to, and she was also breathless. He took her by her shoulders. "We are alike, you and I," he breathed.

"No, we are not," she tried.

He grinned. "Both odd, eccentric—and misunderstood. They talk about us behind our back." He shrugged. "But we do not care. We live as we please."

Her heart was racing with alarming speed. "Please release me," she whispered, and her mind raced as well. There was some truth to what he said. Dear God, no one understood her—except for her father and except, she thought, for Bragg. But he was also very, very wrong. "I care what people say, what they think, and I think you do, too."

He released her and laughed. "No, Francesca, in that you are so wrong. I do not give a damn what the world says about me. I did, once, a long time ago. But I have since outgrown my folly and seen the error of such thinking."

"I don't believe that," she whispered, unable to look away.

He tilted up her chin. "How can you and your sister be so different? She is so proper, so legitimate, and you are a woman of passionate inclinations. How?"

"I am a reformer," Francesca said, wondering if he was going to kiss her and terrified that he would. Her entire body was shaking, but she was not quite immune to his charm and his masculine appeal. How could she be? "Please, remove your hand from my face."

"Why? Because you are saving yourself for your husband? Or my brother?" But he dropped his hand, and the glance he gave her was piercing.

She backed away. But even the distance of several feet and a good-sized chair did not feel like a safe distance or a good barrier. "I am not an adventuress."

He gave her a crooked grin. "How easily I could disprove that."

She wet her lips. "Please don't."

He met her gaze and a silence fell, hard, between them. "I am sorry," he said, shocking her. "It is the liquor. I like you, Miss Cahill, and I apologize."

"No, I understand, and it is not the liquor; it is your pain and grief speaking today, so eloquently."

He gave her an angry look and walked back to the bar. She saw him lurch slightly as he did so, and she was stunned, realizing he was far more inebriated than she had thought. "Mr. Hart? May I ask you some questions?"

He sighed, taking his drink and flopping in a big red chair. "Only if you must."

She gingerly took a chair facing him. A small table remained between them. It was foolish to hope that any object might keep him at bay, should he truly decide to act the cad and make improper advances.

He laughed. "I said I would not bite, and I won't. I can control myself, my dear Francesca. If I choose to."

She was rigid again. She clutched her palms tightly together. "I trust you," she lied.

"Bullshit," he said.

She flushed.

"Surely you have heard worse?"

"Would you speak that way in front of Connie?" Francesca asked tersely.

He eyed her, and it was lazy, sensual, considering. "Yes. I speak as I choose, always. If someone does not like it, they need not share my company again. It is actually quite simple."

Her eyes widened. "I don't think there is a single simple aspect to you or anything that you do."

He grinned, pleased. "And you are also astute. I begin to fully understand Bragg's fatal attraction. So. How is your sister? You know, the two of you could be twins, you so resemble one another. Except that you are an inch or two taller, and you have more golden tones in your hair and your skin, and even in your mouth." His gaze moved to her lips. It was considering and speculative now.

She sat up straighter.

"I am not being suggestive, although you have a lush and lovely mouth, Francesca. I am an art connoisseur. Art is about color and shape, at first glance. It is about form and arrangement—at second glance. More importantly, it is a story, about life. Ultimately, it is about the artist and, dare I say it, God." He grinned. Francesca stared at him in shock. "Or the Devil," he added, his smile widening.

He continued while she remained speechless. "If I cannot comprehend the vague nuances between tones of pink and gold, then I cannot comprehend form, arrangement, the larger story, life, or the pain or passion of the artist—now can I? And if that were the case, I should not be a collector of art." He smiled at her, now sprawled so indolently in his chair that Francesca wondered if he would drop his drink. "Color is but the mundane and contemporary tip of the prehistoric iceberg," he said.

"I see." She realized she was whispering. This man was not at all what the world might think or claim—oh no. "The Randalls hate you," she abruptly changed the topic.

He grinned, apparently not disturbed. "Not half as much as I hate them."

She leaned slightly forward. "Did you kill your father, Mr. Hart?"

"Calder. No." He did not look away.

And as she stared into his eyes, she thought that she believed him, but she was too unsettled by his presence and his behavior to be sure. For how could she analyze anything when her heart was racing and she was so discomfited by his every word and every action? "Were you blackmailing Randall . . . Calder?"

"Blackmailing him?" Hart erupted into laughter. "Is that a joke?"

"No. It is what Mary claims."

He laughed again. "That man-hater." He shook his head. "I first met my father face-to-face when I was sixteen years old. That year—" He stopped.

"What?"

He looked away, his entire face rigid. "That year, I was a fool. I had . . . expectations. They quickly changed." He smiled at her, but it did not reach his eyes. "I have not had anything to do with that family ever since. They are certainly not my family. I despise them all. I would not bother to blackmail Randall. Why give myself such a headache?" he asked.

Francesca bit her lip. "Perhaps it would please you to frighten him."

He shook his head. "You mean, to torture him? Actually, it would please me, but the flip side of that coin is that any involvement with them would torture me far more than it would torture them." He stared at her.

She knew he meant every word. His plight moved her, yet she had to remain somewhat objective now. "But you had dinner with Randall at your club last Tuesday."

He sat up. "Oh ho. So the little sleuth is as clever as she appears. Are you blushing, Francesca? I seem to make you blush."

"You are changing the topic."

His grin flashed. "Yes, I did try. Randall approached me. He seemed desperate. I agreed to meet him for supper. I

haven't seen him socially in years, Francesca. And I do mean
years."

"What did he want?"

"Money. Isn't that what we all want?" He smiled at her.

"No, Calder. Some of us want love, liberty, and happiness."

"Money buys it all, except for love, which is an illusion."

She stared and thought, *Dear God, he truly believes it.* "I
shall debate you on that point some other time, Calder."

He grinned. "And I shall look forward to the debate."

Only he could make it sound so sexual, as if a debate were
the prelude to far more intimate activities. She ignored the
remark. "I understand he was deeply in debt."

"Deeply." Hart seemed pleased.

"And? Did you loan him the money?"

Hart stared at her, his eyes wide. "Are you serious?" He
chuckled. "No, I did not. Not a single penny."

Francesca was appalled. "You would not lend your own
father a dime?"

"Paul Randall was not my father. He gave up that claim
many years ago." Hart was cool.

"But . . . how could you refuse Randall? You have so
much."

"Easily, my dear. I do have so much. I have enough money
to buy this city and everyone in it two times over." He stared,
his eyes dark and hard. "And I have earned every cent that I
possess—the hard way. It is my wealth—to do with as I
choose." He seemed angry.

She didn't want him angry. "Would you care to join the
Ladies Society for the Eradication of Tenements? There is a
place on the board," she said. Actually, she was the society's
only member thus far.

He stared—and he laughed.

She smiled. "We could use a sponsor, Hart."

"Thank you, Francesca. Thank you for that."

She blinked. He wasn't laughing now. Instead, he seemed
very serious—and very intent. It was a moment before she
could look away, and when she had, she was shaken.

Then he yawned.

She hid a smile.

"Good God, I apologize," he said, standing. Clearly he wished to end the interview, and as he stood, he staggered.

"Oh, dear," Francesca whispered. "Calder, how much have you had to drink?"

He looked at her, his eyes half-hooded now, but with sleepiness. "Don't know. Why? Do you care?" His tone had turned into a purr.

She fought to ignore the suggestive sound. "Before I go, may I ask a few more questions?"

He waved at her, an affirmative, while moving to the sofa. He was lurching on his feet now, and he half-sat and half-collapsed onto the plush cushions. Before her very eyes, he lay down on his back.

"You didn't mean it, did you, when you called Mary a man-hater? She certainly loved her father," Francesca said.

"She is a man-hater, Francesca." His eyes closed. "And I imagine that sometime soon she will realize her inclinations lie elsewhere."

"Elsewhere?" It was so odd, talking to a man who had lain down in front of you as if this were an everyday occurrence.

"I promise you that it is only a matter of time before she takes a lover—who is female," he murmured. He sighed then, flinging one arm over his face.

Francesca gaped. Did Mary prefer women to men? Could Hart be right? Her thoughts instantly veered to Daisy and Rose. "Calder, someone claims you were not with Daisy and Rose on Friday night."

He lifted his arm and blinked at her. "So my sweet Daisy broke?"

She flushed at his use of language. "No. She did not. It was an outsider who overheard them." She was anxious now. "Is it true?"

He nodded and sighed, stretching out more fully on his back now, his eyes once again closed.

Francesca stared down at him. This was too intimate, she had to leave, but she had to know. "Then *where* were you,

Calder? On the night of the murder, at seven P.M., where were you?"

His arm remained high above his head, but he turned his face toward her and opened his eyes and their gazes locked. His eyes were hazel, she realized suddenly, not brown as she had thought. She saw shades of green and gold and brown in them, as well as orange. Worse, they slid over her slowly, with enjoyment, even, from her face to her toes—before lifting to her face once more. "I was here," he said.

"Here?" Relief filled her. "Why didn't you just say so? You have a houseful of servants—"

He cut her off, his eyes drifting closed. "No. Here, alone. I dismissed everyone."

She stared, and as comprehension hit her, she was horrified.

His arm shifted, falling over his chest. His breathing had become deep and even.

Francesca finally clasped her cheeks, which were warm and damp. She brushed off the perspiration, and as she stared down at him, some of the tension generated from their duel dissipated. But hardly enough.

He had been in this monstrous house, alone, on the night of the murder?

Abruptly Francesca turned, weaving through chairs and tables, settees and ottomans, and finally arriving at the door. Alfred materialized a moment later, at the end of the hall. "Alfred, how much has Mr. Hart drunk?"

"He has been drinking ever since you called yesterday afternoon," the Englishman said, revealing a glimmer of anxiety as he spoke.

Francesca gasped. "Oh, dear! Alfred, please bring a tray of sandwiches into Hart's study. He is asleep now, but leave them beside him, within reach."

Alfred nodded, about to leave. But Francesca plucked his sleeve. "And take away those whiskey bottles from the bar. Hide them—lock them up."

Alfred paled. "Miss Cahill?"

She folded her arms. "He should grieve for his father properly, Alfred. Do you not agree?"

The butler hesitated. "Indeed I do. But he will dismiss me from my post."

"Blame me."

His eyes widened almost imperceptibly—and then he smiled. "Indeed I shall." He started to go.

"There is one more thing. Did Hart dismiss the staff on Friday night?" It was too incredible to be believed, she thought. And if it were true—and it could not be—no one would believe it. No one. Not the police—and not a jury.

Alfred nodded. "Yes, he did."

Francesca knew she gaped. "But . . . why?"

Alfred hesitated.

"My dear good man," she said, "I only wish to help your employer. You do not betray any confidences by speaking with me."

Alfred nodded slowly. "He dismisses the staff from time to time, perhaps two or three times a month."

Francesca stared. "But this house is huge. It is a mausoleum. He dismissed *everyone*?"

"Everyone," Alfred said with emphasis.

"But . . . why?"

"I do not know."

Francesca could not imagine anyone being alone in a house of this size. "Does . . . he entertain on those nights?" It was the only possible explanation. Perhaps he gave parties like Stanford White.

"We wondered about that, madam. But one of the maids did snoop. No. He does not entertain. He wanders about, alone." He paused, as if he might say more but was thinking the better of it.

"And?"

"He drinks and wanders about from room to room, apparently viewing his paintings and sculptures."

Francesca was shaken. "And on Friday night? When did he get home? At what time did he dismiss the staff?"

"He returned home a bit after six, I believe, looking somewhat dour, and instantly ordered everyone out."

Francesca's heart lurched. Calder had no alibi between six and nine on the night of the murder. Dear God, it did not look good. "Thank you, Alfred."

He nodded, then said, "No, thank *you*, Miss Cahill." He left.

She hesitated, remaining stunned. Why come home, dismiss everyone, and then go to White's party a few hours later? Terribly disturbed, she returned to Hart's library. He was so still it was almost as if he were not breathing. Alarmed, she went to his side, then was pleased to see the slight rise and fall of his chest beneath the velvet smoking jacket.

She felt sorry for him. He was a complicated man, and she suspected his wounds ran deep.

And now, should anyone ever learn the truth of his whereabouts on Friday night, he was in deep trouble indeed.

Francesca looked around. The draperies had been left open. It was snowing steadily now outside. From this window, she had a view of the empty lot to the north of his property. In this distance, she saw a four-in-hand on the avenue, shrouded in the falling snow and the yellow glow of the streetlights.

She walked over to each of the three large windows and closed the curtains. Then she took a cashmere throw from a chair before the fireplace, and she returned to Hart's side. She laid it over him, carefully so she would not awaken him. As carefully, she removed each of his slippers. Then she smiled a little, satisfied.

"Perhaps you wish to tuck me into bed?" he murmured, making her start with surprise.

She stiffened. "I did not mean to awaken you," she managed.

"Any time." His eyes did not even open.

She stared. "Hart?" she whispered.

His breathing seemed deep and even. He seemed to be sleeping once again. There was no answer.

Francesca turned slowly and again she made her way

through the elegant but overfurnished room and to the door. She paused, and an odd urge made her look back. He was asleep, or very close to it. He hadn't moved since first lying down on the couch.

Even in sleep, he appeared intriguing and dangerous.

He was, she decided, a very interesting man.

She left.

FOURTEEN

Her coach was moving down Fifth Avenue, following another brougham. Because it was a Sunday night and snowing, there was no other traffic directly ahead, and the pace was a swift one. Francesca stared west, at Central Park, which appeared magical in the glow of falling snow and the dull yellow lights cast from the tall iron street lamps. She was glum. Hart was an unusual man, and she was more convinced than ever that he was not as bad as he clearly wished the world to think him to be. But he was in trouble, and he had lied to the police, creating a false alibi. No good could come of that, it only made him look guiltier, and while she remained convinced he was not capable of murder, much less murdering his own father, she was afraid of what was going to happen when the truth came out.

Unfortunately, she would have to tell Bragg what she had just learned. She could not keep something so momentous from him, and maybe he could help. Francesca felt certain that, when push came to shove, the blood Bragg shared with Hart would win out over any enmity between the two of them.

She glanced out of the other passenger window, aware that they were passing her own house. She sighed, her thoughts turning abruptly to her sister. Where could she be?

Bragg had said she was in a hotel somewhere. But Connie would never let the world know of her difficulties, especially her marital ones. Francesca doubted she would move into a hotel. If only she had not packed a trunk. Then Francesca would be certain she had merely gone out with the girls for the day.

She sighed again and realized they were approaching 59th Street. The posh and elegant Plaza Hotel was on her right and just ahead. It was Connie's favorite lunch spot. She often met her girlfriends there. . . . Francesca sat up like a shot.

Beth Anne Holmes.

Beth Anne was Connie's best friend, and her only unmarried one. Francesca pounded on the partition. "Jennings! We must detour to the Holmes house!" she cried. Her heart was pounding like mad. *Of course. Connie had to be at Beth Anne's. And why hadn't she thought of it sooner?*

But then, Neil had only insisted that Connie had left him a few hours ago. And she had only disappeared that morning.

Five minutes later the brougham was pausing in front of a large house that took up the corner of 38th and Fifth. Francesca had hoped to see one of the Montrose coaches in front, but to her shock, she saw the second Cahill carriage parked on the street instead. Francesca knew who was calling upon the Holmes family: Julia.

Julia had realized Connie was gone, and she had quickly come to the conclusion Francesca had just reached. Francesca leaped out of the carriage before Jennings had fully stopped it. She flew across the drive and up the front steps of the house. Her knock was greeted instantly by a houseman. She was not close to Beth Anne and hardly ever called—she did not know the servant and he did not know her. But before she could even introduce herself, she could hear voices coming from the parlor, and even from behind closed doors she recognized both Beth Anne's voice and her mother's.

"I am Francesca Cahill. I believe my mother is here," she said breathlessly.

"Mrs. Cahill is in the blue room," the servant said, waiting for her muff, hat, coat, and gloves.

Impatiently Francesca shed everything, practically thrusting her outerwear into the manservant's arms and racing to the pair of teakwood doors on the entry hall's other side before he had a chance to dispose of anything, much less lead her there. Francesca flung open both doors.

Connie sat on one of the room's two blue-and-gold-striped sofas. Julia sat in a bergere adjacent to the sofa, patting Connie's hand. Beth Anne, a plump and pretty girl with freckles on her nose and curly red hair, was standing. Connie appeared

oddly calm, as if she had not just taken her children and left
her husband. In fact, sitting there in a simple navy blue suit,
one magnificently cut and stitched, with her hands clasped in
her lap, she seemed beautiful, elegant, and composed. But she
was so still that she could have been sitting for her portrait.
She was so still that it was eerie.

Everyone looked at Francesca at once.

Julia said, grimly, "So you have told your sister that Montrose has a lover?"

Francesca nodded, suddenly realizing which direction the
wind was blowing. "Con? Thank God you are all right!" She
rushed forward.

Connie gazed at her steadily. She attempted a smile. It was
brittle and heartbreaking. "Yes, I am fine," she said.

Francesca sank down beside her sister, taking both of her
hands. Connie looked as if she might break into pieces at any
moment, as if she were the most fragile of porcelain dolls.

"How could you tell her such a thing?" Beth Anne cried
angrily. Her green eyes were flashing.

Francesca turned incredulously. "She asked me if I knew
something! Was I to lie?" Beth Anne was a gossip. In fact,
she could not keep a secret if her life—or someone else's—
depended upon it. Francesca felt that Beth Anne had some
nerve criticizing her now.

"I do not think it was your place to say anything—and we
all know how often you say the wrong thing!" Beth Anne
cried.

"Please don't fight," Connie said quietly but tersely. Her
voice was high with tension.

"I wish you had come to me first," Julia said, intervening.

Francesca looked at her mother and tensed. "He does have
a lover, Mama. I saw them. And I cannot lie to Connie."

Julia stared at her. "We shall speak privately in a moment,
Francesca."

Francesca stiffened, about to protest. Then she shook her
head, becoming angry. Clearly she was going to be blamed,
when this was all Neil's fault. She faced Connie. "I have been

so worried about you." She sat down and took her hand. "*Are you all right?*"

Connie said, "I am fine," in the exact same odd, detached tone of voice. She pulled her hand away from Francesca's grasp. Her smile remained, as if carved upon her face. Clearly she was not fine.

"Connie, we have been so worried and . . . Neil is worried, too," Francesca said.

Connie looked at her. Her eyes were oddly wild while she remained so still. She did not comment upon what Francesca had said.

"Would you dare to meddle again?" Beth Anne cried.

Francesca stood, glaring at Beth Anne. "He is worried. He is worried and filled with remorse. I am certain of it!"

"Just as you are certain Neil betrayed Connie?" Beth Anne challenged. "What if this has been a mistake? I find it hard to believe that Neil would ever betray Connie."

Francesca wanted to shout at Beth Anne that no mistake had been made—that she had seen them in the act of fornication. Instead, she glanced at Connie, who had tears sparkling in her eyes, and then she looked at Julia. Julia stood up.

"Ladies, this is not the time to argue over spilled milk. Beth Anne, we appreciate how much you love Connie, but this is a family matter."

Beth Anne looked ready to burst into tears. "Mrs. Cahill, you know I have been Connie's best friend for years. I don't think Francesca had any right to spy on Neil, or any right to tell Connie what she did."

"I could not lie to my own sister! I never expected Connie to leave her husband!" Francesca cried.

"Connie had the perfect life! And you have simply ruined it," Beth Anne said harshly.

Francesca stiffened. "I did not force Montrose upon . . ." She stopped. "Upon another woman!"

"*If* there was another woman!" Beth Anne flared.

Francesca wanted to throttle her. She was the biggest pain in the neck! How could Connie tolerate her?

"Please," Connie said. "Do not fight."

Beth Anne sat down on Connie's other side and hugged her. "Everything will be fine. I am certain of it." Over Connie's head, she gave Francesca a dark look, as if this were all, entirely, Francesca's fault.

"Beth Anne, I know how close you and Connie are, but Francesca is her sister, and they are even closer. Would you give us a few moments alone?" Julia asked.

Beth Anne stared, as if incredulous and disbelieving. She glanced at Connie, but Connie did not defend her. "Very well," she finally said, but she shot Francesca an ugly look as she got to her feet.

Francesca refrained from glaring back. The truth was, it was hard to be patient or pleasant around Beth Anne. Francesca had never really cared for her, and she found her the busiest body there was.

"And, Beth Anne? We all know you would never breathe a word of this to anyone," Julia said with a smile. "It will only hurt Connie more should anyone learn what has happened."

"My mouth is sealed," Beth Anne said firmly.

Francesca made a disparaging sound.

Beth Anne looked at her and left the room.

A silence fell. Francesca said, "If I have done the wrong thing, then I am terribly sorry."

Connie looked down at her lap. "You did not do the wrong thing, Fran," she said, low. "I asked you what you knew, and you told me. Thank you."

Julia said, "Are you certain that you did not make a mistake, Francesca?"

"I am positive, Mama," Francesca said, glancing at Connie. But Connie did not speak.

"Well, what has been done is done. There is no preventing spilled milk. Now we must think of the future." Julia sat down on Connie's other side. "You must go home, dear. Before you do cause a scandal."

Connie nodded. "I know." She did not seem thrilled with the prospect.

Francesca was flooded with relief. "Neil does love you, Con. I am convinced of it."

Connie looked at her. "Perhaps."

Francesca felt her heart breaking all over again. She glanced at Julia. Julia gave her a look of approval. She said, "Dear, I am not exactly surprised that Montrose has wandered. It is the way of the world. Few men are capable of fidelity in the long run."

Francesca gasped. "Mama! Surely you do not think most men stray?"

"I do. Or rather, I think most exceptional men wander, at times. But I never expected this to happen so early in your marriage. Your heart is broken now. It will mend. And I agree with Francesca. Montrose loves you. But now, you must go home, before you cause a scandal."

"How easy it is for you to say," Connie whispered.

"Connie, the longer you stay here, the more likely it is that society will learn what happened. You should go back to Neil tonight, as if nothing is wrong. In fact, stun him with your kindness. His guilt will know no bounds."

Francesca said, "I think she should put him on the carpet. I would."

Julia looked at her sharply. "Marriage lasts a lifetime, Francesca. And waging war upon one's spouse hardly enhances a union. Connie must go back and pick up as if nothing were amiss. Enough has been said. Neil knows she knows. In little subtle ways, Connie can make it clear that this will not be tolerated again. Andrew will weigh in, as well. Discreetly. After all, should Neil truly incur the displeasure of the family, his future would be threatened."

Francesca was stunned. Did Julia truly mean that Andrew might threaten Neil with disinheritance? She was shaken. And surely she did not really expect Connie to go home as if nothing were wrong?

"Are we in agreement?" Julia asked, clasping Connie's shoulder.

Connie gazed at her mother. "Mama . . . it is too soon," she said.

Francesca felt every bit of her sister's anguish then. "Could another day or so really matter? She and the girls are well off here."

"Francesca, every day matters!" Julia exclaimed. "Connie, you must return tonight. Especially as Neil thinks you have left him on a somewhat permanent basis."

Connie said quietly, "He knows I would not do that."

"But you packed a trunk. You left no word," Julia admonished. "When you return home, tell him you left him a note. That you decided to take the girls on holiday. That a maid must have misplaced your note and this has all been a misunderstanding."

Francesca wanted to protest. She stared at Julia, aghast. This was not right! Neil's treachery could not be simply swept under the rug.

Connie nodded.

Finally Francesca could bear it no more. "Mama, I think this is wrong, terribly so. I think Connie should confront Neil. But not in a combative manner, of course. They must discuss this, to ensure that it does not happen again."

"Francesca, you are twenty years old, and more often than not, your nose is in a book. I have not a doubt as to how this entire sordid affair should be handled, and that is that. Connie?"

Connie took a breath and nodded. "I think you are right, Mama," she said.

Francesca felt like pulling her own hair out. Her frustration knew no bounds.

"Well, that is settled, then," Julia said with some cheer. "Francesca, let us go."

Francesca wished to stay but realized Julia was not about to allow it. But before leaving, she hugged her sister, hard. "Con? If you want to talk, call me on the telephone. Or just come to the house."

Connie met her gaze. "Thank you, Fran."

"And I am truly sorry. And if I did speak up wrongly, I am even sorrier."

"No, you did what was right." Connie managed a smile,

finally standing. She seemed very tired. She walked them to the door but did not leave the salon.

When they were in the entry, awaiting their coats, Julia turned to Francesca. "Dear, I know how much you love your sister. And your desire to help others is so endearing—most of the time. But sometimes it has an opposite effect. I happen to know that you always mean well. I just wish you were less impulsive."

Francesca was somewhat relieved. The worst had passed; there would be no terrible tongue-lashing. "I had decided not to say a word. But when Connie asked me what I knew, I could not lie."

"No one was asking you to lie, Francesca." Julia sighed. "Sometimes, people wish to pretend that all is well. In fact, it has been my experience that more often than not, that is the case. I believe Neil is very fond of Connie, and he certainly adores the girls. Whatever prompted him to stray, I am quite certain it would have passed. I wish you had come to me, instead of to your sister. I am not sure she needed to learn of this." Her glance was rather reproving. "You could have put her off and avoided telling her the truth."

Bragg had said the same thing, although for different reasons. He was worried about Connie's fragility, and after seeing her a moment ago, Francesca was now worried, too. "Maybe you are right. But what I really am is worried. Mama, I am not sure that Connie should go home. She is in such an odd state!"

"Of course she must go home," Julia said firmly. She took her hand and smiled, but it was a sad smile indeed. "I have no doubt that in the end, they will successfully reconcile."

"Connie is so distraught," Francesca returned.

"She is distraught, but then, how could she not be?" Julia sighed. "She is so used to things being easy for her. She has had so little adversity in her life—if she has had any at all. Yes, this is a terrible blow. Perhaps, in the end, this will be good for her . . . and her marriage."

"How can you say that?" Francesca asked, with surprise and real curiosity.

Julia smiled a little. "Your sister will emerge much stronger from this crisis. Of that I have no doubt. But more importantly, it is never too soon to realize that we enter this world alone, and we leave it alone."

"Mother!" Francesca was stunned. "You have been married to Father for over twenty years. Successfully, I might add. That was a very negative thing to say."

"Francesca, never be deceived. No matter how much I love you, no matter how much your father loves you, or Evans or Connie, you are here alone. Ultimately, your fate rests in your own hands, whatever it might be."

Francesca shivered. "I do hope you are not telling me that in the end, there is no one you can count on other than yourself, ultimately?"

Julia smiled just a bit and did not reply. And that was an affirmation.

"What happened, Mama, to make you feel so alone? Papa loves you. We all do."

"Even I have my secrets," Julia said, standing and looking down at her. "We all do—and that is as it should be."

Francesca was bemused.

"So. Where are you off to at this hour, Francesca?" Julia asked as they finally were helped on with their coats.

Francesca hesitated. Numerous excuses and denials sprang to mind. Then, "I was on my way to bring an important bit of information to the police commissioner's attention. It is very important, Mama."

"Francesca, you are not involved in police business again?" Julia was incredulous.

"Not exactly. But this should please you—I called on Calder Hart. And he gave me the information I must pass on to Bragg."

Julia stared. "You called on Hart? Francesca! He must be the one to court you!"

Francesca hid a smile. "I called on him, Mama; I did not go courting him. You know, I think you should call on him yourself. If you state that you are my mother, I am sure he will receive you." She continued to keep a straight face. One visit to Hart and her mother would dismiss him as a marriage prospect.

"You are up to something. And I will think about it. But you are right; I am pleased you called on him. What time is it?"

"A bit past seven. I can be home by eight, I promise," Francesca said, crossing her fingers behind her back. Half past eight was more likely, or even nine o'clock. But she would deal with that matter when the time came.

"I know you will go home and then steal out of the house at some horrendously late hour if I refuse. So go, but be back by eight-thirty." There was a warning in her tone.

"You can be the most wonderful mother," Francesca cried, impulsively hugging her. "And I shall be back on time, I swear."

Julia smiled fondly and Francesca dashed from the house.

Peter, Bragg's man, answered the door before she had even finished knocking. The big blond man looked down at her, his expression inscrutable. Francesca beamed. "Good evening, Peter. Is it not a lovely night?" She nodded her head toward the street, now dusted with an inch of snow. The few carriages that passed by were also snow-clad, and two of the neighborhood children were out, tossing snowballs at each other not far from Bragg's house. A spaniel puppy was chasing the snowballs amid shrieks and laughter.

"Good evening, Miss Cahill. The commissioner is in his study."

Francesca walked past the giant man, well aware of her rapidly pounding pulse. She had butterflies in her stomach, too. *Oh, well. So much for detachment and professionalism,* she thought, continuing to smile.

She followed Peter down the hall. The one single time she had been in Bragg's home, she had been in the parlor, which was at the end of the house. The door was open now, but no lights were on, and no fire danced in the hearth.

Peter knocked and then pushed open a door to the left of the parlor, saying, "Miss Cahill, sir."

Francesca stepped inside.

Bragg was sitting at a large desk, oddly placed in the center of the room. One old and very frayed armchair was placed facing the room's hearth, which was small. There a small fire crackled. A bookcase crammed with books covered another wall; windows looked out on the small backyard. Boxes, opened but unpacked, were everywhere. They contained books and journals.

It was a reminder that he had only returned to New York recently, in order to accept his appointment as police commissioner.

Bragg had leaped to his feet as she entered. He was in his shirtsleeves, which were rolled up to his elbows, and a dark vest, which was open. Even his shirt was unbuttoned at the throat, revealing a hollow there and a few dark hairs. He smiled, obviously pleased to see her. "Francesca, what an unexpected surprise."

"You cannot get rid of me, I fear."

He laughed. "Do you not remember, I learn fast? And that fact I learned weeks ago, during the Burton Affair."

Francesca found it hard to remove her gaze from him. He seemed bigger somehow, perhaps because when he was clad only in his shirt and vest, one became aware of how broad his shoulders were, how strong and muscular his arms. And in the shadowy room, in the firelight, his eyes appeared darker than they were. He, too, seemed to be scrutinizing her. Not glancing away, she murmured, "You need a decorator, Bragg."

"I know. Is that another one of your many and unique talents?" He moved out from behind the desk, coming toward her slowly. Not taking his eyes from her face, he said, "Peter, bring Miss Cahill a sherry, please. Or would you prefer a glass of wine?"

She wet her lips, which had become dry. Her body felt taut, as if riddled with tension. "A sherry would be perfect," she said. "Wine tends to go straight to my head, making it rather mushy."

He smiled, his gaze still on hers. "A mushy-headed Fran-

cesca. That might be an interesting change. I will have a glass
of red wine, Peter. Burgundy, if you will. Open a bottle if
none is left over from supper."

Peter left.

"Does he speak?" Francesca opened the top button of her
shirtwaist, at her throat.

"Infrequently," Bragg said, his gaze moving to her fingers.
"When he does, it is usually worthwhile to attend to what he
has to say." It lifted again to her face.

Francesca nodded. "I imagine so."

"Shall we go into the parlor? You seem warm. It is warm
in here. And I am afraid the only chair I can offer you is
rather shabby, and the cushion rather thin."

She eyed him, then reached down to test the cushion,
which needed new stuffing. "Actually, decorating is not a talent of mine, but it is one of Connie's." Thinking about her
sister made her frown with the worry she could not shake.

"Then perhaps we shall enlist her aid. Francesca? What is
wrong?"

She straightened and met his gaze. As usual, it was intense
and riveted upon her. Her butterflies increased. The feeling
was a heady one. The night felt immense, as did the possibilities. It was almost as if anything could happen—as if anything would happen.

And he had said "we."

"I am sure Connie could be enticed into sprucing up your
home," she said softly.

He touched her arm. "Has something happened that I do
not know about?" he asked with concern.

Her heart melted then and there. "She spent last night at
her best friend's. Mama and I found her, and Mama insisted
she go home. Connie has agreed. She is so distraught, Bragg.
I am somehow afraid for her. And I do not like Mama pushing
her." Her tone sounded imploring to her own ears.

His hand briefly cupped her shoulder. The gesture was
meant to comfort, but it did more than that; it caused her
pulse to soar. As if he sensed her reaction, as quickly, he
removed it. "I am sorry. But I do think they will work this

out eventually. Things, however, might get worse before they improve," he said.

"Oh, dear. Do not speak that way!" Francesca hoped fervently that he was wrong. "Mama has actually instructed Connie on how to behave—even on constructing an excuse for last night. I do wish she would let Connie manage her marriage her own way."

"Your mother is a very strong woman. I imagine Connie is accustomed to doing as Julia asks."

"Yes, she is," Francesca said, even more worried now. She sighed.

He brushed a stray tendril of light blond hair from her face. She stiffened; he said, "There has been a betrayal of trust. Trust is no easy thing to give in the first place, but to win it anew, that is even harder. A reconciliation will take some time."

"Do you always have to be so wise?" she asked, her heart beating frantically, and their gazes locked.

He stared and a long and intense moment seemed to pass. He said, "You give me so much more credit than I am due."

"I don't think so." She knew she did not.

His gaze slipped over her. It moved across her mouth and down her bodice, and he turned away almost simultaneously, but she had seen it and she sensed what it meant. She was thrilled. He was aware of her now, as she was of him.

"Do you enjoy working in here?" Francesca asked, smiling and breathless.

"Actually, I do." He gave her a sidelong glance, which she now could not decipher. "There are no distractions, not even the telephone, for that is in my parlor. And upstairs I have installed another telephone, in my bedroom."

She blinked. "You have a *telephone* in your *bedroom*?" It was unheard of.

"I do get calls in the middle of the night," he said. "It is the nature of my job."

"I suppose so," she said, blushing. She should not imagine him in bed, half-undressed, on the telephone, conducting business—but she did. She already knew how he would look without his shirt, for she had held him in her arms and she knew his body was a lean and muscular one. She tried to shake free of her unwelcome thoughts. She had called on him for a reason—and she had limited time. "I have news, Bragg."

"I did not think this a social call," he said, touching her elbow to guide her to the parlor. "In fact, I have played a little mental game with myself, deciding the number of hours it would be before you popped up again."

His tone was so warm that she could only smile. "And how many hours did you decide it would be before our paths did cross again?" He had been thinking about her, too. She was elated.

"Unfortunately, I have guessed rather poorly," he said, wry. "I had expected to hear from you late tomorrow morning. I had decided upon eleven A.M."

"Ah. I am at least sixteen hours in advance of your estimation. I am keeping you on your toes." She grinned.

"I suspect you wish to keep me on my toes. But the evening hours hardly count—or so I have now decided."

"You cannot change the rules in the middle of the game!" she cried, delighted.

"Why not? It is my game," he said softly. His eyes danced. They wound up lingering on her mouth again.

Francesca had to pause. Tonight, surely, when they were alone like this, with just the small fire for company, he would hold her and kiss her. She was certain of it. She wanted nothing more. "But you do business in the middle of the night; you have a telephone by your bed; you have proven that."

"For emergencies only." But he was smiling at her.

"But you never know when I shall have an emergency to present to you," she rebutted with her own smile. "Was it not midnight that I sent Joel over with news of a murder?"

He laughed and shook his head. "I concede defeat. You are absolutely right. Next time, you may determine the rules, Francesca." He ceased smiling. His stare was unwavering now. It was also heated.

And her breathing became suspended as well. "I had better

write this down and record this moment for posterity," she said softly.

"Perhaps we had better keep our understanding an oral one. God forbid a rabid journalist learns that the police commissioner of New York City allows a mere slip of a Barnard student to set the rules of the game."

She wondered if he thought her petite, and she did not mind. "You are right."

"The parlor?" he asked, taking her arm and gesturing with his head. He stood so near her now that they were hip-to-hip.

Her arm seemed to tingle beneath his hand. "I do not mind staying in your office. I rather like this room." It was so full of his energy, his essence, and his character, she thought. Her gaze fell on the closest box of books. They were law books, she saw, undoubtedly acquired during his years at Harvard Law School or perhaps even when he had worked in Washington, D.C., as an attorney defending the poor, the falsely accused, and the unfortunate.

"Only you would like so dour a room." He released her and she gingerly sat down in the big chair. To her surprise, it was like sitting on a cloud, and every inch of it reminded her of Bragg. She inhaled his strong, masculine scent. "How long have you had this chair?"

"Too many years," he said flatly.

No wonder she liked it, she thought. The chair smelled like him—woodsy yet urbane, musky yet fresh. She leaned back and to her surprise, the chair tilted abruptly backward while an attached ottoman shot out, elevating her feet. "Oh!"

"I forgot to tell you, the chair reclines." He quickly leaned over the chair, a hand on each arm. As he pulled it upright, she looked at his face, which was now mere inches from hers. He paused, staring back.

Francesca could not help herself. She looked at his mouth and recalled how his lips had tasted and felt. Her heartbeat had become a drumroll. "Bragg?" she breathed.

Bragg straightened abruptly, releasing the chair and moving away from her so quickly it was as if he leaped away. "So what news?" he said roughly, shoving his hands in the pockets of his trousers as if that might keep them there and prevent them from straying elsewhere.

She stared, dismayed. She thought his hands had been trembling, but she was not sure. And he could have kissed her, so easily, but he had not. Disappointment seared her.

Bragg looked at her. His eyes were hot.

Why, in God's name, hadn't he kissed her?

Didn't he want her, too?

She felt her cheeks' heat. "I have a lot of news," she said hoarsely, wetting her lips and climbing out of the chair. This time, he did not reach out to help her. This time, he kept his distance from her. "I am quite certain that Bill Randall was the intruder at Georgette de Labouche's house when I was hiding in the kitchen."

"Quite certain?" Bragg returned, and it was a shot. Relief covered his chiseled features now. "He has stated he did not arrive in the city until the following afternoon. That was Saturday."

"I am very certain, Bragg," Francesca said.

Bragg stared and said, "Then he lied to us, and from the way you have described his behavior, he went into Miss de Labouche's knowing his father was dead. Had he been surprised by the sight of his father's body, he would have shouted for help and called the police." Bragg was grim. "My coroner has stated that the murder did take place between six and eight in the evening. If Randall was the intruder, it was midnight when he entered Miss de Labouche's home—four to six hours after the murder. The question is, why? Why did he go there, and did he know that his father was already dead? For if he did, and that question is a very serious one, then he knew of the murder, and undoubtedly he knows the identity of the killer as well."

Francesca stood. "I am almost positive that he was not surprised to find his father dead, Bragg."

Bragg frowned. "God, 'almost' is not good enough."

"I know. I am sorry. Do not forget, I was hiding near the kitchen—he was in the hall and the parlor."

"If he was not surprised, the killer must be Mrs. Randall or Mary."

"Who else could it be—if he was not surprised? Still, having met them both, I feel certain neither Henrietta nor her daughter is involved. Unless one of them is a fantastic actress. What about Randall's debtors? Could the killer have been one of them?"

"I am already on that angle, Francesca. I have a team of detectives interviewing everyone he owed money to. So far, it is a dead end. His debts were legitimate ones, owed to three different bankers, and while the sums were tidy, these gentlemen have outstanding reputations and are, I believe, pillars of New York society. It would be shocking if any one of them would murder over the debt Randall owed."

Francesca sighed. "That is too bad."

He gave her a look. "I hate to say this, but Georgette de Labouche is still a possible suspect. I wonder if she knew Bill Randall?"

"I was there, Bragg. My every sense says she is innocent."

"Perhaps you are entirely wrong about Bill Randall. What if you have mistakenly identified young Randall as the intruder? What if it was someone else? I shall telegraph the police in Philadelphia and see if they might spare a man to go round to the university and learn anything regarding Bill Randall's departure."

Francesca knew she was not wrong. She had seen Bill Randall at the de Labouche house that night. "I have more news," Francesca said with a small grimace.

He smiled. "Not good, I take it?"

"No, it is not good." She had become quite nervous now. "Hart lied. He was not with Daisy and Rose on the night of the murder, Bragg." She met his gaze and did not look away. "He confessed the truth to me."

Bragg stared, his eyes widening. "*He* told *you* that?"

She nodded, wringing her hands. "Nicely, I might add."

A thundercloud was descending over his expression. He paced to her. "And why, might I ask, would my half brother confess to you that his alibi was a bogus one?" His tone was harsh.

"Because I am a good sleuth," she said quickly. "Please, do not overreact. There is no need to get angry!"

His expression grew darker. "There is every reason to get angry. I asked you to stay away from him, Francesca. You said that you would. Where did this conversation take place?"

"You should thank me for my sleuthing," she said. "And I never said I would stay away from him—you took my silence as compliance."

"That is wonderful!" He was sardonic. "You did not answer my question," he said.

The door opened then as Peter entered the room. Francesca accepted a sherry with some relief and watched Bragg indicate wordlessly to Peter that he put the wineglass on his desk. The big man did so and left. "Well?" Bragg demanded. He had not taken his eyes off of her for a second. He reminded her of an arctic wolf, the kind she had read about in Jack London's books. Waiting and predatory, with golden, glowing eyes.

"I called on him at home earlier this evening," she said grimly. "He was quite drunk, and that is why, I suspect, he volunteered the truth."

Bragg cursed. "Damn it, Francesca! Will you ever do as I ask?"

She flinched a little. "But are you not happy that I have gotten to the truth? The bad news is, he dismissed the staff that night, a habit of his, I have learned, and was alone, at home, from just past six until he went to White's party."

Bragg cursed. But this time, she knew, it was in reaction to the trouble his half brother was getting himself deeper and deeper into. Bragg stepped closer, his eyes on her face. "And what else did my saintly brother have to say—and do?"

Francesca was surprised—she had expected Bragg to comment on the fact that Calder Hart was now an even stronger suspect in the murder. She shrugged, hoping to be nonchalant. "That was about it. He was foxed, Bragg. By the time I left,

he had fallen asleep. I do believe he was drinking himself
into a stupor because of his grief."

"Did he try to seduce you?" Bragg asked, his gaze intent.

Francesca gasped, their eyes locking. "What?"

"You heard me." His entire face was hard and set.

She could not help herself. "Do not be jealous, Bragg."
And the moment the words were out, she was mortified.

But he did not respond to that. "Did he or did he not try
to seduce you?" he demanded.

"Not really."

His hand shot out and he grasped her wrist. "*Not really*?
What the hell does that mean?" He was towering over her
now.

She stared into angry golden eyes, just inches from hers.
His face was but an inch or two from hers. "It means 'not
really.' " She was breathless and a bit frightened by his anger
but even more thrilled, in an ancient, elemental way. Was this
how it had felt, hundreds of years ago, to be a damsel fought
over by two charging knights?

"My brother tries to seduce every woman who crosses his
path," he said, his tone dangerous, his breath feathering her
cheek. "Did he kiss you?"

"No!" she cried, aghast. But she did not pull away; she
did not move. "Bragg, he did not!"

Bragg did not release her. His arm somehow brushed her
breast.

"Calder happens to know how we—" She stopped
abruptly, out of breath. She had been about to say that Hart
knew how they felt about each other, but that would not do,
oh no. It was becoming difficult to defend herself, to speak.

"So now it is Calder? And Calder happens to know what?"
His eyes gleamed. He leaned closer.

"Are you manhandling me?" Francesca asked roughly.
"You and Hart have far more in common than either one of
you knows."

"Going over there, especially if he was drunk, was a dangerous proposition. And we have nothing in common, except
for our mother, Lily Hart. *Nothing*."

Bragg had mentioned his mother but briefly once before and not by name. "He was a gentleman."

"Oh, really?" Bragg laughed. "Please, Francesca. If he did not try to seduce you, it was only because he was too drunk to do so. Trust me." And he released her.

She was disappointed, dismayed. "He is merely a flirt. At least, I think that is what he is. And I believe he did not try anything improper because he has a bit of a gentleman buried within him, that and for other reasons."

"Do not delude yourself." He walked away from her and stared down at his wine, but he made no move to touch it. His broad shoulders were stiff and set with tension. Was it a sexual tension, or an angry one, or both? Slowly he looked up. "What other reasons?" His tone remained harsh.

She stiffened. How could she say that Calder Hart knew they had strong feelings for each other and, because Bragg was his half brother, that had held him back? For that was what Francesca believed, and that was what she had hoped. "Do you not know the saying that blood is thicker than water?" she said softly.

"In our case, there is more water than blood between us," he returned swiftly.

"I give up. For now," Francesca said with a sigh. "But one day I should like to know just why the two of you have taken such hostile positions against each other."

Bragg stared. "The subject of Calder and myself is off-limits, Francesca," he warned.

"Why?" The question just popped out.

"That is not your affair," he said darkly.

His words hurt her. "But we are friends. Or so I thought."

He lifted his wineglass and held it to his chest, staring at her. "Yes, we are certainly friends. But some things are private and sacred. In this instance, you must respect my wishes, for to fail to do so would be a terrible invasion of my privacy."

Of course, if he so insisted, then he was right, and she had no choice but to turn away from the entire subject of his relationship with his half brother. Still, Francesca knew there

would come a time and place when reconciling the two brothers would be appropriate. Because blood was thicker than
water, and because Bragg was wrong—Hart wasn't as horrid
as Bragg claimed, as Hart himself claimed.

"I can see those little wheels in your mind spinning and
spinning," Bragg said softly, from the distance where he now
stood.

She started, having been completely immersed in her
thoughts and a new and accompanying resolve. Her gaze
lifted instantly to his.

He had, she realized, put half the length of the room between them.

"No schemes, Francesca. Do you not have enough with
which to occupy yourself now? We must find Georgette de
Labouche, and Hart is becoming even more of a suspect."

"You are right," she said, wanting to close the distance
between them but afraid to try to do so. Why hadn't he kissed
her? "I have Joel working on finding Georgette de Labouche.
Once he learns who her friends are, I shall start interviewing
them. As for Hart . . ." She trailed off. It was hard to focus
on the case now. "We must not let the press get wind of this."

"It will only make my job harder," Bragg agreed, taking
his first sip of red wine.

"And it will further ruin Hart's less than stellar reputation,"
Francesca said, watching him.

"Even he would not care about that," Bragg said.

He was probably right. Francesca heard the clock striking
once on the half hour. Startled, she glanced around the room
and found a huge antique grandfather clock standing in the
corner. It was a half past eight—already. Her dismay inten-
sified with sickening force. She was not ready to go, oh no.

"Are you Cinderella tonight?" Bragg asked with some
amusement.

"Actually, I am. I have been warned by Julia in no uncertain terms that I must be home by eight-thirty." She stared at
him.

He did not move away from his desk, where he stood.
"Then you must leave, by all means." His jaw tightened.

Francesca could not prevent herself from moving to him. He stood motionless, his eyes upon her, as she approached. She set her sherry down on the desk by his lean, hard hip. And she faced him, looking up.

"Where do we go from here, Bragg?" she whispered. And too late, even though she had meant to pose the question as a professional one, she realized it had not been a professional one at all; it had been entirely personal. And to make matters worse, her tone had been soft and husky, seductive, a tone she had never heard coming from herself before.

He stood still.

Oh, God, she thought, *how bold can one be?* She swallowed. "I meant," she began thickly.

"I know what you meant." He set his glass down as well. He faced her, his hands fisted at his sides. "I shall speak with Hart tomorrow—at length. And you shall find Miss de Labouche." His jaw was flexing. She saw his temples throb.

He had known what she meant, Francesca was certain. She should play along with him, now. She said, "That is not what I meant. I meant where do *we* go from here?"

"Nowhere," he said flatly.

"What?" she gasped.

"Are you trying to seduce me?" he demanded then. "Do you know how hard it is, to be alone with you like this—at such an hour? You do realize, of course, that your being here like this, even innocently, would destroy your reputation and your prospects—should anyone realize that you were here . . . with me?"

She wet her lips. He was angry, and she did not understand. "No one knows. And I do not care about my reputation—or my prospects."

"But I do!" he cried. He reached out as if to grab her by the shoulders, then dropped his hands. "As long as we discuss police affairs, I can manage this, Francesca. But when you cast your eyes at me and start making innuendos, I cannot. I am not a saint. I am a man. A man who has his hands tied behind him, where you are concerned. We go nowhere from here," he stated harshly.

She was breathing hard now. She could understand why he did not wish to kiss her and compromise her; she was genteel, he was a gentleman and in public service, and it was wrong. But why not court her?

Her temples throbbed. The question was on the tip of her tongue. Did she dare ask it? Did she dare find out just why he kept pulling away from her?

"Why are you looking at me as if, on the one hand, you wish to devour me and, on the other, I am hurting you unbearably?" he demanded. He finally touched her cheek, briefly. "I have done my absolute best to conduct myself in a proper and restrained manner around you, Francesca."

She inhaled. "You kissed me."

Their gazes locked. "I was exhausted, overworked, drunk."

"I know," she said softly, and her gesture was not conscious or planned—she reached out and cupped his face and the feel of his unshaven skin, his hard jaw, and the edge of his mouth beneath her palm made her faint with need and desire.

He inhaled harshly and seized her hand, but he did not remove it from his cheek. Instead, he held it there and turned his face, kissing her palm heatedly. Francesca cried out.

And somehow she was in his arms, but his grasp was brutal, and he anchored her by the hair pinned at her nape, and his mouth claimed hers, the way she had dreamed it would. Hot, hard, insistent. His tongue thrust past her lips. Francesca felt the wall at her back. She felt her pins falling out, her hair falling down. She felt his loins, heavy and aroused, against her own hips. He kissed her as if he wished to take her there and then.

She found his shoulders and clung to them, for her life.

With his tongue deep inside her, he moved his hands down her back and somehow found her hips. He held her hard against his body, and she became even more aware of his huge arousal. She had to moan, but that only made him slide one hand farther down her backside, anchoring her to him.

She wanted to die. She wanted to fly. She wanted, desperately, to tear off his clothes and then her own.

Suddenly he tore his mouth away from hers, and his lips pressed against the side of her neck, again and again, just as his hips pressed against hers, urgently, demandingly, and then he pushed her face into the crook between his neck and shoulder, and he simply held her, hard and tight, against his own shaking body.

She was shaking, too. Like a leaf. Francesca became aware of her thundering heartbeat and his, an answering drumroll against her breasts. She became aware of his rigid stance, of the power, barely controlled and leashed, within his body, within him. His legs were rock-hard, braced against her thighs, almost hurting her with their strength. His arousal remained obvious, insistent. This man was doing everything he could not to give in to his most basic instincts, she realized. He was doing everything he could to treat her with respect.

It took a long time, but finally, her breathing began to slow.

His heartbeat also began to steady.

His trembling eased and ceased.

Finally, he straightened and looked into her eyes. Francesca could not smile or speak. She was stunned with the intensity of the passion she had felt, from both him and herself. The passion—the urgency. She could only stare—until she realized how dire his expression was. How dire, how grim.

Fear flooded her.

"Bragg?" she whispered. Something was wrong, terribly so, and his name came out frightened and unsure. She was frightened and uncertain now. "What is it?"

"I am corrupting you," he said tersely. "You had better go; you are late. But tomorrow, Francesca, we must talk, once and for all."

And somehow she knew it was a conversation to be avoided, at all costs.

FIFTEEN

Francesca gave up trying to decide what Bragg might wish to say to her the next time that they spoke. But unease filled her—and it was accompanied by dread. No good, she thought, would come of their conversation.

She was also late. Francesca wished she had not broken her word to Julia, because next time, her mother might not be so accommodating when she wished to run about the city at an unusual hour. She hoped Julia had retired for the evening. That would make life so much simpler—for the moment. Because Francesca could not shake the feeling that life would never be simple again.

Jennings had reached the corner of 63d Street and Fifth Avenue and was turning onto the avenue. The brief snowfall had ceased. Fifth Avenue and the park were carpeted with fresh snow. Snow dusted the trees and sat atop the park's stone walls. Stars were emerging in the blue-black night, along with a sliver of incandescent moon. It was a beautiful sight, but Francesca sank deeper into her gloom, failing to appreciate it. On the corner ahead, she could make out the high, steeply pitched roof, the turrets and chimneys of the Cahill mansion. As she espied it, she noticed her brother striding down the steps and out of his private entrance on 62d Street.

Her coach crept forward steadily, the clopping of hoofbeats muffled by the snow. Evan started on foot toward Fifth, his hands in the pockets of his coat, his head down, a scarf thrown carelessly about his shoulders. He had not worn his hat. As he was walking, he must be on the way to the Metropolitan Club, which was but a half-block down, or some other establishment that was almost as close. Her heart sank a bit further. It was Sunday evening. Couldn't he stay home?

And where was he going—or rather, whom was he meeting—and why?

"Jennings, pull up, please. I wish to speak with my brother."

The coach was braked immediately. As it slowed, Evan looked up, and seeing the Cahill brougham, he halted, waiting. Francesca unlatched and pushed open her window, recalling their rather nasty argument the day before. "Hello," she said with feigned cheerfulness. "Is it warm enough to walk? I am on my way home. Do you wish to wait and use the coach?"

"Hello, Fran," Evan said, coming up to the door and peering through the window at her. "I am only going to the club, so I am on foot." He smiled at her. Apparently all was forgotten, if not forgiven. But then, Evan was not one to hold a grudge.

Except, apparently, with Andrew, in the matter of his forthcoming marriage.

"The Metropolitan?" Francesca asked. "Come in out of the cold. Jennings will drop you there."

Evan hesitated, then opened her door and leaped in. "It's actually a nice evening," he said, settling down beside her. "It's warmed up, with the snow and all."

"I would hardly know," Francesca said, frowning now.

"What's wrong?"

"Everything." She tried to smile at him and failed.

"Is it Connie? At least you and mother have seen her. She'll be fine, Fran," he said, patting her knee with real affection. "By now she is home, and she and Neil have begun to patch things up."

Did he really think it would be so easy? Was she the only one who was worried about Connie? Francesca looked at him. "Spoken from a man with a mistress," she could not help herself from murmuring.

Evan had leaned forward. "Jennings, drop me up at the club, please, and then take Francesca home."

"Yes, sir," Jennings replied, and the coach rolled forward.

Evan turned to her. "Fran, I am not married yet. And Sarah

Channing hardly loves me. I think she is afraid of me, if you wish to know the truth. She would not care if she knew about Grace Conway."

"You mistake her quiet manner for timidity and shyness. I did, too, at first."

He sighed. "Please, do not go on and on about the merits of Sarah Channing. Is that why you have waylaid me? I know you wish to speak with me. I can see it in your eyes." He sighed again, more heavily. "I am prepared. Do your worst."

"What does that mean?"

He folded his arms, regarding her. "I am expecting a lecture, about not breaking things off with a certain lady whom I am very fond of. I am sorry we shouted at one another last night, Fran. It is not your affair, but that did not excuse my temper. I blame my lapse on a rather improper amount of gin."

"You got soused. I've never seen you that way before," Francesca said, and it was the truth.

"It is simple. I am a man on his way to the gallows. Why not drown my sorrows?" He smiled at her, but it did not reach his blue eyes.

Francesca hated seeing such sadness there. And she was angry with Andrew for not thinking of his son's feelings, for refusing to even consider undoing the match. She smiled and brushed a stray lock of black hair from his eyes. "Evan, let's call on Sarah tomorrow together," Francesca said impulsively.

"Let's not."

"So now you dislike her? I refuse to believe that; you are too much a gentleman."

"I neither like her nor dislike her, but I saw her the other night. At the opera, remember? You were there. I was courteous and attentive and she, well, perhaps I had better not say." He turned away, but not before she saw him grimace.

"It's important. Please," Francesca cajoled. "You may feel differently about her when we are through."

"I might feel differently about her if she had an opinion and dared to utter it," he said with real exasperation. "And have you noticed that she is reed-thin and as plain as a door-knob?"

"She is petite. She has the most beautiful brown eyes I have ever seen. Her complexion is porcelain-perfect—"

"Enough! If you think to convince me that she is pretty, you will not succeed. She is plain, Fran. Plain, plain, plain." He scowled. "And I am being kind."

"I think you are determined to resist her." It was a sudden insight, one that Francesca hoped was true. The brougham had halted before the imposing granite building that was the club. "I think you would resist any lady Papa brought to you for the purpose of marriage. Perhaps you are simply not ready to wed."

"How astute! Unfortunately, Papa is stone-deaf on this particular subject. The man dictates my entire future, like a tyrant, and will not heed one word I have said." He turned a dark gaze on her. "Or that you have said, on my behalf, and I thank you again, for that."

Francesca had pleaded his case, in vain. She had been shocked by her father's refusal to reconsider the union. "Let's take this one step at a time. It is a long time until June. Much can happen between now and then. Why don't we call on Sarah together, you and I?"

"It is a long time until June!" he exclaimed, incredulous. "June is four months away!"

"Are you panicking?" she asked with worry.

"Wouldn't you? If Mother had done this to you, if, say, Mr. Wily was to be your husband in June, wouldn't you be in a panic?"

She met his gaze and for the very first time she truly understood his plight. "I would not walk down the aisle," she said simply.

He grimaced. "But you would not then be thrown in debtor's prison."

That was true. "Oh, Evan. Well, either you must fall in love with Sarah, or we must find a way out of this. I shall begin working on your dilemma immediately."

He smiled at her and kissed her forehead. "If this were not so dire, I would be frightened."

"Do not be afraid. I shall think this through very carefully, I promise you."

"The way you did with Connie?" He grinned and reached for the door.

She ignored that. "Tomorrow afternoon at four?" Francesca asked. She would show him Sarah's studio. Perhaps, when he saw his fiancée's talent and when he saw her with fire in her eyes, his feelings would take a turn for the better. Surely it could not hurt. Meanwhile, she would do her best to come up with a plan, at least to postpone the nuptials.

"Very well." Evan was about to rise. Francesca restrained him.

"Now what?" he asked, but not with any rancor.

"Evan, something you said to me last night has truly been bothering me."

He searched her gaze, no longer smiling. "I was drunk."

She winced. "Yes, you were. And I do hope you are not intending to drown your sorrows tonight?"

"No, of course not."

She hesitated again.

"Spit it out, Fran. As I know that you will, sooner or later."

She crossed her arms. "Well, last week my understanding was that your debts were of a certain sum." It was a sum she would never forget, for it was vast—impossible. Evan owed $133,000 in gaming debts.

Evan's eyes became hooded. "I do not think my debts are your concern, Fran." His tone was even and he turned to leave.

"Wait! But they are my concern! When you are my brother and I adore you! When Papa is forcing you to marry—"

He cut her off. "He is blackmailing me. Let's not mince words now."

She shivered, taken aback. But he was right, as much as she hated to admit it. In her heart, she still could not believe what Papa was doing. "You haven't been gambling again, have you?"

His face changed. It closed completely, and his eyes became cold. "I am late," he said.

Dismay flooded her. "Do you think to gamble to spite him now? Evan, what if we can raise the money to pay off your debts? Do not increase them!" she cried as he leaped out of the coach.

He stared at her as he closed the door. "No one will lend me that kind of money."

"Perhaps not. But how do we know if we do not try?" she cried.

He shoved his hands in his pockets and stared.

Francesca realized that she was perspiring. "Stay away from the tables. Gaming will not solve anything." He did not move and he did not speak. "And Papa has asked me to speak to you. He says you have ignored him." She waited anxiously for his response.

It was a bitter laugh. "What a coward he is," he said. "Do not bring me any messages from him. And I have not ignored him, Fran; I have cut him out of my life—and my heart."

"Evan!" she cried, aghast. But he was walking away. Francesca unlatched the window, opened it, and poked her head out. "You do not mean that! Papa loves you, just as I know you love him!"

Evan faced her, walking backward. "Love? Like hell he loves me, because if he did, he would not force me to marry some homely little spinster that no man would ever look at twice, a woman whom I find completely boring, a woman whom I shall have to tolerate for the rest of my life. As far as I am concerned, he has lost his rights as my father. I do not *have* a father, Fran." He turned on his heel and strode up the wide granite steps of the Metropolitan Club, where two liveried doormen immediately let him in.

Francesca realized her eyes had filled with tears. She rapped on the partition and said, "Jennings, I will go home now."

MONDAY, FEBRUARY 3, 1902—11:45 A.M.

The old stone church was on the corner of Lexington Avenue and 58th Street. Francesca stepped down from her cab as several mourners entered the eighteenth-century Presbyterian church, their faces suitably somber, heads down. Francesca paused, clutching her purse, just outside of the entrance. She had read that Paul Randall's funeral service was to take place that day at noon, followed by a burial just north of the city in a popular Yonkers cemetery. She had skipped her eleven o'clock biology class in order to attend the church service. Her every instinct had told her that she must not miss the funeral, even though one of her teachers had warned her that she had been absent far too frequently last month.

Sleuthing and the pursuit of a higher education did not, apparently, go hand in hand.

Carriages and taxis continued to pause at the curb to discharge their passengers. Lexington Avenue remained both busy and noisy, mostly because of a series of passing electric trolleys, each one on the heels of another. Francesca was about to go inside when she saw a gleaming cream-colored motorcar rolling to a stop beside a parked carriage, clearly double-parking. It was a Daimler, and there was no mistaking the driver.

The engine died and Bragg got out of the car, his dark brown overcoat left open and swinging about him. As he strode toward her with his agile yet purposeful stride, her heart skidded. He was devastating in appearance this morning, oh, yes. His tawny good looks were just so unusual, so striking.

He had seen her and he smiled, crossing over to the sidewalk carefully, behind the carriage. "Good morning," he said, his regard somehow far too intent. Or was it intimate?

She couldn't help herself; in spite of how dire he had sounded last night, she smiled happily, pleased to see him, to be with him. "Great minds think alike," she said lightly and breathlessly.

"Indeed they do." His gaze moved over her face. "I received a telegram this morning."

Francesca became alert. "From Philadelphia?"

"Do you read minds? Or only mine?" he said teasingly.

She smiled and waited for him to share with her whatever the telegram had contained.

"Bill Randall has a roommate on campus. Alistair Farlane states the last time he saw Bill was Thursday morning. If Bill was in Philadelphia Friday night, as he has claimed, he did not sleep in his college dormitory, or at least, not in his room."

"So I was right," Francesca breathed, watching another taxi pausing at the curb. A woman was inside. "Bill is our intruder."

"It looks that way." Bragg turned. A buxom woman alighted to the street, but she was not Georgette de Labouche.

Their eyes met. "I was hoping she might show up," Francesca confessed.

"I doubt that she will. Any leads?"

She hesitated. "One. I will let you know if it comes to anything."

"I would hope so." He began to smile at her, his gaze soft, and then he glanced sharply aside. But Francesca had also seen the Randall family alighting from a taxi at the exact same time.

Bill Randall was on the curb, helping his mother out of the hansom. In the broad light of day, his face seemed pale and angular, his lanky body far more than slender. In fact, he had a tired and worn, if not sallow, look about him. Was he worried? Overtired? Or merely in the throes of anguish? And why had he lied about when he had arrived in the city—if he did not have something to hide?

"Careful, Mother," he said. "There is melting slush all about."

"Thank you, dear," Henrietta returned weakly, clinging to him as she eased her plump bulk onto the sidewalk. She wore a dark coat, beneath which was a black ensemble, and a black hat with several roses and a half-veil. Francesca tried to discern her state of mind, but it was hard to see through the veil. She clutched a wadded-up handkerchief in one hand, which she kept pressing to her eyes, beneath the veil. Clearly she was still distraught.

"Mary? It's slippery," Bill warned, after leaving his mother on the curb.

Francesca saw Mary posed to alight from the hansom, a too-thin figure in a too-big beige coat, her pinched white face ravaged from days of crying. Her eyes remained red and swollen, as did her nose, in general doing little to aid her in her appearance. She was wearing a hat, sans veil, but her hair seemed unkempt beneath it, shiny tendrils escaping this way and that. She was clutching a faded brown velvet purse almost compulsively.

Francesca felt a pressure on her arm. She glanced at Bragg. He met her gaze and they moved over to Henrietta, who was, for the moment, standing alone.

"Mrs. Randall?" Bragg said softly. "We have come to pay our respects."

She choked on a sob and looked up at them, and as quickly away. "Commissioner Bragg," she gasped, surprised. "Oh, I did not expect you. . . ." She glanced up again, briefly, this time at Francesca. "And Miss Cahill," she breathed. Her gloved fist found her mouth as she fought more sobs.

"We are very sorry," Francesca said, deeply disturbed. She quickly slid off her gloves and clasped the woman's hands, which remained gloved. "If there is anything we can do," she added, encouraging the woman to meet her gaze.

"No, no, thank you," she murmured, and she refused to look up.

Francesca glanced up at Bragg and met his eyes. His expression was wry; he knew exactly what she was up to, she thought.

"We appreciate the offer," Bill Randall said tersely, taking Henrietta's arm and looping it tightly and possessively in his. "Hello, Commissioner. Miss Cahill. Have you found the killer?" His tone was high.

Francesca slipped her gloves back on. Mary was standing beside them. Her eyes were wide, intense, and even angry. "I have heard of no arrests!" she exclaimed.

"There have been no arrests, but we are working round-the-clock on this one," Bragg said calmly. "We shall find our man."

"But you know who murdered our father!" Mary cried, pointing her finger at Bragg. It was shaking.

"Actually, I do not," Bragg said. He nodded politely, as if to leave.

Francesca's insides tightened as she saw Hart climbing out of the most elegant, and by far the largest, coach that had stopped on the block. He was stunning, as always, in a coal black suit and coat. Like Bragg, he wore no hat.

"Perhaps it is time for you to recuse yourself from the investigation," Bill Randall said stiffly. "Have you read today's editorial in the *Times,* Commissioner?"

"I'm afraid not, and if the need arises, you may be sure that I will recuse myself. Shall we go in?" Bragg asked, unperturbed. If he had seen Hart, he gave no sign. Still, Francesca knew he never missed a trick.

Hart was studying them all as he approached. In fact, once he had seen them all, there was no question that he intended to greet them, instead of entering the church. Francesca felt her tension soar. Unquestionably, a scene was in the making.

He met her gaze and winked.

She felt like strangling him. Could he not go inside and behave himself?

Bragg's gaze had become strangely hooded, but Francesca knew he also watched Hart approaching, and she felt that he only pretended indifference. And at that moment Mary turned, saw Calder Hart, and cried out. "There he is! The murderer of our father!" she screamed shrilly.

Hart laughed and paused before the group. Several mourners whirled on the steps of the church in order to gape. Francesca tried to catch his eye, so she could silently convey to him that he must leave the Randalls alone. But now he was not looking at her.

"Henrietta," he intoned, "my dear, dear . . . what? Stepmother? I see you are incoherent with grief. And Billy. You have actually come home to bury your beloved father. And Mary. My sweet, innocent, adoring little sister. May I give one and all my deepest and most sincere regrets?" he asked, and he was laughing still.

Henrietta sank into Bill's arms, apparently in a dead faint.

"Arrest him!" Mary shouted, stomping one foot. "Arrest this . . . this despicable murdering bastard!"

Hart laughed harder.

Bragg turned cold eyes on him. "How clever," he said.

Hart shrugged. "I did my best."

"As usual," Bragg murmured. "Are you happy now?"

"Very." Hart grinned.

Francesca looked from the one to the other and realized that Bragg had expected Hart to show up at the service, in just such a provocative manner.

Suddenly a small man in a suit and top hat was shoving a notepad in front of Mary's face. "Would you swear in court that your half brother murdered your father, Miss Randall?" he demanded, prepared to scribble her response.

Francesca groaned.

"I most certainly would!" Mary cried, practically jumping up and down. "There is no doubt in my mind."

"That is slander, tsk-tsk. Play with fire and you shall get burned," Hart said, clearly not alarmed.

Francesca caught his eye. He was truly enjoying himself.

"Someone help me get Mother inside," Bill huffed, holding her up in his arms. Her head lolled to the side. And she had, of course, dropped her handkerchief.

No one moved.

Except Bragg, who had taken the notepad out of the man's hands and now threw it in the street. "Get lost," he said. "Before I take today's *Tribune* and use it to render you speechless."

The reporter blanched and fled. And standing behind him was Arthur Kurland, the reprehensible reporter from the *Sun*.

"Will someone, anyone, help me with Mother?" Bill asked heavily again.

Hart chuckled and held out his arm to Francesca. "May I?"

She shook her head no, and as she did so, she saw Henrietta slam closed one eye beneath the veil. Francesca froze as Bragg put his arm underneath the heavyset woman in order to help Bill. Henrietta Randall was pretending to swoon.

When the woman was standing rather solidly, moaning and pretending to have regained consciousness, Bragg stepped aside.

Kurland took his notepad from his breast pocket. "Miss Randall seems to have no doubts as to who murdered her father," he said to Bragg. "Have you officially interrogated your *brother*, Commissioner? Does he have an alibi for the night of the murder? I believe he was at White's party—but the victim died earlier in the evening."

"No comment," Bragg said brusquely.

Francesca's insides seemed to curdle. She did not like Kurland's expression, much less his question. And now the reporter from the *Sun* was staring at Hart.

"May I ask you some questions?" Kurland asked.

"No." Hart turned away brusquely.

"Perhaps I shall interview two young ladies . . . er, two young women!" Kurland called to his back.

Francesca froze. He knew. He knew about Hart's lie; somehow he had uncovered the truth.

Hart whirled, his expression black with rage. Kurland took a step backward, but Hart stalked him. "You may speak with anyone you wish," Hart ground out softly.

"Did you lie about your whereabouts that evening?" Kurland cried, clearly frightened.

Suddenly Hart had the man by the throat. "Prepare yourself for my lawsuit," he said viciously as Kurland began to choke.

"Calder!" Francesca screamed.

Bragg grabbed his brother. "Let him go, Calder! Let him be!"

Hart released the reporter, who doubled over, choking and gasping for air.

Bragg dragged Hart away. "Are you insane?" he hissed. "You may as well have begged the man to set his sights upon you! He will gun for you now."

Hart shrugged Bragg off as Francesca came up to them. "I

lost my temper," he said. His gaze turned to Francesca. Their eyes met.

"I did not say a word to anyone—except Bragg," she said quickly. "Calder, I had to tell him. Because you are in trouble now, even though I know you are innocent." She spoke very softly, so no one might overhear them.

He stared at her. "I spoke to you in confidence."

"I know. I'm sorry. I did not feel that I had a choice." Hart straightened his suit, then looked at Bragg.

"I have not said a word, not even to my foremost detective. Kurland has done his own homework," Bragg said grimly.

Hart brushed some dust from his sleeve. "Apparently."

"Why did you lie in the first place?" Bragg asked quietly.

"Why not?" Hart said with a shrug.

Bragg stared grimly. Then he glanced at Francesca. "I am going inside with the Randalls. I shall try to speak with Bill after the service."

Francesca nodded, relieved that the intense moment had passed. She smiled a little at him, and he smiled in return. And for one moment, their gazes held.

She watched him walk over to the family, admiring the set of his shoulders, the length of his stride. Hart breathed, "Star-crossed lovers. And so the drama goes on."

She flinched. "What are you talking about?"

"You and my brother," he said, his dark eyes upon her.

Dread filled her. A very vivid and bittersweet memory of last night assailed her. "Why would we be star-crossed? What do you know that I do not?"

His eyes widened slightly with surprise. "Well, well. My brother has been keeping secrets. I do believe it is time for the service to begin. Shall we?" He held his arm out to her.

Francesca nodded, finally smiling and about to give him her arm when someone brushed her from behind. Startled, she whirled and came face-to-face with a stranger.

The man said in a hushed and urgent whisper, "I must speak to you, Miss Cahill. Alone, after the service."

"What?" she cried.

"Ssh." The man stood eye-to-eye with her. He wore a

proper although ill-fitting suit and coat, his brown fedora pulled low over swarthy and rather rough, although attractive, features. Had he not been in a suit, he might have been a prizefighter, for although he was not tall, he had broad shoulders and an equally broad chest. Francesca guessed him to be about thirty. "Make sure you get rid of the police commissioner."

She gaped, looking into a pair of startling sea green eyes.

"Francesca?" Hart said from behind her, with concern.

"I am Mark Anthony," the stranger said.

She gasped. And before she could react, he rushed away.

SIXTEEN

Had Hart not been present, she would have shouted after Anthony or followed him. She did not know what he wanted, but there had been no mistaking the urgency in his tone. She could not wait to speak with him now. Francesca was elated. She had found Mark Anthony! Or rather, he had found her!

"Good news?"

The sexy murmur was breathed into her ear and it tickled her skin. She looked up, into Hart's bemused and beguiling dark eyes. "You are the busiest body I know," she said, almost meaning it.

He grinned, his spirits obviously having rebounded. "But that excludes yourself."

She ignored that. What did Anthony want? She was on pins and needles now.

"And who is that prizefighter?"

She blinked. "Excuse me?"

"You are very distracted, Francesca. Clearly that gentleman is preoccupying your thoughts now—although I daresay he looked rather disreputable. Who is he?"

Francesca was saved from answering when a church clock began striking the noon hour, somewhere close by.

Instantly bells all over the city began ringing. The effect was, as always, magnificent.

Hart laughed. "I am heartbroken that you find me so uninteresting. Let's go in. The service is about to begin."

She gave him her arm, relieved that he did not press her about Anthony. They started forward. "So why did you come, Hart? Why are you really here?"

He shrugged. "To let them know they will not keep me away."

"I think you are here to mourn your father's passing," she said pointedly.

"How romantic you are," he said, somewhat fondly. And then he stopped in his tracks.

His action halted her, as well. She followed his gaze and saw Neil striding toward them. Her heart stopped and she stared.

Montrose seemed ravaged. He looked terrible—as if he had not slept in days. He had not shaved, either, and with his rumpled suit, he looked incredibly dissipated. What was this? Montrose was clearly looking for her—he must have gone to the house and learned that she was attending the Randall funeral. But why was he there? Hadn't Connie gone home last night? Or had she returned, but things had worsened, instead of getting better?

"Now what could this be?" Hart murmured.

Francesca tensed, dropping Hart's arm. "Calder, I must speak with Neil. I will be in shortly," she said.

Hart followed her regard. "Are you certain you wish to be left alone with him? He seems to have taken a turn for the worse. And what *is* wrong with your brother-in-law?"

She bit her lip. "I have no idea," she lied.

Hart gave her a look and a shake of his head, clearly aware of her pretense, and he moved away. Francesca took a deep breath. Across an expanse of about ten feet, her gaze locked with Neil's. There was no mistaking how distraught he was. "You must be looking for me," she said, not moving.

"Yes, I am," he said grimly.

Francesca realized she had begun to tremble. She moved closer to Neil, aware that Hart had paused on the church steps, ostensibly to roll a cigarette. She knew his game—he was determined to eavesdrop upon them—but could not even begin to brood upon it now. "What is it? It's Connie, isn't it? Is she all right?" She tried to keep her voice down so Hart could not overhear.

"How would I know whether she is all right or not when I haven't seen her in two days?" he returned unevenly.

Francesca felt herself blanch. "Connie did not come home?" she gasped.

"No, she did not! Do you know where she is? Have you seen her?" he demanded.

She could only stare. Why hadn't Connie returned? Last night she had said that she would.

"Francesca, I am here to ask you for your help. As you now consider yourself a sleuth, I am here asking you to find my wife, before any more damage is done." His turquoise eyes held hers.

"I saw her last night. She went to Beth Anne's."

Relief flooded his features. "And the girls?"

"They are fine." Francesca bit her lip, uncertain of what to say.

And suddenly Neil was angry. "Why is she doing this? Does she want the whole world to know of our impasse? Or does she think to humiliate me? We have had callers, Francesca. I have told our friends that Connie is not well, and that she is abed. But very soon, the entire world as we know it shall know that she has left me!"

"Neil." She took his hand. "She is coming home; I am certain of it."

"She had better," he said grimly. And it was a threat.

Francesca stiffened. "What?"

"How much more of this kind of behavior do you think I can—or will—take?" he asked.

"What does that mean?" she asked cautiously.

"It means that I am becoming angry," he said. "I am truly sorry for what I have done, and if I could, I would change the past. But I cannot, damn it. And enough is enough."

Francesca stared and their gazes held. In that moment, she knew he genuinely regretted what he had done, and she found that she herself could—and did—forgive him. In that moment, she recalled why she had loved Neil from the moment she had met him, when he had come to court her sister five years ago. He was a noble man after all. Perhaps his only flaw was that he was human.

"I want my family back. I want her back, now. But perhaps by the time she decides to come back, it will be too late," he said grimly.

"Neil! You do not mean that!" Francesca cried, horrified.

"I came here to ask you to find my wife. But now I know where she is. I am expecting her to come home—today." He gave her a long, dark look—one filled with warning.

"I understand," Francesca said.

"Good." He turned on his heel and strode away.

"Oh, Neil," she whispered, and she shivered, but he was already gone, moving rapidly down the street, his strides long and angry. Francesca closed her eyes. She had a terrible feeling that this might not end the way everyone was predicting. Connie and Neil were not behaving like mature or sensible adults. Connie hadn't come home, and Neil was becoming angry. And clearly the longer this impasse went on, the worse it would become. And had Neil been suggesting that he might not take Connie back if she did not return swiftly? Francesca hoped not. She refused to believe it.

"So your sister has left Montrose."

Francesca stiffened with dread. Just then, Hart was the very last man on the face of the planet with whom she wished to speak—especially about Connie and Montrose. Slowly she turned.

His gaze was filled with speculation. He smiled a little at her and said nothing more, staring after Montrose.

Which was worse than any mockery could ever be.

The service was over and the mourners were standing and crowding into the aisle of the church in order to leave. Francesca waited her turn, Hart behind her. As they had entered the church together, somewhat late, they had sat together as well, in one of the last of the occupied pews. The church had not been full. Francesca had counted twenty-three mourners.

Bill Randall had given a loving eulogy, during which Henrietta and Mary had wept—or so it had appeared. Apparently Paul had been a warm and wonderful father. Or so Bill was now claiming.

Georgette de Labouche had not appeared at her lover's funeral. Was she truly that frightened of the police? Or was she, Francesca wondered suddenly, heartless?

She stepped into the aisle, aware of Hart exerting a small pressure upon her arm with which to guide her. It was most unnecessary; still, she rather enjoyed his attention. She glanced toward the front of the church; Bragg had sat behind the family in the second row of pews, and he was regarding the crowd now as he waited to step into the aisle himself. She felt certain he was filing away information to himself on all those who were in attendance, hoping for a clue that might lead them to Randall's killer. As she filed out, she saw, from the corner of her eye, his gaze veer to her and Hart.

She debated telling him about Mark Anthony, then decided she would meet Georgette's brother first, briefly, to see what it was that he wanted. She smiled to herself then, having a mental image of herself handing over Georgette de Labouche to Bragg. He would be quite impressed with her sleuthing indeed.

Across the crowded church, she smiled at him.

He did not seem to notice.

Sobering, Francesca finally reached the steps of the church and found herself standing on the street outside with Hart. She instantly saw Anthony. He was seated inside a livery that was double-parked next to another vehicle, a few coaches up the block from where Bragg had left his motorcar. Anthony was watching out his window, undoubtedly for her, and when he saw her, their gazes locked. Immediately he pulled the shade down.

Francesca turned to Hart to murmur some kind of pleasantry, but saw Bragg emerging onto the stone steps. Hart said, "May I give you a lift? It would be my pleasure."

As always, when he spoke, he somehow insinuated his warm tone with an inflection that was utterly sensual and rather irresistible; she looked up and saw him smiling, his eyes warm. It was so easy to understand why someone like Daisy should be fond of him. "I appreciate the offer, but I have some errands to run," she said quickly.

Speculation filled his gaze. "I should still be delighted to drop you wherever your errands may take you," he said, his gaze sliding over her features, rather lingeringly, one by one.

It was as if he enjoyed every aspect of her appearance and was, indeed, savoring it.

She flushed a little. She had to meet Anthony; she declined. The words were hardly out of her mouth when Bragg stepped up to them by the curb and said, "That will not be possible, Calder."

It was funny, how quickly Calder's posture changed. Before Bragg had even completed his sentence, Calder's hands fell to his sides, his shoulders straightened and stiffened, and his smile became a sneer. Even the warm light in his eyes changed, turning into something sardonic and mocking. "Anything is possible," Hart returned smoothly. "And I fear my heart is broken now." He smiled at Francesca with a flash of his white teeth, placing his hand upon his chest. He was clearly in jest, and Francesca did smile in return.

Bragg faced his half brother more squarely. "I have some questions to ask you. I am afraid they cannot wait. I shall be happy to give you a lift so we can speak, but it would be more convenient if we went to my office." He gestured toward his motorcar.

Hart's eyes seemed to flicker just barely with surprise or something else. "I am afraid I have appointments, back-to-back, this entire afternoon. It *is* Monday."

"I am sorry, but you will have to cancel one or two, depending upon how long this will take." Bragg remained courteous but firm.

"I am afraid my meetings are extremely important ones. Some of us do work for our livings." Hart grinned. It was mirthless.

"I am afraid I am not giving you an option. Be sensible, Calder. You have lied—to the authorities, I might add—and you are the victim's son. I need to solve this case, and perhaps you can be of help. Let's go. Send your driver on. This will not take that long—not if you cooperate."

Hart no longer smiled. He stared back at Bragg. "Perhaps you are feeling pressure to question me—because less than an hour ago a reporter cast aspersions upon your management of this investigation?"

Bragg stared as coldly. "Perhaps. You may think what you will. But I will ask you some questions, come hell or high water. Today," he added flatly.

Francesca wanted to butt in. She did not dare.

"I am a busy man," Hart snapped.

"You may ride with me, or, if you prefer, I can call for a police wagon," Bragg said in a too-silken tone.

Francesca realized what was happening. His simple request to ask a few informal questions was escalating dangerously now. "Bragg!" she cried, dismayed. He was taking Calder downtown for questioning? To police headquarters? Was this truly necessary? "Surely you can quickly ask Hart some questions now! Here!"

Bragg shot her an annoyed look. "We will speak later, Francesca," he said, and it was an extremely firm dismissal.

But she did not move. She did not dare, as she sensed an imminent conflagration. It felt like it might be a horrific hurricane.

Hart said, "It is one o'clock. I have a meeting in half an hour in my Pearl Street office with two Englishmen who happen to be two emissaries from China. I have worked long and hard for this appointment, and I do not intend to miss it. A huge shipping contract depends upon it."

"And I have a dead man on my hands—one who happens to be your father. Let's go." Bragg's eyes had darkened impossibly. Francesca sensed that he was losing his temper now. He gripped Hart's arm.

Anger flooded Hart's face. He shrugged Bragg off. "So now you pull rank on me? Is this because, for once in your life, you have the power to do so?"

"No, Calder, this is because your father is dead, murdered, in fact, and you knowingly lied to me about your whereabouts on the evening of the murder, digging yourself into quite the hole," Bragg replied coldly.

Hart stared. "No. You are in your shining glory and we both know it. This once, you have power. This once, you can actually force me to your will. This is not about Randall, Rick. This is about you and me."

Bragg laughed, and it was such a cold sound that Francesca felt chills rippling up and down her body. "I should have expected you to think in such a way. After all, you have no honor, so you would not understand the notions most of us live by. It is my duty to find Randall's killer, whoever he— or she—might be. It is also my duty to question you, now, about your misleading testimony. You have lied to the authorities, Calder. That was not a good idea. It is a criminal offense."

"So charge me," Hart said coldly, and he began to walk away.

And Francesca saw the anger flood Bragg's face. Impulsively she reached out and grabbed him, crying, "Let him go. He did not do it, Bragg!"

"You stay out of this," he said, his tone amazingly level and calm. She quickly dropped her hand.

"Hart. Do not make me arrest you."

Hart stiffened. He stopped in his tracks and he turned. "Perhaps I shall. Rathe and Grace would love you for that." He laughed. It was an ugly sound.

"You may come downtown willingly, or I shall have my roundsmen bring you down. But we will speak, in my office, privately—one way or another."

Hart stared, and he shook his head no.

Francesca ran to him. "Hart! You must go. You must answer Bragg's questions! Forget that he is your brother; he is the police commissioner. He is not doing this to hurt you. He must find your father's killer! And you did lie," she cried pleadingly, lowering her voice for this last declaration.

He met her gaze. "I did trust you," he said.

She flushed and bit her lip. She realized that her hand was clamped on his arm. Even through his coat and jacket, she could feel an arm of steel. "I had to tell Bragg. After all, he is your brother, and I know you did not murder your father. Still, that lie is so suspicious. We want to *help* you, Calder."

"No. *You* want to help me. Your golden lover would love nothing more than to put me behind bars—in his jail cell."

She gasped, about to protest, but it was Bragg who did so. "That is not true. And you know it."

Calder's gaze slid over his half brother like a sleek snake shedding his skin.

"Please do not make this worse than it has to be," Francesca said softly. "Please, Calder."

His gaze seemed to soften as he glanced at her. He then glanced at his pocket watch and nodded. "Very well." Then, "Only a beautiful and determined woman could work such wiles on me in this particular instance." He shook his head again, as if not quite understanding himself.

Francesca stepped back, inordinately relieved. She turned to Bragg, smiling.

He did not smile back. His look was hard and cold—and directed at her. She flinched. He was angry with her, too? But she was only trying to help him—and to smooth over the brewing conflict.

"Let's go," he said to Hart.

"In a moment. I wish to speak with my driver," Hart said, already walking away as if indifferent now to the meeting he had resisted so furiously just a moment before.

Francesca trembled a little.

Bragg said to her, "Do not interfere in police business again. I mean it." And even though he did not raise his voice, Francesca saw the anger in his eyes, and she recoiled, crushed.

He wasn't angry—he was livid.

He walked away.

Anthony did not step out of his coach. But after Bragg had driven off with Hart, Francesca went to the hired hansom and stepped up and into it. She sat down facing him, her back to the driver, arranging her navy blue skirts as she did so.

Under other circumstances, she would be filled with curiosity as to what he wanted. Now, she felt ill. Bragg was so angry with her, and it was unfair. And she hated leaving the two brothers alone—she would die to be a fly on the wall of Bragg's office.

Did she dare?

"Thanks, Miss Cahill, for meeting me," Anthony said, interrupting her thoughts. He had removed his hat, which lay on the torn squab beside his thigh. His hair was that unusual shade that was neither blond nor brown but somewhere in between. A long lock fell over one eye. The carriage began to move away from the curb.

"Where are we going?" Francesca cried, startled and instantly frightened. Of course, he could not be abducting her!

"Georgette wants to speak to you. It is urgent," he returned, his gaze unwavering.

Francesca stared. His powerful body seemed stiff with tension, yet his face appeared relaxed, and his eyes were veiled—she could not read his emotions. Then, "Where is she?"

He grimaced. "You know she thinks the coppers suspect her of murdering Randall—the man she loved. She will not come forward, and she will not reveal where she is. But she *must* talk to you," he said with some urgency.

"And I wish nothing more than to speak with her," Francesca said, worried. The livery had turned onto Lexington Avenue and was moving slowly downtown, crushed by an electric trolley, a horse-drawn omnibus, and several huge lorries. "This is very unorthodox."

"Yes, it is, but murder is hardly orthodox, now is it?" He smiled a little then. When he smiled he had a dimple, and that, paired with the cleft in his chin, his green eyes, and his high cheekbones, gave him a very roguish look. Mark Anthony was short, and Francesca suspected he was exactly her height of five feet, five inches tall, but she doubted that deterred the ladies from admiring him.

She did not relax and she did not smile back. "If she will not reveal her whereabouts, how can she be certain that I will not do so?"

"Isn't she your client?" He grinned, his eyes wide with feigned innocence.

Their gazes met. Francesca flushed. Somehow, word had gotten back to Georgette that Francesca was claiming to represent her. She could only assume the culprit to be her new assistant, Joel. "It is not quite official," Francesca murmured. "But I have been hoping that she would allow me to sleuth on her behalf."

"How much?"

"I beg your pardon?"

"How much will you charge her?" He leaned back now in his seat. As he did so, his brown suit jacket opened, revealing a gun. Francesca stared at it. It was tucked into the waistband of his pants. Perhaps he *was* a boxer. His abdomen was absolutely flat and appeared to be as hard as his chest looked.

He followed her gaze but only said, "My gun has nothing to do with you. I always carry it; it's for self-protection."

"It has been my experience that only criminals and law enforcement officials carry weapons," Francesca said tightly.

His brows lifted. "Are you calling me a crook?" He grinned. His grin was lopsided.

"I meant no such thing." She was perspiring. She did not particularly trust this man. Worse, he carried a weapon. But she had to speak with Georgette. "My intention was to represent your sister for free," Francesca said tersely.

He looked at her oddly, with amusement. "Really? That's so kind of you." He leaned forward. "Well, it's been my experience that nobody does nothing for nothing." He sat back up.

"I do not believe she killed anyone," Francesca said, and even as she was speaking, she wondered if this man was the killer. He carried a gun. It was not a small gun—and the murder weapon had been found—but he looked like the kind of man who lived outside of the law, as he pleased. He was dressed like a gentleman, but that did not fool Francesca. She sensed he was not of her ilk and he never would be. In fact, in a way, he reminded her of Calder Hart. But on the other hand, Hart seemed like a perfect gentleman in comparison to Anthony.

God, was she riding about the city with a killer? And what if this was a trap?

"And I do things for free, as you put it, for others who

have need of me in one way or another," Francesca added primly. She stared at his rough-hewn face. Now she was noticing a scar by his left eye. His brows were darker than his hair and very pronounced.

"My sister has no need of charity, not from anyone," Mark Anthony said, and he chuckled.

She could not understand the source of his amusement. "To the contrary, your sister is a prime suspect in the Randall Killing, as far as the police commissioner is concerned," Francesca said. And the moment the words popped out, she regretted them.

"Really? Is that what that damned leatherhead thinks?" Anthony's lips took on a vicious twist.

Francesca did not particularly care for his sudden anger. "He has several suspects," she managed. "But in any case, to offer my services for free is not about charity, Mr. Anthony. I do not think your sister a murderess. I suspect she would not hire me, should I demand a fee, so it is the interest of serving justice that motivates me."

He stared at her, his sea green eyes incredulous. "Only the rich," he said with a shake of his head. His wavy hair was too long; it reached his shirt collar.

Francesca shrugged. "I have no inclination to change your worldview."

"My what?" He stared. "Just listen carefully, Miss Cahill. Be ready at seven tonight. I'll come round and take you to Georgette."

She was surprised. "But that is not where we are now going?"

He also seemed surprised. "No, that is not where we are going. I only asked to speak to you. I'll pick you up tonight."

She stared at him. Did she dare venture out into the city with this man, whom she did not know or trust?

She could not refuse Mark Anthony. But she would bring Joel, and maybe, this time, she would tell Bragg where she was going, and why.

"All right. But I shall bring my assistant with me."

He folded brawny arms over his broad chest. "The kid?" He laughed.

"Yes."

He continued to grin, shaking his head. "OK. But no coppers. Especially not your *friend*, Bragg." His grin was gone. He stared coldly at her.

Chills swept over her. She bit her lip. She did not dare bring Bragg—and what had that inflection meant?

"I mean it. I see a single fly, and no Georgette."

She nodded slowly, reluctant and filled with regret.

He rapped on the partition to gain the driver's attention. "Pull over," he said.

Francesca glanced out of her window—they had reached 39th Street. The neighborhood was a commercial one, and it seemed to be filled with immigrant workmen, hurrying to and fro with their equipment, bundles, and carts. Wagons and lorries predominated in the traffic; she saw neither a trolley nor a cab anywhere in sight. She did not especially wish to walk around this neighborhood alone.

But Mark Anthony was the one to leap out of the cab. He slapped on his fedora and banged on the hansom. "Take the lady anywhere she wishes to go," he said, not looking at the driver. "It was a pleasure meeting you, Miss Cahill. Sorry, but you'll have to pay the fare."

She looked into his dancing eyes and was not amused. "Don't you need my address?"

"For the 'Marble Palace'? I don't think so." He laughed again and rapped his fist on the cab to tell the driver he could go.

"One more thing," Francesca said. "Is your name really Mark Anthony?"

He laughed. "It's one of them." He turned and as suddenly he faced her again. "By the way, Georgette is *not* my sister." And laughing, he strode away.

Surprised, Francesca stared after him. What was this? Anthony was not Georgette's brother? Who was he, then?

Francesca did not like this sudden turn of events. Surely he was not Georgette's lover—she had been Randall's mistress. But something was definitely amiss, and she had no intention of walking into a trap. Her every instinct was telling her that Anthony was involved in the Randall murder. But was he a killer? He would certainly have the motive if he were Georgette's lover.

He made a much better suspect than either Georgette de Labouche or Hart.

Francesca trembled, but not with fear. She realized she was on the verge of finding a killer.

"Where to, miss?"

She swiftly gathered her thoughts. And determination overcame her. "Police headquarters," she said.

The headquarters of the city's police department was just beyond Mulberry Bend, an impoverished neighborhood of saloons and cribs frequented by gangs and thugs, where every possible type of criminal business was conducted. In fact, pickpockets, hoodlums, prostitutes, and crooks of all sorts were not swayed by the proximity of police headquarters and ran their affairs as if roundsmen were not standing on nearby street corners. Every time Francesca came to 300 Mulberry, she was amazed anew by the audacity of the local populace and the indifference of the police force.

Now she paid the cabbie a ridiculous fare, quite certain she was being swindled—although he insisted his fare for waiting on the street was a dollar an hour. Two roundsmen were standing in front of the brownstone that housed the police, looking bored and watching boys playing jacks out of the corner of their eye. A woman in a fur coat dyed a shocking burgundy, who was clearly a prostitute, stood just across the dirty brown street from the coppers, and she was clearly trying to attract business for herself. Two men sat on an opposite stoop, swilling beer, Francesca presumed, from pails. She doubted either one could stand upright.

Francesca stepped gingerly over a pile of manure, then avoided a pile of slushy garbage, making it safely to the curb. Bragg's roadster stood out like a sore thumb, parked right in front of the brownstone. It had attracted a crowd of gawking men and boys and two more ladies of ill repute.

The roundsmen glanced at her as she walked past them and inside. Francesca knew from experience that ladies did not *ever* enter the premises.

As usual, the scene inside the reception room was rather frenetic: several uniformed officers were behind a long desk, one of whom she recognized. Numerous citizens sat on a wooden bench, apparently waiting their turn to speak to or complain to the police. Two civilians, one a man and the other a woman, both in the shabby and threadbare garb of underpaid and overworked laborers, were speaking with different officers, loudly and unhappily. Francesca gathered that the man had had his purse cut, but she could not overhear the woman's complaints.

Another man stood a few feet from them in manacles. He seemed bored and sullen; clearly he was a criminal about to be arrested, and an officer was gripping his arm firmly, as if afraid he might escape. Several reporters also hovered about the front desk—in their shabby suits, bowler hats, and oversize overcoats, they stood out as journalists awaiting a scoop. One seemed to be arguing with a sergeant.

Francesca was relieved; Arthur Kurland was not in sight.

And in the background, adding to the din of arguments and conversation, typewriters were clacking and the telegraph was pinging. Somewhere, a telephone was also ringing.

Francesca approached the front desk. The burly bald officer saw her and smiled. "Hello, Miss Cahill," he said.

She was elated and she smiled at him. "Sergeant O'Malley, how are you?"

"Fine, thank you, ma'am. The commissioner is in. Go right up," he said, smiling at her.

Francesca was about to thank him when another officer walked over to them. He was also in his thirties, but he had a full head of dark hair. "Commissioner has asked not to be disturbed, O'Malley," he said. "Who's this?" He peered at her through horn-rimmed spectacles.

"Miss Cahill, a friend of the c'mish."

Francesca smiled and extended her hand bravely. The second officer had an additional bar above his lapel; clearly he outranked O'Malley.

"Captain Shea," he said, looking at her hand as if he did not know what it was. Finally, he took it.

"I am a good family friend," Francesca said brightly. "And, in fact, I helped Mr. Bragg solve the Burton Abduction."

He squinted at her. "You're the dame—I mean the lady—who was imprisoned, right? With the boy? Yeah, that was you!"

She nodded proudly. "Yes, that was I."

Shea absorbed that. "Bragg doesn't want to be disturbed, but why don't you go on up and take a seat? I'm sure he'll see you when his business is concluded."

Francesca beamed at him, thanked him, and made her way to the elevator. It was wonderful, being able to walk right into police headquarters and then be treated with such deference. She wondered if she should have shown O'Malley and Shea her business cards.

The cage arrived. Francesca was about to open it—there was no elevator man in this building—when someone tapped her shoulder. Francesca turned, and instantly her heart sank like a rock to her feet.

For the small reporter who had tried to question Mary Randall outside of the church, and who had then had his notebook torn out of his hand by Bragg, stood facing her with bright eyes and a wide smile. "Might we have a word, Miss Cahill?"

The last person she wished to speak with was a darned reporter; she knew now from experience how much trouble that might bring. "I'm afraid I am late." She felt how brittle her smile was—it felt more like a baring of her teeth—and she started to move into the elevator.

He barred her way. "Do you think Calder Hart is guilty?"

"No, I do not," she snapped.

"Why? Even Bragg thinks him guilty."

"Oh? Has he said that? And I do not recall your name, sir," she said coldly.

"Walter Isaacson, with the *Trib*. If Bragg does not think him guilty, then why drag him downtown? And how well do you know Hart, Miss Cahill?" He smiled at her.

She stiffened. "I will not even presume to tell you why the commissioner does anything. You will have to ask him that. You are blocking my way."

"Calder Hart is rather notorious. And he's the city's most eligible bachelor. Is he courting you? Is that why you are so eager to defend him?"

She felt herself flush and saw the light in his eyes, which reminded her of a cash register ringing. *Aha!* it seemed to say. "I have only met Mr. Hart for the first time the other day. Not that I see how it is your business, Mr. Isaacson. But I am a very good judge of character, and I feel certain he is innocent of the Randall Killing."

"What did you and Hart talk about at the church today? Did he escort you to the service?"

She blinked at him. "What?"

"I saw the two of you sitting together. Clearly you have known him more than a few days. Where was he on the night of the murder? He has refused to speak with the press, and that has not been a good idea. The city wants answers, Miss Cahill. Perhaps you can provide them?"

She looked down at the small, wiry man, despising him. "I have nothing to say. Now, will you excuse me or should I call the police? And then who shall explain that you will not allow me to get into the elevator?"

He stepped away. "I do apologize, Miss Cahill, if I have inconvenienced you," he said, seeming sincere. "I am only trying to get to the truth."

Briefly their eyes met. Walter was, she thought, about her own age, and he wore large wire eyeglasses, making his eyes seem huge behind the lenses. Briefly, he seemed to be telling the truth. *The truth*. She wanted to find it, too. "Good day." She nodded and stepped into the cage, pulling the slatted iron door closed with effort. She released the lever, then looked through the iron bars at Isaacson. He stared and she stared back as the cage began to ascend to the second floor. Finally, he was out of sight.

Thank God.

Bragg's office was on the second floor. Francesca had no intention of taking a seat on the wood bench in the hall outside his door. None of the passing police officers paid her any mind, the doors closest to his office were closed, and at the end of the hall everyone worked in one room, with small desks on top of desks. Francesca went right up to his door. The top half was thick frosted glass, and she could not see through it. But she could certainly hear.

They were arguing.

And as she had feared, it was about to become a brawl.

Francesca dashed inside.

SEVENTEEN

Hart walked into Bragg's office, his hands moving to his hips. As Bragg shut the door behind them, Hart glanced around at the Spartan quarters. He saw two desks, piles of files and folders, books, and journals. The desk where his half brother worked contained a telephone. It was not a comfortable room. There was one chair, with a rattan back, that rocked behind the desk, and two worn and shabby chairs in front, for visitors. He eyed Bragg but did not make a mocking comment, even though one would be richly deserved.

Hart watched Bragg move to his desk, but he did not sit down. That left both men facing each other in the center of the room. Because it was the middle of the winter, the room's single window was closed, effectively shutting out all of the sounds from the street below. The office had a rather unpleasant view of almost the entire block of Mulberry Street and its inhabitants, all of whom were riffraff and crooks—and that included the police. Just below the window, Bragg's automobile could be seen. It was ridiculously incongruous, gleaming, expensive, brand-new, sitting there amid the muck and grime of the street and its residents.

"Why the false alibi?" Bragg asked calmly, cutting into the brief silence.

"Why not?" Hart smiled and shrugged. He would never give his half brother an inch.

"Might I presume you wished to make the investigation of your father's death a more difficult one? Or did you only hope to make my life more difficult—as usual?"

Bragg had remained calm. Hart grinned. "Would you have believed me if I had told you the truth?" he challenged.

"No."

"I did not think so." Hart moved to the scarred wood mantel over the fireplace. It needed beeswax and hours of polishing. He lifted a framed photograph of Rick standing with a beautiful red-haired woman, who was exactly Hart's own age, with two boys and a little girl. Everyone was smiling. The woman was Rick's half sister, Lucy Savage, and the children were hers.

He considered Lucy a sister, but she wasn't his sister, for they shared not one drop of blood.

There were other pictures on the mantel, including one of Rick with the city's mayor, Seth Lowe, and another of him standing on the steps of a building that was perhaps a federal one with Theodore Roosevelt. Hart wondered where the rest of the family photographs were. Undoubtedly Rick had dozens.

Bragg sighed and walked over to his desk. He lifted a thin folder from it and turned back to Hart. "Spending a part of the night alone in a mansion like yours will not hold up in a court of law. In fact, a good prosecuting attorney will work such an alibi against you very quickly, and very easily."

"I have assumed so," Hart said. Softly he added, "And you will hardly shed a tear if I am carted off to jail."

Bragg stared, his gaze hard. "Not if you are guilty, Calder. Not if, this single time, you have gone too far."

"And if I haven't?"

"If you have not broken the law, then I will find out who has."

"Such determination," Hart mocked. "As always, the good brother rides his white charger in the pursuit of liberty and justice."

Bragg's jaw tightened and he stepped up to his brother. They stood almost eye-to-eye. Bragg was an inch taller, actually, and Hart knew he was about ten pounds heavier, for his frame was larger, his shoulders wider. "Why in God's name did you dismiss the staff for the evening?"

"I felt like it," was Hart's easy reply.

Bragg stared. "I happen to know how much you have hated Randall your entire life. I was there, remember?" he said softly—and not pleasantly.

Hart refused to ever think about their childhood, before Lily had died. "I will even swear to it in court," Hart returned easily. "Yes, Rick, I hated my own father. Tsk-tsk. What a horrid man I am." Hart shuddered and then he laughed.

"Save the theatrics for an audience who is interested; I am not," Bragg snapped. "The real question is, did you or didn't you do the deed?"

"I am not going to keep repeating myself."

"So why the lie? Please answer me, Calder."

"Let's just say that I have an amazing instinct for self-preservation," he said.

Bragg stared. "Yes, you do. You always have." He sighed. "The truth is, I think you are too smart to have murdered Randall in such a stupid manner. The truth is, while you are extremely hot-tempered and as passionate, you are one of the most intelligent men that I know. The crime was not one of passion. It was premeditated. Randall was shot from behind. Someone followed him to Miss de Labouche's with the intention of killing him there."

"Bravo," Hart said. He happened to agree with Bragg.

"As much as you hated your father, you have hated him for years. So why murder him now? I cannot find motivation," Bragg said.

Hart watched him closely. He did not speak.

"Oh, come. Or do you hate me so much that you will not share your insights with me?"

Hart smiled. "It's not my place to do your job. I mean, you did take this thankless position." He shook his head. "Even though we grew up together, your ambitions never cease to amaze me. Why would anyone want to be the city's chief of police?"

"I am the city's police commissioner—I have yet to appoint a chief of police. And someone has to take on the corruption in the ranks." Bragg sank one hip down on the edge of his desk. "But I do not expect you to understand what, precisely, motivates me."

"Doesn't being so good all the time get old? Tiresome? Boring, even?" Hart knew that it must.

"We are talking about who might want Randall dead."

"Other than myself? I have no idea. I have had nothing to do with the man. As you should know."

"I heard you dined with him on Tuesday. Did he seem anxious, upset? Even frightened, perhaps?"

"No."

"Why the sudden friendship? And when was the last time you sat down with your father?"

"I had never sat down with him before. He came to me. I was rather intrigued." But he had been more than intrigued. Ridiculously, a boy still dwelled deep within him, and that boy had been eager to meet his father for a simple meal. Until the true reason for the invitation had come to light.

"What did he want? Or was he suddenly regretting never becoming better acquainted with you?" Bragg asked.

"He wanted money. I refused." Hart shrugged.

"Just like that?"

He felt his jaw grind down. "Just like that. It was quite enjoyable, actually, to watch him grovel."

Bragg stood. "I thought by now you might have changed a bit. But you haven't changed. You were a cruel and troublesome boy, and you are still cruel and troublesome. Has it ever occurred to you that you might wish to grow up?"

That was it. Hart put his nose against Bragg's. "Don't you dare judge me. You are nothing but a repressed bastion of jumbled-up social mores, and all because you wish to please and appease Rathe and Grace. I find it appalling hypocrisy. At least I am honest. I hated Randall. I live for the attainment of pleasure. Which money buys, I might add—and which I have vast sums of. There is no hypocrisy here."

"Like hell there isn't. You are a desperate one, and do not deny it. You are desperate for attention, and thus you never cease your outrageous behavior. And it has worked!" Bragg exclaimed. "You turned my father's hair gray. You made my mother cry herself to bed at nights. Until you ran away at sixteen—to find Randall, I might add—you had their attention, and mine, night and day! And until Friday night, you have gained the attention of most of this city, with your flam-

262   BRENDA JOYCE

boyant and self-indulgent ways. But I do believe Randall's murder has truly put you in the limelight. And if you weren't so clever, I would be convinced that this, then, was the climax of your desperation."

Hart was shaking. "I was very clear. I said do not judge me." He clenched his fists hard, because he so badly wanted to smash his brother's nose.

"Then stop breaking rules. Stop behaving like a delinquent child. Delinquent children get their ears pulled and their bottoms spanked. Unfortunately, Lily did not think to punish you, and so here you are, incorrigible to the end."

"Do not ever speak her name to me again!" Hart shouted.

"She was my mother, too, and there is no reason we should bury her memory—she was a good mother, damn it," Bragg said, his voice raised.

"Fuck this." Hart strode for the door. He ached to throttle his brother. He hated thinking about their mother. Beautiful, tired, worn . . . hurt . . . dying.

Bragg grabbed his shoulder. "We are not through. I am certain you know something you are not telling me."

Hart stiffened but did not turn. "Get your fucking hand off of me before I break it, Commissioner." He meant his every word. Never had he exercised more self-restraint.

Bragg released him. "You know who killed Randall, don't you?"

Slowly he turned. "And if I did, you would be the last person I would tell."

"Why? Because you are protecting the murderer? Or because you hate me so?"

"Take your pick. Either answer might be right," Hart snarled.

"If you know who killed Randall, I demand you tell me, Calder."

Hart smiled. His mouth felt like plastic. "I know nothing. Enjoy your job. It suits you, Rick. King of the coppers."

"Maybe a night in the Tombs will suit you."

Hart froze. He turned. "Try it. My lawyers will have me

out in one hour—if you dare to press any charges against me."

"Maybe I should test the capabilities of your lawyers," Bragg said.

Their gazes locked. It was there now, between them, in the open, the rivalry that Hart could not ever recall not being present, the hostility, and the need to know who was stronger, better, smarter. As little boys, their battles had usually ended in a draw. As often as Lily had dragged Bragg off of Hart's back, she had dragged Hart off of his older brother. Once, there had been a piece of Bragg's ear in Hart's mouth as she did so. The scar Bragg still wore, to this day, was a tiny one, but it remained.

"Go right ahead," Hart returned, relishing the war.

Rick just looked at him, and this time he did not take the gauntlet. He shook his head in disgust.

They stared at each other, and as they did, the door flung open, hitting Hart in the back. He flinched, about to murder the intruder.

But it was a woman, a very beautiful and interesting woman, and he calmed, growing watchful.

Bragg had his gaze on her as well. Of course.

"Please, stop!" Francesca cried wildly.

The surprise vanished from Bragg's face. Annoyance replaced it.

Francesca flushed. "Please. You are brothers. Please." She hesitated, tears coming to her eyes. "This is too awful," she said when neither man moved or spoke. "Think of what this would do to your parents, Rathe and Grace."

Hart made a derisive sound. "I have no parents," he said. "My parents are dead. Rathe and Grace are *his* parents."

"They wanted nothing more than to become your parents, but you would not let them," Bragg said quietly now.

"My lawyers are waiting to hear from you," Hart returned caustically, his gaze dark. He nodded at Francesca and strode from the room.

Francesca shivered.

Bragg turned away, and she heard him sigh heavily.

Francesca walked up to him. Without thinking about it, she covered his shoulder with her palm. The muscles there were a huge, hard knot. "I am so sorry, Bragg," she whispered.

He sighed again. "I know you are. He is impossible." Suddenly he turned. "Listen to me carefully, Francesca, for I know you well enough now to know that you are a rescuer, and I also know Calder, who is a seducer. Calder cannot be rescued. His demons are of his own making. Save your compassion, pity, and time for someone who shall benefit from it."

Francesca studied him. "That's not fair. There is always hope and . . ." She hesitated.

"And what? And he is not bad? He is bad!" Bragg cried.

He had taken the word right out of her mouth. "I think you are right. I think he wants attention and the only way he knows how to get it is by seeming to be bad."

"He has a cruel side. I warn you, Francesca, I grew up with him. Jesus, he was my little brother. Our mother was always so tired. I was responsible for Calder when we were boys, even when I was no more than four or five. I recall worrying about him, dragging him out of scrapes, maneuvering him out of harm's way. I remember once he was almost run over by a carter, except that I ran into the street and pushed him aside. I remember he stole a purse, which I replaced before the theft could be remarked. Believe me, he was always in trouble, and it was always of his own making." Bragg turned away, moving to the mantel, staring at it. No one had bothered to make a fire for the city's police commissioner.

Francesca felt her heart warming, for she could imagine Bragg as a little blond boy, holding Calder's hand, telling him what to do and how to do it. Except Calder would have been angry and obstinate, refusing to obey and comply. Instead of adoring and respecting his older brother, he would have fought Bragg tooth and nail.

"I don't recall this, but Lily told me that she had a difficult birth with Calder and was bed-ridden for several weeks afterward," Bragg murmured. "I wasn't much past two years

old when he was born, but she said she showed me how to
hold him and give him a bottle of cow's milk. She could not
nurse him herself," he added, looking at her, his gaze somber
with the memories he was unearthing now.

"So he is two years younger than yourself?" Francesca
asked.

"And a few months."

"Was Randall in the picture when he was born?"

"No. Her relationship with Randall was a brief one." His
gaze held hers steadily. "And when she realized she was dying, she contacted my father and Calder's. Rathe came; Randall did not."

"Poor Calder," Francesca cried, taking Bragg's hand.
Somehow, it was so natural and right to slip her small palm
in his larger one. Briefly their hands tightened around each
other. "When was this?"

" 'Eighty-six," he said, removing his hand from hers and
stepping farther away from her.

She felt more than his need to withdraw; she felt the brief
moment of memory and the pain it still caused. "Can you talk
about it?" she asked softly.

"Of course." He sent her a small smile but avoided her
eyes. "She died of peritonitis, a cancer of the colon. She knew
she was dying for many months—we all knew. My father
had no idea I existed, and neither did Randall know about
Calder. She sent them both letters. Rathe came immediately.
As it turned out, Lily had only just begun to work in a dance
hall when she met my father. She was only seventeen, fresh
off of a farm, and he took her out of the hall and set her up—
for a while." His smile was brief, strained, sad. "Rathe was
a terrible womanizer before he fell in love with Grace. He
enjoyed my mother's company for several months, then
moved on and did not ever look back. Lily was proud, even
as a young, frightened, and pregnant girl. She went back to
work until the pregnancy became obvious, had me, met Randall, who was the second and the last of the men that were in
her life. I think becoming pregnant again made her realize
she must find another way to provide an income for herself

and her new family. From the time Calder was born until she died, she worked in sweatshops as a seamstress. I recall her bringing her pieces home and sewing until she fell asleep in the wee hours of the morning. She would fall asleep at our flat's single table, by the light of a single candle."

"That is so terrible," Francesca whispered. She imagined Bragg as a boy creeping over to that table and blowing the candle out.

He shrugged. "Rathe got her letter and came right away. He was married, and they already had three children. He not only took me; he took Calder when he realized that Randall would not." He regarded Francesca. "He went to Randall himself, Francesca, begging him to take his own son in. That is the kind of man that he was."

"I look forward to meeting him—and his wife," Francesca said earnestly.

"You shall, as they are returning to the city. They are currently residing in Texas, where my grandparents, my sister, and her family live. You will like them. You remind me of Grace. She is a fervent reformer, like you. She has been an active suffragette since the seventies," he added.

Francesca smiled with excitement. "Oh, we shall get along well indeed," she cried. Grace Bragg must have some wonderful stories to tell.

"I have no doubt." His smile was wry. He sent her a glance that seemed very affectionate, and he walked behind his desk and sat down. Francesca watched him steeple his hands and knew he was now thinking about Calder and the case.

She gingerly sat in one of the chairs facing him. How painful it must have been, to watch your mother dying and then to have to leave to join a brand-new family, people who were complete strangers. Bragg would have been twelve years old at the time, Calder ten. Other brothers might have become close in such a circumstance, but that had not been the case with Bragg and Hart. That, too, was sad.

Francesca could not begin to imagine how difficult it had been.

She realized Bragg was watching her. He said softly, "You

do not have to look at me like that. There is no need for pity, although some sorrow is in order. It all worked out for the best. If Lily had not died, Francesca, I do not know what kind of man I would have become. And the same is true for Calder."

She nodded. "But the story still hurts me in my heart. It always will."

His gaze moved over her face. "And that is why you are so special," he said.

She stiffened, her pulse beginning to pound. "Am I special, Bragg?"

He looked away, his jaw flexing. Clearly he had spoken without thought, as, clearly, he did not like his choice of words. "You know you are unique." He continued to avoid her regard.

She bit her lip. Too well, she now recalled his words last night. She did not want to think about them now, as they had sounded so ominous. And Hart had said they were star-crossed. "Am I special to you?"

He jerked, meeting her gaze. Somehow, he was on his feet. "Francesca."

She was also standing. "You kissed me last night. Again."

It was a moment before he could speak. "Believe me, I have not forgotten."

She would have been elated, except that his expression was so daunting, so grim. "What is it? What is it that you wish to say to me? Why do you kiss me as if you cannot live without me and then look at me as if the world is about to end?"

"Because I do not want to hurt you."

She felt her ears begin to ring. She gripped the edge of his desk. She felt light-headed now. "There is something, isn't there? There is something between us. Something wrong."

"Yes."

Oh, God. She must not faint. "You have a commitment," she whispered, slowly going into shock. "An understanding. Something."

"Yes."

"Oh, God," she said, realizing her world was about to end. "There is another woman."

"I did not want to tell you this way. I did not want this to happen."

"There is another woman?" She gasped in disbelief.

"Yes."

She stared at him, in shock.

He stared back.

"I do not understand," she heard herself say. But of course she did not understand. She loved Rick Bragg. She had fallen in love with him within moments of their meeting. He was the most honorable and committed man she had ever met. And he loved her. She felt certain of it.

No, she did not understand.

Commitments, understandings, could be broken.

And surely he did not love someone else.

"Francesca," Bragg said. Suddenly he had come out from behind his desk and he had looped his arm around her waist. "Sit down."

She looked into his golden eyes and he looked back and she trusted him completely. "Tell me," she whispered, sagging against his body.

"I am married," he said.

EIGHTEEN

Francesca looked at him and knew she had misheard. For this was certainly not a possibility; she had not read one word in the newspapers about a wife, and he had no wife at No. 11 Madison Avenue. No, she had misheard; either that or she was dreaming.

"Francesca?" he asked tersely, his gaze unwavering upon her face.

She turned and found herself in the circle of his arms. "I thought you just said that you were married," she said unsteadily.

"I did," he returned unsteadily.

She pushed him away, overcome with disbelief. This had to be a dream of the worst sort, a nightmare! This could *not* be possible. She had expected some kind of understanding, a pre-engagement, perhaps. Something that might, ultimately, be changed or broken. But not a marriage. A marriage was *impossible*.

But she had not misheard. He had not denied it.

And last night he had kissed her, wildly, passionately, and uncontrollably.

She stiffened.

"Don't look at me that way!" Bragg said quickly. "This is not at all what you are thinking."

In that one moment, she imagined another woman—a wife. Someone beautiful, intelligent; someone who shared his bed, his life. In that one single moment, Francesca felt hatred.

"Francesca," he said tersely, "I have not seen my wife in four years."

The hatred, as unfamiliar to her as the air on the moon might be, vanished. "What?" She reached for the arm of the chair; otherwise, she would surely fall down.

"I have never wanted to make this explanation to you," Bragg said harshly. "Damn it, Francesca, I have never intended for there to be anything between us."

"Then you should not have kissed me—twice."

He stared at her. There was genuine anguish in his eyes.

"Are you going to say anything?" she cried. "I mean . . ." She stopped. She had been about to shout that he had just ruined her life. She had intended to marry him and spend her life with him, fighting the ills of society, fighting for the prevalence of justice, the pursuit of liberty. Of course, he did not know the extent of her feelings; he had only witnessed her passion. "Do you love her?" she heard herself ask harshly.

Something very close to hatred filled his eyes. But it wasn't hatred, and when he spoke, she heard the distaste in his tone and knew she had just glimpsed revulsion. "No."

She did not move. She stared at him, beginning to feel her heart ripping apart inside of her breast. Oh, how painful it was. How could this be happening? "You kissed me. You misled me."

"I did not mean to. It is very hard, fighting my feelings for you. Francesca, you seem to think me a saint. I am not a saint; I am nothing but a man in a moral dilemma of his own making."

The tears welled, finally. It was becoming difficult to breathe. "Who is she? Where is she? Why haven't you seen her in four years?"

"Please don't cry," he whispered, touching her face.

Fury galvanized her. "Don't touch me! Don't ever touch me again!"

He dropped his hand, blanching. "I will tell you everything, but do not hate me. I cannot live with that."

"I don't know how I feel right now. No. I know how I feel. I feel betrayed. Crushed. Run over by a lorry." She felt tears trickling down her cheeks.

"You and I have only known one another a few weeks. We only met on the eighteenth of January," he whispered.

He knew the exact date they had first met. Francesca hugged herself, biting her lower lip, hoping to keep it from trembling like a mewling baby's. It did not work. "How could you kiss me when you knew you had a wife waiting for you, somewhere else? My God, I thought you were honorable."

"My wife is not waiting for me. Although perhaps she is waiting for me to drop dead." He stared grimly at her.

Her heart felt as if it had stopped. "You don't mean that." Did he? Did his wife hate him enough to wish him dead? Should she care? Of course she should not, but she did!

"Oh, I do mean it. Leigh Anne would be free at last if I died."

Her name was Leigh Anne. "Why isn't she with you? Where is she? Why haven't you seen her in years?"

His gaze was searching. "Do you want to sit down?" He gestured at the chair. He seemed afraid to touch her, as he should well be.

"No," she snapped.

"Very well." He looked so unhappy now. Was it due to the prospect of sharing this truth with her? Or did merely speaking about his ill-fated marriage bring him such distress?

"She is from Boston," Bragg said slowly. "I met her in my first year at Harvard Law School. I fell instantly, madly, in love." He stopped, grimacing. Francesca winced. "I asked her to marry me within the first three months of our having met. Rathe begged me to wait; I refused to listen."

His every word was cutting into her like a little, finely honed knife. "She must be very special," Francesca said bitterly. "For you to have been so smitten so instantly."

"She looks like an angel, a blue-eyed, dark-haired angel. I could not see past her face and form. Francesca, there is little angelic about her."

His wife was so gorgeous that she looked like an angel. Another knife wound. Oh, well. Maybe this conversation would kill her. That might be the proper ending to this oh, so sordid and ugly affair.

She must not weep now.

"I am hurting you. I am sorry."

She shrugged. "So you married her right away."

"By the end of my first year at law school." He studied
her. "I was a fool."

She stared at him, wishing he would expound upon the
why and how of it, but he did not. "What happened?"

"Simply? I refused an offer in one of the nation's top legal
firms, an offer that would have taken us to Washington, D.C.,
and I opened up a private practice instead. A practice of criminal law, one that was not very lucrative." He smiled sardonically. "The poor and the indigent cannot afford legal fees,
you see."

Her heart tried to move her with love and compassion;
Francesca refused to heed it. "And?"

"Leigh Anne told me I was a sorry fool, and she left me.
She packed her bags, went to Europe, and has been there ever
since."

Francesca stared. "I am not sure I understand," she said
slowly.

"She expected a life of wealth and glamour. After all, she
was marrying a Bragg. She knew I had political aspirations
as well. Somehow, she failed to truly understand me. She
could not accept a life of genteel poverty, with her husband
working long into the night to defend people she would cross
the street to avoid. She did not like going to parties alone and
being asked where her husband was. When she went to Europe she told me, very explicitly, that she would come back
when I accepted the position I had turned down, or another
of similar prestige and economy."

Francesca's eyes felt wide. "She blackmailed you?"

"Yes, she did. That August, three months after she had
left, I went after her, truly thinking her a good-hearted person
who had committed a folly, erroneously believing that she
loved me and that she had missed me and that she would
come back." His eyes were now impossible to read. "I found
her in the south of France, with her lover, and I returned
home."

Her heart won. "Oh, Bragg!" Francesca cried, appalled.
She reached out to touch him, realized what she was about,
and dropped her hand before making any physical contact.

"Do not feel sorry for me. I am paying for my stupidity
and my rashness, for my complete lack of judgment." He
shrugged. "She remains in Europe. Although we do not communicate, we have an understanding. She does as she pleases
and I pay her bills."

Francesca stared. "She is an awful woman," she heard herself whisper.

"Do not pity me, as I cannot stand her and I prefer that
we remain separated. I am sorry she spends so much of my
money, but that cannot be helped." His eyes were dark. He
jammed both hands in the pockets of his trousers.

Francesca wanted to ask a dozen questions. Did he have
any feelings for her? Did she still have a lover? Would he
ever consider a divorce? She wet her lips and asked, carefully,
"But you did go to Washington. I seem to recall an article I
read that clearly stated you were practicing in the capital before accepting this appointment."

"I took on a partner in Boston and left my practice there
in his capable and fervent hands. I moved to D.C. to continue
the very same work, but at the same time I could also devote
my spare time to the politics of this nation. You know I am
invested in public service, Francesca," he said.

She nodded. "Your father took a position in Cleveland's
first administration, did he not?"

He smiled briefly at her, pleased. "Yes, he did. He was
secretary of commerce. My first years with Rathe and Grace
were in Washington, D.C."

Clearly the memories were good ones. Francesca had almost smiled. "Why didn't she come back? Why doesn't she
come back now?"

"I still live in genteel poverty, Francesca," he said evenly.
"I did not take lucrative cases in D.C., where much of my
work was done gratuitously, and my position now pays very
little, as I am sure you must know."

Francesca just could not understand a woman so motivated
by wealth and position. On the other hand, she saw it every
day, for the debutantes seeking husbands in her social circle
all were determined to marry either money or a title. "Maybe

she will see the light, one day," Francesca somehow offered.

He stared at her. "I do not want her here. Not now, not ever."

"So you would never forgive her?" Did that mean he still loved her?

"I could forgive her the dozens of lovers. I could forgive her for spending every cent I earn. Yes, I could forgive her, easily, in fact. I may never forgive myself for ruining my own private life, but her character is defective and she I can forgive. But I do not love her, and what is even worse, I do not like her, and worse than that, I have no respect. We have *nothing* in common. Living apart is the best solution to a terrible mismatch."

She couldn't help thinking about Connie and Montrose—but they were not a mismatch.

"Do you hate me, Francesca?"

His soft words, uttered firmly and without hesitation, cut into her thoughts. She looked into his eyes. Damn it, her heart still trusted him. Her heart would not take this for an answer, for *the* answer, and it seemed to have a will of its own, beating inside of her breast with compassion, understanding, and love. "I could never hate you," she heard herself say.

He did not move.

Nor did she.

The silence had become infused with tension. And the tension of betrayal and anger had changed. Francesca was breathless and disbelieving. He had just told her that he had a wife, yet she was standing there, and for her, nothing had changed. Dear God, he remained a man she admired, respected, trusted, and still loved. He remained the man she wanted, not just with all of her heart but with her treacherous body as well.

"I have to go."

"You must," he agreed tightly.

Francesca turned, felt more tears welling, and, somewhat blinded by them, moved to the door. Before she could open it his hand pressed upon it, so she could not open it if she had tried. Francesca froze.

"I can't let you leave, like this, after this," he said roughly.

She turned and was so close to being in his arms. "I don't want to leave like this." Their eyes met and held. "But you are forbidden to me now. You will never divorce her, will you?" The question just popped out. But the moment was too intense, the stakes too high, for her to regret it.

He hesitated. "No. A divorce would never allow me into a significant public office."

"One day, you will run for the Senate."

"Yes. One day. In the future."

She started to cry. "And I will be proud of you."

"I know you will," he whispered. "Francesca, please."

"No." She shook her head. "I have to go." She turned blindly, tugging at the door.

He opened it for her, as she could not seem to do so. "When will I see you again?"

She fled into the corridor. She didn't know, but that wasn't why she did not answer him. She simply could not speak.

She paused on the wide front step before the house where she lived with her husband and her daughters, the house that Papa had built for them as a wedding gift. Connie stared at the front door, trembling and trying to breathe properly. She reminded herself that this was her house as well as Neil's and that she should have gone home last night, as she had promised Mama she would do, and that everything would be fine, just fine—that everything *was* fine. But she saw not the gleaming teakwood door she faced, which was closed in front of her; instead, she saw Neil.

And in her mind's eye, he was with the beautiful Eliza Burton.

What was she doing? Why was she there? This no longer felt like home.

"Lady Montrose?" Mrs. Partridge asked, standing behind her with Charlotte at her side and Lucinda in her arms. "Shall we go in?"

Connie heard her, but only vaguely, as if from a distance, or as if she were in a dream. Last night she had intended to do as Julia had asked. But when she had gone to her room she had sat down in front of the fire, staring mindlessly at it, and the dancing flames had reminded her of hell, and that had frightened her enough to take a small dose of laudanum. No, what had frightened her had been the eeriest and most hor-rifying thought—what if she were dead and her life, exactly as it was, with a treacherous husband, was hell?

Of course, the laudanum had soothed her and caused her to lie down. She had not risen again until the following morn-ing, and somehow, it had taken all day to pack up the single trunk she shared with the girls.

"Lady Montrose?" Mrs. Partridge's voice was soft with concern. "Let us go in. Lucinda must be fed."

Images of her life rolled through her mind, all of them having occurred from the moment she had met Neil. That first heart-wrenching introduction, his first kiss, the whirlwind of parties and balls, their wedding celebration, their wedding night. Connie started, as Mrs. Partridge tugged on her hand.

"What?" she said, fixing a smile upon her face.

"We should go inside," Mrs. Partridge said. She was a tall, thin woman with kind blue eyes, and her gaze, behind her spectacles, was so worried it gave Connie a moment's pause.

What was she so worried about? "Of course we must go inside." Connie pushed open the door. Mrs. Partridge was acting strangely, she decided, as if they had been loitering on the front step.

A doorman instantly held the door open as Charlotte raced past everyone, shrieking, "Daddy! Daddy!"

Connie felt a huge weight settling about her neck and shoulders. She felt the tension inside of her body, already as tight as a wire, escalating uncontrollably. *Neil,* she thought, and a huge wave of grief crushed her.

He appeared at the other end of the entrance hall, and for one moment, as Charlotte charged toward him, his gaze locked with Connie's. Her heart skipped too many beats to count. He looked terrible, as if he were ill, and he certainly appeared unkempt, but more important, he was so terribly grim.

But certainly that was not because of her.

"Daddy!" Charlotte screamed, and Neil caught her and lifted her high, his expression changing. He laughed, whirling his three-year-old daughter about, then hugged her hard to his chest. "Baby, I have missed you!"

"Me, too, Daddy," Charlotte laughed. She was a platinum blond child and she could pose for an artist who wished to render blue-eyed angels upon his canvas. Connie thought that she was very much like her aunt, Francesca—she was too smart and too stubborn; that is, she was a handful.

Neil released his daughter, who ran off into the house, looking for her King Charles spaniel puppy, a Christmas gift from her Uncle Evan. Connie glanced at Mrs. Partridge, but she was already excusing herself and following Charlotte. She paused briefly so Neil could touch the sleeping infant's chubby cheek with his fingertips. He kissed her high forehead, and then the nanny and the baby left the hall.

Connie realized that he hadn't moved since they had entered the house. She did not know if she could move. The distance of the hall separated her and her husband, and the doorman stood behind, having closed the door. Now behind Neil, their butler appeared, clearly wishing a word with her.

Neil moved. He strode purposefully toward her, his turquoise gaze never leaving her face. In an almost detached way, she noticed that, even disheveled, he remained powerfully stunning, disturbingly so. She felt herself tremble again.

What was she doing? She did not want to be there, in this house, with him, like this.

She wanted to go back to a better place and time, when there had been love and respect.

"Connie." He kissed her cheek, but his lips did not quite touch her skin. Again, his intense gaze held hers. She dropped her eyes, avoiding it—avoiding him.

But Mama was right. She had to go home. This was where she lived. And she did not want the world to know about the discord in her life.

"Hello, Neil." She smiled brightly, not quite meeting his gaze. "We have had the most wonderful time. It has been an adventure for Charlotte! I am so pleased that Beth Anne invited us for the weekend," she said, wondering if her tone sounded as strained as her words felt. And she dared to glance directly at him.

He simply stared at her, as if she were some odd act in a circus.

She continued to smile brightly. "James wishes to speak with me. Have you told him what we shall have for supper?"

"No," he said slowly. "I have not. You are the one who prepares the menus."

That was true. He was clearly chastising her, wasn't he, for not having been home to take care of the task? She stiffened, as it was not fair—she ran a nearly perfect home and this was the first time she had not set a day's menu or rather, two days'. "Then I shall speak with James now. I am rather tired," she added, glancing past him at their butler. "So I shall retire to my rooms in order to rest before we dine."

The butler came forward and Connie quickly requested a meal she knew would please her husband and be possible for Cook and his staff to buy and prepare in several hours' time. James thanked her and hurried away. Connie smiled at Neil without really looking at him, and she started upstairs. To her dismay, he fell right into step behind her.

Her heart began to pound, hard. What was he doing? What did he want? He was so close behind her that she could feel her trailing skirts brushing the tips of his shoes.

"I wish to speak with you," he said quietly.

Alarm filled her, but she did not pause. And she thought, *What if I have gone too far? What if he thinks to leave me?*

She could not breathe easily now. How she wished for a sherry or a dose of laudanum. "Very well," she said, as lightly as possible.

Inside her sitting room, which was attached to the huge, lavishly appointed master bedroom that they shared, she paused, not quite facing him. And he gripped her arm. "Please look at me," he said.

She inhaled, hearing the contained anger in his tone, and she turned slowly, daring to meet his eyes. "Neil?"

"Don't you ever do such a thing again," he said, releasing her. "And I mean it."

She stared at him and was both afraid and angry herself. "What?"

"You disappeared. You took the girls—my daughters—and disappeared. I have been frantic with worry," he said tightly.

Had he been worried about her as well as his daughters? "Neil, didn't you see my note?" she asked unsteadily now. Julia's instructions filled her mind, but she hated lying. It did not feel right to lie to Neil, no matter the circumstances.

"What note?"

"Why, I left you a note telling you where we were off to for the weekend. In fact, I was surprised not to hear from you in return. As I said, Charlotte had a most wonderful time. Beth Anne's nieces were staying over, on a holiday from Pittsburgh. They are a bit older than Charlotte, and you know how she adores older children." Connie managed a smile that felt frozen.

"You left me a note telling me that you were going to Beth Anne's for the weekend?" he asked, at once incredulous and suspicious.

Somehow, she nodded. "I would hardly take the girls and vanish," she heard herself say.

He stared at her, wetting his lips. Then, "Connie, you frightened me."

She felt her heart quicken in response to his words. She turned away. She did not want to hear him now.

He seized her arm. "Don't turn from me, and damn it, don't smile at me as if I am some fool you are entertaining for supper! I can see past that smile, Connie. I can see how distressed you are. We must talk."

His hand was large, strong, and oh, so familiar on her arm. God, she had forgotten, briefly, how much she loved his touch—how much she loved him. But she must not allow those feelings now—or must she? Her mind seemed to spin crazily. It was hard to think. "I am tired," she said. She faced him and smiled another time.

His gaze was searching and agonized. Then, "Your rest can wait."

She did not like his firm tone. When he was decisive, there was no getting around him. What did he wish to speak about? Surely not his sordid affair? "Very well." She walked away and he released her. She sat down on the gold-and-white settee in the room's large sitting area, clasping her hands in her lap.

"I never meant to hurt you," he said slowly.

Connie knew she should not speak, but she heard herself say, "Then you should not have taken a lover."

His jaw flexed. "I tried not to."

What did that mean? Unease assailed her. She truly did not wish to continue in this vein. "I am sure you were seduced. Neil, I am very tired." She stood, intending to go to bed. She had one dose of laudanum left. She had been intending to save it for after supper, but now she changed her mind. She would dose herself now.

He strode to her and took her arm. "I was not seduced! Lucinda is eight months old, and we have had relations less than half a dozen times since her birth, not to mention the fact that during your pregnancy it was even less! I know you do not like that part of our marriage, Connie. I have tried, repeatedly, not to bother you with my more basic needs."

Whatever was he speaking about? She blinked at him, beginning to blush. He wished to discuss . . . the s-word? "This is not a seemly subject," she managed.

"Not seemly? Damn it, I am a man, and I have a beautiful wife, a wife whom I happen to love. A wife who I believe loves me, but who does not care for physical relations. I know how proper you are. I know you are embarrassed now. To hell with that!" he cried.

She was embarrassed. But she was also shocked. It was true that they had not made love that often since the baby had been born, but when they did, it was wonderful. And she had hated him seeing and touching her when her body was grossly fat while carrying the child, because Neil expected her to be beautiful—he would not love her if she was not.

She did like the most intimate aspect of their marriage. She more than liked it, if she dared to be honest with herself. His touch made her tremble, and dear God, he knew how to make her body explode. Surely he knew that? It was just so hard to know when and where to cross the line between proper and indecent behavior. It was hard to be a lady when he was touching her and kissing her. God forbid she might act like a trollop or, worse, a whore.

He stared down at her. He was blushing, too. "Connie, I have known from the beginning of our marriage that you do not like sharing my bed. Unfortunately, I am a very virile man. It has been very hard for me, controlling my needs. *I did not mean to stray.* I have tried to live a very celibate life. In fact, no one has tried harder than I have. But I failed. I failed and I am sorry and it will not happen again. *I never meant to hurt you.*"

She stared at him and wanted to tell him that his touch was exquisite and that being joined together into one being was heaven. But she could not speak. She did not dare speak openly about such a subject.

Was this, then, all her fault?

He faced her gravely, both hands fisted on his hips. "However, I made you a promise, one I intend to keep. It will not happen again—even if you lock me out of our bedroom." And a questioning light appeared in his eyes.

She didn't know what to say. She could hardly breathe. Somehow, she smiled. "I am not locking you out of our bedroom, Neil."

Relief filled his gaze. "Thank you." He studied her and then his gaze slipped past her, to the open doorway of the room they shared. It was dominated by a large canopied bed.

She followed his regard by shifting slightly. She looked at their bed and felt her cheeks warm. What should she say, or do, now?

Julia had instructed her to pretend that nothing was amiss. But something was amiss. He had turned to another woman instead of to her, because she wasn't perfect after all.

Connie inhaled, stabbed with pain.

"Are you all right?" he asked.

"I am fine," she said.

He studied her. "I wish you would tell me the truth. I wish you would shout and scream and even throw something at me."

He did not mean it; it was impossible. She stared. She would *never* indulge in such behavior.

He sighed heavily. "I will see you at supper," he said. He glanced again at the doorway of their bedroom.

She sensed what he wanted. But it was only the afternoon, and good God, she had only just returned home! Still, she should do something now. She should somehow invite him in. She should take him to bed, following Julia's advice. For then they could truly pretend that this had never happened. . . .

But it had.

And Connie did not now have a clue as to how to even begin to approach her husband in such a forward fashion.

Neil walked out.

She closed her eyes, wanting to call out to him. She did not.

Instead, she sat down, dazed, and it was several moments before she felt the tears sliding down her face.

He had been forty-five minutes late to his meeting, but he had sent a message to the gentlemen awaiting him, and that had saved the day. Now their lawyers would haggle over the more minute details of the agreements that had been made, enabling him to gain another shipping contract with China.

Hart did not care.

He was on his way home now after what had been an unusually long day. He was aware of his mood being foul, although not precisely why. He was in his coach, crossing 33d and Broadway. He had a function to attend at eight, and it required a damn tuxedo.

Impulsively he rapped on the partition, alerting his driver. "Raoul, Madam Pinke's."

The coach made a right, heading east. Hart leaned back in

his seat, an image of Daisy filling his mind, followed by one
of Rose. But the tension within him was so vast that those
images—and the anticipation—could not make him smile.
Then he thought about his damn brother.

He was partially, Hart decided, the reason for his mood.
Rick had decided to pull rank on him, but that was merely
amusing. His stint with power would be brief enough. Even
if he did last an entire year in the job, Hart doubted Lowe
would get re-elected, and Rick would move on.

It was a shame that that absurd appointment had brought
him back to New York City. Now their paths kept crossing,
to everyone's annoyance. They would cross even more once
Rathe and Grace Bragg returned to the city.

It was even more of a shame that Rick was so damn dedicated to his job. Who the hell cared who had murdered Paul
Randall?

No one cared, Hart thought somewhat savagely. Not he
himself, not Randall's grieving wife, and not his man-hating
daughter or his student son.

No, his mistress cared. She had lost her sugar daddy.
Georgette de Labouche cared—and so did Rick.

Hart laughed silently, but that helped nothing. He seemed
to have a headache—the same one that had bothered him all
day. Randall was dead. So what? He had been murdered three
days ago in his mistress's home. Who cared? He did not care.
He was glad the man was dead. He hadn't lied when he had
said he was happy about it. He had truly hated the man.

The man he had spoken with exactly twice.

The man who had also hated him.

The coach halted, but not at 48th Street and Third, for that
establishment had been closed down and boarded up. The
new premises were five blocks south and one avenue west.
Hart watched a well-dressed gentleman enter a nondescript
brick house, his pace brisk, a walking stick in hand.

But did he *really* know that Randall had hated him? They
had only spoken twice!

He had always been intending to confront Randall one day,

far into the future, and maybe even beat the shit out of him, in order to find out the truth.

"Sir?" The big, overweight man who was more of a body-guard than a driver had slid open the partition. "We are here, Mr. Hart," Raoul Torelli said.

Hart started, so immersed in his dark thoughts that he hadn't realized they were at his destination. Grimly he launched himself from the coach. He was not going to think about Randall again.

He bounded across the sidewalk and up the house's front steps. He was ushered inside the house almost immediately—already it had been painted the sensual salmon color Madam Pinke was famous for, the same color as her old establishment. Madam Pinke greeted him instantly, receiving him in a small office set off of the larger salon, where the gentleman he had noticed upon the street was waiting. "Hart! This is a surprise. Have I made an error? I don't have you down in my books." She embraced him and pretended to kiss his cheek.

He didn't bother to smile. "I would like to see Daisy, and I will be brief."

Her eyes widened. "Daisy has a six o'clock appointment. I have another girl—"

"I don't want anyone else," he said, and he heard how dangerous he sounded. He opened his billfold and handed her several hundred dollars, and then he turned and walked out of the room. He heard her quickly count the money, and then she called after him, "Upstairs, second door on your right. A half hour, Mr. Hart!"

Like hell, he thought, his black humor increasing. This situation was intolerable. For he was not a patient man in the best of circumstances. He had stumbled across the girls by chance two or three weeks ago. He had espied Daisy at the sale counter of B. Altman's on a weekend—he had been there with a married woman who wished to pick up some absurd item. It had not taken him long to strike up a conversation, and he had quickly realized the kind of woman Daisy was and the luck he was in. An appointment with her and Rose had immediately followed—within hours of that first meeting.

And he had not been disappointed; to the contrary.

But dealing with Madam Pinke was no longer acceptable. He did not have the patience for it. She was an avaricious fool.

He bounded up the stairs, suddenly hot and explosive. He reminded himself not to rush, as rushing ruined everything for everyone. Trying to control his sudden wild impatience—he was already erect—he knocked.

The door opened and Daisy stood there, the loveliest sight he had ever seen in his entire life.

And he met her sky blue gaze, looked at her breathtaking face, and smiled. "Sweet, sweet Daisy," he murmured. "You shall be my salvation today."

"Hart!" She was surprised, but then she smiled, and it was genuine—it reached her gorgeous eyes. "What is this? Has Madam Pinke let you up?" She looked at him coyly, speaking in that soft, breathy manner she had.

His answer was to stroll past her, and she closed the door. She was wearing a short red-and-orange kimono, exquisitely embroidered with black and gold, that barely covered her loins. In fact, her buttocks peeked out from behind, an enchanting sight. She was, without a question, the most beautiful woman he had ever seen. She had a quality that was ethereal, yet she was one of the earthiest women he knew. "She has," he said, loosening his tie.

She smiled again. "How lucky I am. Is Rose coming to join us?"

He could not tell if she wished for Rose to be there or not. "I did not ask for her," he said, removing his tie. Perhaps he should have. Watching two exquisite women in bed together was a delicious prelude to his making love to them both. In fact, it was one of the finer things in life.

"Good," Daisy said, moving gracefully away to a bar cart where she lifted a decanter. She glanced directly at him over her shoulder. "Then I shall have you all to myself. For *only* the second time."

He realized she was pleased. And that pleased him. Still, had he only been with her alone once? "Yes, you have me all to yourself. How lucky you are."

She returned his smile. "My only fear is you will exhaust me for the rest of this evening."

His smile vanished. "How long have you been with Madam Pinke, Daisy?"

She approached him, handing him a scotch, neat. Both pale brows lifted. "Perhaps two months. I do believe I told you we only just came to town."

He was an inquisitive man, and he had asked her and Rose several questions, but their reluctance to tell him of their past had made him desist. The only fact he had learned was that they were from another northeastern city and they had arrived in New York together, two months ago. How mysterious it was. "I think it has been two months too long," he said, taking a long sip of the scotch.

She arched a look at him. "I am not unhappy."

"But the real question is, are you happy?" he asked. He took another sip of scotch and cupped her jaw. "You remind me of a butterfly, my sweet. A precious, rare, and delicate butterfly. And as such, you need a gilded cage filled with elegant appointments, and with a door that is not locked."

She stared at him.

He stared back, smiling softly, because he did like her, when a disturbing image of Randall, begging him for cash, came to mind. He stiffened, refusing to entertain it. "You are too good for this place."

Daisy's eyes changed. The open look vanished, replaced by caution. He already knew she often played dumb, but that she was as smart as anyone. "I am hardly too good for this place, Calder," she said in her soft and breathy voice.

"I want to make you my mistress," he said, setting his drink down and cupping her shoulders.

She had stiffened beneath the stunning and short but otherwise unrevealing kimono. "I beg your pardon?"

He felt her mind race. "You heard me. I will take care of you in a most spectacular way. You shall have your own apartment, furnished as you like. I shall buy you clothes and baubles. Expensive baubles." He smiled. "We shall make an agreement, for, say, six months. When the six months is up, you may leave if you choose to do so, or I may ask you to leave, or we may renew our arrangement. But for those six months, you will be my mistress, and I will take care of you." He smiled into her eyes. And he slid his hands under her kimono, moving them back to her bare shoulders, but opening the belted garment as he did so. He glanced at her small, perfect breasts.

But she remained stiff, even though she inhaled when he knuckled her. "But what about Rose?"

"I do not wish to make Rose my mistress, Daisy. It is you I wish to have at my beck and call. And you would be at my disposal, dear, night and day, as I choose." He tugged the kimono and let it fall to the floor. She wore only white lace garters, white stockings, and high-heeled shoes. "You are perfection. And perfection such as yours should almost never be covered up." He slid his hands down her long, supple back.

She said, arching a little toward him, "How can I leave Rose? She is my . . . sister."

He returned, "I am exceedingly generous with my mistresses when the relationship ends. When our relationship ends, you will have such a handsome settlement that you and Rose will be able to buy your own house and retire from this life, if that is what you wish. Or perhaps you will start your own house." He rubbed his knuckle lower, down her rib cage, then over her navel. She shivered. "Ask anyone, dear."

"I have already heard that about you," she said breathlessly.

His knuckle moved over her belly, approaching her pubis, which was completely shaved and bare. "You will not be sorry," he promised. "But if I find that you are not loyal to me, I will throw you out instantly. And that includes with Rose," he said flatly.

She stared at him thoughtfully, considering the fact that he had stopped stroking her just inches away from her sex, and given its condition, he could see that she was swelling. "I can leave after six months?" she murmured.

He smiled, for he had her. "Yes, sweet Daisy. But not a day before."

"I must speak with Rose," she said, smiling now, "but I do not think she will mind too much. Well, she will be upset at first, but I do think I can bring her around, and thus my answer is yes."

He grinned at her. "And you do not wish to know how much I will give you when we part ways?"

"I trust you, Calder. You are the only man I know whom I do trust." She did not smile now.

He thought about all the questions she had never answered. One day he would learn her secrets. He turned abruptly and sat down in a big armchair, aware of her surprise and disappointment. His gaze slid over her slender body, lingering on her long legs and the perfect juncture between them.

"But I have heard you have a mistress," she murmured, not moving.

"Our agreement stipulates only that you be faithful to me—and I will not tolerate jealousy," he said easily. "I am not a faithful man."

She laughed softly. "And I am not jealous. So you will have two mistresses?"

He reached out and touched her soft, warm inner thigh with a fingertip. He trailed it upward. "I have not seen her in a week; she knows the end is near. No. I am sending her on her way, even as we speak."

Daisy took a step closer, the easier for him to toy with her. "You seem preoccupied today, Calder. I want to take your mind off of whatever it is that is disturbing you."

Randall's image flashed. God, he hated the man! And the man had hated him. Most definitely. He was an idiot to think otherwise.

He pulled Daisy down so she sat on his lap, straddling it. He smiled at her, banishing all thoughts of his dead father from his mind. Holding her head, he pulled her face close and whispered, "You are going to take care of me first, and then I shall take care of you."

She smiled.

He decided not to kiss her. He slid his finger down her perfect, stunning body, low and lower still. He dipped it into the folds of her sex, and then he began to rotate it around her clitoris, slowly, thoughtfully, expertly. As he had thought, she was already moist and quickly growing ready for him.

She inhaled. "I thought—"

"Ssh," he said, and he laid his head back against the chair and watched her as he played with her. He watched her face and chest flush with desire. He felt her grow slick and wet beneath his hand. He had been hard before even stepping into the room. God, she was so lovely.

Daisy gasped, reaching for his trousers.

He pulled her hand away. "I want to watch you come first," he said.

She met his gaze, her blue eyes already glazed and unfocused. "You need me, Calder," she whispered. "Not the other way around."

"But I enjoy watching you writhe upon my lap," he murmured, and he slowly pushed her upper body backward, holding her legs in place. Daisy was as supple as she appeared to be, and she arched over until her head reached the floor. He bent, and began licking her sex.

She came.

Gasping at first, then crying out, and it was a genuine climax.

He had warned her to never pretend otherwise with him.

He smiled, pleased, and tasted her one more time, until she went limp in his arms, practically sliding through them to the floor. He let her down gently and stood up. "Christ," he said, opening his trousers, staring down at her. It was, perhaps, the most erotic sight, a stunning woman sprawled naked at your feet. "Tell me what you want," he said softly.

She looked up, panting. And her gaze settled on his huge arousal. She smiled. "You know what I want. I want that."

He did not move. No, it was power, not eroticism, that dominated the moment. Her legs were wide. She was wet, willing, and absolutely submissive. He could do with her whatever it was that he chose. "Get up," he said softly.

Daisy rolled over gracefully and shifted fluidly onto her knees, and with a soft moan she began rubbing her face all over his penis. Her hair became sticky, wet. Then her small tongue darted out, tasting the tip, his seed.

He wanted to grab her head and ram down her throat. He did not.

She flicked her tongue over him, around him, teasing him now the way he had her. And finally, when perspiration was streaming down his body, she sucked him into her mouth and down her throat.

Finally, he grabbed her head, clasping it.

He pumped into her.

He reached down and lifted her to her feet with one strong arm. Almost simultaneously, he moved her backward and pushed her down partially onto the bed. She lay with her hips on the very edge, both feet on the floor, her legs wide open for him. "Do as you will, Calder," she whispered, not moving.

He studied her and smiled, removing his jacket and unbuttoning his shirt. "You are magnificent, just like that," he said.

"So are you," she said huskily, smiling. Her gaze was on his distended shaft.

He flung his shirt on the floor and stepped out of his shoes, trousers, and underwear. He did not rush.

"Hurry," she whispered.

"I don't think so," he said, and when he moved over her, it was not to penetrate her. Instead, he rubbed himself over her sex, between her legs, and then between her buttocks, until she was writhing and gasping for air. "Do you like being teased, sweet Daisy?" he murmured.

"Yes, yes . . . yes!"

He laughed and rubbed the swollen tip of his penis over her clitoris, very, very deliberately, watching the flush on her neck increase. Suddenly she began to cry out.

And as she started to spasm he thrust inside of her, hard, almost viciously. *This* was what he wanted. *This* was where he needed to be. And no damn ghost could take *this* away from him, now could he?

The explosion came. Stunning, fiery, intense. Fire and

light. Followed by darkness and death. Hart collapsed on top of Daisy.

And when he could breathe, they were both fully on her bed, in each other's arms. He held her, stroking her fine, silken platinum hair. Randall leered at him suddenly, as if he were actually in the room. Stiffening, Hart kissed the top of her head.

And he was disbelieving. Even the act of sex could not chase away this particular dead man.

Damn it. He had to face the truth. He was pissed.

Royally so.

Because someone had gone and killed his father, and now he would never know what the man had really felt for him.

"Calder? Are you all right?" Daisy shifted to look up at him.

The concern in her eyes was real. But she was now his, bought and paid for by him. This was what he had wanted, but in that moment, it felt tainted.

He smiled at her. "I still want you," he said.

NINETEEN

"Miss Cahill, you have a caller."

Francesca had been studying—with very little interest and even less attention. The words on the page of *Madame Bovary* kept blurring and jumbling, not making any sense. It just hurt so much.

She would never be Bragg's wife.

She would never share his life.

They could remain friends, but that was all it would ever be.

The book slipped from her hands to the floor. Somehow, another stray tear had escaped. How long, she wondered, did it take one to recover from a broken heart?

In that moment, she did not think she would ever recover.

Francesca wiped her eyes and looked up at the housemaid who stood in the doorway of her large bedroom, a room recently painted a mauve-colored pink. She had no wish to entertain a caller now, and she glanced at the bronze Louis IV clock on the pale marble mantel above the fireplace where a fire crackled on the iron grate. Francesca started—it was already 7:00 P.M.! She had forgotten all about Mark Anthony! Clearly he had come to fetch her.

Her heart lurched. She must dismiss her grief now, or at least pretend to. She had a case to solve. But where was Joel? He had not yet appeared, and she was afraid to go out with Anthony alone. What if Anthony was the killer? For if he was not Georgette's brother, then who was he, and why was he so immersed in her affairs? It was still not too late to back out of the evening's undertaking, or to call Bragg on the telephone and tell him what she was doing. And if Joel did not arrive soon, she would have to go with Anthony alone.

She stood up. She was not going to call Bragg. He would

think that she was chasing him, which she was not, by God.

But more important, it would hurt too much to hear his voice now.

Fortunately, her parents were out for the evening, so it would be easy to sneak out. A throbbing began behind both temples, painful and distinct. "Thank you, Melinda. I am coming right down. Who is it?"

"It is Mr. Hart, miss," the elderly maid said, holding up a small silver tray.

Francesca's heart turned over and then began a series of rapid heartbeats. Hart was here? At this hour?

She did not have to lift the calling card to recognize it, but she did. "Thank you. Tell him I shall be right down."

The maid left and Francesca stared at his card, wondering what he could possibly want. And it was a somewhat odd hour to call. In general, one received callers from noon until four or five in the afternoon. It was quite understood that after four or five, a lady was either resting for the evening's events or preparing for them. Of course, Hart didn't give a fig for convention.

She smiled at that thought and walked into her bathroom. She ceased smiling the moment she saw her reflection—she still looked miserable, and her eyes remained somewhat red and quite puffy from crying. She sighed. A touch of rouge on her lips and cheeks hardly helped. Francesca wiped it off, grabbed her purse so she would not have to return to get it later, and hurried downstairs.

If only this day had never happened.

But that would not change the fact that Bragg was married.

If only her heart would stop hurting her. At least then there would not be a constant reminder of her grief.

Hart was in the reception room, a room usually reserved for greeting large numbers of guests as they arrived for either a party or a ball. He was studying a landscape by a French painter, Corot. Upon hearing her pause on the threshold he turned and smiled at her. "I find Corot far too tame for my tastes," he said in a genial manner.

Her heart fluttered a little as she looked at him. He was

wearing a tuxedo; clearly he was on his way to an evening affair. Like most gentlemen, he looked his most dashing in formal wear. Tonight, Francesca imagined more than a few women would try to catch his eye and win his heart. She wondered if a woman existed who might be capable of that last feat. "Good evening, Calder. This is a surprise."

He smiled as he crossed the room, approaching. "A pleasant one, I hope."

"Of course it is a pleasant one," she said.

His gaze moved over her features, slowly, but differently from the time when he had been drunk. Then, his gaze had been heavy and sensual; now, it was sharp. Francesca avoided eye contact, aware of flushing. "Have you been crying?" he asked with no preamble.

"I am allergic to peanuts," she said with a poor imitation of a smile.

He took her arm. "Don't lie to me."

She started. "I—"

"You have been crying. It is obvious. What has my brother done?"

She stared. Her heart beat heavily now.

His gaze was searching. He said, "I decided, impulsively, I admit, to stop by on my way out for the evening. I want to thank you for your kindness earlier today." His gaze remained intense, holding hers.

She wasn't sure which kindness he referred to. At the church or at Bragg's office? She smiled, this time slightly, but it was genuine. "Why would I be unkind?"

He smiled in return. "Clearly you do not have an unkind bone in your body. I find that charming."

Her heart seemed to skip. He was still holding her arm. Francesca stepped away from him.

He regarded her shrewdly. "I both compel and repel you."

She was surprised. "You do not repel me, Calder."

"Perhaps a better choice of words is *compel and frighten*." It was not a question.

She inhaled. This was not a good topic of conversation,

she decided. "Why have you called? Surely not merely to tell me I am kind?"

"That is why I called. To thank you for your kindness and to tell you, as it is genuine, I find it refreshing." He shrugged.

He was being sincere, and that was refreshing as well, Francesca realized. There was, thus far, no trace of mockery in his tone or in any of his words. "You are welcome," she said, smiling in return.

"I owe you, Francesca," he said flatly.

"You owe me nothing," she replied, startled.

He continued to smile, and it was clear he felt that he owed her a kindness, or something, in return for her actions that day. "So why did you walk in here looking so distressed?" he asked.

Her smile vanished. She turned away. She hesitated, but could not think clearly and could not decide what—or what not—to say.

He came up behind her. "I think I know."

His breath feathered her nape. She turned, stepping back, hoping that was not a habit of his. "I am a bit crushed," she said in an understatement that was even a lie.

"I see."

She hugged herself. "Bragg has a wife. I am afraid I had no idea, and I have some small affection for him." She forced a smile. "Or I did," she lied yet again.

He cupped her cheek. "Poor Francesca."

She stared, wide-eyed.

He dropped his hand. "I was wondering where this little drama would lead. So he finally found the courage to tell you. Well, I cannot applaud him, really. You should be angry, my dear. He should have told you the minute you met. So what will you do now?" His gaze remained on hers.

"Well, there is nothing to do, of course," Francesca said lightly. She started to turn away; he caught her hand. Perhaps Hart was right. Bragg should have told her sooner.

"Please, my dear. I am a man of the world. You are in love. Your heart is broken. Do not lie to me."

She wanted to cry. She did not. She could only stare.

"Let me advise you, Francesca. My brother is a very honorable man. And you, you are a gentlewoman, an innocent with future prospects."

"I do not care about any future prospects!" she cried, interrupting him.

"Hush." His thumb touched her lower lip.

Shocked, Francesca pulled away, her gaze wide and on his.

"You know, I might very well become jealous," he said, staring thoughtfully at her.

"Please," she began.

He shook his head, as if to clear it. "Bragg can exercise incredible self-restraint. He will never cross the line with you. So you must forget this infatuation of yours and move on. Otherwise, it will only bring you heartbreak and grief—not to mention the waste of much time."

"It already has," she muttered.

"I can see that." He sighed. "Were *you* not involved, this would have been a most amusing melodrama. As it is, I admit, I look at you and am somewhat moved." He shook his head again.

"I don't know what to say." She hesitated. "Does Bragg love his wife? At all?"

Hart laughed. "She's a bitch."

Francesca gasped.

"Forgive me. But you did ask. She is also a slut, by the way. I do believe her current lover is a Spanish count." He shook his head. "If I were Bragg, and I do mean literally, I would bring her here, force her to live with me, and keep her on a very short leash. Instead, he lets her roam Europe with her string of paramours, living in the lap of luxury, as if she were a queen, which she believes she is. He continues to pay her exorbitant bills, bills he cannot afford, by the way, and chooses to look the other way."

Was Leigh Anne really so bad? Oddly, Francesca was relieved. And he had not answered her question.

As if reading her thoughts, Hart said, "No, my dear, sweet Francesca, Bragg does not love Leigh Anne. But she is the cross he has decided he will bear, as he is too proper to get rid of her—one way or another."

Francesca gasped. "Surely you did not mean whatever it is you sounded as if you were saying!"

He laughed. "You are so naïve. That is also charming. Which world have you grown up in? The real world, or one of poetry, novels, and schoolbooks?"

Francesca did not bother to answer. She sank down on a love seat. *At least Bragg did not love his wife. At least she was truly a horrible woman.* Then she realized the train of her thoughts and she was angry. She must get over him! In that, Hart was right. Because there simply was no hope.

He sat down right beside her, and as he was a muscular man, the small love seat instantly became too crowded. He took her hand. "You are so despondent. I confess, I do not ·like seeing you this way. I am on my way to a black-tie supper. Why don't you join me? I will wait for you to change and we shall be fashionably late." He smiled at her.

Francesca tried to tug her hand from his, but it was impossible. So she stood up, and he had to let her palm go. "I do appreciate the offer, and your *kindness,* Calder, but I am afraid I must decline."

He slowly rose. "Why? So you can mope about this empty house?" His gaze was searching; she avoided it.

For it was after seven o'clock. Anthony was waiting for her. She would solve this case—alone. Without Bragg. As they were no longer a team.

Even that notion hurt.

"I am afraid a bit of moping is just what the doctor has ordered," Francesca said with a small smile.

He studied her, too closely, and said, "I have good instincts, and I think you are up to something, but for the life of me, I have no idea what that something might be."

"What, me?" Francesca gasped, her eyes wide and, she hoped, innocent. She batted her lashes at him.

He laughed, caught her by the waist, and pulled her shamelessly close—completely up against his side. He pecked her cheek; his lips seemed to make her skin burn. "Forget it,

Francesca. You shall never be the coquette. I am off, then. If you need me, your good deeds of these past few days shall be reciprocated. You may call anytime, night or day." He winked at her. "Even if I am indisposed, I shall accept your call."

Francesca was thoroughly taken aback. She walked him to the door. "Thank you, Calder. I do appreciate that."

"You should. I cannot recall ever making such an offer before. Now. Chin up. Forget my duty-shackled brother. No good can come of it, not for either of you. There are other fish in the sea. Trust me." He grinned at her and received his hat and coat from a servant.

As he did, a maid hurried up to her. "Miss Cahill? I am so sorry, but this came earlier and Penelope forgot to give it to you."

Francesca accepted a small and oddly stained paper from her as Calder shrugged on his coat. She opened it and instantly saw a child's labored scrawl, and knew the note was from Joel even before she read it.

Mis Cahill. cant come tonite. Sorry. Joel.

Her heart sank.

"Trouble?"

She jerked and looked up at Hart, who was watching her closely. Darn it, but now she would have to meet Anthony alone. "No." She smiled. A doorman was opening the front door for him. Francesca said, "So we remain friends after all."

"Yes, we do," he said with a merry glint in his eyes. "I *am* one to hold a grudge, but not against a beautiful, clever, *and* kind woman." He bowed elaborately at her.

She laughed.

"I like that sound," he said, and with a parting smile he left.

Francesca paused, watching him stride down the steps and to his elegant, overly large coach, one drawn by four stunning blacks. A footman in dark livery opened the door for him and he disappeared inside. The coach moved around the circular half of the drive, the team quite spectacular, and down it, toward the avenue on the other side. Francesca sighed.

That had been like being in the eye of a hurricane, she decided. One false step, and she might have found herself in gale winds. She didn't know whether to be pleased or alarmed. Of course, having such a man as a friend could not hurt. Especially given her current new line of work.

She watched a shadow detach itself from a large oak tree by the house and take on the shape of a man. He approached the house swiftly.

Mark Anthony. Tension overcame her. She would have to go alone. Breathlessly Francesca turned. "Wallace, please get my coat and hat. I am going out."

She was on her way to catch a killer.

Only now, she was afraid.

Mark Anthony had had another hired fare waiting for them on the avenue, and this time, to his credit, he paid the fare when they arrived at their destination, a small hotel on the corner of Broadway and Houston Street. During the ride downtown he did not speak, although he remained watchful. "This is it," he said, gesturing for her to precede him up the hotel's front steps.

The hotel was called the Grande, rather inappropriately, as it was a run-down four-story brick building that looked neither inviting nor luxurious. "After you," Mark Anthony said with a smile.

Francesca hesitated. She was extremely nervous, and the fact that Anthony had not been talkative during the cab ride had not helped calm her down. "I thought Georgette did not want her whereabouts known," she said, stalling. Her mind raced. Should she go up? She desperately wanted to speak to Georgette. What if this was a trap? But if this was a trap, what kind of trap could it be?

Anthony smiled at her with his cocky grin. "I just took the room two hours ago," he said.

That did not ease her fears.

He looked directly at her. "Why are you so nervous? I

thought you believed my *sister* to be innocent." He grinned as he said "sister."

"I do," she said tersely.

"Are you afraid of me?" He was mockingly incredulous.

She could not answer him.

"Listen." His smile faded. "I might be a lot of things, but in my own way, I'm a gentleman."

Francesca knew her expression had become disbelieving.

He jabbed his hand at her. "What that means is that I don't hurt ladies."

She looked at him. Did that mean he hurt other kinds of people?

"Oh, forget it." He seemed disgusted. "Do you want to see Georgette or not?"

Francesca found herself nodding. She told herself that first thing tomorrow, she would purchase a gun just in case she ever had the need to protect herself. Perhaps Calder would help her.

Anthony nodded gruffly and gestured for her to precede him in. Francesca lifted her skirts and did so, entering a small lobby with a dilapidated couch and a threadbare rug. It was empty except for the clerk reading a newspaper behind the reception desk.

Anthony ignored him and they walked up the unlit narrow stairs to the second floor. He knocked on door 200.

"Who is it?" Georgette asked in a low and fearful voice from the other side of the door.

"It's me—an' Miss Cahill," Anthony returned.

The door was unchained and unbolted. Francesca stepped into a small bedroom with a single bed, on chair, a bureau, and wall pegs. There were no personal items in the room, so clearly Anthony had been telling the truth about only renting it a few hours ago.

Relief filled Georgette's eyes, but whether it was at the sight of Francesca or Anthony, Francesca did not know. Georgette had eyes only for Francesca. She looked extremely agitated, at once nervous and distraught. "Miss Cahill," she cried, "I am so glad you have come!"

"Please, think nothing of it. I am worried about you, Miss de Labouche," Francesca said, clasping the other woman's hand briefly.

"And I am so worried, too!" Georgette cried. "The boy said you are working for me. But I have not hired you! Then Sean said you were doing so for free. Is that true?"

Francesca nodded and glanced at Anthony, who was standing with his brawny arms folded across his broad chest, watching them both with interest. So that was his real name. Or at least, so she assumed.

"He also said that you said the police do think I am the murderess!"

Francesca gripped her elbow. "Please, Georgette. Your disappearance has only heightened the police commissioner's suspicions. You must trust me now. You must come with me, to police headquarters. He wishes, dearly, to speak with you."

Georgette looked fearfully at Anthony. He said, "Can you swear, on the Bible, that she will not be arrested?"

Francesca looked at him. She looked back at Georgette. They were both waiting. She wet her lips. "That would be an impossible promise to make."

"I thought so," he said.

"I didn't do it. You still believe me, don't you?" Georgette asked, tugging on her sleeve.

"Yes, I do," Francesca said. "But why are you so afraid?"

"Because I am the mistress. I am the other woman, the cheap woman, the immoral one—the whore! Whom shall they blame? I mean, I think she did it—his wife. They've hated each other for years! But it happened in my house. I am the one who will go to jail for this. I am the one who will hang, because I am not a real lady!"

"You will not go to jail, because you are innocent," Francesca said firmly. "And we do not hang murderers, Miss de Labouche."

"But you can't promise me that!" Georgette cried.

"You convince the police commissioner, being as he is your *friend* and all," Anthony said softly.

Francesca looked at him. Their eyes locked. "What did that innuendo mean?" she asked stiffly.

He smiled at her. And he shrugged.

"Bragg happens to be married. Did you know that?" she flashed. She felt dangerous now.

He stared, his smile disappearing. "No, I did not. That's news. What's the deal? His wife a crazy woman, locked up in an attic somewhere?"

"That's not amusing. She lives in Europe," Francesca said tersely.

"He's still your friend. It's the word on the street. You can walk into his office anytime, they say. So convince him Georgette is innocent."

Francesca was so angry—and she did not know where the anger had come from. She marched over to Anthony and faced him down. In her one-inch heels, they were exactly the same height, meaning they stood eye-to-eye and nose-to-nose now. Of course, her bonnet actually gave her an inch or two in the end result. "Look, Mr. Anthony, or Sean, or whatever your name is. Just what is it to you? Why are you so bent on protecting Miss de Labouche? Who is she, to you? Are you her *friend*?" she demanded furiously.

"Well, well, the little Fifth Avenue lady has claws." Anthony grinned at her, as if amused. "Georgette and I are old *friends,* if you know what I mean."

"You were lovers," Francesca said.

"My, someone is awfully curious," Anthony said, his green eyes sparkling with mischief.

Georgette stepped between them. "We haven't been lovers in years, but we have remained good friends, that is all," Georgette said.

Francesca regarded her. "Your neighbors think he is your brother."

She shrugged. "You know how people talk. It's easier to say he's my brother. That way he can call and tongues don't wag."

Francesca believed her. She turned back to Anthony. "Did you know Randall? Had you ever met him?"

"Nope, but I knew of him, and I'd seen him around. We didn't run in the same circles," he said wryly.

"Did he treat Georgette well?"

Anthony stared. "If you're asking me if I liked him, the answer is . . ." He shrugged emphatically. "Georgette's a grown woman. She got a good deal. He paid the rent, the staff, bought her a few trinkets, some clothes. I've seen better and I've seen worse. He didn't beat her, or hurt her in any way. I'd never heard her say he was mean or jealous. It was OK. It was good for Georgette."

Francesca didn't know whether to believe him or not. She looked at Georgette, who was an attractive, lush woman—the kind of woman whose attentions many men would enjoy and covet. Did Anthony still like her in that way? Had he been jealous—and enough so to kill Randall?

He smirked at her. "Don't look at me. I had no damn reason to kill him. The one thing I'm not is a killer."

Francesca thought she just might believe him. But she saw Anthony's eyes go past her, to where Georgette stood, and there was a warning in them. Francesca turned.

Georgette looked about to cry. She began wringing her hands convulsively. "Sean—"

"Shut up," he said harshly.

Tears filled her eyes.

"What is it?" Francesca asked quickly. "What are the two of you hiding?"

Georgette began to cry.

"Shit," Anthony said. "Look at what you've done." He was angry, and Francesca stepped away from him—but he was moving to Georgette. He put his arm around her and she wept on his shoulder.

They were still intimate, Francesca realized with a start. She felt certain.

He murmured, "Miss Cahill is going to go. I'll drop her at the police station. She'll convince the commissioner you're innocent and in no time you can go home. Don't cry."

"My life is over. I'm going to jail," she wept.

A frisson swept over Francesca.

"Sean . . ." It was a plea.

"No!"

Georgette pulled away. "Someone's going to find out! That little busybody overheard you and Paul on the street! She's bound to have told the police already. I know Mary from years of being with Paul; trust me!"

Conversations flashed through Francesca's mind. Mary, tight-lipped and filled with anger, saying, *Hart was blackmailing my father. . . . I overheard them on the day of the murder.*

She had been speaking about Calder Hart. But Hart had been in Baltimore, or en route from Baltimore, at the time.

Anthony's jaw was clenched. "Not another word," he warned.

But Hart wouldn't have condescended to blackmail his father anyway—no matter what. Francesca looked at the two of them, seized with total comprehension. "You were blackmailing him, weren't you? The two of you? Or was it only Anthony? Mary overheard a conversation on the morning of the murder, and she thought it was between Randall and Hart, but Hart wasn't in the city at the time. It was you," she said, looking at Anthony. "Randall was arguing with *you.*"

Anthony's jaw tensed. Georgette cried, "I didn't know about the blackmail, I swear, not until it was too late, and even then, I had nothing to do with it!"

Francesca felt the horror begin.

Anthony's eyes locked with hers.

His eyes were so cold now. They were cold enough to be the eyes of a killer.

Francesca tried to discern just how far behind her the door was. Because she had to make a run for it, now.

"Christ," Anthony said in real disgust. Then, "Not another word, Georgette. And as for you, Miss Cahill, you have just ruined my evening."

TWENTY

Francesca stood unmoving by the door, her pulse pounding so rapidly now, she felt as if she had the strength of several men. She *had* to make a run for it. Georgette was grabbing Anthony's arm. "This isn't her fault. She is trying to help us!"

"Like hell she is. Did you have to tell her about the damned stupid blackmail scheme?" Anthony asked grimly.

"It was stupid! And Paul did not deserve it!" Georgette cried.

Francesca moved the tiniest step backward. Her hands were now at her sides.

"Forget Paul, because he's dead. Now what? She knows about the blackmail, and this makes me—and you, Georgette—look damn bad. And by 'bad' I do mean guilty." Anthony rolled his eyes.

"They already think I'm guilty."

"That's right, they do, so you have just nailed down your own coffin. What the hell are we going to do with her?"

Georgette stopped crying. "We're going to send her home."

"She won't go home. She'll go right to Bragg with a mouthful of stories. Damn it." Anthony glared at Francesca.

She had managed to move another inch backward, and she felt certain that she could touch the doorknob if she tried. If her memory served her correctly, it had not been chained or locked when she and Anthony had entered the room.

Anthony sighed. "I need to think." He looked down grimly at his scuffed brown shoes.

Francesca turned, and she had been right: she could reach the knob—she wrenched open the door.

"Damn!" Anthony shouted, reaching for her.

Francesca felt his hand grazing her sleeve, but she was moving so quickly that he did not catch hold of her. She fled down the narrow hall, with Anthony just steps behind.

But the stairwell was blocked. Someone was coming up. "Move!" Francesca shouted frantically, barging into the man. Anthony would catch her now!

They collided and the man gripped her shoulders.

"Let me go!" Francesca screamed, aware of Anthony behind her on the second-floor landing, just inches away and poised to seize her as well. And then she met the man's dark, familiar eyes.

"Francesca, it's me!" Calder Hart was shouting.

She was stunned.

"Police!" someone shouted from below as a horde of racing footsteps sounded. A whistle blew.

"Shit!" Anthony cried, whirling.

Hart shoved Francesca to the wall as Anthony fled, a half a dozen policemen racing up the stairs. Bragg was at their head.

As he raced past Francesca he glanced at her but did not stop.

At the end of the hall was a window. Anthony wrestled it open, clearly intending to jump to the ground two floors below, even at the risk of breaking his legs—or his neck. Bragg collared him.

Instantly Anthony straightened, lifting both hands into the air. "I give up," he said.

"That's good," Bragg returned, pushing him face-first into the wall. "Search him," he said to his men. "Then cuff him and throw him in the wagon and book him on suspicion of murder."

Francesca suddenly sank against the wall. It was only then that she realized Calder Hart had his arm securely around her waist and was holding her upright. She tore her gaze from Bragg, Anthony, and the policemen to Hart. His eyes were already on her face.

"Are you all right?" he asked.

She nodded. And she felt her knees give way.

Instantly his grip tightened. He lifted her, holding her upright against his side.

"How . . . ?" she began, trailing off.

"I followed you." He smiled briefly at her. "When I left your house, I was highly suspicious. As well as curious. When I saw you leave with this man, I grew even more, well, let's leave it at curious. When you entered the hotel with him, I learned his name from the clerk." He shook his head. "Francesca, Randall told me that he was a blackmail victim the night we met at the Republican Club, and when he did, of course I forced Anthony's name out of him. The moment I realized who you were with, I went round the corner to the local police precinct and had Bragg telegraphed." He smiled now. It reached his eyes. "The timing was rather fortunate, was it not?"

She nodded. "Thank you," she said. And then she stiffened.

Bragg had come to stand behind her. Slowly Francesca turned.

His amber eyes were searching. His gaze seemed to penetrate not just her own eyes, but to the depths of her heart and soul. Her heart lurched in response and began anew a frantic beating. Francesca knew she would never hate this man.

Staring back at him, into his golden eyes, at his unique and stunning features, she knew she would be connected to him for all time.

"Are you all right?" he asked softly, and she knew he referred not just to her physical state of being but to her emotional well-being as well. After all, they had not spoken since he had made his devastating declaration of the truth. She couldn't nod.

"I am trying. . . . It is hard."

He reached out, as if to take her hand, in a gesture she had come to know. But instead, he hesitated, and their gazes met and held again. And she saw his strength and will power then. She saw his resignation. He dropped his hand without touching her. "I'm going to have to speak with you, Francesca. Professionally, of course."

Francesca nodded. Her heart was breaking all over again. How could it still hurt like this? Would the anguish ever end?

She did not think so.

She thought, perhaps, it would dull, but she would carry the ache around with her for the rest of her life. She loved him that much.

"She's tired. She's been through hell. Let her go home and get some rest," Hart said grimly. "And then I would suggest that you stay as far away from her as possible."

Francesca realized his arm was still around her in a very intimate way. She slipped free. He was also angry. How odd. "That's all right. I can come downtown now. I prefer to help."

Bragg's jaw flexed. "No. My brother is correct. Hart, take her home, please, if you don't mind?"

Hart smiled. "It will be my pleasure."

Francesca stared at Bragg. She did not want to go. She wanted to stay there, on that small stairwell, with him. And if Hart hadn't been present, she did not think she could have stopped herself from reaching out and touching Bragg's cheek, his jaw. He seemed so distressed, too.

He stared back, a painful light in his eyes. "Can I stop by early in the morning?"

She nodded. "Of course, Bragg. You need not even ask."

"Is nine all right?" His gaze slipped over her features again, this time lingering on her mouth.

She nodded again. He was thinking about the kisses they had shared and she knew it. And now he looked so grim and unhappy.

Hart made a sound. It was one of disgust. "I shall be downstairs. I cannot watch this," he said.

She didn't speak. She couldn't. She was feeling so drained that it was almost like being lifeless.

The police were hustling Anthony toward them. He looked unhappy and grim. Francesca got off the stairwell to let them pass. He looked right at her. "I didn't do it," he said.

Francesca looked away, ignoring him.

Georgette was next. One officer escorted her downstairs.

She looked at Francesca, tears in her eyes. "You have to help us," she said. "We are innocent."

Francesca closed her eyes tightly. When she opened them, her gaze met Bragg's.

"You have done good work today," he said softly. "You are a fine sleuth, Francesca."

Her heart soared to impossible heights. "Thank you," she whispered, desperately wanting to reach for his hand.

He seemed to want to say more. He hesitated. Then, "I shall see you tomorrow then. At nine."

"Tomorrow," she echoed. And Francesca felt a tear sliding down her cheek. She was aghast. She tried to turn away.

He caught her by her arms. "Please don't cry. Your sorrow is killing me," he whispered.

"I am not crying," she lied. She smiled as bravely as possible up at him.

He hesitated and she thought, stunned, that he was about to kiss her.

Then footsteps sounded once, twice below them on the stairs. Hart said loudly, "I cannot leave the two of you for a second. I am putting Francesca in my coach. I am going downtown with you, Rick."

Bragg stepped away from her. "That is a good idea," he said.

Hart's elegant brougham was even more luxurious inside than out. Francesca sank in the corner of a plush red leather seat, found a fur throw, and wrapped herself in it, as if the sable might become a safe cocoon in which to hide. She should be pleased, she knew, for they had found Randall's killer; instead, she kept recalling the look in Bragg's eyes when she had turned away and gone downstairs. He was as anguished as she was, Francesca thought glumly.

She closed her eyes and suddenly heard Anthony saying, as clear as day, *I didn't do it.* Her eyes flew open.

She did not want to envision him now. Especially not while making that statement—his gaze had been hard but di-

rect. He *had* been blackmailing Paul Randall, with or without
Georgette's prior knowledge and help.

Another image and recollection assailed her strongly. "We
are innocent," Georgette had said, looking at Fran as directly.

Francesca sat up grimly. In spite of her grief, it was impossible now not to think about the two of them more fully.
And what about the fact that Bill Randall had been to Georgette's house after the murder? Francesca did not think she
was mistaken about having seen him there. If only Joel had
been present, if only he had seen Bill as well! But she felt
certain Bill had been to the house and that he had known his
father was dead. Which meant he knew the killer, or was
protecting the killer. Francesca could not imagine him and
Anthony as partners. That was inconceivable.

And committing blackmail did not necessarily mean that
one could commit cold-blooded murder.

Something wasn't right.

*I am the other woman, the cheap woman, the immoral
one—the whore! Whom shall they blame? . . . I think she did
it . . .*

Francesca stiffened. Why hadn't she paid more attention
to Georgette when she had been accusing Henrietta of killing
her husband? Perhaps because it had been so clichéd and the
widow was the obvious choice for the mistress to point the
finger at. But there hadn't been any hatred in Georgette's
words. She had been frightened, yes, but she had been impassioned as well. What else had she claimed?

They've hated each other for years!

Dear God, Henrietta had been faking her tears at the funeral. Not only did Francesca know that from watching her,
but she had picked up the handkerchief Henrietta had dropped
and it had been as dry as a bone. Her swoon had been a matter
of theatrics as well.

Francesca's pulse raced with excitement. Oh, my. It looked
as if they had apprehended the wrong person. But this would
make so much sense and it would explain Bill's actions. For
who had more motivation than the long-suffering widow?

She rapped on the partition and when it was opened by

the driver, she said, "Number Eighty-nine East Fifty-seventh
Street, please. I must make a stop and I won't be long."

"As you wish, miss," the coachman replied.

It was only half past eight, but Francesca was told that the
Randalls were not receiving callers at this hour. She was also
told that Mr. Randall would receive her tomorrow at noon.
Francesca barely heard the maid, because from where she
stood in the foyer, she could look right down the hall, and at
its end the parlor door was ajar. Light spilled from that room.
She could also hear voices coming from within, and even
though she could not see anyone, one of the voices was
Mary's.

Francesca smiled at the maid. "I shall return on the morrow, then," she said, and the door was closed before her.
Francesca did not move.

She heard no lock turning, but it was early yet, too early
to lock the doors.

Francesca counted to a thousand, slowly. Then, shoving
aside any twinges of guilt, she tested the doorknob. As she
had thought, the door had not been locked yet.

She was becoming rather adept at trespassing, she thought,
slipping into the empty foyer. Just a week or so ago, she had
entered the Burton household in the exact same—and ille-
gal—manner. The second time was much easier than the first.
There was almost no guilt, but there was fear. If Henrietta
was a killer, Francesca might well be in trouble if caught.

The parlor door remained ajar. Now she could hear Bill's
voice, but not what he was saying. Francesca debated eavesdropping, and her need to know more won. Her fear increased
as she moved cautiously down the hallway and tried to blend
into the wall at its end. But she could hear them clearly now.

"Don't you think you have had one glass too many of
sherry?" Bill asked calmly.

"Not really. It has been a gruesome day," Mary returned
sharply. "They are all gruesome days, now."

"Far more gruesome for me than you," Bill said darkly. "I

do look forward to returning to the university—that is, if I can afford the tuition."

A silence fell. It was brooding.

Francesca could hear her own breathing. It was tense and labored and she sought to relax.

Then, "At least we do not have to live with his hypocrisy anymore," Mary said bitterly.

"But the question is, how shall we live? He has left us nothing. He has left me nothing. I am his heir and I am penniless." Bill was angry. "At least you will marry—if you can bring yourself to do it."

"I am never marrying," Mary said vehemently. "You know how I feel about that. More so now than ever. How could Papa have done this to us? How?"

"I don't know why you never saw the truth. After all, Calder Hart has been in our midst for ten years."

"But that was before he met Mama! He explained to me so carefully and I understood completely. But then"—she paused—"I was only eight years old when I met that bastard brother of ours. Papa could have told me he had come to us from the moon and I would have believed him." She sounded tearful. "But you should have told me about her! I should have known about the whore! I am always the last to know everything in this house."

"Poor Mary."

They were silent now, but Francesca stiffened. Was that footsteps she was hearing? She felt herself tremble. Someone was coming downstairs!

She froze. Unfortunately, there was no place to hide and no way to make herself invisible. Was Henrietta approaching, or a servant? The hall was dimly lit, but if the person on the stairs intended to visit the parlor, she would be caught like a mouse in a trap. Sweat trickled down her temples and inside of her bodice. Damn it. Perhaps this was not a good idea.

"I am going to take Miss de Labouche to court. I intend to wrest that house from her," Bill suddenly said. "I could kill father for leaving it to her!"

Francesca had stopped breathing. The intruder had reached

the ground floor. She held her breath and heard the person
moving away from where she stood, toward the front door.
A moment later the person opened a side door and disappeared into another room.

Francesca started to sigh and heard, "Good. And meanwhile, they will hang Hart." Mary was vicious. She laughed,
but the sound turned into a sob. "He has no alibi, he despised
Father, and he will be the first to admit it. God, if only he
had really killed Father!" She started to cry.

Francesca started. What was this? Elation filled her. So the
Randalls knew Hart was innocent . . . which seemed to mean
that they knew the identity of the killer.

"Mary . . . enough. I am going to bed," Bill said abruptly.

Breathless now, Francesca realized that she must either
leave the house or do what she intended in the first place,
which was interview Henrietta. And there was no time to
procrastinate. She started to inch down the wall, away from
the parlor, afraid of making a sound and being caught with
her hand in the safe, so to speak.

Then she gave it up. Her strides increased; she reached the
stairs. Her pulse was rioting and sweat was gathering beneath
her chemise, between her breasts. She did not dare breathe
easier as she bounded swiftly up the stairs.

Only a single light was shining on the second floor. But
the door to Henrietta's sitting room was wide open, and she
could be seen sitting at her desk, a pen in hand. She was
writing a letter or a note and Francesca watched her breathlessly. She was an innocuous-looking woman. Plump, well-
dressed, quiet of manner. She did not seem at all like a murderess.

Francesca stepped into the room.

"Mary?" Henrietta turned, but she was not smiling. And
her eyes went wide in shock.

Francesca closed the door behind her. "I am so sorry to
intrude, Mrs. Randall, but I must have a word with you."

It was a moment before Henrietta spoke. "How did you
get up here? Who allowed you in?" She did not stand.

"I do apologize for letting myself in," Francesca said,

watching her closely. She was dry-eyed. She did not appear grief-stricken. "Your son gave a wonderful eulogy today."

"I think you should leave." Henrietta calmly clasped her hands in her lap.

"An innocent man has been arrested for your husband's murder, Mrs. Randall."

Henrietta did not even lift a brow. "And that affects me how?"

"Do you not care?"

She opened her mouth and closed it. "Of course I care." Francesca waited.

"I mean, I want to see my husband's murderer brought to justice. I certainly do."

Francesca sighed. Clearly there had been no love in this marriage. "I am sorry, Henrietta, so sorry, that you have shared most of your life with a man you did not care for."

Henrietta stared. "I loved Paul."

"Did you?"

"Of course."

"But he has been keeping Georgette, a beautiful, younger woman, for years. He has been visiting her like clockwork, every Tuesday and Friday night. He has bought her jewels and furs," Francesca said, not wanting to be mean, but trying to provoke a reaction. "And you have known about it."

Henrietta stared, her expression rather strained. "I am no fool," she said. "Of course I knew."

"How long have you known?"

Henrietta stared. "Forever. Paul has never been faithful to me for a day in his life. Miss de Labouche was not the first, and had he lived, she would not be the last." She remained calm, although tense. "Why are you here, Miss Cahill?"

Francesca was grim. She wet her lips. "Did you follow your husband to his mistress's house on Friday evening and shoot him in the back of the head?" Francesca asked.

Henrietta stared.

"Do not answer her, Mother!" Bill exclaimed from behind Francesca.

Francesca whirled, her heart sinking with stunning force,

to find Bill and Mary standing there, having come into the room undetected. Bill was angry, and justifiably so, while Mary's face was starkly white and pinched with fear.

Mary's face was pinched with fear.

Henrietta was also staring at her children, now on her feet. "Yes," she said, ashen. "I have disliked my husband for years. I grew tired of it all. We argued that morning, over money, of course, and I followed him and shot him in the back of the head."

"Mother!" Bill shouted.

Mary remained tight-lipped, white, and silent.

Francesca looked at Henrietta, who was lying. Oh, dear. What did she do now?

"I am very sorry, Miss Cahill, but you have gone too far," Bill said from behind her.

Francesca turned and met his cold gray eyes. And too late, she saw the gun he held in his hand. *He was going to shoot her.*

But before she could react, he raised the butt and struck her on the head with it.

There was a huge lancing pain, and then there was blackness.

TWENTY-ONE

MONDAY, FEBRUARY 3, 1902—10:00 P.M.

Francesca became aware of a pain arcing through her head. And for one moment, as she fought unconsciousness, she was confused.

Then the heavy blackness dimmed, lifting. As she awoke, the pain increased, and she realized that she was lying down. She stirred, her eyes fluttering open—only to find that she could not move her arms or her legs.

Her eyes flew open as she tried to sit up, but she was incapable of all movement except in her fingers and toes. The comprehension was brutal. *She was tied to a bed.*

Francesca looked from the plain whitewashed ceiling down to her arms and legs and saw that rope bound her wrists and ankles. The bed was simple and placed against one wall, several shelves above it. The room was feminine but neither cozy nor comfortable. The truth struck her then.

Bill Randall had hit her from behind with a heavy object and now she was tied to Mary's bed.

Oh, God. She had never expected this. Henrietta was so mild-mannered; Francesca had actually expected some kind of guilty and stricken confession. Instead, she was tied up—she was a prisoner, for God's sake.

But surely, surely, they would not harm her, would they? Or worse?

But she was already harmed, she reminded herself grimly.

And then she had a truly terrible thought. What if Bragg found her this way?

She flushed, anticipating her humiliation—it would know no bounds. She had to free herself.

Suddenly the bedroom door opened and Bill Randall was standing there.

Francesca met his dark gaze. It was so dispassionate that

fear assailed her. *She was in grave danger indeed.*

"What are you going to do with me?" she whispered.

"I don't know." He stood in the threshold but did not come forward. "Why did you have to snoop, Miss Cahill? Why could you not be like other young ladies your age? Now I have a terrible dilemma. I must protect my family. No matter the cost."

She tried to breathe normally, for it was a way of controlling her fear. "You will never get away with this."

"There is always a way when one is truly motivated," he said, and he turned abruptly and closed the door behind him. Francesca did not hear it lock.

She tugged on the ropes, but to no avail. All she did was become warm and begin sweating. She felt tears of real fear trying to form in her eyes, and sternly she told herself she must remain calm—she must think.

After all, she was a clever woman. She prided herself on her intelligence. Her intelligence was what must save her now.

Did Randall think to kill her?

She shivered, sick to her stomach at the thought.

And then she heard footsteps at the door. They were not Randall's; they were far too soft. She tensed.

The door slowly creaked open and Henrietta stood there. Their gazes locked.

And Henrietta appeared to be on the verge of genuine tears.

Hope flared within Francesca. "Two wrongs do not make a right," she whispered.

Henrietta gazed at her. "Why did you have to come?"

"You know why. Your husband was murdered. No matter how horrible he has been to you and your family, no one deserves that." She did not take her gaze from the other woman's.

Henrietta wet her lips. "I am so sorry," she said.

"Please untie me," Francesca tried. To her own ears, it sounded as if she were begging.

Tears filled Henrietta's eyes. "I can't."

"But Bill will never get away with this. You know he will not."

"He is very clever," she said, ashen.

"You will be all alone when this is over. Your entire family will be taken from you."

A tear fell. It trickled down her face. "I love my children," she whispered. "How could this have happened?"

"I know you love them. And they love you."

Another tear fell. "They deserve better than this."

"Yes, they do. Please, Henrietta. Before this gets out of hand."

Henrietta stared at her, and for one moment Francesca thought she would comply, but instead, she turned and left, not quite closing the door after her.

Francesca collapsed into the mattress. Now what? And no one knew where she was—no! Hart's driver was outside!

That gave her hope. But what if they killed her before the driver suspected anything?

She tested the rope again. It was the kind of cord used to tie parcels for the postal office. She would never be able to break it. Francesca wiggled her wrists, praying that if she tried long enough, she might wiggle her wrists free. After a long moment, it seemed that the bonds were loosening, but her wrists were becoming burned. Francesca stared at the cord there. It was only her imagination, she decided grimly, for the bonds had not loosened at all.

She flopped back on the bed, tired from her efforts and trying to hold the fear at bay. A cramp seized her calf.

Francesca cried out, shaking her leg wildly to alleviate the terrible feeling, and when it had passed, she realized that the loop on her right ankle was far looser than all the other ones. Perhaps there was hope after all! She began to work her ankle in circular motions, breathless with hope, a silent prayer in her mind—and after several long moments, she slipped her foot free.

She could only stare in disbelief at her freed foot. But now what?

There were two shelves above the bed. And the bed was

placed with one side along the wall. She looked up and saw several knickknacks and books. Then she saw the porcelain doll.

She stared, trying to stay calm, but her breathing increased with excitement. She raised her leg experimentally—she could reach the shelf and she could easily knock the doll down.

Her decision was made. Wishing she did not have shoes on, Francesca raised her leg and carefully maneuvered her foot behind the doll. Her intention was to knock the doll to the bed, move it to the wall, and break it. But if the doll did not land on the bed, in the vicinity of her foot, she was back where she had started.

She pushed the doll off of the shelf.

It fell right onto the bed, not near her foot—but near her right hand.

She wanted to shout with relief. She caught it with her fingertips and took a deep, deep breath; then she flung it at the wall by her feet.

It broke, making a brief shattering sound.

Francesca did not pause. She used her foot to push the pieces toward her other hand, a laborious process that took several long minutes. But finally a shard was within reach, and she grabbed it with the fingertips of her left hand. Dear God, she was halfway home!

Drenched with perspiration, she began to maneuver the shard into position until she could saw at the cord around her wrist. It was far easier than she had thought it would be. In a moment, her hand was free.

She wanted to shout with joy.

Instead, Francesca untied herself rapidly and sat up, panting now. She did not pause. She leaped from the bed, dashing to the door. She halted there, straining to hear.

No one seemed to be present.

It was now or never. She would have to race downstairs and to the front door, avoiding detection. And she must not fail. . . . She ran.

Reaching the stairs and pounding down them.

Bill appeared upstairs, coming from one of the bedrooms. "What the hell!" he exclaimed. "She's escaped!"

Francesca reached the ground floor. The front door was just ahead. Never had she run faster. She heard Bill thudding down the stairs in hot pursuit.

She was going to make it. Barely. She was an arm's length from the door. And he was not close enough to grab her.

Francesca seized the doorknob—but it did not budge.

It was locked.

Too late, she realized that it had been a servant coming downstairs earlier and that he or she had locked the door while she eavesdropped in the hallway.

Bill clamped his hand down on her shoulder. "Christ Almighty! How the hell did you get free?" he cried, whirling her about to face him.

Francesca smiled brightly but did not even think. They were both standing on the small rug in the entryway. Mary was now coming downstairs as well. Francesca dug her heel into the rug, and when it caught, she yanked with all of her strength upon it. Bill gasped, thrown off balance as the rug was pulled forward, falling backward, into his sister.

Francesca fled through the closest doorway.

Mark Anthony slouched in the small wooden chair in the tiny bare room used for interrogations. Two detectives sat facing him across a small and rickety wooden table. Bragg stood with his arms folded across his chest, leaning against the closed door of the room. A single lightbulb glared from the ceiling above. The room stank of sweat, tobacco, and blood.

The prevailing silence had been a long one.

"C'mish?" one of the detectives asked, looking over his shoulder at Bragg.

Bragg shoved himself off of the wall. "Last chance," he said softly.

"Fuck you," Anthony said, but not particularly harshly. He had a black eye. The officer who had delivered it had received an instant suspension. There was nothing like making a point. The days of beating and torture were over.

"Throw him in the Tombs." Bragg stalked out of the room, not bothering to close the door behind him. And the moment he had left the prisoner, his thoughts veered uncontrollably, and an image of Francesca filled his mind.

There was no mistaking the terrible accompanying feeling of loss and anguish. It was a feeling he had never before experienced, not like this. He had been ill ever since telling her about his wife, and the only way to avoid the pain and the grief was to concentrate on his work.

How had this happened? They had only just met. How *could* this have happened?

Very easily, he thought, as she was the kind of woman a man might meet once in a lifetime, if he was very lucky.

"Wait!" Anthony shouted.

Relieved, Bragg whirled and re-entered the interrogation room. He stared coldly at Anthony and did not speak.

"I didn't do it," Anthony began.

"You're wasting my time," Bragg said, turning to leave.

"Damn it, I didn't! Why would I kill the bastard? Georgette had a sweet deal. She's my friend. We go back fifteen years, maybe more. Blackmail is one thing. OK, I blackmailed the gent. But I didn't off him," Anthony growled.

Bragg walked out.

"Are you going to release me?" Anthony shouted after him.

He did not answer. He was grim. Francesca tried to penetrate his thoughts again, but he shoved her away. Brooding solved nothing, and he had a case to conclude. Determined not to suffer another distraction that came from the heart, he walked briskly down the corridor, refusing to dwell on his personal life, even though that task seemed a monumental one now. Funny, but it was so easy to forget Leigh Anne even existed, and with Francesca, whom he had only just met, the opposite was true.

His strides brisk, he passed numerous policemen, all of whom looked at him and then, sensing the brewing storm, as quickly looked away. He entered the reception lobby of headquarters. It was a Monday night, so it was relatively quiet there: one gentleman in a top hat was making a complaint, one shabby fellow with holes in his breeches was being booked, and only one or two telegraphs were ringing. Conversation remained hushed. A drunk was in the holding pen behind the front desk, but he had passed out. Georgette de Labouche was in a separate but adjoining cell, and she stood upon glimpsing Bragg, gripping the iron bars. He had intended to ignore her; instead, upon impulse, he wheeled and walked over to her. "How long have you known Anthony?"

"Fifteen years or so," she replied. Then, "My only crime is taking good care of Paul, Commissioner. And Sean's a lot of things, but he isn't a killer."

Bragg did not tell her that he agreed with that. "Is there any detail of that night that you have forgotten to tell me?" he asked.

"No. I have told you everything! I asked Miss Cahill to hide the body because I was so frightened. And when she refused, I decided to run away. Now I know it was stupid . . ." Tears filled her eyes. Then she blinked, her eyes widening, the tears gone.

She had remembered something. "What is it?" he asked sharply.

"Oh, dear. There is one thing, but I don't see how it could be important. When I was about to sneak out of the house, I saw Paul's son walk in. I do not know him except by sight, and I have no idea what he wanted, but he went up the hall, I think into the parlor, where Paul's body was. I ran out then."

Elation seared him. "Thank you, Miss de Labouche." He turned to go.

"When will we be released?"

"Soon," he said.

Bragg turned and as he did so, someone fell into step beside him. "Sean Mackenzie is a well-known swindler and con man. Is he being charged now with Randall's murder? And if so, why? What is his game?"

Christ—it was after ten at night. Did these vultures ever sleep? Bragg vaguely recognized the reporter as that especially irritating newshound from the *Sun*—the one who often sat outside of Bragg's home on Madison Square, snooping and spying upon him and all of his affairs there, both his personal as well as his professional ones. And who had opened his mouth and blabbed about Mackenzie, whose alias was Mark Anthony? Another fly would fall.

"It is after working hours," Bragg said succinctly. "I suggest you leave these premises before I have you thrown out—on your rather large ass."

Kurland dared to smile at him. "The city never sleeps," he began.

Bragg seized him by the throat and threw him against the wall. Kurland cried out. A dozen police officers came rushing over, but no one tried to intervene. "I said leave," Bragg said, and he released the man, shaken by his inexplicable and uncontrollable loss of temper. The rage had been red-hot.

Kurland had turned white. He loosened his collar and gulped air. Finally he said, "Thanks, C'mish. I needed that. I can see we have truly reformed the city's finest." He grinned and then seemed to realize he was pressing his luck, for he blanched anew and quickly left.

Bragg rigidly watched him go, dismayed by his own behavior. His brief attack would undoubtedly be in the morning's paper, made out to be far worse than it was. Damn it. The mayor would demand an explanation—and there was no reasonable one to make. Police commissioners did not attack civilians, or even criminals for that matter.

"Someone is in a fine humor indeed," his half brother drawled from behind him.

This was just what he needed now. Bragg turned, his men having quickly dispersed, no one speaking, everyone hushed and avoiding him now as if he carried the plague.

"What do you want now, Calder?" His tone sounded weary to his own ears. It crossed his mind that there was something he must say to Francesca, or something that he must do, yet in truth, nothing could change the facts of his life, and everything pertinent had been said.

"I cannot believe what I just saw." Hart was laughing. "My

lily-white brother has assaulted someone. My lily-white brother who is a police officer!" He was crowing, in fact.

"I have a murderer to arrest. I have no time for this."

Hart's smile vanished. "Anthony is not the one?"

"No, he is not." Bragg walked away from Hart and ordered a dozen officers to assemble for a raid.

Hart had followed him and when he had finished directing his captain, Bragg faced him, irritated. "Why are you here? What do you want?"

Hart studied him. He seemed serious now. "I want you to leave Francesca alone."

Bragg stiffened, all thought of the imminent arrest vanishing from his mind. "Actually, I want *you* to leave her alone, Calder," he said coldly. "But I believe I have already stated that."

Hart's smile was mirthless. "But I am not the one who has a wife, and I am not the one who has misled her, nor am I the one currently breaking her heart."

Unfortunately, he happened to be right. "And since when is it Francesca?"

Hart smiled. "We are friends."

"You just met her!" He felt explosive. He could not seem to get a grip on himself these days. "And you do not even know what it is to have a lady for a friend."

"Perhaps not. Until now. But oddly, I have become inexplicably fond of her, and I do not like what has happened."

Bragg felt his temper imploding. "Never think to come between myself and Francesca," he warned.

Hart smiled, and it was colder than before. "My dear brother, there is no 'you and Francesca.' There will never be a 'you and Francesca.' She is young and with prospects; you are married and too honorable to ruin her. What a shame. She will get over you, and she will fall in love with someone else. It is the way of the world." He was not mocking now.

"Just what are you saying?" Bragg asked, incredulous. Did his amoral brother think to amuse himself with Francesca? Or to *pursue* her?

Of course he did. Calder pursued everything in skirts.

"I am saying you should do what is truly honorable, you should exit her life, until her wounds heal, and then, perhaps, you might be somewhat of a casual friend, a kind of acquaintance."

He was right again. Bragg stared. Finally he managed, "So you can enter it?"

"How jealous you are!" Hart laughed. "I have not one honorable bone in my body, and not one marital intention, and Francesca shall remain my friend, and that is that. Nothing more. What? Do not tell me you are afraid I will think to court her?" He was truly amused.

Bragg was not relieved. "You have come all this way to tell me to leave Francesca alone? I can hardly believe it."

Hart studied him. "Actually, I cannot believe it of myself, either. But I have owed her one, and now the debt is repaid."

Bragg hardly knew what to think. "You are acting out of character, my friend, and I have business to conclude." He walked away. "It is time for Bill Randall to come downtown."

"Don't let her get away!" Mary shouted wildly.

Francesca ran through a dark and unlit dining room and into a brightly lit kitchen. She heard Randall curse and set chase. The maid who had answered the door earlier was drying plates and putting them in a cupboard. "Help! Call the police! They have murdered their father!" Francesca shouted at the stunned girl, dashing across the kitchen.

Bill Randall was just entering the room, Mary behind him. "There's nowhere to go, Miss Cahill!" he shouted.

There was a back door. Francesca was on her way to it when it crossed her mind that the yard out back might be closed off and she would truly be trapped if she went outside. Out of the corner of her eye, she saw several cast-iron pots and pans on the stove. She did not even think. She grabbed one, whirled, and struck out at Bill Randall, who was directly behind her, as hard as she could.

The fry pan hit him squarely on one side of the face, and the blow halted him in his tracks.

Their eyes met, his wide with shock.

And then he collapsed to the floor.

"You have killed him!" Mary screamed from the dining room doorway.

Francesca thought she might be right, but never mind that now. Clutching the big heavy iron pan, she looked up from the unconscious, or dead, man sprawled at her feet. Mary faced her, yards away, as white as a sheet. The housemaid had disappeared, Francesca hoped to scream her lungs out for the police. Mary and Francesca stared at each other. Neither moved.

A rigid silence fell.

Francesca knew she had to do something, but what? She elevated the pan threateningly as a plan occurred to her. "Do not move. Or you shall be next."

Mary remained frozen.

Francesca wondered how long she could hold the heavy pan in such a manner, and she also did not think she could actually hit Mary with it—the girl remained just barely out of reach. But Mexican standoffs could be broken. She said, "See if your brother is dead."

"No," Mary said. Her tone was ice-cold. "Do you take me for a fool, Miss Cahill?"

"No," Francesca said, not quite calmly, "I take you for a ruthless murderess."

Mary smiled. "How clever you are. But can you prove it? And will you?"

Francesca wet her lips. "I don't think I will have to."

"I shall never confess," Mary returned, her eyes glittering. And she reached into her bodice.

Somehow, Francesca knew a small derringer was there. And as Mary pulled the dainty but deadly pistol out, Francesca heaved the cast-iron pan. The gun went off, the pan struck Mary's temple, and the girl crumbled at Francesca's feet.

Francesca cried out, swaying uncontrollably from the momentum of her blow.

Francesca stared down at them both. She began to shake. Oh, God. Had she killed them both?

Someone groaned. It was Bill Randall. And then Mary tried to get onto her hands and knees, but she failed, collapsing once again.

Henrietta appeared in the kitchen doorway. She looked at her daughter and son, both lying in a heap on the floor, and burst into tears.

"It is over, Henrietta," Francesca said, as kindly as possible. "I know you were trying to protect Mary, but she must pay for her crimes."

"I never wanted to hurt anybody!" Henrietta cried. "But dear God, something is wrong with my daughter, terribly so."

Francesca agreed silently with that—in fact, something was wrong with everyone in the Randall family—but she did not voice her opinions aloud. Instead, as Bill stirred again, she tightened her grasp on the frying pan when there was a movement in the opposite doorway. She looked up and her gaze locked with Bragg's.

His golden eyes were wide and riveted upon the kitchen scene—upon her.

Just in the nick of time, she managed to think, lowering the pan at long last.

Behind him stood several officers. Relief flooded her now. "I have found your killer, Bragg," she said.

Slowly, looking at the heap of humanity at her feet and then back at her face, he smiled. "Yes, I can see that," he said. And then his expression changed. "Jesus, Francesca! You are bleeding!"

She looked down, saw red, and realized he was right.

TWENTY-TWO

Francesca realized that she had rubbed her wrists raw in the process of freeing herself. But before she could tell Bragg that she was fine, he was at her side, holding her hand up so he could inspect it. He stared at the abrasions and then looked up. "I thought you had been shot," he said grimly.

Francesca now saw Mary's small gun lying on the floor, not far from where she had fallen. "No. I . . ." She hesitated.

"Thank God you are all right," he said, his amber eyes on hers.

Her heart melted and sang all at once. "I am truly fine, Bragg," she said softly. There was no mistaking his concern for her welfare. But then it flickered through her mind that his concern changed nothing and that Hart was right—they were star-crossed lovers now.

Randall's murderer was about to be arrested. The crime had been solved. She had narrowly escaped God only knew what fate, and she was with Bragg. Her pleasure had been intense, and now it started to crumble, piece by piece and slowly.

His gaze did not waver. "You are going to tell me why you are here and what happened," he said. "Of course."

She smiled. "Of course."

Bragg nodded to his men then. "Escort Bill and Mary Randall to headquarters. Put them in separate cells. There is to be no conversation between them." He turned to Henrietta, who had sat down in a kitchen chair and was as white as a ghost. "Mrs. Randall, will you wait for me in the parlor? I am afraid we must speak."

She nodded with resignation.

"Murphy, escort her, please."

The burly detective went over to the plump woman, helped her to her feet, and guided her from the kitchen.

"They may need a physician," Francesca remarked. Mary was moaning now, but she hadn't moved.

"Undoubtedly," Bragg said. Then, "How did you realize that the killer was Mary?"

"At first I thought it was Henrietta," she said. "It was the way both Georgette and Anthony claimed their innocence. But after speaking with Henrietta, I realized she was innocent, too, and trying to protect her daughter. The giveaway was the glance she exchanged with Bill over Mary's head when I was trying to speak with her. I realized they both sought to protect Mary. I also saw how frightened Mary was, and the truth was crystal clear." She dreaded having to tell him everything that had happened that evening. But of course, she must.

Bill Randall was recovering consciousness, and two officers had him on his feet. Mary still lay prone. Briefly Francesca and Bragg turned to watch Bill being pushed and dragged out. He did give her an ugly look before he disappeared from view.

"You have made an enemy," Bragg said flatly. "Francesca, this sleuthing penchant of yours will not do."

"But I solved the case, Bragg," she said with real satisfaction. Then, upon seeing his look, she added quickly, "With your help."

"Of course." He shook his head. "What happened to your wrists?"

Bill Randall was going to be charged for his efforts to conceal his sister's crime. If Francesca did not tell Bragg what he had done to her, he would not be charged for assaulting her. "He hit me over the head, knocked me out, and tied me up," she said lightly.

"What!" he exclaimed, a shout. His eyes were wide with shock.

She was wide-eyed with what she hoped was both nonchalance and innocence. She kept a bright smile in place. "But I am fine. As you can see. No worse for wear. Not at all." She decided not to tell him that her head hurt and that she had to see a doctor.

"Francesca, you are not fine; your wrists are bruised and

bleeding, and you could have been seriously hurt. Mary shot at you, too, did she not? I can smell it," he said.

The acrid smell of the fired gun did hang in the air. Francesca was meek. "Well, you have jogged my memory. Yes, she did try to shoot me."

"What am I going to do with you?" he cried. "How can I convince you to cease this crime-solving profession you have taken to?"

She met his gaze. He was so concerned for her welfare. She was fiercely—foolishly—glad. "Bragg, surely you agree that I am a good sleuth?"

"I refuse to agree," he growled. "And if your wrists weren't raw, I would grab them and shake some sense into you. Instead, I am directing you home. Put salve on them—at once."

"Yes, Commissioner," she said with a smile and what she hoped was a properly obedient tone.

"Am I amusing you?"

"Never," she said. She hesitated, her eyes sparkling, and said, "We did it again, Bragg."

He sighed.

TUESDAY, FEBRUARY 4, 1902—2:00 P.M.
Francesca was on time for the lunch date she had made with her sister that following day, but Connie had arrived early and was already seated at their linen-clad table in the large high-ceilinged and elegant dining room of the Plaza Hotel. Connie smiled as Francesca sat down opposite her. She looked very well, stunning, in fact, and Francesca hoped it had something to do with the fact that she had returned home.

The restaurant was full, as it was well into the lunch hour. Francesca smiled at her sister. "You look so well. How is it possible? I could barely sleep all night—I am a wreck." She had been thinking about the events of the evening, replaying them in her mind, and she had been thinking about Bragg.

"You appear a bit tired," Connie said, her blue regard scanning her. Then she noticed the slight scabs forming on Francesca's wrists. "Fran! What happened!"

"Con! Last night I found Randall's killer!" Francesca exclaimed with a grin.

Several heads turned in their direction.

"You did?" Connie's eyes widened with surprise. "Who was it? And what happened to your wrists?"

Francesca lowered her voice. "First of all, I am not going to tell you why my wrists are bruised, because you will tell Mama."

Connie was taken aback. "That's not fair." Then, her eyes narrowing with suspicion, "What have you done?"

The truth was, Francesca was dying to tell Connie everything, including the fact that Bragg had a wife, albeit a horrid one. She leaned forward. "Swear on the Bible that you will not tell *anyone*."

"You are so dramatic!" Connie complained. "All right. I shan't tell a soul, not even Neil."

Francesca took a good hard look at her sister, who realized what she had said and looked away. "How is Neil?" Francesca whispered.

Connie studied the napkin on her lap. "Fine." She looked up, clearly not about to discuss her private life. "So? Why are you hurt?"

Francesca wanted to know more, but she would wait until Connie wished to tell her. "I am not really hurt." Dr. Finney had examined her head and told her she was quite fortunate, as she did not have a concussion, just a small bump. Because Francesca had not wanted him to visit her at home, she had gone directly to his house from the Randalls'. Finney had been the family doctor ever since they had first moved to the city, and, still excited from the evening, Francesca had told him everything. He had sternly advised her to give up sleuthing, ordering her to rest for a few days.

Francesca quickly told Connie what had happened, the version an annotated one. Then, as her sister gaped at her speechlessly, "It will be in the afternoon papers, I am sure. Can you believe it was Mary? Apparently she went berserk when she learned he had a mistress, and she followed him to Miss de Labouche's house and shot him right in the back of the head."

Francesca was breathless. "That is premeditated, Con."

Connie stared, ashen. "Fran, you could have been killed by that horrid Bill Randall!"

"I don't think he would have gone that far," Francesca said. "And then Mary went running to her brother, who had come home for the weekend, begging him to help her dispose of the body and hide her ghastly crime. But Miss de Labouche had already come to me, as I was leaving Stanford White's party. As I had sent for the police, it was too late for Bill and Mary to get rid of their father's corpse." Francesca shook her head, excited even to be discussing the case. "Apparently they both hate their father, or at least his memory, as he has left them nothing in the way of an inheritance."

"Good lord," Connie said again. Then she reached out and clasped Francesca's hand. "Please tell me that this is the end of your sleuthing?"

"How can it be!" Francesca cried passionately. "I am an excellent crime-solver. Even Bragg admitted that."

Connie stared, anxiety written all over her face. Finally she sighed. "And how is your romance with our handsome and interesting police commissioner proceeding?"

Francesca sat back in her chair. Briefly, for a few minutes, she had somehow forgotten about Bragg's wife and the fact that Bragg and she must now remain just friends. She thought about how upset he had been last night when he had thought she had been shot. She had *not* told Connie about that. She sighed. She still carried the pain of grief with her like a hand weight used by gymnasts and muscle men. "Bragg is married."

Connie's eyes popped. "What?!"

"Bragg is married; he has a wife."

Connie sat there, stunned, and then she took Francesca's hand from across the table. "Oh my God. And he has kept this a secret from society?" She was stricken, aghast.

And Fran felt her anguish surge forth, for it had only been buried, relegated to some deep hiding place within her. "He hasn't seen her in four years, Con. She lives in Europe. They are separated, and they have been since the first few months of their marriage. There is no love between them."

Connie squeezed her hand. "I am so sorry, Fran. I confess, I had no idea. . . . I am in shock." Suddenly she flushed. "He is a terrible man! You would think he might have found a moment to tell you this, weeks ago, when the two of you first met!"

Francesca stiffened. "We were only friends, and we did not meet until January eighteenth. Neither one of us was looking for a romance."

"You defend him now?" Connie was incredulous. "You should be angry, no, furious!"

Francesca did not hesitate. "We are still friends." She was not going to tell her sister or anyone how painful the marriage was for Bragg or how awful his wife was. That was his private affair.

Connie stared. "No, Fran, you are still in love, and that will not do! The man is in politics. He will never divorce, so unless his wife suddenly dies, there is no hope. You must forget him now and move on." She was firm.

"The way you have forgotten Neil?" The words just popped out.

Connie flushed. "That is different. We are married, and we have two children."

"Love has many guises," Francesca said, meaning it.

"Oh, God. You are the most stubborn person I know! I am afraid for you now!" Connie cried.

And deep in her own heart, Francesca was also afraid, for herself, for Bragg. Because the bond between them felt somehow stronger with every passing moment, not the other way. But she removed her hand from her sister's, so she could pat Connie's reassuringly. "Don't worry about me. I am fine."

Connie eyed her, then said, "Did you see the *Sun* this morning? Apparently he struck a reporter last night at police headquarters."

Francesca had seen the article, and she was dying of curiosity and eaten with apprehension to know just what had transpired. Diverted from her own personal fate, she said, "I saw. I know the reporter. I am certain the article was a highly distorted version of the truth."

"Yes. I cannot imagine Commissioner Bragg striking anyone. He is quite the gentleman—or so I thought, until today."

"He *is* a gentleman," Francesca said firmly. And he was, even though he had grown up on the Lower East Side in a tenement and had belonged to a gang. A few weeks ago she had seen him in a brutal fight with the thug Gordino. Bragg was capable of losing his temper and his better judgment, and he knew how to fight with the most vicious sort. But that did not change the fact that he was a man of honor. Still, Francesca felt there was a bit of truth to the article, and she hoped, fervently, that if there was, it would not cost him his job.

"There was a suggestion in the article that the man who was attacked might sue," Connie said.

"I know; I read it. Don't you think we should order?" Francesca asked, worried about Bragg. Perhaps she would make a trip downtown to headquarters to find out what was happening now with the Randall case—and to learn what had really happened with that miserable Arthur Kurland.

"Good afternoon, ladies." A familiar and oh, too sensual drawl caused Francesca to start and look up.

Calder Hart smiled at her and her sister, standing beside their table, a dashing figure in a dark gray business suit.

"Mr. Hart!" Connie cried, smiling as if very pleased to see him. "What an unexpected surprise."

His gaze moved over her slowly, as if relishing the view, before he spoke. "And I do hope it is as pleasant for you as it is for me, Lady Montrose. You are, beyond a doubt, the loveliest woman in this dining room."

Connie flushed. "How could it not be a pleasure to see you?" she murmured.

And Francesca looked from Hart's smiling countenance to her sister's blushing one and she was stunned. What was this?

And had Hart not noticed that the two sisters were almost identical? Indeed, strangers often assumed them to be twins!

"And you do flatter me overly, I fear," Connie added.

"I am a connoisseur of many things, including beauty," he

remarked. He turned toward Francesca. "And how are you today, Francesca?"

She felt herself flushing as well. She stared at him. "Very well, thank you."

"You look tired." But his eyes were warm.

She did not rate the flattery her sister did? "I am tired." Her expression felt mulish now.

"Busy sleuthing, I believe?" Both slashing brows lifted.

"You know?"

"Bragg called me last night. I understand you apprehended my vicious half sister and her equally reprehensible brother yourself. With a fry pan," he added, a twinkle in his eyes.

Before Francesca could respond, Connie cried accusingly, "Francesca! I thought Bragg was with you!"

She glanced gingerly at her sister. "Well, Bragg did show up a minute later, and I do mean a minute."

"You cannot go about apprehending killers by yourself," Connie said firmly.

"I am in absolute agreement with your sister," Hart said, his eyes still sparkling. He reached into his interior breast pocket and handed Francesca an envelope.

"What is this?" she asked, bewildered.

"A bank note." He smiled. "I am accepting your offer to join the board of the Ladies Society for the Eradication of Tenements."

Francesca gaped and as she opened the envelope, Hart looked at Connie. She glanced at the bank note and froze— it was for $5,000. "Hart!" she cried, stunned. "Thank you!"

"You are welcome," he said, but his gaze had slipped to Connie's décolletage. Her beautiful rose-and-ivory-striped ensemble was form-fitting but modest, not low-cut, and absolutely appropriate for day, but his glance was unmistakable.

Francesca felt herself scowl. It was stupid to wonder, but had he ever looked at her that way?

Yes, he had, she decided, when he had been outrageously drunk.

Connie leaned toward Francesca to peek at the note. Her

eyes became round. "Oh. Mr. Hart, that is terribly generous of you."

Hart smiled into her eyes. "It is my pleasure to aid your sister in her efforts at reform."

"Obviously." Connie smiled back, into his eyes. "More citizens of this city should be like you."

He laughed at that. "I do not think so. So, what shall *we* do about Francesca's penchant for sleuthing?" he asked Connie with a dimple.

"I think we shall have to convince my *little* sister of our way of thinking," Connie said lightly, clearly enjoying the flirtation.

He did not look away. "A joint effort is clearly called for."

"She can be very stubborn," Connie warned.

"So can I," he said softly. "And you, Lady Montrose? Do you have a stubborn streak?"

Francesca looked from the one to the other and knew her eyes were impossibly wide. This had to be stopped!

"Determination is not considered ladylike," Connie said softly. "Would you have me share my secrets with you?"

"I am very good at keeping a lady's secrets," Hart murmured. "And yours I would love to share."

Connie's complexion had turned pink again. "I rather believe you," she murmured in return, glancing coyly aside. "You might get me in trouble, Mr. Hart."

"I might," he agreed, causing both sisters to stare at him.

Connie flushed. "You are shockingly bold."

"I am well aware of it. Perhaps you will come to enjoy my boldness."

She gazed at him with a soft, slight smile. "Perhaps."

"Ahh." His smile widened now. "Does this mean you will finally, at last, accept my invitation to lunch?"

"It has only been three days since you tendered it," Connie smiled.

"Four, if you count today," he countered quickly.

Francesca could not believe what she was witnessing. Did they even know she was still present? She opened her mouth to say something, anything, and said, "I wonder if *Neil* has heard the news. Do you think he knows we caught your *father's* killer?"

She was ignored—as if she hadn't spoken, as if she did not exist. Connie said, "Four then. I had not realized you were counting the days."

"How could I not? When I offer up an invitation to the most enchanting woman I have met in years, I do not forget it. So? Will you accept my invitation?" he pressed, his gaze steady and intent.

"Nothing would pleasure me more," Connie said, no longer smiling but staring back at him.

They regarded each other for an interminable moment.

"Connie!" Francesca finally gasped, shocked.

Hart grinned, the moment broken. "I must check my schedule, but I do believe I am free this Friday. Say, at one?"

"Friday at one o'clock would be perfect."

Hart nodded at her, still smiling—as if the cat had already eaten up all the cream. "I shall be in touch with the details," he said. He bowed, then looked at Francesca. "Will you be joining us?" His eyes were gleaming with amusement.

"Francesca is busy on Friday," Connie said quickly, before Francesca could even open her mouth. "Aren't you?"

Hart seemed to choke back a laugh.

Francesca looked at her sister and wondered what would happen if she reached across the table and actually tried to throttle her. "I happen to be free on Friday," she said.

Connie gave her a perfect smile. "You have forgotten that you have an engagement," she said sweetly.

Francesca gave her a look that should have killed; unfortunately, it did not.

Hart had to laugh out loud. Heads did turn at the happy and robust sound. "Good day, ladies. And, Francesca?" His smile vanished. "Thank you," he said.

She looked into his dark eyes and saw the sincerity there and felt an odd pang. "You're welcome, Calder," she said softly.

He bowed at them both and left the restaurant with long, graceful strides. Both men and women turned to watch him go. Whispers as well as stares trailed in his wake.

Francesca turned to see Connie gazing after him, her blue eyes almost shining and certainly thoughtful. "What are you thinking?" she cried. "Have you lost your mind? Have you forgotten that you are married?" she demanded.

It was a moment before Connie replied, and not until Hart had exited the dining room. "I have hardly forgotten that I am a married woman with two children," Connie said calmly.

"You were flirting with Hart," Francesca accused.

"So? That is hardly a crime." Connie was serene. "I see my friends flirting with gentlemen other than their husbands all the time."

"But you are not a flirt!"

"I have decided to try it as a pastime; it seems rather enjoyable."

Francesca gaped. "Con, he is notorious for his liaisons, and I do believe married women are his *specialty.*"

Connie smiled. "I suppose we shall see."

"What? Wait!" Francesca was horrified. "Is this your idea of vengeance?"

"Francesca, do not be absurd. A charming man has asked me to lunch, and I have accepted. It is no more than that—a casual, and I do mean casual, flirtation." But she looked like the cat that had swallowed the canary. Indeed, she continued to smile, an expression Francesca had not seen in days.

"Well, let me tell you something," Francesca said in a huff. "If you play with fire, you shall get burned."

Connie shrugged with nonchalance. "Not if one holds the match very carefully," she said.

After a meal that had tasted very much like cardboard—during which Connie seemed to be in extraordinary spirits—they paid their bill and left the dining room. The lobby of the Plaza was a vast room with huge Corinthian columns and an atrium in its center. The moment the two women paused on its threshold, Francesca saw a cluster of gentlemen entering through the hotel's front entrance. In their midst was Bragg.

Quite literally, her heart missed a beat.

She froze in mid-stride.

He was surrounded by newsmen, she realized, as every single one was holding a small notebook and a lead pencil. But he stopped speaking in mid-sentence, and like herself, he halted.

Across the spacious room, through the huge potted palms, in spite of the atrium, in spite of everyone coming and going, he looked at her and their gazes met.

It should have been impossible, given the distance and space between them, but it was not.

"Fran?" Connie said with worry.

Francesca didn't hear her. Smiling, she moved toward him. It was almost as if a magnet were luring her there.

Bragg detached himself from the reporters, as if he, too, were being pulled toward her. Somewhere between the atrium and the long walnut-and-marble reception desk, they paused. He was smiling, too.

"Good afternoon, Francesca," Bragg said softly.

"Hello, Bragg. It's a bit late for lunch, is it not?"

His gaze was searching. "Yes, it is. How are you?"

Her own gaze searched his as well. "I am fine. A bit tired, I suppose."

"Yes, and you should be. I am tired, too."

She touched his sleeve, too briefly for anyone to notice. "How late did you work last night?" She had already noticed the slight discoloration beneath his eyes and the fact that if he had used a razor that morning, he had done so too swiftly for it to have been thorough.

"Late." He smiled. "Well after midnight. Mary has admitted everything."

"She was eager to speak?"

"It seems that way. She is a very troubled young lady."

Francesca nodded. "And Bill?"

His gaze never left hers. "He is being charged with conspiracy and assault." His eyes changed. "You did not tell me that he hit you on the head with a lamp."

"I didn't know. But I saw Dr. Finney, and I am fine. There shall be no permanent damage." She smiled.

He smiled back and took her hand and lifted it in order to look at her wrist. He nodded and met her gaze again, dropping her hand. "The abrasions are healing well."

"Yes." How easily his touch could arouse her, she thought.

"And other than having been hit on the head with a lamp and having rope burns on your wrist and being tired, how are you today?" he asked.

"Well enough," she said, but only after a hesitation.

He was the one to pause now. His gaze was so somber. "Will you step outside with me for a moment?"

She wanted nothing more. "Of course."

He grasped her elbow, but only for the barest of moments, and they walked through the library, careful not to look at anyone, careful not to touch. Still, Francesca felt her skirts brush his trousered leg as they stepped out into the brilliant winter sun. The day was dazzling in brightness.

She squinted and faced him where they stood beneath the hotel's majestic bronze awning, within a stone's throw of the park. "It is an unusual day," she remarked. She was achingly aware of him.

"And I hope you shall find the time to enjoy it," he returned. "You deserve a holiday."

She studied him with a smile. "I have no time for a holiday. I fear to fail all my courses if I do not do some serious studying indeed."

He laughed. "Then by all means, it is off to the library with you." He quickly sobered. Then, "Francesca, I keep thinking that there is something that I must say to you."

"Yes, I have that feeling, too." Her pulse raced now.

He shook his head. "But all has been said, I fear."

Her heart skipped a series of beats. "Do you really believe that?" she asked softly.

He hesitated. "No."

She gazed up at him and he gazed back. So desperately, she wanted to move into the circle of his arms. It would be so right.

But she did not, as it was not right. She felt a tear shimmer on her lashes.

Abruptly he reached out his hand. She did not hesitate,

and she slipped her palm into his. His grip tightened.

Briefly, she closed her eyes. There was something magical about the feeling of her palm enfolded in his. There was something so right it was almost impossible to describe. Her hand fit in his, the way she had somehow come to belong in his life, in its very center—the way he now belonged in her life, at its core. Yet it was also painful, and forbidden now.

"Anything I say will only make things worse," he said, very low. And he slid his hand from hers, slowly and reluctantly.

"I don't think so," she said, glancing at the two liveried doormen out of the corner of her eye. But if they had noticed the city's married police commissioner holding her hand, they were not batting an eye.

"What is it that you wish me to say?" he asked, low and strained. "I am so sorry, to have hurt you and to have misled you, but I cannot wish we had not met, because I treasure our friendship, and wishing that my own circumstances were different would be a useless and pitiful act. There is a saying—I made my bed and now I shall sleep in it."

"Do not punish yourself for making a mistake when you were young and far less wise than you are now."

"Only you would say something like that to me, now," he said softly. "It is why—" He stopped.

Her pulse accelerated. "It is what?" she asked softly.

"There is no point," he began intensely.

She grasped his wrist. "Yes, there is! *Do you love me?*" She could hardly believe herself. She no longer cared if she broke every rule of etiquette.

"Yes," he said, his golden eyes riveted upon her face.

She nodded, feeling tears well. She was not surprised, for she had known what his answer would be. "I love you, too, Bragg," she said, very careful to keep her voice down.

"Damn it," he said, and he took her hand firmly in his and he held it, hard, as if daring society to look at them and speculate and point fingers and cast shadows.

It was hard to speak now. A tear interfered with her vision. "What do we do now?" she asked quietly. "Where do we go from here?"

"I do not know," he said. His smile appeared fragile. "But I wish that I did."

Her own smile felt fragile in return.

"Miz Cahill!" someone shouted.

Only a reporter would shout her name that way. Francesca stiffened; Bragg released her hand, and they turned as Walter Isaacson from the *Tribune* came hurrying out of the hotel's front doors. Two other journalists were with him. "Is it true that you apprehended Mary Randall and her brother last night? By yourself?" he cried, rushing over to them.

Francesca looked past the reporters at Bragg. He smiled at her, with encouragement. She turned. "Yes, it is true."

"But how did you know she was the killer? Did you suspect her all along? And how is it that you came to be involved in the first place?" Isaacson rapidly asked her. All three men held pencils, prepared to write down her every word.

"Well," Francesca began, quite pleased with the attention— though her parents would surely lock her in her room for days, months, even years, if they knew the truth, so she must carefully choose her words—"it is a long story, but one I am glad to supply." She looked past Isaacson and his colleagues.

Bragg had walked over to the hotel doors, where he paused. Silhouetted against the bronze and glass, he made a magnificent sight: a tall man with tawny, sun-streaked hair, high, high cheekbones and nearly olive skin, and strong, broad shoulders. Their gazes locked; he saluted her. In his eyes was far more than love; there was respect and, she thought, admiration.

Francesca smiled in return, and against all common sense and better judgment, her heart did sing and exult. She turned back to the reporters. "Now where was I?" she asked.

All three newsmen began firing questions at her. "How did you become involved in the Randall Killing?"

"Weren't you involved in the Burton Abduction?"

"Are you intending to become the city's first policewoman?"

Francesca was about to reply when she noticed a blue-eyed woman in a worn, hooded cloak standing behind Isaacson.

She was staring at Francesca so intently it was as if her eyes might burn a hole through Francesca's clothing. Francesca started, tensing.

"Which clue led you to Mary Randall?"

Francesca returned her attention to the journalists, held up her hands, and as she started to speak, glanced back at the hotel's bronze doors. Bragg was gone.

She turned back to the newshounds. It did not matter. There would be another day, and another case for them to solve together—of that she did not have a single doubt. In fact, she would go downtown to Headquarters later that day; she had forgotten to ask him about the Kurland incident. And as for the road they must travel, she only knew that it would be exciting indeed, with Bragg at her side. She would worry about the rest of it another time.

Then she felt the woman's eyes upon her again. Francesca looked her way, and their gazes locked.

The woman seemed to realize that she was staring, because she flushed and began to back away.

"Miss Cahill? Which clue led you to the murderer?"

Francesca knew that she was not imagining it. The other woman, who was close to Francesca's own age, *had* been staring and was extremely upset and afraid. What was this? "Miss? Wait!" she called impulsively.

The woman whirled. As she did so, her hood fell back to reveal rich, chocolate-brown hair. She ran down the steps to the curb.

"Wait!" Francesca shouted, rushing after her.

Her cry only made the woman run faster. Francesca suddenly realized that a brougham was approaching and that the young woman was running directly into its path.

"Stop!" she screamed, halting at the curb.

Too late, the woman realized the danger from the oncoming vehicle. She froze in her tracks, her eyes wide with terror.

The coachman saw her, too. He jammed down the brake, cursing at her. The two bays reared as he wildly tried to rein them in.

Francesca dove after the woman, knocking her down and out of the way of the two plunging horses and the carriage.

She felt a carriage wheel graze her shoulder as the coach passed. It slowed and then stopped a short distance away.

The woman blinked up at her, and for one moment, they stared into each other's eyes. Francesca knew the woman's terror had nothing to do with almost being hit by a carriage.

Francesca had landed on top of her, and she quickly rolled off, still stunned. The woman leapt up, and without a word, she lifted her coat and skirts and ran.

"Wait," Francesca gasped, still sitting in the middle of the street as three reporters and half a dozen bystanders rushed to her. "Are you all right, Miss?" someone asked.

"Miss Cahill! Who was that?" This from Isaacson.

A crowd had gathered around her. "Did you see that? The woman must have been mad, to run in front of a coach like that!" "Maybe a lunatic, from the looks of her."

Someone was shoving through the crowd. Francesca felt him before she saw him, and she turned and looked up, meeting his eyes. Bragg knelt. "Are you all right?" he demanded.

She nodded, her wind having returned, and he helped her to her feet. She leaned into him, shaking a bit from the close encounter. "There's a woman in danger, Bragg. She wanted to approach me, I am certain of it, but then she ran away, and was almost run over!"

He held her upper arms. His gaze was concerned and grim. "You don't know that, Francesca. I was just coming out of the hotel to speak with you again, and I saw you chasing her into the street. You have no facts."

"I am certain she wished to speak with me!" Francesca cried, as he released her. Suddenly she realized just what was happening. She blinked at him, and in spite of the danger the mysterious woman was undoubtedly in, she did smile, just a bit.

"Oh, no," Bragg said, with a soft groan. "I know exactly what you are thinking."

"There is another crime to solve," she said sweetly.

"Francesca! You were almost killed last night—"

"Balderdash," she said.

He stared.

She grinned.

**THE ADVENTURES OF FRANCESCA CAHILL WILL
CONTINUE! TURN THE PAGE FOR A SNEAK PREVIEW
OF**

DEADLY AFFAIRS

(ON SALE IN APRIL 2002)

AND

DEADLY DESIRE

(ON SALE IN MAY 2002)

DEADLY AFFAIRS

"You have a caller, Francesca."

Francesca halted at the sound of her mother's voice, having just handed her coat, hat, muff, and gloves to a servant. She slowly turned, with dread.

For the voice had been sharp. Now, disapproval covered Julia's attractive face. She was an older image of both daughters: blond, blue-eyed, with classic and fine features. Although over forty, she remained slim and glamorous; many men her own age often eyed her in a covert manner.

"Good day, Mama," Francesca said nervously. She had seen *The Sun*. Francesca would wager her life on it.

Julia Van Wyck Cahill was magnificently attired, clearly dressed for an early evening affair. Her sapphire-blue gown revealed a slim and pleasing figure, while two tiers of sapphires adorned her neck. Before she could answer, Andrew appeared on the stairs, in a white dinner jacket and satin-trimmed black trousers. He took one look at Francesca and his expression became pinched, with disbelief and accusation warring in his eyes.

"I can explain," Francesca whispered.

"What can you explain?" Andrew demanded, halting beside his wife. "That you have made the front page of *The Sun*? That you once again immersed yourself in a dangerous affair? One belonging, I believe, to the police?"

Francesca inhaled. How to begin? Before she could speak, her mother interrupted.

"I am aghast. I am aghast that my daughter would confront a killer and place herself in unspeakable danger. This shall not continue, Francesca. You have gone too far." Julia turned and nodded at a servant, who was holding her magnificent sable coat for her. She allowed him to slip it over her shoulders.

"I am beginning to wonder if my brilliant daughter has truly lost her mind," Andrew said.

Francesca cringed. Papa never spoke to her in such a manner. "I helped the police enormously," Francesca murmured. The fact was, she had solved the case at the eleventh hour.

"You have been up to your ears in police affairs ever since Bragg arrived in town," Julia said sharply. "Do you think I am blind, Francesca? I can see what is happening."

"Nothing is happening," Francesca tried, stealing a glance at her father. He knew about Bragg's married state, she thought suddenly. This was the secret he had been keeping. But why hadn't he told her?

"We are on our way out for the evening, but we shall speak tomorrow morning, Francesca." Julia gave her a look that was filled with warning, and did not look at her again while Andrew donned his coat. But her father met her gaze, shaking his head, looking so terribly grim that Francesca knew she was in a kind of trouble she had never dreamed of. There was no relief when they left the house. But what could they do? She was a grown woman.

Francesca relaxed slightly. She would worry about her parents tomorrow. She turned as Bette handed her a delicately engraved calling card on a small sterling tray. Francesca studied the card for a moment, curiously; she did not believe she had ever met a Mrs. Lincoln Stuart. She thanked Bette and entered the far salon.

It was beautifully appointed, but small, and used for more intimate gatherings, such as a single caller. It was painted a pale, dusky yellow, and most of the furnishings were in various shades of yellow or gold, with several red and navy-blue accents. The moment Francesca entered the room, she saw Mrs. Lincoln Stuart. She had been sitting on a sofa at the room's other end, but upon espying Francesca, she instantly stood. Francesca smiled and approached.

Mrs. Lincoln Stuart twisted her hands.

Francesca saw that she was a few years older than her. She was rather plain in appearance, her features usual and unsurprising. But her hair was a beautiful cascade of chestnut curls, and it was what one noticed first. She was very well-dressed, in a green floral suit and skirt, and she wore a rather large, yellow diamond ring. Her husband was obviously wealthy. And she was nervous and distressed.

"Miss Cahill. I do hope you do not mind me calling like this," Mrs. Stuart said in a husky voice, one filled with tension. Worry was expressed in her eyes.

Francesca smiled warmly, pausing before her. "Of course not," she said politely. "Have we met?"

"No, we have not, but I was given this by a boy the other day." And Mrs. Stuart handed her a card.

Francesca recognized it instantly—how could she not? Tiffany's had printed the cards at her request upon the conclusion of the Burton Affair. It read:

> *Francesca Cahill*
> *Crime-Solver Extraordinaire*
> *No. 810 Fifth Avenue, New York City*
> *All Cases Accepted, No Crime Too Small*

"My assistant, Joel Kennedy, must have handed this to you," Francesca mused, pleased. She had recently assigned him the task of drumming up business for her. She glanced up at Mrs. Stuart. Was she a prospective client? Francesca's heart thudded in anticipation.

"I don't know the boy's name, I only know that I am frightened and I have no one to turn to," Mrs. Stuart cried, her eyes wide. Francesca saw that they were green and lovely. Mrs. Stuart was the kind of woman who had a quiet kind of beauty, one that was not instantly remarkable, she decided.

Francesca also realized that she was on the verge of tears. She took her arm. "Do sit down, and I am sure I can help you, Mrs. Stuart," she said. "No matter what your problem might be." There was no doubt now; Mrs. Stuart had come to her for help. This would be her second official case!

The woman dug a handkerchief out of her velvet purse. It was hunter-green, like the trim on her elegant tea gown. "Please, call me Lydia," she said, dabbing at her eyes. "I saw today's article in *The Sun*, Miss Cahill. You are a heroine, a brave heroine, and when I realized that you are the same woman on this card, I knew it was you to whom I must turn."

"I am hardly a heroine, Lydia," Francesca said, barely containing her excitement. "Excuse me." She rushed to the salon door and closed it, so that no one might overhear the conversation. Her resolve to take a "sabbatical" from sleuthing had vanished. In fact, she forgot all about her studies now. She hurried back to her guest—her *client*—and sat down. What could this woman's problem be? And was she truly going to have, for the very first time, a paying client? In the past, she had offered her services for free. A paying client would truly make her a professional woman.

Lydia managed to smile at her, and she now handed Francesca a small piece of paper, upon which were two names, Rebecca Hopper, and an address, 40 East 30th Street. "What is this?" Francesca asked.

Lydia Stuart's face changed, becoming filled with distaste. "Mrs. Hopper is a widow, and that is where she lives. I believe my husband is having an affair with her, but I want to know the truth."

Francesca stared.

"And I have no doubt that he will be there tonight, as he has said he is working late and he will not be home for supper," Lydia added.

Mrs. Hopper's residence was a corner one, and while all of the lights were on downstairs, only one bedroom upstairs was illuminated. It had been years since Francesca had climbed a tree, and now she was sorry that she had not gone further downtown to locate Joel to do her evening's work for her. He would have been very useful indeed—especially as he did not have cumbersome skirts to deal with.

Huffing and puffing, her hands freezing because she had stripped off her gloves, she sought another foothold in the huge tree she was climbing, clinging to the trunk.

She had decided to tackle Lydia's case head-on. It was nine P.M., and a quick look at the house had shown her that if she climbed the big tree in the yard, she might very well be able to spy upon the lovers directly. In fact, if Lydia were right, this case might be solved before it was even begun.

Francesca made it to the large, higher branch. She clung to it, one leg atop it, both arms around it. Her skirts were in the way; she had not worn men's clothing for she did not have the psychic ability to know when she would be climbing trees. With great effort, she somehow moved her other leg onto the thick branch, and then she hugged it with all her might, afraid she was going to fall. She glanced down.

She was not sure she liked heights. When she had been on the ground, in the yard, the tree had not seemed so tall. Now, looking down, her cheek upon the rough bark, her hands feeling rather scraped and raw, the ground looked very far away.

She had not a doubt that if she fell, the snow would be rock-hard, as it was solidly frozen. It would not break her fall; she might wind up with a broken arm, or God forbid, a broken neck.

But she was determined to ignore her cowardice now. Very, very carefully, Francesca sat up. When she was astride the branch as if it were a horse, she began to breathe easier. This wasn't too bad. She believed she could mange.

Dismayed, she suddenly realized her eyes were still below the window and she could not see into the bedroom in order to learn what was going on. She was going to have to stand up.

But Francesca realized she was turned around the wrong way—the trunk of the tree was behind her. *Oh dear.* This might be far too dangerous a maneuver, she thought.

She could not see into the bedroom, and she was at a grave risk if she tried to turn around. Now what?

There was no choice. She had to turn herself around. She simply had to. *Because Lydia Stuart was her first paying client.*

Francesca lifted her right leg up slowly, until she was able to move it up and over the branch. Now she sat with both legs dangling off the same side of the tree, and her position was precarious at best. She failed to breathe now. She had to reverse herself, but she was afraid to move.

That was when she slipped.

Francesca cried out as she lost her balance and started to slide off the branch. Instantly, desperately, she reached out, trying to grasp the branch with her hands, the bark scraping and abrading her palms, and for one moment, she thought she had succeeded in stopping herself. She gripped the tree, but then her hands failed her and suddenly she was falling through space.

She saw the white snow below, racing towards her face, and she thought, *Oh dear, this is it. It is all over now.*

Whomp.

Francesca landed hard on her shoulder and her side, not her face, her head smacking down last. And then she was spitting out snow.

God, she thought, dazed. Was she intact? Had she broken anything?

She began to move. The snow was not as frozen as she had thought it would be; it was not rock-hard, surprisingly. She wiggled her toes and fingers in the snow, moved her hands and legs.

She froze.

Had she just touched something? Something beneath the snow? Something *sticky*? And *solid*?

Francesca sat up shakily, and as she stood, she looked down at her own hands.

One was pale and white in the moonlight, the other was dark and splotched in places.

She had an inkling. She did not move. She recognized those splotches.

Her heart pumped hard now.

And then she rubbed her fingers together. *Oh, no.*

Francesca was on her knees, tearing at the frozen snow. And as she moved the top layer away, she found a piece of garment.

Francesca stared at a patch of brown wool, and the dark, still not thoroughly frozen, stain upon it.

She touched it.

It was no different than what had been on her fingertips; it was blood, and it was fresh.

Someone was buried in the snow, recently, and maybe the person was alive!

Francesca pawed the snow frantically, shoving it away in clumps, and then she saw the woman's face—she saw the open, sightless blue eyes, and they were glazed in terror.

She saw the throat.

She stood, and unable to help herself, she screamed.

For carved in the once-pristine white skin was a perfect and bloody cross.

DEADLY DESIRE

The Channings lived on the unfashionable West Side of the city. Sarah Channing was becoming a good friend, ever since her engagement to Francesca's brother, Evan. When her father had died, her mother, a rather frivolous and harmless socialite, had inherited his millions and promptly built their new house. As Francesca approached the mansion, which was quite new and horrendously gothic, she clutched her reticule as if she expected a cutpurse to appear and seize it.

Francesca was told by the doorman that Miss Channing was not receiving visitors.

"Would you care to leave your card?" the liveried doorman asked.

"Harold? Who is it?"

Francesca stepped forward at the sound of Mrs. Channing's voice. A not-quite-pretty woman with reddish-blond hair who was extremely well-dressed and somehow reminded one of a flighty, mindless bird was entering the foyer. "Why, Francesca! This is quite the surprise!" She clapped her beringed hands together in childish delight.

Francesca managed a smile. "Hello, Mrs. Channing. I am sorry to hear that Sarah is indisposed. I hope she is not too ill?"

Mrs. Channing's dark eyes widened. Then she put her arm around Francesca and leaned toward her, speaking in a conspiratorial whisper. "Perhaps this is a stroke of fate, indeed. That you should choose this very day to call!"

Francesca looked into her dramatically widened eyes—as there was little else to do, with the other woman's face a mere two inches from her own. "Whatever do you mean, Mrs. Channing?"

"We are in the midst of a crisis," Mrs. Channing said. Her

breath was sweet, as if she had been eating raspberries and chocolates.

Francesca was in no mood for a crisis other than her own. "Perhaps I should leave word that I have called—and come back at another time."

"Oh, no!" Mrs. Channing cried, finally releasing France-sca. "I *told* Sarah we should call for you! But she said you were recovering from that horrid encounter with the Cross Killer, and we mustn't disturb you! But you are a sleuth, dearie, and we do need a sleuth now! Nor do I have the foggiest of whom else to call upon in our time of need!"

Francesca straightened. In spite of her worries, she could not help being intrigued. "You have need of an investigator?" she asked, a familiar tingle now running up and down her spine.

Mrs. Channing nodded eagerly.

"Why, what has happened?"

"Come with me!" Mrs. Channing exclaimed. And she was already hurrying into the hall.

Francesca followed, not bothering to hand off her coat, hat, and single glove. She quickly realized, as they moved down one hall and then another, that they were heading in the di-rection of Sarah's studio. She was perplexed.

Suddenly Mrs. Channing turned and placed her back against the door of Sarah's studio, barring the way. "Prepare yourself," she warned, rather theatrically.

Francesca nodded, holding back a smile, more than in-trigued now. What could be going on?

Mrs. Channing smiled, as if in satisfaction, and she thrust open the door.

Francesca stepped inside. The room was all windows, and brilliantly lit. She cried out.

Someone had been on a rampage in the room.

Canvases, palettes, and jars were overturned. Paint was splattered across the floor and walls, the effect vivid, brilliant, and disturbing. Amidst the yellows, blues, and greens, there were slashes of black and dark, dark red. For an instant, Fran-cesca thought the red was blood.

She rushed forward, kneeled, and dabbed her finger into a drying pool of dark red. It was paint, not blood.

Then she saw the canvas lying face up on the floor.

It had been slashed into ribbons.

"Sarah! I cannot believe what happened!" Francesca cried. She had been pacing in a huge, mostly gilded salon, which was as overdone as the outside of the house. A bear rug complete with head and fangs competed with the Orientals on the floor; chairs had hooves and claws for feet, and one lamp had a tusk for a pull cord. Mr. Channing, God rest his soul, had been a hunter and a collector of strange and exotic objects. Apparently his widow was continuing his hobby.

Sarah had just entered the room. She was a small and plain brunette, although her eyes were huge and pretty. Today, she was wearing a drab blue dress covered with splotches of paint. She appeared very pale, her nose and eyes red. Clearly, she had been weeping. "Francesca? What are you doing here?" she asked softly—brokenly.

Francesca forgot all about her own problems. She rushed forward and embraced her friend. "You poor dear! Who would do such a thing?"

Sarah trembled in her arms. "I told Mother not to call you! You have a badly burned hand and you are recuperating!"

Francesca stepped back. "Your mother did not telephone me. I called upon you, dear."

Their eyes met. Tears welled in Sarah's. "I did not want to bother you, not now, not after what happened on Tuesday," referring to the aftermath of the Channing ball.

Francesca took Sarah's hand with her own good one. "How could you *not* call me? I am your friend! Sarah, we must catch this miserable culprit! Have you called the police?" Her heart skipped madly. These days, the police and Rick Bragg were one and the same and never mind what Connie had said a few minutes ago.

"Not yet. I have been too devastated. I just found out this morning," Sarah said, and she was shaking visibly.

Mrs. Channing stepped into the room. "Sarah gets up before dawn. She takes a tea and goes directly into her studio. She will spend the entire day there, if I do not rescue her from her frenzy."

Francesca looked from mother to daughter. "So you found your studio that way when you went down this morning?" she asked.

Sarah nodded.

"Why don't you girls sit down? Francesca, have you had lunch?" Mrs. Channing asked.

"No, but I would like a moment alone with Sarah, if you don't mind, Mrs. Channing."

Mrs. Channing seemed taken àback.

Francesca smiled, politely but firmly. "Do you wish me to take—and solve—the case? If so, I need to interview your daughter."

"Oh, of course! My, Francesca, you are so professional." Then Mrs. Channing smiled. "I shall have a small meal put out anyway. Do as you shall, then, Francesca." She left, closing the door behind her.

"Francesca, how can you take my case now when you are hurt? Besides, didn't you promise to rest for a few weeks?" Sarah looked her directly in the eye.

She had, and she had mentioned her resolve to Sarah. "Never you mind, my hand is healing very well, Finny said so himself. I would never let down a friend in need." Francesca smiled and guided her to a couch, where they both sat down. She leaned forward eagerly. "What time did you first enter your studio?"

"It was five-fifteen. I get up at five on most mornings, and go directly there." She smiled a little. "And I take coffee, not tea, black with one sugar."

Francesca patted her hand. "And when were you last in your studio? On Friday morning?"

Sarah nodded. "I worked there until about noon on Friday." Suddenly she covered her heart with her hand. "Francesca, I am so shocked. And worse, I feel ill. I feel . . . raped, I suppose. Or I imagine that this is what being raped feels like. I am shocked and sad and angry and I cannot stop crying! Why would someone do this? Why?" she cried, a tear sliding down her cheek.

Francesca sat up straighter. "I don't know. I have no idea. But whoever it was, he got into this house to do his deadly deed sometime between noon on Friday and five-fifteen Saturday morning. I shall have to interview the entire household staff. Are there any new employees?"

"I don't know. Also, we were out last night," Sarah said. "We went to the ballet. But still, there is a houseful of servants, and a doorman is always on the front door."

"Still, a single doorman can fall asleep," Francesca mused. "I shall have to speak to the doorman who was on last night while you were out."

"That would be Harris," Sarah said. "He has been with us forever, it seems."

"And when you are out, where is the rest of the staff?"

"In their rooms on the fourth floor," Sarah said. Suddenly she sighed, the sound filled with grief. "Why, Francesca? Why?"

"I don't know. But I shall find out. Sarah, do you have any enemies?" And even as she asked, the question felt ridiculous. Who would dislike, no, hate, Sarah Channing enough to do something like this? She was a sweet young girl, and so reclusive that she hardly had any friends, much less enemies.

Sarah blinked at her. "I hardly think so. Why would someone hate *me*? There is nothing to be jealous of."

Francesca considered that. "I don't know. It is absurd. But you are a wealthy young woman, and you are engaged to my brother, who is quite the catch."

"I don't think either reason is sufficient for someone to break into this house and destroy my studio," Sarah said tersely. "Do you?"

"No, I do not. But people can be strange." She was reflective now. Her last three cases had certainly proven that, and more. She had learned there was a goodly share of insanity going about undetected. "Perhaps you turned a client down? Perhaps you portrayed a client in a way he or she did not care for?"

Sarah sighed again, heavily. "Francesca, I cannot recall anyone being angry with me for a painting. And—I do not have clients. I am hardly an artist. Everyone I have painted has agreed to sit for me, usually quite happily." Suddenly Sarah smiled. "Well, I do have one client." Her smile widened.

Francesca knew exactly whom she was talking about and tensed. "You mean Calder Hart?"

Sarah nodded, beaming. "He commissioned your portrait. Surely you haven't forgotten?"

"How could I?" Francesca said sourly. "I hate to disappoint you, but Hart only asked for my portrait because he was angry with me. We have patched things up, and he will hardly want my portrait now."

Sarah blinked at her. "Oh, I do think you are wrong. You are an amazing woman, and Hart sees that. He is very eager to have your portrait, I am certain of it."

Her tension—and dismay—increased. Francesca recalled the Channing ball, which for her, personally, had been a disaster—and the moment when Hart had looked at her in her disheveled state, a state induced by spending quite a few minutes upon a sofa in Bragg's arms. The look he had given her had been thoroughly unpleasant; he had known what she had been doing, and he had been quite clear that he did not approve of her interest in his *married* brother. (He had also, several times, admitted how perfect she and Bragg were for one another.) And then he had told Sarah that he wished to commission a portrait. Of Francesca—in her daring red dress, with her hair down, and her straps slipping, and her lips bee-stung.

Francesca flushed now. She hated recalling that nasty exchange. It was not Hart's business if she remained enamored of his half brother. In fact, she had told him so several times.

"Francesca, you aren't changing your mind, are you?" Sarah asked breathlessly.

Now it was Francesca's turn to sigh—almost. Instead, she muffled the sound. Sarah had begged her to sit for the portrait.

This was her chance to gain a foothold in the world of art. It was, in fact, a huge coup to have Hart commission a portrait from her. "If he remains serious, of course I have not changed my mind," Francesca said, rather glumly. "I promised, and it would be the most stunning opportunity for you. But Sarah, do not be disappointed if Hart is no longer interested."

Sarah grinned. "Yesterday he dropped off a check. A deposit, if you will. He has paid me half of the commission in advance."

"Why, that's unheard of!" Francesca cried, stunned and furious.

Sarah lightly touched her arm. "You see, he is deadly serious."

Francesca stood, about to pace. Then she decided to dismiss Hart from her mind, as he had the knack of annoying her even when he was not present. "We have a case to solve. In fact, I shall go home, fetch Joel, and see if there is any word out on the street about the who or the why of this. Then I shall go down to Police Headquarters, as this is a crime, and it must be reported. First, however, I wish to interview Harris, the doorman." She wanted a head start on the case before the police became involved.

Sarah nodded. "I can see that, in spite of the unhappy circumstances, you are thrilled to be back at what you love most—sleuthing."

Francesca smiled a little. "I cannot seem to help myself, I guess. We are very alike, you and I."

"I realize that. Although no one would ever know it to look at us, as you are so beautiful and so full of life, while I am drab and shy."

"You are not drab! You are not shy!" Francesca rushed to her and hugged her.

"I do not mind being drab and shy. You know I do not care what others think. I only care about my art." Her eyes changed, glowing now, with anger. "I want to know who did this, Francesca, and I want to know why."

"I shall not let you down," Francesca vowed. And she meant it.

THE
CHASE

BRENDA JOYCE

NEW YORK TIMES BESTSELLING AUTHOR

CLAIRE HAYDEN has no idea that her world is about to be shattered: at the conclusion of her husband's fortieth birthday party, he is found murdered, his throat cut with a WWII thumb knife. He has no enemies, no one seeking revenge, no one who would want him dead. But the mysterious Ian Marshall, an acquaintance of her husband's, seems to know something. Because someone has been killing this way for decades. Someone whose crimes go back to WWII. Someone who has been a hunter . . . and the hunted. As Claire and Ian team up to find the killer, they can no longer deny the powerful feelings they have for one another. Then Ian makes a shocking revelation: the murderer may be someone Claire has known all her life . . .

"Joyce excels at creating twists and turns in her characters' personal lives."
—*Publishers Weekly*

ON SALE JULY 2002
FROM ST. MARTIN'S PRESS